Chain Reaction

by

Andrew Atiyah

Prologue

The fly crashed against the window pane buzzing frantically in its futile bid to escape. I watched and listened with increasing irritation before I stormed across the room and swatted the hapless insect with my paper.

The fly crashed against the window pane buzzing frantically in its futile bid to escape. I watched and listened with increasing irritation before I stormed across the room, released the sash and pulled open the window to grant the hapless insect its freedom.

Life is but a game of chance as I know better than most. For me, the five minutes which it took to rummage through my school locker in a desperate search for Weller's Advanced Latin Text shaped my life so completely that virtually nothing of my past remained intact.

Of course I did not know it at the time, anymore than the fly anticipated my intention as I strode across the room with a rolled up copy of the Times in my grasp. What came to pass that morning in August 1950 was no more than the inevitable next link in the chain reaction which had begun after I had finally pulled the textbook from my locker and started the walk home.

One

August 13th 1950

I was enjoying a breakfast of boiled eggs, toast and tea whilst perusing the Sunday Times, dressing-gowned and slippered looking forward to a relaxing and leisurely morning when there was a sharp ratter-tat-tat on the front door.

"Bugger." I whispered to myself as I yawned and stretched my way down the corridor to open the door.

On the front step was an anxious looking Lucy.

"Someone has just confessed to the murder of Stanley Jakes."

Smile frozen on my lips and comfortable morning over I ushered Lucy through the front door as my mind slipped back to 1939 when it had all started.

Stanley Jakes had been bludgeoned to death with a hammer in the autumn of that year with the finger of suspicion firmly pointing at my best friend Billy Cosgrove whose cause had not exactly been helped when he disappeared three days later leaving a blood-stained hammer concealed beneath floor boards in his bedroom. His disappearance was taken as further proof, if proof was needed, of his guilt and when the war came along his trail was well and truly scrubbed clean. Nothing had been seen or heard of Billy Cosgrove since.

Eleven years on, we were slowly emerging from the post war world of rationing and shortages and it was all too easy for me to bury the past. I had built a comfortable new life and the world I shared with Billy Cosgrove seemed nothing more than a distant memory, although, as I followed Lucy up the corridor it was with a vivid clarity that I recalled our first meeting. It was my final year at St Benedict's College when walking home along Elm Grove that I had caught sight of Billy Cosgrove and Stanley Jakes arguing outside the Albany Tavern. Angry words were exchanged before an inebriated Jakes lurched away toward Albert Road. As he did so he aimed a hefty kick at one of Billy's young friends scattering his precious collection of cigarette cards across the pavement.

What the argument was about I had no idea but I clearly remember Billy's parting shot, which he delivered with fury. "I swear that I'll kill you Jakes, if you lay a finger on my sister or my friends again." Nothing more than empty rhetoric at the time maybe but words which came back to haunt me 18 months later, nonetheless.

A strange circumstance in which to start a friendship but then again the friendship between Billy and me was anything but ordinary. Whilst I lived with my father at Liongate, the second largest private house in Southsea and had plans to go to University in Oxford the following autumn, Billy worked as an apprentice electrician in the dockyard and shared a small terraced house with the five members of his family. According to the social conventions of the time we were not meant to be friends but somehow we put aside our differences as we watched the world move inexorably toward war. It was in Billy's company that I grew up. I had been an isolated and reclusive teenager and Billy the antidote I needed.

With thoughts of Billy washing through my mind I followed Lucy into the sitting room and sat down beside her. Rather than launching into an explanation of what she had learnt she put her head in her hands and cried. Awkwardly I slid across the settee toward her and placed am arm around her shoulders. "It must have been quite a shock, how did you hear?" I asked.

"A policeman came on Friday; Inspector Hanaho." She said, looking up with moist eyes and pulling out the Inspector's card from her handbag. "I just don't know what to think anymore, William. I have spent ten years hoping to hear from Billy and then this. Is it good news or will it just lead to more heartache? I can't say the policeman gave me grounds for much optimism."

"First things first Lucy, who has confessed?" I asked, anxious to hear the story.

"Some chap in prison on the Isle of Wight called Clive Davenport. Apparently he has terminal cancer and is not expected to live long so wants to make a clean breast of it before he dies."

I had heard of terminally ill prisoners wanting to unburden themselves before meeting their maker and assumed it was a divine insurance policy to be cashed in at the Pearly Gates. My brain was working overtime trying to work out what it might mean for Billy, the hope, of course was that the confession would lead to his warrant being withdrawn which would flush him from his hiding place.

That was assuming Billy was still alive and indeed that he *wanted* to be found. Since Billy's disappearance we had been through the small matter of World War II so to my mind there was more than an even chance Billy was dead. And even if he was alive he could have washed up more or less anywhere from Adelaide to Aylesbury so how we were to find him, heaven only knew. The world of the living was a big place and if you added the dead too it would be a tall order to bring him home, particularly if he was not able or willing to come in voluntarily.

I did not air my doubts to Lucy but instead, hoping for more information, asked her what else Inspector Hanaho had to say. Neither did I, at this juncture, mention my previous encounter with the duplicitous Inspector.

"Nothing much but he does want you to call by the station as I think he has some questions for you."

Lucy then looked up and sighed. "It's up to us to see this through. You do know that, don't you William?" She placed her hands on mine and gave me a look I was helpless to resist. I was sixteen years old when I had first met Lucy and she had held a spell over me ever since. "If this chap Davenport really did kill Jakes we *have* to find Billy." She pleaded.

Whilst the possibility of the hangman's noose had awaited Billy our efforts to track him down were to say the least, half-hearted. Yes, we had gone through the official channels and made a few discreet enquiries but always with a fear of where it may lead. With Davenport's confession I sensed that Lucy was hoping that we could start searching afresh without worrying about the consequences. But I rather suspected there would be a few hoops to jump through first.

For Lucy the burden of coping with Billy's loss was made infinitely worse by her guilt. It was Jakes' unwanted attentions which had started the feud between Jakes and Billy in the first place. Stanley Jakes was not used to being turned down and had reacted badly to Lucy's rejection and even more so, by the manner of it. Lucy had not been shy in her derision, telling Jakes she would not date him if he was the last man left on Earth. From that moment forth Jakes took every opportunity to avenge his injured pride and Billy became Lucy's protector.

Two

My previous encounter with Inspector Hanaho did not bode well for the success of the interview that Lucy had arranged for me for that afternoon. Although only a handful of words had been exchanged the encounter had left me with a bitter taste. It was a Saturday in September 1938 when I had finally cajoled Billy into letting me tag along to a football match at Fratton Park. Billy had planned to meet friends for a pre match beer at the Talbot so we had hopped off the trolley-bus on Francis Avenue.

Our timing could not have been worse as we ran into Jakes and two of his henchmen. They had just pulled up to the kerb in a shining black open topped sports car and emerged wearing expensive long coats and the latest in fashionable hats, looking the world like they had just arrived from a second rate Hollywood film set and totally at odds with their shabby surroundings. After a few insults were exchanged they bundled Billy down an alley between the houses and gave him a good beating, while I stood helpless.

Billy was seventeen at the time and tall for his age but no match for the three men. The attack was short but brutal and left Billy badly bruised, dazed and disorientated. I sat him on the pavement whilst his attackers nonchalantly sauntered off toward the Talbot at the end of the street. A witness to the assault had flagged down a police car in Goldsmith Avenue and I was glad when a police constable arrived a few minutes later.

I was brought up in a world with an unwavering belief in British justice and was fully expecting to see Jakes and his accomplices hauled off to the Police Station but instead, much to my astonishment, watched as they left the pub a short while later, in good humour with the police sergeant and two constables following on their coattails. The sergeant's expression hardened as he walked along the pavement toward us.

"Cuff him, Jones. We're having the pleasure of his company tonight." He gestured toward Billy. Before I could protest he pointed in my direction and barked. "And before you say a word get home now or you'll be coming along too!"

Constable Jones looked uncomfortable as he bundled a sorry looking Billy into the back of a waiting Black Maria whilst the scowling Sergeant strode off in the opposite direction.

I had often dreamed of getting my own back on Hanaho and was not in a conciliatory mood when I was showed into a sparsely furnished interview room at the Kings Road Police Station that afternoon. He turned-up a few minutes later looking pasty faced and overweight; too much good living, not enough exercise and a prime candidate for a cardiac arrest, I thought. Hitching up his trousers the corpulent policemen launched straight-in.

"Good afternoon Mr. Goldhawk, thank you for coming but I fear that I cannot give you good news if you are looking for a reprieve for Cosgrove. I have interviewed Mr. Davenport and have no doubt in my mind that his confession is totally fabricated. The fact is that he has made a life-long habit of lying. And I can't see this leopard changing his spots, can you?" He asked with a disingenuous smile, challenging me to disagree with the official line.

My suspicion of a cover-up was confirmed. If the Inspector expected me to meekly submit to his strong-arm tactic he was mistaken, I had no intention of giving him the satisfaction.

"Have you got a transcript of the interview with Mr. Davenport?"

"Of course we keep a record of what was said Mr. Goldhawk but that's police business and not for the public. Clive Davenport has convictions stretching back thirty years; he's been tried and found guilty in Courts in Hampshire, London and East Anglia. He's been in contempt for perjury and is an inveterate liar with only one saving grace; he's never actually been convicted of any form of violent crime. Not only is Davenport a totally untrustworthy witness but he's as gentle as a pussycat. Mr. Davenport did not kill Stanley Jakes and I strongly recommend that you take that message back to the Cosgrove family and persuade them that digging up the past won't get Billy off the hook."

My hackles were up as I listened to the overbearing policeman. "My solicitor will be in touch and we will be looking for assurances that the confession is investigated by the book, Inspector." I retorted, doing my damnedest to wipe the smirk off his face. "Whatever your own pre-conceptions, the police have a duty to investigate thoroughly. Maybe Davenport is an unreliable witness but why would a man on his death bed want to confess to a murder he didn't commit?"

I was pleased to have removed some of the bravado from Hanaho's manner. He was a man who gave the impression of being unfamiliar with the concept of conciliation and expected to get his own way irrespective of justice or reason. His puffy cheeks reddened and the pitch of his voice rose by an octave. If not exactly rattled, he was at least alerted to my intentions not to be brow beaten.

"I hope you are not questioning my professional integrity?" He spat and without giving me a chance to reply, went on. "I think we have concluded our business for the day."

"Inspector, before you go, may I ask you what your connection was with Stanley Jakes? You know as well as I that as senior investigating officer you must be seen to be impartial. But I have it on good authority that you shared a business interest with the deceased. Would you like to comment?" I looked up at the Inspector, my gaze steady.

"Mr. Goldhawk." Hanaho replied. "You are an accountant I understand? How about leaving this to the professionals? I do not appreciate your insinuations. I will let you know if there are any further developments." He gathered together his papers before giving me a perfunctory nod and turning on his heels.

But before he closed the door behind him he turned back to me and whispered menacingly. "Don't mess with me *Mr. Goldhawk.* You will regret it. Believe me."

I had spent twelve years harboring a grudge against Hanaho and I had no intention of treading carefully. I had always disliked bullies and Hanaho was the worst kind, a bully with authority. Feeling glad that I had riled the inspector I made my way along the corridor to the exit.

Three

When I reached home I wanted to talk to Helen and explain the day's developments so arranged to meet her at the Dolphin Hotel in the High Street later that evening. As well as my fiancée Helen was my confidante and my *pro bono* legal advisor. Whilst the war had intervened to curtail my university ambitions, Helen had determinedly pursued her goal and emerged with a 1st class law degree from Oxford before returning to the south coast as a solicitor. It surprised no one when Helen Crawford became the youngest ever partner at Shawcrofts at the tender age of twenty five.

I had met Helen just before the War but somewhat reluctant to give away my freedom it took until the spring of 1949 before we finally agreed to tie the knot. Whilst Helen had put her not inconsiderable intellect behind her education, I had opted for working for the Admiralty in London during the war years and returned home to Portsmouth as an articled clerk with Surtees, Hancock and Lampson (Chartered Accountants). As Helen was only too fond of reminding me, I achieved partnership status, three years her senior at the *less* than tender age of twenty eight. She may well have added too, that my partnership was earned on the back of work from my future father-in-law's business, rather than from the merits of my own hard work but she tactfully declined to rub salt into the wound.

I wanted Helen's professional advice about the developments in Billy's case but was concerned that her smoldering antipathy toward Lucy may cloud her judgment. Helen was jealous of the close bond that Lucy and I shared even though I was always careful to play down our past relationship. We found a table at the back of the lounge-bar and I broached the subject with care.

"I had an interesting afternoon at the Police Station and I don't think you would have approved of the Inspector's tactics!" I said before going on to abstract the details of my interview.

“So, how was Lucy?” Helen asked just a little frostily but as I glanced up I could tell that her professional interest was piqued and that she would soon forget the discomfort she felt at the thought of Lucy and me spending a morning together.

I had been quietly proud of the way I had handled my interview with Hanaho but Helen shot me down in flames.

“Your objective, William, is to persuade the police and the Court to withdraw Billy’s warrant so that he can come home without being arrested. And to do that you need to convince them that Davenport’s confession is genuine. Your little spat with the Inspector, although understandable, as the man is an arse, was not the wisest move, was it? In fact if you antagonise him you’ll make matters worse.” She scalded me, before adding. “The police are closing ranks and you have got to find a weak link.”

“But surely they can’t just ignore the evidence? If Davenport has signed a statement confessing to the murder the police will have to investigate won’t they?” I asked.

“I think you’re being a little naïve, William. Of course the police will go through the motions, that’s why they contacted the Cosgrove family but an investigation is meaningless if all the parties involved have a vested interest in the same outcome. I know how people like Hanaho work and they have no problem in bending the rules when it suits them. I think the best thing we can do is call Hanaho’s bluff and arrange a meeting with Clive Davenport ourselves. After all, the Prison Governor is hardly going to find it unusual for a Portsmouth solicitor to request a visit, is he? I’ll send a letter tomorrow.”

A local solicitor by the name of Sebastian Harris had acted for Billy’s family in the weeks immediately after his disappearance but after eleven years’ worth of dust had accumulated on the Cosgrove file I imagined that he would be happy enough to pass the reins to Helen. I had previously encountered Harris at an engagement at the factory of Helen's father, Sir Marcus Crawford on the Isle of Wight and I was anxious to meet again to run though the events of those weeks back in 1939, just before and after Billy disappeared. When telephoning, however, I was informed by his secretary that he was working abroad and not due back to England for a few weeks so we penciled in a meeting for early January.

As far as Helen was concerned our discussion about Billy was over and she determinedly steered the conversation toward her favourite topic, our forthcoming wedding. Fortunately the Dolphin served good ale which soothed my nerves as I politely smiled with feigned interest in the colour and material of the bridesmaids' dresses. As the evening wore on my mind slipped away from the wedding and back to Billy Cosgrove. I felt my cheeks flush with shame as I thought about how I had used the war as a convenient excuse to hang Billy out to dry. Lucy's insinuation was right, it was inexcusable that I had done so little to help track down my best friend.

With conversation grinding to a halt I paid the bill and Helen dropped me off home in her new sports car. Her perfunctory peck on the cheek revealed her disappointment at my lack of interest in the wedding, something else to feed my guilt, I sighed to myself as I walked-up the steps to my front door. I hoped that we were not drifting into a marriage right for neither of us.

* * *

The following morning I made my way down stairs to retrieve the Times which I had heard drop through the letterbox. On the mat by the paper was a slightly tatty envelope with my name written in a scruffy hand. There was no stamp.

Intrigued, I slid my thumb under the envelope seal, opened it and pulled out a single sheet of writing paper. The note, short and to the point read:

Meet at the Wellington Arms at 7pm on Friday if you want to know the truth about Billy Cosgrove.

Four

I saw little of Helen the following week as she had been visiting her family on the Isle of Wight and was surprised to see her ensconced on my settee reading a book when I returned home from work one evening. As I walked through the door she waved what looked like an official envelope in my direction and smiled.

"Governor Michael Groves has cleared us to visit Clive Davenport on Friday. I hope you're not too busy at work?"

"Well done honey, that's great news."

"And don't 'honey' me, you delinquent." Helen responded, before playfully launching herself at me. Our lighthearted wrestling turned to pursuits of a more amorous nature and we soon adjourned to the bedroom, minus several items of clothing. One of the terms of our engagement was the instatement of sexual relations which Helen had hitherto banned; some compensation for the ceding of my freedom!

Later, as we lay in bed my thoughts once again strayed back to Billy Cosgrove.

"Helen, honey, listen, I've been thinking about Billy. He was only eighteen when he disappeared and he had hardly ventured further north than Copnor Bridge. Billy was a local lad through and through. He had no bank account, no spare clothes and just a few shillings to his name. What would he have done? Where would he have gone?" I tried to put myself in his shoes but stuck fast.

"The war had just started and Billy wanted to enlist in the Royal Navy but couldn't bring himself to leave Lucy at the mercy of Stanley Jakes. So he arranged to meet Jakes on some pretext or other and battered him to death." hypothesised Helen. "He covered his tracks and hid the murder weapon under floorboards in his bedroom. Because of the history between Billy and Jakes the police were soon onto him and found the damning evidence in his room. Billy realised the game was up and had no choice but to flee or face the gallows. He scraped together a few shillings and made his escape.

He had no friends or family outside Portsmouth so where would he go? The obvious destination would be London, quick and cheap to get to and the easiest place in the world to lose yourself if you don't want to be found. From there he may have assumed a false identity, joined-up and....well who knows?" She finished somewhat lamely.

"If he doesn't want to be found it will be nearly impossible for us to track him down though won't it? Where would we start looking? Even if your theory is correct that was twelve long years ago. And anyway I don't believe for a single minute he is guilty. He was framed once by Hanaho and I'd lay a pound to a penny he was framed a second time." I replied in frustration.

"You can't think like that William, we must clear his name and hope that he comes home of his own accord." Helen, forever the pragmatist concluded and in my heart, I agreed.

I had no end of advice from all quarters over the next few days as word of Davenport's confession spread. The one common thread was the visceral distrust of the local constabulary. There was plenty of anecdotal evidence against them too and murmurs of dissatisfaction straddled all sectors of the community but there was precious little in the way of hard-facts to back up the hearsay. What concerned me most was the Constabulary's lack of accountability or any mechanism for independent investigation. From what I could make out, unless local politicians or newspaper editors were prepared to put their necks on the block, there was not a great deal that could be done to bring a renegade policeman to book.

Perhaps it was because of my instincts as an auditor that I was particularly irked by the absence of accountability within the police authorities and I expressed my disquiet to my senior partner and mentor Brian Surtees the following morning. He made no secret of his unease at my extra curricula activity as I gave a blow by blow account of my interview with Hanaho. But Brian had always fought my corner and I felt I owed it to him to keep him informed. He sat behind his antique wooden desk and peered over the top of his glasses which were perched half way down his nose and warned me gently:

"Be careful William. It doesn't do to upset the establishment. It maybe that what you say is true and the police should be held accountable for their excesses but is it your job to bring this to the attention of the public? Or is that the job of your MP or local councillor? If you'll excuse the footballing metaphor pass the ball to someone more qualified to score.

As Chartered Accountants we adhere to certain standards and chasing around upsetting the local constabulary may not be a good career move. We are a conservative bunch, William. I have sympathy with your motive and do not wish to prevent you doing what you must but be careful."

I admired Brian and at one level wanted to heed his wise words but my instinct for justice took precedence. To my eternal shame I had stood idle for far too long whilst my friend Billy was stuck in limbo. It was time to stand up and be counted.

Five

I met Helen at the Ferry Port on the Hard at 8.30am on Friday morning. She looked fabulous in her professional outfit; moderately high heels and gray suit which accentuated her female form to perfection. I gave her a peck on the cheek and we walked up the ramp to the terminal to buy our tickets.

"The prison is just outside Newport and there is a train which takes us all the way from Ryde." Helen told me, as I fumbled around in my jacket pocket looking for change. It was unseasonably warm for September, even so early in the morning as we stood on the jetty enjoying the sun and speculating about the interview to come. "What do we know about Clive Davenport?" Helen asked.

I dug around in my brief case and pulled out a pad of paper on which I had made a few brief notes. "Well he's 52 and has spent eight of the last 25 years incarcerated mostly for white collar crime; fraud, selling counterfeit goods and a couple of counts of bribing public officials. He has no history of violence, pleaded guilty in 1948 at Winchester Assizes and was sentenced to four years. He is due for parole in April but it rather looks like he won't make it."

"He doesn't sound like a cold blooded killer, does he?" Helen commented as we made our way up the gangway and onto the deck of the paddle steamer.

We alighted from the ferry half an hour later and walked the few yards across the jetty to the train station where we jumped aboard the old fashioned steam train just as it pulled away from the platform. While Helen put the short journey to good use by re-reading her papers I sat and watched from the window as we passed through the gently undulating countryside of the Island. I thought about Billy and once again berated myself for my complacency. He was hardly more than a boy when he was separated from his family and thrown onto the streets and there was no way I could avoid the uncomfortable truth.

I was jolted from my reveries as the train squealed to a halt at Newport Station and Helen clicked her fingers in-front of my eyes. “Come on William, wake up we have work to do.”

We walked the final leg of our journey through an avenue of coppiced beech trees to the entrance of the prison. Once inside we were searched and our identification examined before a prison guard led us through a warren of corridors to the hospital wing where we were shown into a small and sparsely furnished room with a rickety old wooden table and four scruffy chairs. A few minutes elapsed before the guard reappeared handcuffed to the gaunt figure of the prisoner. Although not quite at death’s door his sallow complexion and rasping cough betrayed his illness.

Once inside the room the outer door was locked and the guard removed the handcuffs. The man gave a wan smile and sat down heavily. The prison guard stood by the door just in ear shot and reminded us that we had 30 minutes.

Helen took charge: “Good morning Mr. Davenport, my name is Helen Crawford from Shawcrofts Solicitors and this is William Goldhawk who has an interest in the case of the murder of Stanley Jakes. His close friend Billy Cosgrove has an arrest warrant served on him for the crime. We have been informed by the police that you have confessed to the murder and we would like to ask you some questions.”

“Fire away, Miss Crawford.” Replied the man.

“Mr. Davenport, Jakes was murdered in October 1939 and it’s now September 1950. Why have you waited so long to confess?”

“With my record I can hardly describe myself as a saintly character now can I? But I do have a conscience. When they charged that boy with the murder I felt bad. Maybe not bad enough to risk the hangman's noose but bad nevertheless. When the doc' told me my lung cancer would kill me I thought, what the hell I'm going to die anyway so if the boy's still alive let's give him a chance."

"The police came last week and they claim your confession is a pack of lies. What do you say to that?" Helen continued.

Davenport, struggling for breath, answered with a shrug. "I'm sure the Inspector has his reasons but doubt they have much to do with justice. I told him I wanted to make a full written statement confessing to the murder but he refused to listen and wouldn't even provide me with pen and paper."

"We only have twenty-five minutes Mr. Davenport so why don't you tell us in your own words about the events which led to the murder?"

"Well it's a story which began in the mid-thirties. Portsmouth was alive with people in those days, ships in and out of the harbour and traders of all description competing to sell their produce. Did you know that by '39 there were over 20,000 men and women working in the dockyards building and repairing the navy's warships? When the siren sounded at the end of each day thousands of workers were disgorged through the Main Gate and into the streets beyond. Queen Street and the Hard were packed to the rafters, people queuing 100 deep to catch the trams and trolley-busses to take them home and bicycles weaving in and out trying to avoid a collision. It was pandemonium.

Everyone had a few pennies to spend but the real money was with the ships, some naval, some merchant which were regular visitors to the harbour. Ships steamed in and out every day, many just to refuel or replenish depleted supplies and mostly they had neither the time nor the inclination to buy stuff with much concern for how much it cost. They just wanted it easy and most importantly they wanted it fast, and that's where I came in. I'd hang around the docks and whenever a ship arrived I'd hunt down the purser or whoever bought their supplies. It was a matter of keeping your eyes peeled and being the first on the scene.

We'd get hold of literally anything from sacks of potatoes, fruit, fresh meat, tins of beans, tomatoes, tea and coffee, cigarettes, pots and pans, books, clothing. You name it and we got it. And of course we bought stuff from the ships too, especially souvenirs from America and the far-east which we'd store in lock-ups around Landport and flog up in London. And we made good money.

I remember one day, not long after the War started a rusty old tanker steamed into port which had been requisitioned by the Royal Navy. This ship had seen better days to say the least and was due to be scrapped before the Navy stepped in. It arrived in Portsmouth empty. I mean *totally* empty. The skeleton crew, which brought her down from Newcastle ditched everything that wasn't battened down into the North Sea. The ship was due to steam to Malta four days later to service the Fleet in the Med and I re-fitted her from top to bottom earning myself six months wages in two weeks!"

"Is this all relevant Mr. Davenport?" Helen asked brusquely, pointedly looking at her watch.

"Just setting the scene love, we have plenty of time yet…as long my lungs don't give out on me." Davenport replied with grimace.

"How did Jakes fit in to all this?" Persisted Helen.

"Well, of course the good times never last forever do they? Looking back it's obvious I suppose that other people would want a slice of the cake and within a couple of months of war breaking out the work started to dry-up. It was harder because there was more competition and my main competitor was none other than Stanley Jakes.

And Jakes was not satisfied with sharing the trade with others, he wanted it all for himself and would use any means to get it. At first it was mostly small bribes, a bottle of Scotch, that sort of thing but it wasn't long before things started turning nasty. One day, it must have been late September, early October I was hanging around the Queens Hotel waiting for a customer when two of Jakes' boys threatened me. They weren't subtle that's for sure! The message was simple, 'stop trading or we will break your legs'. And I knew it was no idle threat as I had seen retribution, Jakes' style, before.

Portsmouth was a lawless City in the thirties and Jakes had contacts. It was pointless even thinking about going to the police. They were involved up to their eyes in corruption so I had little choice but to keep my head down. I had a few loyal customers who kept me in beer money but it was galling watching Jakes swanning around in his swanky car with a different girl on his arm every night."

"Let me get this straight Mr. Davenport, are you insinuating that Stanley Jakes was what...being protected by the police or in league with police in some way?" Helen asked, trying to tease out something more tangible from the prisoner's casual accusation.

"I am not insinuating anything! I'm telling you straight, Sergeant Hanaho was accepting back handers from Jakes, pure and simple. Thing is about Stanley Jakes, he had a big mouth and wasn't shy about telling people his business."

"Right Mr. Davenport, let's move on."

"A few days later, I was trying to cheer myself up with a fried breakfast at the Odeon café in Highland Road when a young lad sidled up to me and handed me a note. Ordinarily I would have taken no notice but the message left me more than a little intrigued suggesting a meeting would be mutually beneficial. And after all, what had I to lose? If I didn't like his proposition I'd quickly be on my way. So I decided to follow the instructions on the note and meet the man that evening at the Canoe Lake.

It was a cold night with clouds obscuring the moon as I found a bench to await the arrival of the mysterious man who had signed himself, 'the professor'. He came a few minutes later and sat down beside me. It was difficult to get much of an impression of the man in the dark but he looked well dressed; expensively dressed with a scarf and hat strategically positioned so there was no possibility of identification. He sat for a short while before he spoke.

'Mr. Davenport, thank you for coming.'

'How do you know my name and what do you want?'

As though I hadn't spoken the professor ploughed on: 'We have a task for you. It's very simple and by midnight tonight it will be completed and you will be walking away with three hundred pounds in your pocket. How does that sound?'

'Look.... Prof' I am really not interested in your scheme.' I lied. In truth I was very interested in the prospect of earning three hundred quid for a couple of hours work.

'Sorry if I have misled you Peter…I can call you Peter?' He asked rhetorically without even a glance in my direction. 'Once you understand the full facts I am sure that you will see that there is no real choice to be made. Can I ask you for your personal question?'

'If you must.' I said with feigned disinterest.

'What is your opinion of Stanley Jakes?'

With three hundred pounds swimming before my eyes I lost my initial reticence and gave an honest answer to his surprising question: 'Stanley Jakes is one of the most objectionable bastards I have ever had the misfortune to run into! He cost me my livelihood.'

'That's good news Clive, because he's going to be dead before the nights out.'

Before I had the chance to lodge a reaction I was aware of a surreal scene unfolding before me. As the clouds scudded across the sky and the moon made a brief appearance the man opened a large Gladstone bag at his feet and pulled out a bottle and two glasses. He unscrewed the cap and poured a generous tot into each glass which he had placed on the bench beside him. Passing a glass to me he said, 'To a better future without Stanley Jakes.'

It was a welcome brandy but did not completely soothe my frayed nerves. The professor was a strange fellow indeed and the direction of his conversation was worrying me. But after a third drink of the sweet and unusual tasting brandy, much of what he said began to fall into place. Indeed I was finding it difficult to argue with his logic. Stanley Jakes was an evil bastard and caused untold misery to the people of Portsmouth so, were I to play a part in his demise, surely I would be rendering the public a useful service?

I was to meet Jakes at the bandstand at midnight where, it had been arranged, we were to exchange money for the photographs in the Gladstone bag. The photographs were of a compromising nature and highly embarrassing for a certain senior figure of the City's establishment and Jakes was prepared to pay one hundred pounds in cash for them. The professor talked me carefully through the plan which involved bashing Stanley Jakes over the back of the head with a hammer when he was on his haunches examining the content of the bag.

What would have seemed an abhorrent and preposterous proposition an hour earlier now made perfect sense. I was to become three hundred pounds richer, I was to get my business back and Portsmouth was to be rid of the lowlife Jakes. As I wandered off to complete my task my head purred. I felt absurdly confident and inexplicably happy at the prospect of the murder I was about to commit.

After changing clothes, at the professor's insistence I made my way to the common. Jakes was waiting inside the bandstand as I arrived. The moon was once again hidden by cloud so it was almost pitch black except the glow of Jakes' cigarette. He greeted me with a nod, and asked, 'You have something for me?'

'In the case.' I replied, as I placed the heavy bag at his feet. 'Here's a torch, make sure you're happy with the contents before we conclude our business.'

As the professor had forecast Stanley Jakes bent over the bag and still feeling calm and serene, I removed the hammer from the deep pocket of my overcoat and brought it down with full force on his head. There was a grotesque crunching sound as the instrument struck his skull and he slumped to the ground. I am sure he was dead instantly but I gave him two more blows to be certain."

"To be clear Mr. Davenport, are you suggesting that something in the brandy gave you the necessary bravado to carry out the murder?" Helen interrupted.

"I wasn't myself Miss Crawford so unless you have a better idea I have to conclude that yes, it was something in the brandy." Davenport replied.

"Please carry on with your story."

"After striking Jakes I retrieved the torch which had fallen through the railings onto the grass and placed the hammer, sticky with blood into the Gladstone bag before rooting around in Jakes' pockets for the money. I then left the scene for my next destination, a lock-up in Greater Southsea Street where I was to leave the bag, wash away any blood, change back into my own clothes and pick-up a further two hundred pounds which was waiting for me. The black-out gave me the cover I needed and it was all absurdly simple. I was to dispose of the key to the lock-up and my business with the enigmatic professor was complete.

With the dawn of the new day how very different it all seemed! I awoke early and was immediately violently sick. My heart beat was hammering in my chest, I was sweating profusely and just the thought of food made me vomit some more. But worst of all was the realisation of the crime I had committed. I felt as though I had slept walked into murder.

The professor was as good as his word though and I was never troubled by the police and as he had predicted someone else was soon under arrest for the crime. My feeling of guilt was immense and I was mightily relieved when I heard young Cosgrove had escaped the clutches of the police."

By this point Clive Davenport was coughing badly and Helen waited for him to catch his breath before asking if we could rely on him to sign a witness statement based on the story he had just told.

Davenport nodded in agreement and Helen added two further questions which she promised the fidgety guard were her last. "Mr. Davenport, can you think of anything which may help us to corroborate your story? Anything you noticed at the scene of the crime which was never reported in the press? And secondly have you got anything else to help us identify the professor; distinguishing marks, facial hair, spectacles…anything at all?"

"The professor was very careful not to reveal himself but I would say he was of average height and build; maybe what…40, 50 years old? The only other thing is that he wasn't local. He had an accent, north country I think. Spectacles, yes maybe but that is just an impression.

I still have the key to the lock-up but unfortunately Hermann Goring's Luftwaffe rather saw to it that any evidence on that front was well and truly buried. The crater is still there I believe, if you want to sift through the debris. Other than that I remember that Jakes had an attaché case with him but I have no idea what it contained. Oh, and his lighter. He had a flip-top style brass cigarette lighter with a motif of some description on the front."

With that, the guard called time and without even the formality of a handshake the prisoner was led away. Clive Davenport looked every inch an affable old uncle rather than a cold blooded killer, I thought, as I watched him shuffle from the room. Could it all be an elaborate hoax I wondered, Clive Davenport having one last laugh at the expense of the local constabulary which had put him away? It certainly seemed possible.

On a number of levels I wanted Clive Davenport's confession to be true. Mostly as a draw to entice Billy home but also to give the local constabulary a bloodied nose. I had good reason not to trust Inspector Hanaho and his cronies and if Davenport's confession bought them to book all well and good. But whether I *did* believe him, I was not entirely sure.

"Extraordinary story but I'm not convinced we have made much progress William." Helen revealed as we took our seats on the train half an hour later. "Even if Davenport is telling the truth I can't see a judge ordering a retrial."

On that somber note we drifted into silence and stared out of the train window with our own thoughts. I wanted to believe Davenport but without something concrete I wondered if our efforts were wasted. And of course, even if we found evidence of his guilt did it still follow that Billy would find his way home? Another question to which I had no answer.

My thoughts drifted to Lucy, another unwanted complication in my life. Lucy's reappearance stirred-up feelings within me which were buried only just beneath the surface. I was in love with Lucy at the point that Billy disappeared and I knew full well a small spark was all that was needed to re-ignite the flame. I turned to face Helen with a feeling of acute discomfort and guilt. My life was so intertwined with Helen's that the consequence of loving another was something that I just could not bring myself to acknowledge. I pushed the thought away and put my arm around Helen's shoulders, as though the act itself would guard against my potential betrayal.

Six

The satisfaction I derived from working with Surtees, Hancock & Lampson had improved markedly over the previous twelve months. Although my agreement to marry Helen had not been overtly influenced by the carrot of the Crawford Electrics' account, at a subliminal level I guiltily accepted it played a part. Working as a junior for a firm of external auditors is as close to slave labour as you can get. The work is tedious beyond measure and the pay outrageously low.

I cannot easily forget the endless hours I spent working my way through voluminous, dusty ledgers in cold, dank offices comparing one set of numbers with another set of numbers. This task is known in auditing circles as 'reconciliation' and I was the worst reconciler in the long and illustrious history of Surtees, Hancock & Lampson. My head swum, my eyes lost focus and my brain refused to co-operate.

Chartered Accountants are, however, by no means, stupid and the conditions under which an articled clerk worked offered the ideal incentive for qualification. And miraculously I passed my examinations at the first time of asking and once Sir Marcus Crawford's signature had ratified Surtees, Hancock & Lampson's appointment as Crawford Electrics' accountant and auditor, my passage to partnership was secure.

The offices of Surtees, Hancock & Lampson were situated in Landport Terrace on the border of Southsea and Portsmouth along with several other accountants and solicitors. Housed in an elegant Georgian terrace on four floors the building, like the partnership itself was the epitome of quiet understatement and professional reserve. The same description could easily be applied to senior partner Brian Surtees who took his rightful place at the head of the Boardroom table.

The Boardroom, on the third floor where prospective clients were courted and current clients entertained was a sumptuous room with a large Edwardian rosewood table as the centerpiece, twelve padded, matching wooden chairs and two leather settees to cater for less formal meetings. Several oils depicting mostly rural scenes and naval battles from Victorian England gave the room an added touch of grandeur.

I took my seat at the table just as Brian Surtees brought our monthly Partners' Meeting to order by reading the previous minutes and giving a resume of the last quarter's management accounts. All was rosy for Surtees, Hancock & Lampson it seemed, as we settled back to bask in our reflective glory. Once the formalities where completed Brian got to the main agenda:

"Crawfords is now by some way the largest client in our portfolio and its importance cannot be overstated." He began, before continuing in the fashion of a Chartered Accountant, to balance good news with bad. "Nor can the additional risk to which it exposes us, likewise, be overstated. Crawfords will represent almost 50% of our fee income this coming year which is frankly far too high. We have had to employ a number of new staff just to cope with their audit. So gentlemen, although Crawfords is an exciting opportunity we must beware the risk.

My recommendation is that William leads the accountancy team and that Douglas takes charge of the audit. Has anyone any objections?" Brian looked around the table at each partner in turn: Douglas Lampson happy to be handed the plum job of managing the audit, Gordon Hancock who was Brian's closest ally, Michael Bridges and me.

"Are we sure that it's the right thing to expose ourselves to so much risk? I am not even sure that it's ethical to advise a client of this size about their financial affairs and at the same time audit their books. Isn't it a bit like marking one's own homework?" Michael was my rival and fieriest critic and I had expected his opposition but to his credit he clearly expressed what everyone in the room had already privately considered.

Brian looked over the top rim of his glasses in my direction and raised his eyebrows to indicate that he wanted me to answer.

"Of course there is always risk but even if Crawfords cancelled the contract tomorrow we are protected by a 12 month contract so would have time to restructure. We can't just pass up an opportunity to grow and earn good returns for fear that we will one day lose the client." Warming to the task, I added. "We would be better off putting some of the fee income from Crawfords into a contingency fund which could offset some of the risk."

Michael was not yet beaten though and replied. "That's all very well but we still have the conflict of interest to consider. How can we advise on financial matters in one breath and then audit their books in the next?"

Gordon Hancock, the most cautious of our partners had been at least partially swayed by Michael's argument. "Of course, in a sense Michael is right. We really need to be careful here."

The battle lines were drawn and Brian was left to adjudicate. Very calmly but decisively he came down in my favour but did so, so smoothly that it appeared to be a perfectly crafted compromise.

"The audit team and the accounts team must be seen to be operating entirely independently. Michael, I would like you to join Douglas on the audit and I will lend my experience to William so that we may advise our client on best practice and offer any financial help we are able. Of course we will continue to monitor and review the situation and will discuss it again at our next partners' meeting."

I felt reasonably satisfied with my day's work as I left the office at around 6.30pm for my rendezvous with my mysterious letter writing friend. I arrived at the Wellington Arms ten minute early and found a quiet table in the corner. With a pint of bitter to hand I opened-up a copy of the Portsmouth Evening News to await their arrival. I was hoping that the paper had uncovered the story of Davenport's confession but there was no mention of it. We needed maximum publicity and I made a mental note to consult Lucy and Helen.

A tall, middle aged man, bald on top with a graying but luxurious moustache arrived on the dot of 7.30 looking decidedly uncomfortable. I had little doubt that he was my man. I made eye contact and he nervously introduced himself as an off duty Sam Jones of the Hampshire Police. He joined me in a pint of bitter and after a few minutes of awkward small talk I steered him toward the business of the evening: "So Sam, what is it that you want to say?"

"You don't remember me do you?" He started, looking up for confirmation. "I was with Inspector Hanaho or sergeant as he was then, when your friend Billy Cosgrove was arrested after his fight with Jakes, Riley and Buchanan. Before the War, like."

"Well well I do remember you Constable Jones. What a stitch-up that was, I have never forgiven your boss for that. It was no *fight*; it was an assault plain and simple!" I replied with feeling.

"And you have good reason to be angry, Mr. Goldhawk. It was a stitch-up. More importantly, every copper at the Station knows that Billy Cosgrove didn't murder Stanley Jakes. In the early thirties I walked the beat around central Southsea and Billy was a good kid, always looking out for the younger ones. I'm telling you Mr. Goldhawk, Billy Cosgrove is no more a murderer than you or I."

"How can you be so sure? After all, he hated Jakes didn't he?" I said, playing the devil's advocate to try and prise more from the suddenly loquacious policeman.

"He did hate Stanley Jakes of course but then who didn't? That's the point Mr. Goldhawk, Jakes had so many enemies! And I'm telling you straight, Billy's no murderer." He looked at me as though willing me to believe him but at the same time not to ask any more awkward questions.

"But what about the hammer that was found in his room?" I persisted.

"Yes well of course but.....look Mr. Goldhawk I really can't say anymore, I've said too much already. And what I've told you is strictly off the record. I really hope you find Billy and that it works out in the end, like. Be very careful with Inspector Hanaho. He had more than a passing acquaintanceship with Jakes as you well know. And he'll do his best to undermine Davenport's confession." With that, Jones stood and without a word more left the pub.

Exhilarated at a clear indication of Billy's innocence but frustrated at not getting anything more concrete from Jones I finished my beer in two gulps and made for the door. Cutting across the Common I walked up into Southsea toward Lucy's flat. I promised her an update and had plenty to tell. She answered her door and my heart missed a beat, with no effort Lucy always looked dazzling and that night was no exception.

We talked at length about everything that had happened and Lucy burst into tears when she heard what Sam Jones said. "I know Billy's innocent." She said. "But I am just so glad to hear that there are other people out there who think so too."

"The constable wanted to tell me something more Lucy, I am sure of it." I finished, trying to understand what it may have been.

"It's something to do with that loathsome Inspector Hanaho I expect." Lucy had been angry and dumbstruck when I told her of the conduct of the bellicose Inspector. Our investigations had so far produced more questions than answers but I strongly suspected that the Inspector held the key.

Seven

One Monday later in the month I was joined by Michael Bridges on an excursion to London to meet the John Benison and his team of accountants at Crawford's prestigious head office in Spital Square. I declined Michael's offer of a lift in his new red Alfa Romeo sports car and chose instead the more sedate but reliable 9.20am express from Portsmouth Harbour to Waterloo.

We found seats in the first class compartment and I flipped open my brief case searching for an excuse to avoid conversation with my companion but to no avail. Michael Bridges liked to talk; and talk he did for the majority of our two hour journey. He was particularly interested in the idea of me furnishing him with details of Lucy Cosgrove, spotted in the reception as Surtees, Hancock & Lampson the previous week. Of course, I spared Lucy the trouble of having to fend off his advances and side-stepped his appeal.

The journey was not a complete waste of time however, as I received a small but useful snippet of information from Michael; the address in New Road of Constable Sam Jones who by a fortunate coincidence belonged to same billiard club as him. After my tantalising encounter with the policeman at the Wellington I rather wanted to pay him another visit. He knew more than he had let on and I needed to know what.

The meeting at Crawfords was a formality and little more than an exercise in public relations. We all shook each others' hands, smiled and exchanged pleasantries for an hour over lunch, before shuffling a few papers back and forth across the desk. We were then introduced to other members of staff and given a tour of the splendidly appointed premises. Having arrived at Spital Square at 1pm, Michael was back on the train heading south by 3.15pm.

Rather than leaving with Michael I jumped on the underground to Russell Square for my appointment with Dr. Nichol, arranged for me by Lucy. I did not really know what to expect of Dr. Nichol: an academic wearing a dusty tweed Jacket working in a book lined study with learned papers strewn across his desk; a scientist peering at specimens under a microscope in a laboratory; or a physician working in a hospital ward treating patients with brain disorders? I was shown into an office where a Doctor, wearing a white coat was seated behind a large and orderly desk. A medical man I decided.

With a friendly smile he shook my hand and introduced himself. "I'm Doctor Andrew Nichol and I am pleased to meet you. I have been looking forward to our chat, it sounds intriguing. Somewhat like a modern day Sherlock Holmes story." He rubbed his hands together in anticipation of our conversation.

Dr. Nichol was a leading British expert in neurological disorder specialising in how chemicals affect the brain's functions. I was interested to find out if the effects that Davenport described were fact or fiction and whether some cocktail of drugs could induce the almost dream like state which had led him to battering Jakes to death. I explained in as much detail as I could about the circumstances of the case and Dr. Nichol listened intently. Once my narrative was complete he rubbed his chin as though in deep thought.

"Very interesting. Yes, very interesting indeed! I would dearly love to meet the fellow who mixed this little cocktail."

"So you think Mr. Davenport could be telling the truth?" I asked, my hopes starting to rise.

"To me this sounds very much like a hallucinogenic drug of some description, either based on mescaline or more likely LCD. Hallucinogens are unstable and the reaction in the subject hard to predict. What's so interesting about this case is that it sounds as though the professor successfully anticipated exactly how the subject would react."

"Do you think that's possible?"

"There's been a lot of experimentation with drugs over the last thirty years but most of it 'underground'. These drugs are generally considered unsafe by the establishment so we do not prescribe them. It's difficult to be sure of course but I am inclined to believe Mr. Davenport. His description is too precise to be made up without a deep understanding of how these hallucinogens would affect the workings of the brain."

"And this LCD, could it be diluted in brandy and absorbed into the blood stream as quickly as Davenport described?" I asked.

"Absolutely, an alcoholic drink of the strength of brandy would disguise the bitter taste and it's very possible that the drugs would start having an almost immediate effect on the brains functions. The drugs work by disrupting your nerve cells which pulse up and down the spinal cord to the brain. They distort your view of the world. In the case of Mr. Davenport it would seem it blocked the inhibitions which would normally have prevented him from committing cold blooded murder."

Dr. Nichol obligingly agreed to write me a letter confirming his opinions which I hoped would add to the weight of evidence we were building to support Mr. Davenport's confession. Feeling vindicated in my decision to approach Dr. Nichol I jumped on the Piccadilly line back to Waterloo before catching the early evening train home.

Once I had taken my seat in an empty carriage my thoughts strayed to events at Southsea Police Station which I hoped to read about in the Portsmouth Evening News later that night. Lucy had planned a banner waving protest at the Station that lunchtime. I picked-up a copy of the paper at Fratton Station before catching a taxi home and judging from the front page story the event had been an unqualified success. The Cosgrove family, friends and neighbours had turned-out in force.

Eight

'I murdered Jakes!' ran the front page headline accompanied by a photograph of Clive Davenport.

The report continued:

> A terminally ill prisoner serving time at his Majesty's pleasure on the Isle of Wight has confessed to the murder of Stanley Jakes. The eleven year old murder of local businessman Jakes and the mysterious disappearance of prime suspect Billy Cosgrove took a dramatic twist when it was revealed today that an inmate of Coneyhurst Prison had confessed to the murder.
>
> The police have remained tight lipped but quashed rumours that Billy Cosgrove's arrest warrant will be revoked. Billy Cosgrove disappeared a few days after the blood stained body of Jakes had been discovered, bludgeoned to death in the bandstand on Southsea seafront. A police spokesman said: "It was far too early to speculate but we urge Mr. Cosgrove to come forward. If he is innocent he has nothing to hide and we will be able to eliminate him from our enquiries. In the meantime we continue to investigate the claims of Mr. Davenport. We will keep the press informed of any further developments."
>
> Over one hundred demonstrators assembled on the steps of Southsea Police Station to protest at what they claim is a police cover-up. Miss Lucy Cosgrove, Billy's sister is convinced that her brother was framed and that the only evidence against him was the murder weapon which she alleges was planted in his bedroom.
>
> Miss Cosgrove further asserts that correct procedures were not followed at the time the police raided their house in 1939 when the blood stained hammer was supposedly

found under floor boards in Billy's bedroom. She stated in 1939 and repeated again today that three officers forced their way into the suspect's house with no search warrant.

Miss Cosgrove waved a copy of Clive Davenport's confession under the nose of Chief Superintendent Nigel Parker as he left the station this evening. Mr. Parker's response was a brusque, "no comment."

The Portsmouth Evening News proved to be a more than useful ally in our attempt to ratchet up the pressure on the police. I had spoken to the Editor, Simon Griffin and passed him a copy of Dr. Nichol's testimony and his editorial the following Thursday was more than we could have hoped for.

I sat with Lucy in her kitchen and over a cup of tea we read and re-read Simon Griffin's damning indictment of the local constabulary. Lucy was unable to believe quite what an impact her protest had made and hoped that finally Billy would be cleared to come home.

My strong impression was that Simon Griffin had something of an axe to grind with the local police and our story gave him the ammunition he needed. But whatever his motivation we were exceedingly pleased for the support. His editorial read:

Corruption in High Places

The British Empire, the most far reaching the world has ever seen, was built on the rule of law; fair treatment for all, enshrined in a judicial system evolved over the centuries. Every citizen of the British Empire has the right to expect protection from criminality and excessive wrong-doing. And yet, in the year AD 1950, within the shores of our proud nation we are subjected to the fetid odor of corruption from the very institution established to protect us.

Superintendent Nigel Parker, you are accused of undermining the confidence of the people of Portsmouth in your ability to maintain law and order. It is disgraceful that Inspector Hanaho, a known former associate of the murder victim, Stanley Jakes, has remained the investigating officer in this case. You have left it to a 27 year old librarian to bring to the attention of us all, the shameful cover-up which has left an innocent man in exile.

Why Superintendent, have you not provided a copy of the search warrant used to gain access to the home of Mr. Cosgrove in 1939? Why Superintendent did you not investigate Mr. Davenport's confession in a timely and rigorous fashion? Why Superintendent did you leave it to Lucy Cosgrove to investigate the efficacy of the hallucinogenic drugs on which Davenport's confession rests? Why Superintendent is Mr. Cosgrove still subject to an arrest warrant when he has nothing left to answer?

If you have a shred of substantiated evidence to support your case against Mr. Cosgrove we want to hear it. Otherwise, allow him to return home without fear of the hangman's noose.

Nine

Six weeks later, in early December we finally received the news that we hoped for, the police had caved in and had applied to the Court to have Billy's arrest warrant quashed. Davenport was close to death but his confession was being thoroughly investigated and Inspector Hanaho had been removed from the case. For us it was a victory, but a hollow one unless it led to Billy finding his way home. Lucy was ecstatic but I was cautious and preached patience.

It had been a whirlwind few weeks and I was happy to return to the humdrum of office life. I sat at my desk one morning, attempting to decipher some new guidelines from the Board of Trade when Douglas Lampson put his head around my door and asked if I could spare a minute. I nodded, only too pleased for the interruption.

"Nothing to worry about I am sure William but nevertheless I felt I should alert you to something I have found." Douglas began, placing an opened ledger somewhat ominously in front of me. "This is all routine stuff really just preparing the way for the Crawford's audit in the new-year. It's just a little strange that some quite large chunks of money are being paid out and no-one in their accounts departments seems able to provide any sort of explanation. There's no audit trail at all; no invoices, delivery notes, purchase orders, nothing."

"I am sure there is a perfectly logical explanation Douglas. When you say large chunks of money, what are we talking about?"

"Well, have a look at this one; £20,000 sterling paid by bankers draft converted to $56,000 US in August. And here." Douglas pointed out another entry showing £16,000 paid by cheque earlier that month.

"So what does the Chief Accountant, John Benison have to say?" I asked, somewhat bemused.

"It's all very odd really. He's a good accountant and knows his stuff but he got very tetchy when I ask him about it; defensive almost. Maybe you should raise it with Sir Marcus? We need to clear it up before the audit, William."

I had a scheduled meeting on the Island with Sir Marcus Crawford for early in the New Year so asked my secretary to add it to our agenda. Reluctantly, I let Douglas go and returned to the less than riveting minutia of the Board of Trade guidelines to taxation on imports.

Life on the domestic front was quiet but as the days rolled into weeks with Christmas only just around the corner I received the expected summons from Lucy. The euphoria of the previous month had day by day, ebbed away as it became clear that Billy was not coming home. I arrived at Lucy's flat to find her in low spirits. She had convinced herself that the battle had been won and her disappointment at her brother's failure to show up was hard for her to bear.

The case had reached the national as well as the local press and his family, friends and supporters had willed Billy to make a triumphant return home. His picture had been emblazoned across the front of most national newspapers and it seemed inconceivable that someone would not come forward with information to help us find him. Had he made it home he would have received a hero's welcome but it was not to be.

I tried to boost Lucy's sagging morale by staying upbeat and offering some practical ideas in our search for Billy but in truth, judged that finding a needle in a haystack would have been simple by comparison to the task which lay before us. Nevertheless, for Lucy's sake I was not conceding defeat quite yet.

Grasping the nettle, I look my leave of Lucy and started the longish walk up toward Copnor to visit Sam Jones. I found walking therapeutic and a good way to organise my thoughts. It was a cold clear evening and I walked briskly to keep the chill at bay. Constable Jones had made it abundantly clear that he had said his piece and would not relish further discussion and it was only instinct on my part that led me to suppose he had further information for me. But as things stood I had little else to go on.

Of course the landscape had changed since my last encounter with the constable. When we met a couple of months earlier at the Wellington Arms I was looking to clear Billy's name, now I was searching for a clue of a different kind. I had got the impression from Jones that he was wrestling with his conscience. He had something more he wanted to tell me but for reasons of his own, was holding back. I wanted to know his secret.

I approached New Road from the west and had a further half a mile or so to walk to reach number eighteen, the address given to me by Michael Bridges. New Road linked Copnor to Fratton and the Jones's home was situated at the far end, near to Copnor Bridge. I was glad to see a light shining from the front room of their terraced house to indicate that someone was at home. I knocked on the door and within a few seconds it was answered by a cheery middle aged woman who I took as Mrs. Jones.

I deftly avoided an explanation for my visit, beyond my need to talk to her husband and she led me into the kitchen and offered me a seat at the table. We were soon joined by a somewhat tetchy Sam Jones who dismissed his wife before rounding on me:

"What do you think you are doing here? I thought I made it clear that I had said all I was prepared to say. Billy Cosgrove has been cleared anyway so I don't quite know what else I can do for you."

Not a great start but hardly unexpected. "Look Sam, I really am sorry to barge in on you like this but I am desperate for a clue that may help us find Billy. Is there anything that you know which may help me?"

“You have no idea what you are getting yourself involved in Mr. Goldhawk. I should never have approached you in the first place. For your own sake just walk out of here and forget Billy Cosgrove. If he’s alive, let him make contact with you when he’s good and ready. That’s the best advice I can give you.” Sam Jones seemed an altogether more decisive and confident man in his own domain.

“That’s a non-starter I’m afraid, you don’t know Lucy, Billy’s sister. She won’t be put off that easily and I promised her that I would do what I could. So I am afraid that with or without your help I will continue looking.” I ploughed on hoping that eventually Sam’s resolve to remain quiet would weaken. “The police must have made efforts to find him surely? After all he was wanted for murder!”

“Look Mr. Goldhawk the truth is that the force did not *want* Billy found. His disappearance was a godsend. Think about it. I really don’t want to have to spell it out.”

My brain was stuck in neutral, whirring away silently without being able to engage the gears. However hard I tried I could not grasp why the police would not want Billy found. It made absolutely no sense to me. I stared at Jones, bewildered, hoping for some sort of explanation.

“I’ve got to hand it to you Mr. Goldhawk you are a cussed bugger, walking all the way from Southsea on the off chance of finding me home. If you are really determined to see this through go and see Betty Gardener at the Station. For pity’s sake make sure it’s on a day when Inspector Hanaho is out or he’ll have your guts for garters. Betty looks after the records and if you ask her nicely she’ll show you the file. Look for the statement of a little girl called Catherine Salter. But please do not let it be known that I spoke to you about this.

Now Mr. Goldhawk, bugger off. I wish you luck. By god you are going to need it.” He shook my hand and gently pushed me toward the door. With an afterthought he added. “And God protect me too, after what I’ve just told you.”

An hour later I was back at Lucy’s flat giving her a blow by blow account of my meeting which between us we tried to decipher. Maybe I should have pushed a little harder to uncover the meaning of Jones’s defining remark but was afraid that being too pushy may have led to him to clam up entirely. The result was that once again we were left with only half the story.

Why were the police happy for Billy to disappear? The only plausible explanation, we agreed, was some kind of cover-up. The convenience of his disappearance was surely that fewer questions would be asked and the murky water left undisturbed.

Ten

I was surprised indeed when a few days later I found another note from Jones pushed through my letterbox suggesting a further meeting. We were only a few days from Christmas, the weather had turned bitterly cold and rather than the cosy warmth of the Wellington Arms, Jones had proposed we met at the rather less enticing Flathouse Quay. For reasons that he explained as 'precautionary,' he had chosen the most isolated spot in the City and left little room for negotiation.

Whether paranoia or prudence I was unsure but felt a little uneasy as I left the house just before 9 o'clock. Only a few days earlier Sam Jones had been explicit in his demand that our communications should cease. He had given me 'insider' information to help me along the way but had made it very clear he intended to say no more.

On the face of it Constable Jones appeared to be public spirited and despite possible repercussions for himself was prepared to assist a fellow citizen battle against the establishment; an establishment of which he was part. That was certainly my hope but I was beginning to suspect his motives. Rather than a philanthropic gesture by the constable I just hoped that I was not being led by the nose up the garden path. With that worrying possibility lodged in a corner of my brain I closed my front door and made my way down the steps and onto the street.

It was a festive Saturday evening with carol singers and party goers out in force and the pubs I passed, en route to the docks were overflowing with good cheer. As I walked along Old Commercial Road past the elegant Georgian terrace, birthplace of Charles Dickens, I was accosted outside the Oliver Twist by a gaggle of lovely ladies with Father Christmas hats, mistletoe and puckered lips. Trying hard not to dampen their good humoured enthusiasm I briefly joined in the revelry before making a diplomatic exit.

Once I had crossed the road I was soon engulfed by the brick built factories and warehouses which comprised the outer development of the commercial docks. What a stark contrast to the streets I had just left behind. Only disjointed voices singing Silent Night reminded me that I was still within spitting distance of the City's pubs. I cursed myself for forgetting a torch as I blundered through the alleyway which ran past the cement works toward my destination, the jetty's beacon at Flathouse Quay.

It was cold, damp and foggy and the weak light of the moon gave me no help finding my way through the urban labyrinth into which I had plunged. The sound of partying was replaced by the blaring of fog horns, the intermittent squawking of the herring gull and the occasional rumble of engines from boats in the harbour, always accompanied by the faint swish of the incoming tide. The docks were otherwise deserted and I soon had trouble with my bearings. The light from the jetty was obscured by the cranes, chimneys and other dockyard paraphernalia and as I passed a familiar landmark, I realised that I had gone around in a full circle.

I was not sure whether to be more annoyed with myself for not bringing a torch or with Jones for his choice of venue. As the swirling fog enveloped me I became more disoriented by the minute and found it almost impossible to distinguish one alleyway from another. My mood was hardly improved when I dashed a shin painfully against some hard unidentifiable object in my path. Breathing deeply in an attempt to recover my equanimity I attempted to manoeuvre myself into a position to get a view of the beacon and regain my bearings.

Much to my relief, I then heard voices close-by. Jones, I hoped, although I had expected him alone. By now the moon had been completely engulfed by the fog and it was pitch black as I groped my way along the wall toward the voices. As I got closer however, I stopped in my tracks. Moving in their direction suddenly seemed like a very unattractive option. Neither one of the voices belonged to Sam Jones.

I came to the intersection where two alleyways crossed and saw torchlight away to my right. It was clear to me now that these men were hunting someone and I had a strong suspicion that I was their prey. I flattened my back to the nearby wall in a bid to remain in the shadows and tried to catch an impression of the whispered conversation. What I heard wafting through the mist confirmed my fears. I was now within a few yards of the two men and in deep trouble.

"What about the copper?" Asked one, in a hoarse whisper.

"Don't concern yourself with 'im." The other replied with a chilling finality. "He's out cold and trussed like a turkey. Keep quiet and listen out, the other one can't be far away."

I retraced my steps in the hope of finding some refuge. My back and outstretched hands followed the contour of the brick wall until I felt a door frame with my gloved left hand. I pushed at the door and was relieved when it creaked open. I felt for a light switch and flicked it on. A light bulb flickered and briefly illuminated a disused factory but quickly fizzled out and I was plunged back into darkness.

Once inside the relative safety of the old factory I took stock. Locked within a maze of pathways and surrounded by the waters of Portsmouth Harbour I knew that a quick escape was out of the question. With what I had just learnt about Jones I decided that, ill equipped as I was, my best chance was to find something I could use as a makeshift weapon and lay in wait.

I got down on my haunches and fumbled around looking for something suitable. There was plenty of debris scattered about and after the flesh crawling sensation of disturbing a loitering rat which used my right arm as a springboard for escape, my fingers curled around a long handled broom.

I took my position behind the door and wrenched the broom head from the handle. In a state of high anxiety my instincts had taken over and my clarity of thought was razor sharp. It seemed inevitable that my pursuers would eventually find their way here and I intended to give them a surprise.

An almost imperceptible crunch of a shoe on concrete and I raised the broom handle above my head. Sure enough, with hinges squealing the door slowly opened and the flash of torch light illuminated the back wall. I waited a fraction of a second more until I got a view of the man's right hand which held a gun. I then cracked my rudimentary weapon down hard across both wrists. With a yelp of surprise he dropped his torch and gun and I jumped onto his back and wrenched his arm upwards. At the same time I issued a clear warning in his ear. "Don't make a sound unless you want a broken arm."

Chartered Accountants are perhaps not best known for their pugnacious qualities but fortunately God had endowed me with a sinewy strength and I had plenty of adrenalin pumping through my body. I placed a foot on the back of the prone figure and picked up both torch and gun before stepping away. Shining the torch into his eyes and training the pistol toward his midriff I gestured for him to put his hands above his head and turn toward the half opened door.

Once outside I gave the man further instructions. "Keep your hands where I can see them and nice and easy lead me to where you left the policeman."

With little choice but to do as I bid, the man, short in height but muscular, stumbled off in what I hoped was the direction of the Quay. Following three paces behind I kept the torch light and the gun trained on the middle of his back. "I am feeling particularly twitchy tonight." I went on. "So please don't make any unexpected moves or my finger may just squeeze a little too hard on the trigger. If your friend turns up just stay calm and advise him to drop his weapon unless you want a bullet in the back."

Maybe I had read too many Biggles' stories in my youth but the adrenalin coursing through my veins had given me a dangerous self-confidence. And it only took a split second for my concentration to waver before I was whacked on the back of the head. Not, of course, that I could recall a great deal about it but I later learnt that my amateurish attempts at being the hero were dashed when villain number two crept up from behind me and acquainted my skull with the butt of his pistol.

Some indeterminate time later I came to with the face of Jones, puffy, bruised and grimy with dried blood, shimmering in and out of focus. He was shaking me and slapping my face as my consciousness returned. "You alright Mr. Goldhawk? Come on man, wake up! It's too cold to hang around here any longer."

As I regained my senses I realized just how cold it was. All my extremities were numb and even talking proved beyond me. The fact that my head felt as though I had just completed twelve rounds with Joe Louis after a night on the tiles didn't help and when I moved other parts of my body showed similar signs of severe distress.

Our attackers had left a torch propped up again the railings with the light illuminating a double wooden door on which was a message, written in what looked alarmingly like blood. My blood I realised as I looked at my hand!

'First and last warning keep your nose out of our business.'

Jones and I stumbled our way back to the main road and after some haggling found a taxi prepared to convey us back to our homes to lick our wounds. The time was certainly not right to pick through the bones of that evening. We agreed to keep our heads down and at least until the dust had settled, thank our good fortune that our bodies had not been dumped in the cold water of the harbour.

Eleven

When I awoke the next morning, I gingerly drew back the covers and got out of bed before hobbling off to the bathroom to assess the damage. I stood naked, in front of the full length mirror and started from the top: face, cut above left eye, bruised right cheekbone and swollen top lip; nose, mouth, jaw in-tact, all functions working no serious damage. Moving down, sized ten boots had been to work on my abdomen, extensively bruised and painful left rib cage, various smaller bruises but otherwise no major concerns. Reproductive organs thankfully untouched. Arms bruised and right elbow grazed and what looked suspiciously like a knife wound across my right palm; long scrape to left shin, self-inflicted; no obvious internal injuries.

The knife wound would leave scarring but other than that I was confident I would recover with no other long-term ill-effects. I ran a bath and after the shock of immersing the open wound in the hot water attempted to soak away my anxieties.

But my brain had other ideas and relaxation was not on my itinerary for the morning. Rather than the warm soapy water soothing my tattered nerves I was taken on a journey into the far recesses of my mind to places I rarely visited.

Everyone, I supposed was an amalgam of their own experiences and I was no different. I was well used to corporal punishment from sadistic teachers in the public school system of the 1930's and rough-house abuse at the hands of local bullies who envied my apparently privileged lifestyle. As a result I was to an extent, inured to physical pain but the psychological impact was harder for me to deal with. Rather than confront my childhood experiences I kept them under lock and key.

I wondered how it must be to root around in the filing cabinet of your mind and retrieve normal happy childhood memories; a bedtime story and a goodnight kiss from mother, a game of French cricket on the lawn with father, an Easter egg hunt with brothers and sisters, mince pies and Father Christmas. The drawer labeled childhood in the filing cabinet of my mind was firmly locked. However deep I delved all I found was the pain, emotional depravation and loneliness.

After my mother had died when I was only four, I had been brought up by my father, Sir Edward Goldhawk JP, at Liongate. As the story went, my young life was blessed with privilege and the trappings that wealth brought with it. I was privately educated and wanted for absolutely nothing. Certainly that was the impression that my father liked to give and I sometimes suspected that he believed his own press.

In many ways my father was the archetypal English gentleman but to me he was cold, aloof and incapable of responding to the needs of a lonely child. With a feeling of melancholy sweeping over me I tried hard to redirect my thoughts but got myself into further trouble by bringing to mind Lucy. My love life was something else that I had failed to confront. I expected visits from both Lucy and Helen that day and had a premonition that the threads of my personal life were just starting to unravel.

***

Lucy came and went and was visibly shocked, confused and frightened by the events I described. She was all for involving the police until I reminded her that one of the two victims was a policeman himself. I soothed her fragility and gently brought her back to an even keel.

Once calmed, I asked Lucy about her interview with Betty Gardener at the police station. She had copied the statement of Catherine Salter and went through it with me. If we had not already suspected the police of corruption perhaps we would have been outraged at their failure to follow-up the lead. Catherine had been eight years old at the time and lived opposite the Red, White and Blue public house in Fawcett Road. She claimed that from the vantage point of her bedroom window, to have watched a man being forcibly bundled into the back of van and driven-off, just at the time that Billy had disappeared.

By the time Lucy was ready to leave she was in better spirits and looked forward to acting the detective and uncovering the present whereabouts of Catherine Salter. We hugged, awkwardly at first but then with warmth as we relaxed in each other's arms. I kissed her on the cheek and lingered just a second longer I should have.

It was early afternoon when Helen breezed in. "My god, what on earth has happened to you? Have you been in a brawl? It's Christmas Eve tomorrow and we are supposed to be going to see The Cocktail Party at the Old Vic, or had you forgotten?" She was spitting fire.

"Oh, Christ… yes, of course. No I hadn't forgotten." I lied unconvincingly. I then went on to tell the story of the previous evening but rather than sympathy I drew more anger.

"I've had it up to here with you William!" Jaw jutting, she used a hand above her head to emphasise the point. "You have become totally obsessed with this Cosgrove business and spend more time with Lucy than with me. If you think I am going to London with you looking like that, think again! You look like an Irish navy after a Saint Patrick's Day bash!

They could have killed you last night! And what next? You are a bloody accountant William, not a comic book superhero!" Without drawing breath Helen continued. "We have no fun anymore and I'm fed up with it William. Michael has been pestering me all week and I've good mind to call him up. At least he knows how to treat a woman!" She finished with a final flourish and a metaphorical punch in solar plexus.

Helen's anger showed little sign of abating and after a few more complaints about my failure as lover and companion she walked out. I was not quite sure how I should react but my indecision perhaps provided the answer. In my heart I knew that I had withdrawn from Helen in recent weeks, not on a conscious level but her intuition was enough to sense my imminent betrayal.

The following day I received a card through my door from Helen suggesting a trial separation which I assumed was a way of removing the immediate pain and feeding it back slowly over an indeterminate period of time. I strongly suspected that our life together was over. Helen and I had planned to spend Christmas with her family at their favourite retreat in Rimini but now it seemed I would be making alternative plans, somewhat nearer to home.

My relationship with Helen's father Sir Marcus had been cordial (maybe more than cordial) but I was not looking forward to our next encounter. He was not prone to mincing his words and I anticipated a fiery exchange of views. Neither did I relish giving the news to Brian Surtees that my engagement to the daughter of our biggest client had been shelved. I wondered whether Brian may regret my recent elevation to partner.

At least the solitude of a solo Christmas would give my body a chance to recuperate and my mind an opportunity to take stock. My father had offered me an olive branch and suggested I lunched with him at Liongate on Christmas Day but I had politely declined that too giving him the excuse of a prior arrangement. My sense of duty dictated that I should call in at some point over the holiday period but that would now be an awkward occasion without Helen on my arm. Helen was about the only part of my life which my father unequivocally approved.

Twelve

Despite the events of the past twenty-four hours I entered the Christmas holiday in a surprisingly sanguine frame of mind. My feelings toward my split with Helen were ambivalent. We had been together many years and had undoubtedly shared good times but I wondered whether our relationship had run its natural course. Although guilt swept in and out with the tide I was looking toward the future with a degree of optimism.

My good mood was in a large part due to the fact that I was to have the pleasure of Lucy's company on the afternoon of Christmas Day. With a cynical disregard for morality I had called the Library the previous morning and 'inadvertently' dropped into a conversation with her good friend, colleague and incorrigible gossip Dot Flanagan the change in my arrangements for Christmas. The deed was sealed when I asked Dot to promise on pain of death not to breathe a word to Lucy.

Although Lucy and I had been friends of sorts since we had been teenagers, most of what we knew about each other had been learnt second hand from mutual acquaintances particularly in the early days of course, from Billy. I hoped that our cosy Christmas on the couch would be an opportunity for us to get to know one another better.

Lucy arrived in the middle of the afternoon and I sat her down on the settee before disappearing into the kitchen to fetch some Christmas cheer. When I reappeared a couple of minutes later laden with mince pies, Christmas cake and sherry I found Lucy scrutinizing the framed photograph on my mantelpiece above the open fire.

"Your mother and father?" she asked using her sleeve to wipe the dusty glass.

"Mother yes, father no." I replied.

She turned and looked at me with a wide smile and asked, incredulous. "William, are you telling me this man is not your father? I am sorry if I sound unconvinced but look, you are the image of him. Tell me about your mother William….and this man who *isn't* your father!"

"If he looks like me it's a pure coincidence I can assure you. Geoffrey is his name and I know nothing about him except that he was killed in the Great War at least three years before I was born. I was four when my mother died and sadly I have very little recollection of her. My father refuses to recognise she even existed. He won't talk to me about her at all. Just before she died she did write me a letter though, with instructions that I should open it on my eighteenth birthday."

"That's so sad William, I am sorry. What did she say in her letter?"

"To this day I've never read it although I had it in my hands once, albeit briefly"

"Tell me what happened, I love stories." With that Lucy made herself comfortable on the far end of the settee with feet curled beneath her.

So I told Lucy the story of how I lost my mother's letter. It was not the story of my childhood but in many ways it captured the essence of my childhood. It centred on a day which saw the beginning of a chain of events which was to shape my life and those around me for many years to come.

"There's no way to soften the edges or blur the reality, my life at Liongate was miserable. My father was aloof when sober and melancholic when drinking. Yes it is true that he was (and is still) a very generous philanthropist and benefactor to all sorts of worthy causes but when I needed him most he went missing. No warm words to soothe me to sleep, no bedtime stories or encouragement to help me on my way. He was no father to me.

We occupied the same space but we were in no sense a family. I spent most of my time locked away in my bedroom and the only succor and comfort I got was from Gladys and Reginald Cobbett the housekeeper and gardener who lived in rooms on the ground floor. They did their best to keep my spirits up and were very kind to me. They talked fondly of my mother and were my only real link with the past. Sunday breakfast at the Cobbetts was one of my few pleasures.

It was a Sunday morning not long before I turned eighteen when, after a good fry-up on the ground floor, Mr. Cobbett suddenly became uncharacteristically serious. I can picture the scene as though it were yesterday. He placed his empty cup on the table in front of him, leaned forward in his chair and cleared his throat. 'Right young William we have something important to talk to you about it and it concerns your mother. Would you like to bring the folder in please Gladys?'

Mrs. Cobbett walked into the back bedroom before returning with a package in her hands which she ceremonially placed on the table in front of me. 'Your mother gave us this in the week before she passed away William and we were instructed to hold onto it until your eighteenth birthday.'

As you will imagine my heart raced. Inside the package were several photographs and an envelope with my name barely legible in ink, faded brown with age. The picture which immediately caught my eye was the one you were looking at earlier. I of course recognised the woman as my mother but had no idea about the man by her side. I turned the print over and on the back was written: 'My dearest Catherine,' and signed 'with love, Geoffrey.' I was told later that Geoffrey was killed in the Great War.

I expected to discover the identity of my mother's mystery friend in the letter and was anxious to get back to my room to read it so I took my leave of the Cobbetts and bounded up the stairs. Maybe it was inevitable that of all the times to choose my father should come hunting for me that very morning. He caught me on the landing and summoned me into his study.

In his usual style he started lecturing me about my friendship with Billy. I knew it was coming as this was only days after the incident with Jakes and co outside the Talbot when Billy had been arrested by Hanaho. 'Now, look here, William! I spend my hard earned money sending you to the best school in Portsmouth and you spurn the opportunity and ignore your classmates in favour of an urchin from the dockyards! Do you not understand William that you have responsibilities? You may be only seventeen but it's a question of position.

I have nothing against the boy personally…what's his name…Billy Cosgrove? But you have got to understand he is essentially a working class boy and you are part of the governing class. Discipline in society is maintained by strict divisions and the boundaries should not be crossed. It really will not do, William.'

I could never really fathom the intensity of the hatred my father seemed to have for my friendship with your brother. It was out of character in many ways. Although he was a snob of sorts he rarely showed much emotion and generally left me to my own devises but there was something about Billy…. I am sure that he was secretly relieved when he heard that he had been arrested. He certainly had a self-righteous look on his face when he told me about it.

I had heard his lectures many times before but on this occasion his tone suggested that he may have some hidden agenda. Given the ruckus in the Talbot I had expected the kitchen sink but his language was actually more conciliatory than usual. My instincts told me to be weary but my ears pricked up.

‘I think I may be at least in part to blame for this rebellion of yours and I want to offer you a deal. No more escapades with Billy Cosgrove and I will give you more responsibilities and pay you a small monthly allowance. After all William, you are my only heir and one day Liongate and everything I own will be yours.’

I could hardly take in what I was hearing. This was a shift of such monumental proportions from the way in which I was normally addressed by my father that I wondered if he had experienced an epiphany. I was literally struck dumb and stared at him in disbelief.

‘Well William, do we have a deal?’

My instinct was to shout ‘No father we do not have a deal! I do not trust you and I have no intention of giving up my friends!’ But of course I did not say that.

What I actually said was, ‘What sort of responsibilities had you in mind father?’

‘Well William, I have been invited to visit the factory of Sir Marcus Crawford on the Isle of Wight. Sir Marcus has put a plane at my disposal and I will be flying from Hilsea. I would like you to accompany me. We can talk more about it then.’

As I sat on the brown leather settee opposite my father digesting the implications of his offer, I absently removed the envelope with my mother’s letter from my shirt pocket. I was so thrown by the unexpected turn of events that I was not conscious of holding the letter and slowing tapping it on the arm of the settee. In two strides my father crossed the room and snatched the envelope from my hand. Looking down and recognizing the writing his control snapped.

I rarely saw my father lose his temper. He was a man always in control of his emotions. Well, a*lmost* always. ‘Where did you get this from William? I am not sure what game you are playing but you are not doing it at my expense. Whilst you are under my roof you'll play by my rules!' His face reddened as he struggled to control his anger.

Why the discovery of the letter caused my father so much anxiety I could not say. It was clear that his meeting with me that morning had been carefully choreographed to lure me into helping him with some scheme and the letter undoubtedly came as a nasty shock. It almost but not quite derailed him. From the brink, he recovered his composure.

'We'll say no more about this William. But I want an assurance from you that you will stop delving into the past and that you will refrain from seeing the boy Cosgrove again. This world is booming William and there is plenty to look forward to. Grab it with both hands, that's my advice. If you keep moping about your mother and the past it won't make you happy, mark my words. Nothing will change the past but the future is in your hands.'

I knew it was pointless making any attempt to appeal to his better nature and short of a physical assault I saw no way of immediately retrieving the letter so I glumly accepted my fate and have regretted my timidity ever since." I looked up at Lucy who had listened politely but I could see that she had something on her mind.

"I can't imagine anyone having anything against Billy. He was no more than a harmless kid really and always looked out for his friends. What could your father have had against him I wonder? And what was in that letter? What could your mother have possibly said that would have made your father so angry? There's more to this than meets the eye."

"Well I don't know Lucy. Perhaps he was genuinely trying to protect me." I replied disingenuously, for in truth I knew I was in denial about my past. My memories were too painful and I had kept my head firmly buried in the sand for many years. If things did not add-up I simply ignored the arithmetic. It was easier that way.

"Well listen carefully William, because I have some news for you. Geoffrey was killed in the Great War you said?" Lucy asked as she walked across to the hearth to retrieve the photograph on the mantelpiece. "Actually *no*, Geoffrey was not killed in the War. Geoffrey he was very much alive when the War finished in 1918."

"What makes you think that Lucy?" I asked sceptically.

"Geoffrey was an officer in the Flying Corp and was alive until at least 1920."

"Go on, illuminate me. How could you possibly know that?" I asked, picking the photograph up and squinting at it under the electric light.

"You do need to look closely I admit but clearly they were married as you can see by their matching wedding rings. Now, do you see the unusual jacket Geoffrey's wearing with the button over lapel? That's standard officer issue for the Flying Corp in WW1."

"So you think Geoffrey was a pilot?"

"Very probably. Now look at the medals pinned to his chest. Recognise them?"

"Not really my area of expertise I'm afraid."

"Well you have the British War Medal, the Victory Medal and here at the end is a DSO an award for gallantry in the face of enemy fire. Not only handsome but brave too."

"How do you know all this?" I asked hardly daring to believe what I was hearing.

"Not bad for a girl, eh? It's what I do William, help people with their research at the Library. Now the thing is these medals were not issued until at least 1920, so Geoffrey was unequivocally not killed in action."

"That can't be Lucy, I was born in 1921! Are you absolutely sure? It doesn't make any sense. If he was my mother's first husband and was alive in 1920 well surely…"

"Yes, William he was alive until *at least* 1920 and I'd go further. Look at the photograph again and tell me what you see in the background?"

"Yes I see what you mean…it was summer! He was alive in the summer of 1920 and I was born in the spring of 1921!"

I was stunned. Was it possible that this man was my father? It was hard not to notice the resemblance. Like me, the man in the photograph was tall with a fair complexion.

"William, have you got a copy of your birth certificate? That would be the best place to start."

"Um, well I don't know. No I don't think I have. I have a passport but my father organised that for me when I went to America last year."

"We need to get hold of a copy of your birth certificate. That will confirm the name of your father and also give us your mother's maiden name. So you were born on 4th April 1921; where, here in Portsmouth? And what's your full name?"

I confirmed my full name and that I had been born, as far as I knew, at St Mary's Hospital in the city.

"Leave it to me William and I'll see what I can dig out."

The rest of the afternoon was something of a blur as I tried to come to terms with I had learnt. We did later talk about Billy and how we should proceed; with extreme caution, it was agreed after the assault at Flathouse Quay. It was decided I should pay Sam one more visit in a last ditch attempt to find out what he knew. Although I guessed Sam in all likelihood would be doing his best to avoid me. After that our search for Billy would be more discreet and away from the prying eyes of our unseen enemy.

Lucy said very little about Helen and the reasons for our apparent break-up which I had no doubt had been graphically described with numerous embellishments by her friend Dot. But I kept my own council, mostly because I was disconcertingly unmoved by the whole episode and worried that Lucy may take me as callous.

***

Leaving my visit to Liongate until New Year's Eve to give my injuries more time to heal I walked through the garden gate on Sussex Terrace and down the pathway under the cedar to the front door. Since the Cobbetts had died, Liongate held little appeal for me and my visits were infrequent. This particular visit however, held a certain piquancy given my recent discoveries. I had reasoned with myself that until I could prove otherwise I would still take it that Sir Edward was my father but if honest with myself the doubts were difficult to suppress.

Conversation was stilted and awkward and I decided to make my excuses for Helen and pretend nothing was amiss. My father's new wife Elizabeth had gone some way to mellowing my father it seemed as he made more effort than he usually did to show some interest in my life, asking banal questions about my job and indiscreet enquiries about his prospects of becoming a grandfather. After what I considered an appropriate time I stood to take my leave but before I did so I asked my father if he had a copy of my birth certificate. He seemed someone taken aback by my request but recovered quickly and promised to drop a copy in to me during the week.

Thirteen

The New Year came and went and I heard nothing at all from Helen which was something of an irony I thought as I stood on my front step signing for the new Sunbeam which was now parked outside the house. Helen had cajoled me for months into buying a car and having finally succumbed she was not around to share the excitement of its arrival. I tried to remain unmoved but was hit by wave of regret as I took the keys from Henry Dawson, the proprietor of Whites Motors and walked down the steps to inspect my gleaming new machine.

I was given a detailed run through of the car's controls by the thorough Mr. Dawson as flurries of snow began to fall making me feel very glad that the car was fitted with a heater. The cream coloured paint work had been polished to a shine and by the time I was ready to take to the road quite a crowd had gathered to cheer me on; mostly boys from the street, their enthusiasm infectious as they asked question after question of the redoubtable Henry Dawson.

"A 2 litre four cylinder is it sir?" asked one young lad peering under the bonnet.

"Yes, that's right laddie, The Sunbeam-Talbot 90 sports tourer built in Coventry, top speed over 85 miles per hour."

Once behind the wheel I turned the ignition and the engine instantly fired. I shifted the gear lever into first, disengaged the clutch and much to my embarrassment proceeded to kangaroo hop down the road. Once settled though, I soon got the hang of the gearbox and enjoyed the sensation of my first drive in the new car.

The inaugural destination for the Sunbeam was the offices of Mr. Sebastian Harris, former solicitor to the Cosgrove family. My drive took me along the Eastern Road out toward the A3 where I branched-off to the picturesque village of Emsworth, a few miles along the coast. Harris's office overlooked a tidal Mill Pond just off the main road which I approached from the west before carefully manoeuvring the Sunbeam through the wooden gate posts and pulling to a stop next to a blue Bentley which I assumed belonged to Harris.

I had dual purpose to my meeting that morning. Firstly I wished to pick up the Cosgrove file and ascertain whether there was anything more that I should know about the case and secondly I wanted to quiz Mr. Harris about his history with my mother. I felt we had unfinished business from our first encounter on the Isle of Wight.

It was just before the war and I had been visiting Crawford's new factory with my father when the smartly dressed and bespectacled Sebastian Harris strode up and introduced himself. We had chatted for some time, mostly about the state of the world and the Nazi invasion of Czechoslovakia when quite out of the blue and much to my astonishment he told me that he had known my mother.

A strange and unsatisfying dialogue ensued in which Harris recounted his first meeting with her in Paris after the first War and I was left with the distinct impression that I was fed only the scraps from a far more involved story. He was equally unforthcoming when questioned about the portrait of my mother and the uniformed officer and would only tell me that the man I described had, as far as he knew, been killed during the latter stages of the Great War.

As I buttoned up my coat, wrapped a scarf around my exposed neck and opened the car door, snow was falling heavily. It created an attractive panorama of white which covered the path and cottage roofs surrounding the Mill Pond. I slipped and slithered my way to the front of the building and pushed through the door. As I brushed the snow from my shoulders Sebastian Harris was on hand to help me off with my coat.

"Very good to see you again William, it's been a long time." He gave me a warm smile and gestured for me to take a seat in his plush office before he poked his head around the door and asked his secretary to prepare a pot of tea.

As I sat down in the sumptuous leather armchair I took in the classy opulence of my surroundings. I felt somewhat in awe of Sebastian Harris. Whereas I was no more than a parochial boy from Portsmouth, he was a 'citizen of the world', sophisticated and urbane. Furthermore, he was a past master at creating a relaxed and convivial atmosphere. It was hard not to enjoy the company of a man with such style. We talked of this and that for a good few minutes before he turned in his swivel chair and removed a folder from the wooden filing cabinet behind him.

"This is Billy's file, William. As you see it's fairly sparse as of course I never actually had the pleasure of meeting Mr. Cosgrove. I will leave this with you so that you are able to digest the contents at your leisure but there is something important that I do need to tell you about. I have been in two minds now for some time about whether I should disclose this information but my conscience has dictated I should." He pursed his lips and placed his fingers together, a combination designed, I sensed, to accentuate the gravity of what he was about to divulge.

"For this, I will be in breach of the Official Secrets Act for which I could lose my livelihood and my liberty so my decision to talk has not been taken lightly. However." He paused. "I have read all about Miss Cosgrove's efforts to have Billy's arrest warrant overturned and frankly, I was moved. She is a brave and determined young woman and for both your sakes I have come to a decision. But I cannot over-emphasise the need for your assurance that nothing I tell you will go further than you and Miss Cosgrove."

I was taken aback but nodded to convey my understanding.

“I’m afraid that it’s not a story with a happy ending.” He paused again to allow me to absorb the implications of what he had just said.

“Not long after Billy’s disappearance at the end of October 1939, over a period of seven or eight days a number of bodies were washed up in and around Prinsted Harbour…German sailors: and after a frantic search a critically damaged U-boat was found within 200 yards of the entrance to Portsmouth Harbour. Somehow it had avoided detection and almost scuppered the Admiralties defense of the realm strategy overnight. It had serious repercussions for the plans to defend the Naval Base and frankly put the fear of god into the Admiralty.

For the sake of ‘morale’ it was hushed-up and the bodies of the sailors quietly disposed of out in the channel. A few days later, another body was discovered washed-up on Thorney Island and in my capacity as Chairman of the area’s Defense Committee I was called out to supervise its recovery. It was assumed to be another member of the U boat crew but I knew very well that it wasn’t. I had photographs of Billy Cosgrove on file and even in its decomposed state I was sure I was looking at his body.

I was lent on, for reasons of ‘National Security’, to sign papers delivering the body to the Royal Navy for ‘repatriation’ (their term for dumping bodies out to sea, I fear). There are no records of the event, at least no official records, so Billy Cosgrove is still recorded as missing but I regret to tell you that he is dead.”

After another brief pause Harris continued. “I am sorry to be the bearer of such bad news William but I did not want to watch Miss Cosgrove and yourself wasting time in a painful and fruitless search.”

I was shocked and spluttered in reply. “Can I ask if there is any doubt? After all he must have been in the water for some time.”

Harris swiveled once again on his chair and after a short search produced a buff coloured envelope which he handed to me. "This was found on his wrist. Perhaps either you or Miss Cosgrove may be able to identify it?" I pulled out a severely water damaged wrist watch, unrecognizable to me but perhaps not to Lucy.

"Is there anymore that you can tell me? Any sign of a wound which could suggest how he met his death? There was no post mortem I assume?" I asked, hunting blindly for clues.

"I am afraid I really can't help you. I could only guess at his state of mind after being accused of the murder of Jakes: so suicide perhaps or an accident, although that would be stretching credulity. I am sorry but anything I say would be pure speculation."

I did not have the heart for further questions so bid Mr. Harris a good morning and made my way outside to a vista of white.

As I sat in the car, warming the engine and watching the wipers clear the snow from the windscreen a battery of disconnected thoughts bombarded my confused and jaded brain. Although Harris had given no real indication as to how Billy may have died, murder seemed the most likely cause given what I knew of Billy. Certainly I could not see him taking his own life.

So what now? It was a conundrum indeed. Billy was dead and quite possibly murdered but I was powerless to do anything. There was no body and no evidence. However I played my cards it seemed I was destined to lose. And how was I to explain this to Lucy? With that depressing thought I inched the Sunbeam through the gates and out onto the main road back to Portsmouth.

Fourteen

I returned to work the following day and had hardly planted my feet under the desk when I was summoned to the office of Brian Surtees. With a perfunctory knock I entered to find him in conversation with a striking, slightly bohemian looking man with a crop of black hair streaked with grey and dressed in a traditional dark pin striped suit accentuated by a bright yellow tie; a man unlikely to be ignored in a crowd. Brian looked up as I entered and introduced us.

"William, come in and meet Julian Singleton from the Inland Revenue Investigation Department, he is interesting in the Jakes /Cosgrove case and I am hoping you may be able to help each other out. Julian is down from London and has been investigating various cases of tax evasion and fraud in the region. Perhaps I can leave you to expand on this Julian?"

The man smiled as he offered me his hand before beginning his explanation. "My role is primarily to investigate tax fraud and I was interested to hear of your involvement in the case of Stanley Jakes because he is very much on our radar. A small time fraudster in the main but we believe that it may have been his association with some altogether more serious criminals which got him killed.

During mobilization and through the War, Portsmouth, along with London was the main centre for the disbursement of contracts for the Admiralty. Huge sums of money were involved and as most were connected with issues of National Security and speed of manufacture critical, procedures were often circumvented and normal financial safeguards ignored. The result was the potential for fraud on a grand scale with the Inland Revenue losing millions of pounds in tax revenues.

This wasn't helped by the bombing of the Town Hall in January 1941 which destroyed so many of the City's records. Counterfeit operations sprang-up and forged identity papers flooded the city. It became increasingly difficult for us to keep tabs on both individuals and small businesses, with literally thousands of people paying no taxes at all because we had no record that they even existed.

People with debts disappeared and popped-up a few weeks later with new identities and their slates wiped clean. Counterfeit documents were selling in the pubs for five bob a time which was a major problem for a Government desperate to raise money for the War effort. Things have improved since '45 of course but there is an estimated £10 million in unpaid tax that we are still chasing.

Anyway, back to Stanley Jakes. There were a number of extremely large contracts awarded by the Admiralty in the late 1930's and we have serious doubts about their legitimacy. It's been almost impossible to track back through the Navy's own records to get an understanding of what exactly went on. Millions of pounds were spent and much of the money just cannot be traced. We believe Jakes was a pawn in a complex and deadly game of chess and we think that if we can find out who killed him, we may just find out who was the mastermind behind much of the criminal activity in the region.

Now, I am a civil servant and have no authority to investigate a murder so all I can do is rely on the police or other agencies to help me out. Until the last two years of his life Jakes was little more than an itinerant labourer picking up casual work when he was sober (which wasn't very often by all accounts) and spending it in the pub the same evening. And yet when he died he had amassed over £15,000, some in bank accounts under false names and plenty, literally stuffed into a mattress in his bedroom.

Jakes was apt to shout his mouth off which is, we suspect, what did for him in the end. Our mastermind is quiet, discreet, invisible and the inability of Jakes to control his drinking and his tongue was likely his downfall."

I had listened with rapt attention but was unsure exactly where the man was going with this so I asked. “All very interesting but how do I fit into this?”

“I understand from Brian, that you are trying to find Billy Cosgrove which makes us both interested in the same thing. Who killed Jakes and why?”

Given the revelations of Sebastian Harris my interest in finding Billy had, of course, evaporated but I was not in a position to broadcast this, so noncommittally nodded my head and asked Singleton to be more specific.

“Right, well let’s get to the nub. I have to be seen to work the official channels and haven’t the authority to go rooting around the back alleys asking questions and making a nuisance of myself. Of course, in theory this is the job of the police but the local constabulary are not playing ball. I have information but I need someone to do some unofficial ferreting around for me.”

“William, let me declare my interest here.” Interrupted Brian. “I have known Julian for many years and although my instinct is to keep well out of all this subterfuge he has eloquently persuaded me that this investigation is crucial for the region if we are to rid ourselves of the menace of organised crime. So as long you act with extreme caution and keep me in the loop I will give you my backing.”

What could I say? I was left feeling helpless and my only recourse was procrastination. I promised both Brian and Julian Singleton that I would give consideration to their request and provide my answer in due course.

***

All this seemed very unimportant in comparison to the news that I had yet to impart to Lucy about her brother’s death and it was with a heavy heart that I walked down Landport Terrace that lunchtime to meet her. As I arrived Lucy was standing on the steps waiting for me looking lovely as always in her understated fashion. Smiling she greeted me with a kiss on the cheek and linked my arm before steering me up the road toward Betty's Tea Shop.

One of Lucy's most endearing characteristics was her humility. She seemed genuinely oblivious to her own feminine attractiveness and many would-be suitors had been gently cast aside as she paid penance for the part she played in Billy's disappearance. I wondered if the news I had to disclose would enable her to finally put the past to rest but I worried it may have the opposite effect and increase her isolation. Either way I understood that she would need time and space to grieve.

She took the news with an equanimity that I hardly expected but on reflection I realised that she had had twelve years in which to prepare for this eventuality and had probably rehearsed the moment a thousand times in her head. I was less surprised at her unequivocal determination to maintain her struggle for justice. In her mind the fact that Billy was dead had no bearing on her sibling duty to seek out the truth. Her steely eyed look left me in no doubt as to how we were to proceed.

I had hoped but hardly expected Billy's death to bring our investigations to a close but I had no intention of letting Lucy down. After a half drunk cup of tea I walked her back to work. Before she climbed the steps she turned and hugged me and I saw the tears in the corner of her eyes. She held Billy's battered watch tightly in her hand as though it was the last remaining link with her brother.

"We can't say goodbye properly can we William because Billy is not 'officially' dead? But we must walk down to the beach on Saturday, just us two and say our own personal goodbyes. I would feel better."

So that was how we said our farewells to Billy, hand in hand on Southsea beach with a posy of dried flowers which we cast into the surf.

Fifteen

My life dropped into something of a hiatus in the aftermath of the hectic Christmas period as I waited to hear from the two women in my life. I had discovered, second hand that Helen was now seeing Michael Bridges which assuaged my guilt to an extent but I was still anticipating communication from her to formalise the arrangements for our separation. I was more concerned with Lucy though, who seemed to be displaying worrying signs of isolation since she had received confirmation of Billy's death.

A few days later however, I realised that I had seriously underestimated her resilience as she glided into my sitting room looking full of verve. "We need to talk William." With a sunny smile Lucy then put both arms around my neck and kissed me on the lips. I went weak at the knees and lost the capacity for speech.

"Cat got your tongue?" Lucy teased.

The amused look on her face and the glint in her eye reminded me of the Lucy I had fallen madly in love with when I was a gangly sixteen year old, confident, flirtatious and alluring.

"Billy was so full of life and the last thing he would have wanted would be for me to mope about feeling sorry for myself. I owe it to him to look for the truth but I will not let this destroy my life. But it's not your battle anymore William and I will understand if you want to duck out now." Lucy said biting her lip and looking coy in anticipation of me turning down her duplicitous offer.

"You know full well that I would never abandon you. So help me god, I am in this until the bitter end."

"That's jolly good because I have found out where Catherine Salter lives and I thought we should visit her this evening." I had almost forgotten about the young Catherine Salter who had witnessed the abduction of Billy.

I was sorry to dampen the mood but worried that Lucy had not completely grasped the danger of our position. "Whatever happened to Billy we can be pretty certain that somehow he got mixed-up with some pretty ruthless people and if we open this particular Pandora's Box we have no idea what we may find inside Lucy, so prepare for a rough ride."

"Oh William, I love it when you get all protective! Don't worry I'll be careful I promise. Now let's have a cup of tea and have a look at the birth certificate that your father dropped in." Lucy followed me into the dining room and sat at the table whilst I made a pot of tea and retrieved the birth certificate from my brief case.

A couple of minutes later I was back, tray in hands and envelope tucked under my arm. I poured the tea and Lucy examined the birth certificate. "Interesting." She muttered quietly to herself. "I have looked at the photograph again and the earliest it could have been taken was July 1920 exactly nine months before your birth!"

"I know. It doesn't make sense. My mother's maiden name being Smith doesn't exactly help either, does it? How we track her down now heaven only knows. But at least it has squashed any idea that Geoffrey was my father. That was a blow though, I don't mind telling you. I rather took to the idea of being the son of a World War One pilot. Rather romantic don't you think?"

"Let's face it William, you are an accountant so hardly likely to have a flying ace as a father!"

I scowled as Lucy laughed.

"Sorry! Let's move on...I've been doing a bit of digging. Do you remember saying you wanted to give me a ride in your new car? Well how about a trip up to Kent next Saturday?"

I raised my eyebrows to indicate I needed more information.

“Just pick me up at 9.00 o’clock with an overnight bag and all will be revealed.” Lucy answered tantalizingly.

It was four months since Lucy had re-entered my life and I was totally besotted. Life with Helen had been tranquil, ordered and unexciting and my heartbeat had rarely risen about its normal setting. My engagement to Helen was a sort of family contract and had nothing much to do with personal feelings. The Crawfords were old fashioned and duty, status and money were the defining precepts behind choosing a life partner. For them the idea that love should be the predetermining force behind a marriage was something confined to Hollywood movies.

I was hardly different and followed without question the accepted wisdom as espoused by The Tattler that ‘William Goldhawk and Helen Crawford were deeply in love, the darlings of the South Coast Set and destined for a long and happy marriage.’ Nothing, it seemed could touch us and yet we had so easily become unstuck. Helen was attractive, intelligent, sexually provocative and I undoubtedly enjoyed her company on a number of levels. But I wanted to gather Lucy in my arms and hold her tight, protect her at all times and not let her from my sight. I was in love with Lucy in a way that I had never been with Helen.

My worry was that the warmth she displayed in return was more of a sisterly affection and my fear of rejection meant I would say nothing. Whilst we searched out the truth behind Billy’s death I knew that I had the pleasure of her company and for me that was enough, for the time being at least.

“No car ride necessary tonight as Catherine Salter still lives with her mother in the same house as they lived in 1939, on the corner of Heyward Road opposite the Red, White and Blue. Shall we walk around there now?”

"Let's go." I said, pulling Lucy to her feet and heading down the corridor to find my coat. The weather had turned milder but it was still early January so we both added layers before venturing out. It was a short walk up Livingstone Road before zigzagging passed the elegant Thomas Owen properties of Campbell Road and onto Fawcett Road towards our final destination.

The house was a small late Victorian terrace with a front door leading directly off the pavement. I knocked. The woman who opened the door wore a pinny over a floral dress and was probably in her forties. "Can I help you?"

"Are you Mrs. Salter?" I asked, trying to sound friendly and 'unofficial'.

"Who's asking?" The woman replied, immediately on her guard.

"This is Lucy Cosgrove and I am her friend William Goldhawk. We've come to speak to your daughter about her evidence in the Stanley Jakes enquiry."

"I have 'ad the police around and they told me not to say nothing. They warned me that you might call and they said we should not talk to yer." With that the woman pushed to close the door but I wedged my foot on the step and tried to reason with her.

"Look Mrs. Salter we only want five minutes. Billy was Lucy's brother." But my entreaties were ignored as she slammed the door closed.

I turned to Lucy. "Well that went well Holmes. What next?"

"Indeed Dr. Watson, may I suggest we retire to the public house across the street and consult with the landlord?" Lucy replied holding an imaginary pipe to her lips.

I laughed. "Was that supposed to be Sherlock Holmes? May I respectfully suggest you leave that to Basil Rathbone in future?" I got a playful bash on the back of my head for my troubles but we did wander over the road to the Red, White and Blue.

Judging by the leers that Lucy received from the locals the pub was unused to entertaining the fairer sex but nevertheless the main bar offered a cosy and inviting alternative to the drizzle which had just started outside. A warming log fire, Christmas decorations and the soft murmur of a gramophone playing jazz in the background made for a pleasant ambience.

I ordered a pint of bitter for myself and a glass of sherry for Lucy and we found a seat in the corner but before we sat I asked the landlord if he remembered the Billy Cosgrove case. Far more effusive than our friend over the road the bearded publican seemed happy to talk.

"Billy Cosgrove was a good customer. Naught but a young lad mind, when he used to drink here but he was as good a gold. Sat up here at the bar and chatted to all the old folk and used to make them laugh with his jokes and his funny stories. I remember one evening he was impersonating Groucho Marx. It was hilarious. He sat there with a big cigar in his mouth and said. 'I don't care to belong to a club that accepts people like me as members.' And all the old boys laughed, it was like a free cabaret. Mind you he never took it too far or got drunk or gave trouble. He was good lad. Did you know him like?"

"This is Billy's sister Lucy. Now he's been cleared we're trying to piece together what happened to him."

"I remember seeing your picture in the Evening News shoving that confession under the big wig's chin. Good for you love. Well if you find him be sure to bring him in here and he'll get free beer all night, that's a promise."

With that the landlord drifted away to serve another customer and Lucy turned to me with a beseeching look. "Where do we go from here, William? It's so complicated and it seems like someone is always one step ahead of us."

The events of recent weeks had brought into focus our need to embrace the bigger picture. Billy was a side issue, no more than collateral damage in a conflict in which he played a very small part. Without understanding the nature of the struggle in which he had somehow become embroiled our chances of unearthing the truth were all but non-existent. I gave Lucy my blunt assessment and suggested a conversation with the tax investigator, Julian Singleton as my next move.

Julian was bunkered-up as some local hotel for the next few weeks during the course of his investigations so I was fairly sure that he would be more than happy for an impromptu meeting at a local hostelry. After walking Lucy home I phoned the number he had left me with and he enthusiastically confirmed his willingness to meet later that evening. It was to prove an interesting encounter with a sting in the tail.

Sixteen

When I arrived at the Sally-Port, Julian Singleton was seated in a quiet spot in an otherwise busy pub and hailed me as I walked through the door.

"Good to see you William, I've taken the liberty of getting you a pint of Young's Best Bitter. I trust that's to your liking?"

We small talked for some minutes as Julian extolled the virtues of the district of Southsea and his liking for the local ales as well as the sea air. He was a garrulous fellow and judging by the speed in which his beer disappeared, a man who knew how to enjoy himself. I suspected I was in for a long evening but it was Friday night so I was not unduly worried.

I sensed that it was my responsibility to introduce the business of the evening as I had instigated our meeting so I gave a short spiel accepting his proposition of the previous week to help him with his investigations, on the condition that there were no strings attached and I was at liberty to walk away at any time of my choosing. Julian seemed genuinely delighted and gave me an insight into what he had uncovered.

"There is something of the Mafia about the goings on in this city in the thirties and through the War. Profiteering, bribery, extortion and corruption were rife. Even those in public office weren't immune. No-one has ever been brought to book and we would dearly love to find the mastermind - the godfather, if you like - behind the criminal activity of that period. At least five million pounds was embezzled from the public purse by person or persons unknown.

The police are playing everything by the book and all our investigations are being strangled by bureaucracy and red tape. I am the ministry's last chance to get to the root of the problem before the proverbial bulldozers are brought in. Between you and me, if I can't squeeze out a satisfactory result, heads will roll. Very senior figures will be thrown to the lions if you'll excuse my mixed metaphors. It will frankly, be carnage."

"So where do I start?" I asked, feeling suddenly excited by the prospect.

"Fair question. We cannot go in all guns blazing. This requires a subtle mixture of diplomacy and persuasion on your part. It's a question of teasing out information from people and one thing tends to lead to another. Do you recall Stanley Jakes' sidekicks, Eric Riley, Norman Buchanan and Frank Gilbert? Buchanan and Gilbert are rotting in prison but Eric Riley has turned over a new leaf and is now married with children and an honest job. I would like you to talk to Riley and find out all you can about Jakes and what he got up to."

"But will he be prepared to talk to me? I have history with Riley and my experiences so far haven't been promising." I recounted the events of earlier in the evening with Mrs. Salter.

"I'm not saying it will be easy William. See what you can do. Another beer?"

By the time last orders were rung I was on the edge of sobriety. We left the pub together but rather than turn right up the High Street toward residential Southsea, Julian tugged at my sleeve indicating he wanted me to follow him in the opposite direction toward the sea front. We walked through a gap in the sea wall to the deserted beach before Julian looked around to see we were alone. He then opened his attaché case which he had kept a very careful eye on all evening and removed a small, hard object which he placed in my hand. A brisk wind whistled off the sea and chilled me to the bone when I realised what I was holding.

"William, please put this in your pocket. It's a 32 caliber Beretta. I hope you don't ever need it but it just might get you out of trouble one day."

Or into I thought.

And so it did.

Seventeen

I drew back the curtains of my bedroom and looked down on the Sunbeam, nicely polished and ready for our trip. The previous afternoon I had left the car at Whites Motors for a service and walked into town to buy a road atlas. I was looking forward to spending some time with Lucy and a leisurely drive up the A3 through the towns and villages of north east Hampshire and Surrey.

The day had a bitter sweet tinge though as Helen had arranged to empty her belongings from my house whilst I was out; a sad end to our long relationship. But I was determined not to dwell on the past and to enjoy my time with Lucy. She had been secretive all week about the final destination of our trip but as we started our ascent up Butser Hill she decided it was time to divulge.

"You were dead right when you said tracing your mother with the surname Smith would be difficult so I thought we should start with Geoffrey. We're meeting the curator at the RAF archives at Biggin Hill and hope he may be able to point us in the right direction. You have packed the photograph I hope?"

I nodded, smiled to myself and felt grateful to be taken in hand. We chatted of this and that but were mostly silent, enjoying the novelty of the drive and taking in the stark beauty of the English winter countryside.

A little later, as we hit traffic through The Devil's Punchbowl I recounted to Lucy my conversation with Julian Singleton at The Sally-Port on Friday evening. I avoided mention of the evening's finale but outlined my assignment to track down and interrogate Eric Riley and was surprised when she told she was acquainted with Riley's wife Susan.

"She often pops in the library with her two daughters. A nice woman, I believe she teaches at a Southsea Infant School."

“Do you think she knows about her husband’s shady past?” I asked.

“Hard to say, it’s not something of which Eric is likely to feel proud. He’s a proper family man now. I often see the four of them in and around Southsea.” My father’s mantra of information being the key to negotiation sprung to mind. That snippet of gossip from Lucy might just come in handy.

It was almost three o’clock in the afternoon before we pulled into the car park at RAF Biggin Hill and parked in a space ‘reserved for Lucy Cosgrove’. “How did you engineer our special treatment Mata Hari?” I asked.

“I ‘av my vays.” Lucy replied fluttering her eyelids provocatively.

Two World War Two fighter planes stood guard at the entrance to the small enclave now designated to the RAF. As we walked between them Lucy helped me out with a brief explanation: “A Supermarine Spitfire and a Hawker Hurricane the mainstays of the Battle of Britain. The Hurricane was slow and cumbersome in comparison with the Luftwaffe’s Fokkers but the Spitfire was a different matter, nimble and manoeuvrable, a real pleasure to fly. We would not have won the Battle of Britain without them.”

“So which is which?” I asked with a confession of my ignorance.

Lucy pointed out the Spitfire as we walked up the steps to the reception area where we waited a few minutes for the arrival of the curator. A barrel shaped man of middle age, squinting through National Health glasses clumped toward us with hand outstretched and introduced himself as Peter Cahill.

“So glad you could make it Miss Cosgrove it’s an absolute pleasure. I have so enjoyed our correspondence over the last few weeks and I confess that you are far younger than I envisaged a scholar of your distinction to be. I imagined a somewhat dowdier visitor." Peter Cahill finished with a chuckle.

"Flattery will get you everywhere, Mr. Cahill." Lucy replied in her usual self-deprecating style.

Peter Cahill proved to be a genial and generous host, giving his time freely and enthusiastically. We sat over tea and hot crumpets and he gave us an interesting insight into the life of a pilot in the Flying Corp and the RAF. Although he could not identify Geoffrey he gave us a number of leads to pursue.

"You are absolutely right Miss Cosgrove this photograph was indeed taken in the summer of 1920 or later. There are a number of ways in which you could track your man down. His DSO would have been recorded in the London Gazette and often Christian names where included in the citation so by trawling through the papers, which are all archived here at Biggin Hill, for his name you could get lucky. His rank is likely to have been Major or above. Had he gone on to join the RAF after World War One, identification would have been far easier but records from the Flying Corp where mostly lost during the more recent conflict."

"With only a Christian name to go on, trawling through the London Gazette sounds like a long winded job Mr. Cahill?" I interjected.

"Indeed and not foolproof by any means. Hence, I have another suggestion. If you look at the inscription on the reverse of the photograph it is the name of the photographer, A Z Abrahams based down on the Sussex coast in Bexhill. I took the liberty of phoning a cousin in Hastings who tells me that Abrahams still trades in the High Street so I suggest that should be you first port of call. If that proves unsuccessful I will give you the name and address of a retired war time pilot who has something of an encyclopedic knowledge of the Flying Corp."

I consulted the road atlas before we left Biggin Hill to complete the short drive to the White Swan in Tunbridge Wells where we were booked in for the night. We enjoyed a wonderful evening, staring into each other's eyes, holding hands across the table and alternating between sharing our most personal secrets and giggling like school children. If I had any lingering doubts about the depth of my feelings for Lucy they were dispelled during that long, luxurious evening at the White Swan. But if I had hoped that Lucy would furtively offer me the key to her bedroom door and flutter her eyelids in invitation, I was to be disappointed. She left me buoyant but frustrated with a peck on the cheek and a squeeze of the hand. I chided myself for my impatience as I drifted off to sleep.

***

As we drove south toward Bexhill the next morning to visit the photographic establishment of A Z Abrahams I was in good spirits. In love and excited at the prospect of the day ahead, hoping at last to discover the identity of the dashing but mysterious Geoffrey.

Bexhill was a sleepy little town on the Sussex coast and Abrahams was easily found on the main road. It was an old fashioned pharmacy, wooden shelves cluttered with an extensive selection of ointments, lotions and old style medicine bottles. Photography was a clearly a side-line and confined to a small corner of the shop. As we entered an elderly gentleman rose from his chair and welcomed us.

Once we had explained the reason for our visit the man peered at the back of the photograph that I had placed on the counter. "Ah, yes this photograph was taken by my son. 1920 you say?"

"We believe so, yes. Do you have records dating back that far?" I asked.

"Oh yes, back to 1885 actually when my father started the business." He scuttled off and retrieved an old and very dusty ledger from the far recesses of the shop, dropped it on the counter and started flicking through the pages. "Around July you think?"

"Looking at the photograph it looks like mid to late summer so July or August, yes." Lucy replied.

"Nothing in either July or August I'm afraid, I'll try June." But that also drew a blank.

"Well I am sorry I cannot help you.... Ah, no wait one second. Here we are: this photograph was taken at the RAF aerodrome at Lee-On-Solent on the 2nd September 1920. And the invoice was made out to Major G Barrington-Hope, of Lyndhurst in Hampshire."

After offering profuse thanks we made our way back to the car with much to deliberate. "Next stop Lee-on-Solent then, William. Well it gets more curious by the minute. If my calculations are correct Mr and Mrs Barrington-Hope were together seven months before you were born so your mother was two months pregnant when this photograph was taken."

I was at a loss to know what to think and began to wonder if the woman in the photograph was not my mother at all! "Onward and upward." I muttered to myself in resignation. On balance I considered it best to keep moving forward with our investigation and not to tax my brain too much in the interim. It may just be possible to get to Lee-on-Solent before dark I calculated, so chivvied Lucy along, jumped back into the Sunbeam and pointed its nose west along the A259 coast road.

We stopped at Pevensey where I called RAF Lee-on-Solent and arranged to meet Wing Commander Harry Brownfield who helpfully agreed to see what he could dig up before we arrived. It was one of those typical January days, the sky a non-descript grey with an imperceptible misty drizzle hanging in the air. The roads were quiet though and we made good time, by-passing Portsmouth by mid-afternoon and heading south along the Gosport peninsular as the skies darkened.

The Wing Commander, tall, straight-backed and grey moustached greeted us at the gates with a brisk salute. Clearly not a liberal Harry Brownfield pointedly ignored Lucy and directed all conversation toward me, presumably on the basis of my gender. "Well Sir." he began. "I have looked-up the records and Major Barrington-Hope was stationed here just after we were commissioned in 1917. He had been injured in France where he received his DSO and transferred to Lee unfit for active service. It looks as though he lost an arm and was put out to pasture here, training new recruits in the Royal Naval Air Services.

You may care to contact a retired Air Marshall Sir Douglas Evill who was commander here and I understand flew with Barrington-Hope on the Western Front." With that Brownfield jotted down an address and telephone number and handed it to me.

***

Sir Douglas Evill may have retired from the RAF but was still evidently a busy man and unable to fit us into his schedule until the next weekend. However, he told me on the telephone that he had known Geoffrey Barrington-Hope very well and would be happy to accommodate us at his home in Winchester on the following Saturday.

Eighteen

My first day back to work involved an unsatisfying trip to Spital Square to interrogate John Benison, Crawford Electrics' Chief Accountant. With the audit only days away it was essential to have complete confidence in the sales and purchase ledgers but we had still not received a satisfactory explanation for certain high value transactions. And Benison was proving elusive.

I had little choice but to confront Sir Marcus on the subject and approached his office determined but with some trepidation: determined not to be ambushed by the wily Sir Marcus and with trepidation about how he would view my separation from his beloved Helen. As things turned out Sir Marcus was philosophical about my split with his daughter and seemed genuinely sorry to lose me as a potential son-in-law. He confided that he had no such liking for Michael Bridges and hoped his daughter's infatuation with him would be short lived.

On the work front things were more difficult as Sir Marcus tried to smooth talk his way out of divulging the information that I needed. We were standing in the board room which opened out from his office when I broached the subject of the unaccounted for expenditure and in typical style, he put an arm around my shoulder and smiled expansively.

"William, you really have nothing to worry about. I can give you my 100% assurance. We are a complex business turning over millions of pounds selling into worldwide markets. It's just a question of timing you'll find. I'm happy to sign any personal guarantees to that effect." He smiled as though his assurances were enough to stave off any more awkward questions.

"By the way William I was going to ask you whether you would accompany me to Rome next month as I am thinking of setting up a European office in the region and would value your input." Sir Marcus schmoozed.

I stayed firm and gave him the auditor's code. "That's all very well Sir Marcus but my head is on the block here and I will have to sign your accounts off. I have a duty of care to your shareholders and to you as Chairman, for that matter."

"William, of course I understand that, I really don't need a lecture from you on business ethics but it seems you are questioning my integrity. If I tell you that I will offer my personal guarantee then I expect you to accept my explanation as one gentleman to another. Come on William, we have known each other a long time. There are plenty of other firms clambering over each other for our business but I really don't want to have to go elsewhere for my accountants." Sir Marcus finished with a thinly disguised threat.

Before things got heated I decided to alter course and discuss less contentious issues relating to the business and hope that Sir Marcus would heed my appeal and furnish us with all the information required to complete the audit satisfactorily. I nevertheless felt somewhat uneasy with his brush-off and sensed we had stormy waters ahead.

The situation was exacerbated when Michael Bridges announced that previous accounts submitted by Crawfords had been qualified by our predecessors and that there were some very large payments with inadequate supporting documentation, going all the way back to the 1930's. When questioned, Benison had provided a number of invoices relating to 'Consultation' in relation to 'Contract Negotiations' and all from firms no longer trading and with virtually no provenance.

When I had joined Surtees, Hancock and Lampson it was made abundantly clear to me that the firm was built on hard work, openness and most importantly integrity. The rules were not stretched, bent or in any way flexed; however important the client, the same strict standards applied and Crawfords was no exception.

Brian Surtees and Douglas Lampson were disquieted by my report and the firm was put on high alert.

"This is most disturbing." Brian started. "What are they hiding? It's preposterous if Sir Marcus really believes we can just sweep this under the carpet. The exact opposite is true, we will have to be seen to look into every nook and cranny, gentleman. Crawfords may be our largest client but no-one will hold us to ransom."

Nineteen

Saturday shone like a beacon after a particularly irksome few days in the office. I could hardly leave the house fast enough. The Sunbeam's engine turned over sluggishly in the cold of the early morning and I thought I would have to resort to the crank when it suddenly burst into life. Relieved I put her into gear and drove the half mile to pick up Lucy from her seafront flat before we journeyed over Portsdown Hill and across the Rother Valley to Winchester.

Sir Douglas Evill owned a modest stately home, if there was such a thing. Well-proportioned 18th Century, pleasingly lichened stucco frontage with mature tended gardens, it was prepossessing even in mid-winter. The sweeping driveway cut through a manicured lawn and we parked the Sunbeam as unobtrusively as the terrain would allow, between house and garage before walking up to the front door and pulling the bell chord.

A smartly dressed late middle aged man of military bearing opened the door and invited us inside. "Please come in, you must be William Goldhawk and Lucy Cosgrove?" We were shown into the drawing room and offered seats whilst our host organised tea.

"Now, tell me your connection to Major Barrington-Hope, although looking at the uncanny resemblance I suspect I know the answer." He smiled.

I pulled out the well-travelled photograph and handed it to Sir Douglas before offering a brief explanation. "This is Catherine (maiden name, Smith) my mother and her first husband who until last week we knew only as Geoffrey. And strangely, although I am told we look remarkably similar, we are not related."

"Catherine Smith you say? That's strange because I know this woman as Catherine Reneaux before she married Geoffrey Barrington-Hope in Paris in 1919. I was at their wedding. I think you had better tell me all you know and I will do my best to fill in the gaps."

So I told him my story. Sir Douglas leaned back in his chair, removed the pipe from his mouth and started prodding at the tobacco. "Geoffrey Barrington-Hope was a good man; one of the very best in fact. Hoppy we called him; silly nickname but Hope-Hop-Hoppy that's how he came by it. We learnt to fly together at Calshot on the Isle of Wight in the early years of the first war. Hoppy, was a natural, whatever nag he was given he seemed to be able to coax the best out of her. And he loved flying. It was his life.

But one minute..." With that Sir Douglas left us briefly before returning with a map which he spread out on the table. "We were stationed here at St Omer for the early part of the war and were involved in mostly reconnaissance missions, checking out what the enemy was up to. We made propaganda drops, leaflets and that sort of thing and even on occasions dropped a bomb or two from our rickety old planes. One day in July 1916 just after the beginning of the fiasco on the Somme, Hoppy went off on some mission or other and didn't come back. Planes were going down on a regular basis so it was hardly a great shock but Hoppy was popular and something of a talisman so his loss did have an effect on morale. But you got on with it and Hoppy soon became just another statistic; the harsh realities of the front, I'm afraid.

It was Boxing Day 1916 and I was stationed a mile or so behind the front line with the 5th Squadron. We were enjoying an unofficial ceasefire over Christmas, a rare break in hostilities. There were camp fires burning as we took advantage of the lull and dried wet clothes and boots and warmed our freezing limbs. Impromptu carol singing around the fires and football in the snow were surreal sights and sounds amidst the carnage of the War.

I had removed my boots and was cleaning the caked-on mud and warming my stockinged feet when I heard the imperceptible whine of an engine. I looked south and after a minute or two a small biplane appeared out of the sun. At first we all assumed it was the Hun but as it approached I realised it was one our own; an old and battered Sopwith Pup, not from our squadron so I was more than a little intrigued. We watched as the plane circled the airfield a couple of times before coming in unsteadily to land.

Well you can imagine my amazement when old Hoppy pulled off his flying helmet and goggles. He'd lost an arm from the elbow down but otherwise looked in good shape. Talk about a boost to morale. The story of his reappearance spread like wild fire and he was an instant hero. It was quite a story he told. Chased down by three Hun he kept flying south in the forlorn hope of out lasting them but eventually a bullet snapped his tail fin wire and he lost control coming down in fields and flipping over after his undercarriage clipped a tree."

Pointing at a spot on the map, Sir Douglas went on. "He came down here near a small village called Fontaine-Notre-Dame and miraculously not only survived the accident but had the good fortune to be found by the Reneaux family who looked after him and helped him fix up the Pup. Quite amazing how they brought the old girl to life using all sorts of bits and pieces. Hoppy figured on a Christmas ceasefire and took full advantage, somehow getting the Pup airborne and flying with only one arm back over the heads of the Hun and popping her down on our airstrip. Incredible, he was a true hero."

With that he looked down at the photograph he still held in his hands. "He looks every bit the debonair, swashbuckling airman here doesn't he? A true reflection of a brave and resourceful fellow.

Your mother and her sister nursed him back to health. They even amputated his arm after pumping him full of French brandy. Poor old Hoppy didn't drink, so heaven knows how he must have felt when he came-to." Finished Sir Douglas with a slight chuckle.

Before continuing he rose from his seat and left the room again with a gesture of apology but this time came back with a framed photograph which he handed to me. It was inscribed with, 'Geoffrey 'Hoppy' Barrington-Hope, from the boys of Squadron 5'. It showed Geoffrey being hoisted aloft in front of the Sopwith Pup by a number of men, including a young Douglas Evill. "Your mother kindly sent this to me after his death.

Geoffrey had fallen madly in love with Catherine and promised that he would return the minute the war was over. Whether Catherine believed she would ever see him again I do not know but he was true to his word and was knocking on her door as the Armistice was being signed.

The wedding was a joyous occasion in Paris. It combined a wonderfully romantic story with a squadron reunion. Old comrades turned up in force. It was the last I saw of many of them including Geoffrey. The next I heard of him was when I read his obituary in the Times in '23. Tragic, really tragic."

Lucy and I look at each other. "He died in 1923?" We mouthed to each other simultaneously.

I was looking at the map when Sir Douglas returned with a copy of Barrington-Hope's obituary. Peering at the spot where the plane had crashed I asked. "Sir Douglas do you know whether my mother still has family in Fontaine-Notre-Dame? You mentioned a sister?"

"I am afraid I have told you all I know. I joined the RAF and Hoppy, despite his handicap, went on to fly again with Sopwith on a commercial basis. We lost touch after his wedding but please keep-hold of his obituary for the time being. You may find some clues about your mother tucked away in there."

A few minutes later Lucy and I were back in the car on our way across country to Portsmouth. Although the Sunbeam juddered and jolted along the uneven road surface Lucy held fast and read the obituary out loud. And Sir Douglas was proved right, there were indeed clues about my mother. Perhaps, the most striking of which was revealed in the last line '…..Geoffrey William Barrington-Hope married, in 1919, Catherine Claudine Reneaux, who survives him with their two young twin children, son William and daughter Claudine.'

"William Barrington-Hope. So you are the son of a hero after all. And you have a sister!" Lucy looked across to gauge my reaction.

"Don't jump to conclusions Lucy. There is the little matter of the birth certificate to prove otherwise."

"What did Julian Singleton say about the city records after the bombing of the Town Hall?"

I followed Lucy's train of thought and willed her to be right. "But why would my father…or the man who pretends to be my father…want to forge my birth certificate?"

"Surely, because he doesn't want you to find out about your past. That's why he was so angry when he found out about the letter from your mother. It revealed something that he wanted to keep hidden. The question is what?"

"Yes, what indeed?" I mused. I was not quite ready to confront 'my father' yet, but the day was drawing closer.

Twenty

'Geoffrey Barrington-Hope worked for the Sopwith Aviation Company after the war and designed his own prosthetic arm to enable him to continue flying which he did with distinction earning a contract as chief test pilot. Flying out of a small airfield at their Woolston factory in Hampshire, he was killed in a flying accident on July 14th 1923 when the Sopwith Antelope he was testing inexplicably failed and came down in the English Channel. His body was never recovered.'

The obituary went on to describe his exploits in the War but gave very little detail of his personal life, only that he attended a minor public school in Norfolk and his father was a practicing solicitor in Attleborough. My eyes were fixed on the yellowed newsprint in my hands as I contemplated the changes to my own life, so ordered and regulated just a few months earlier.

Was this man my father? Did I have a sister and close family across the channel in France? And what of Sir Edward Goldhawk? If he is not my father what game is he playing? Or perhaps I was looking for something that did not exist; interpreting clues to coalesce with my hopes rather than reality. I needed answers and I was determined to find them.

***

So it was with a new resolve that I approached my interview with Eric Riley, the erstwhile sidekick of Stanley Jakes. Julian Singleton had given me both his home address in Eastney and the address of his office in White Lady's Yard in Landport where he worked in the unlikely capacity of a bookkeeper for Wynyard's fruit and vegetable merchant. I decided catching him at work may prove more conducive to my cause so turned up at his office just before lunchtime.

I was shown in by a secretary with bleached blond hair, a tight hugging skirt and smudged make-up. Riley was obviously unused to visitors at work and his socials skills were in need of refinement. “Yeah, what you after mate?” He asked in a bellicose manner as I found myself in front of his desk.

“Eric Riley? I’m William Goldhawk and I am investigating certain financial irregularities going back to the 1930’s and I wonder if you could help me with a few questions I have about Stanley Jakes?” I asked.

“Thought I recognised you. The answer is no. I had a couple of years as a youngster when I misbehaved and have served a stretch to pay for it. I turned over a new leaf and have nothing to tell you about Jakes.” Riley replied unhelpfully.

“So does your wife Susan know of your association with Stanley Jakes and your little stint behind bars?”

Riley looked up from behind his desk with a resigned expression and muttered some insult under his breath before agreeing to meet at the Ship Hotel in an hour.

The bar at the Ship Hotel was packed and noisy which gave us the anonymity we needed. We sat across a small table were we were able to converse in relative comfort both sustained by a pint of beer and a meat pie. “How were you recruited by Jakes in the first place?” I started.

“We drank in the same pub, the Albany Tavern in Elm Grove. Hard to believe now but I looked up to him. He used to swagger in and was so full of bravado I just got carried along. I was not even quite twenty. Impressionable. I was kicking my heels with no proper job and one day Jakes announced he wanted two ‘associates’ and was prepared to pay three pound a week plus expenses. Of course I jumped at the chance and couldn’t quite believe my luck.

At first I was just running errands, dropping off packages, that sort of thing and I happily took my three quid in cash each Friday afternoon. Things started to change and almost imperceptibly I was dragged into the distribution of contraband as well as other criminal activities. As time went by I became little more than a hired 'heavy' applying pressure and making threats. I didn't like it much but it came with the territory; it was in my job description so to speak.

Honest traders, chancers and thieves were all competing for a share of the work coming out of the expansion of the dockyard and Jakes seized his opportunity. He muscled his way in and pushed most everyone else aside. He set himself up as a sort of 'trade impresario' and even opened an office on the Hard. How he swung it, god only knows but he managed to persuade people that he was an officially sanctioned operation and they channeled their enquiries through his office. He made good money. Looking back you have to admire his enterprise.

I was no more than a dumb teenager and didn't really take in what was going on but I can tell you this much. A number of office boys from London came down to Portsmouth over the summer of '39 to negotiate and draw up the terms and conditions for a couple of very large contracts to supply electrical and mechanical components to the Navy. I don't know exactly what Jakes involvement was but he was looking for action of some sort. He had his claws into those boys make no mistake about that."

"Who was 'the brains' behind all this? Did Jakes really have it in him to organise such a venture?" I asked in surprise.

"I did sometimes wonder if there was someone pulling his strings but I if so they never showed themselves. To be honest you might get more out of Frank Gilbert or better still Norman Buchanan who knew Jakes better than I did. Or maybe you could track down those boys from London; I reckon they could tell you a thing or two about his methods."

I pushed Riley as hard as I could but it was pretty clear he had told me all he had which was not a great deal beyond confirmation of what we already knew. He did though give me the heads-up on Frank Gilbert's imminent release from prison and also, to my surprise offered me a little nugget of gold; Stanley Jakes' 1939 office diary for which I happily paid a king's ransom.

On my way home I called in at The Four Seasons Hotel to find that Julian Singleton was just on his way out of the door. He was in a hurry but quickly scribbled down an address and pulled a photograph from this brief case. "Look William, we need to talk but not right now. I want you to keep tabs on Frank Gilbert who is being released from Oxford Prison on Friday. Here's his photograph and the address of his sister in Havant.

I know it's a tall order but if you have time to keep tabs on his movements it could prove useful. But watch your step, we don't know much about Gilbert but as a rule of thumb learn to trust no-one. He's no hard man like Riley or Buchanan; a smoother operator altogether but that doesn't make him any less dangerous. He has a habit of lurching from prison straight back into trouble and has a reputation for being a little slippery!" And with a condescending pat on the back Julian made to leave, giving me just enough time to hand him Jakes' diary before he disappeared through the revolving door.

Twenty One

I cannot pretend that I was looking forward to my trip to Havant and tailing Frank Gilbert. My accountancy training had hardly qualified me for such a mission and I was not sure that I was up to it. But as it turned-out I need not have worried as neither Frank Gilbert nor Havant played any part in my Saturday, which proved a challenging day for altogether different reasons. In retrospect, the only positive I could draw from my experience from that Saturday was that, in comparison to Sunday, it was a humdinger of a day.

It was early February and we had endured a further spell of cold weather which showed little sign of abating. I wrapped myself up in coat, hat and gloves and walked out to the car replete after a satisfying breakfast. After scraping the ice from the windscreen I wedged myself in the driver's seat and turned the ignition key. It was presumably as the starter motor whined and the engine spluttered into life that the man opened the rear door and edged himself onto the seat behind me.

The first I was aware of his presence was when I felt the barrel of his gun in the nape of my neck. The engine fired and I was given a guttural instruction to drive. Catching sight of the pistol's elongated barrel in the rear view mirror ensured my uninvited guest received full cooperation.

"Where are you taking me?" I asked with a nervous falsetto as we drove along the Eastern Road following signs to London.

"You needn't concern yourself with our destination. You'll know soon enough. Keep driving until I tell you where to turn." He replied in a heavily accented voice.

I was angry with myself for being caught out. After Flathouse Quay I should have learnt my lesson but if truth be known I had an unhappy knack of walking into trouble with my eyes open. The good news was that I had the Berretta in my pocket: the bad news was that I had emptied the bullets on the basis that I would only ever use the weapon as a deterrent. The cold steel of my captor's gun only served to remind me of my current state of impotence.

With that on my mind I drove up the A3, following the route I had taken with Lucy a couple of weeks earlier. We had not travelled far before I was instructed to turn into a quiet side road and pull over. I very much wanted to ask my passenger if he would refrain from sticking his gun barrel into my flesh with such alacrity but somehow felt it would not go down well. Instead I sat stock still and held my breath.

The left rear door opened and another man shuffled in, his identity concealed by scarf and hat.

"Good morning Mr. Goldhawk." he said in an accent that I could not quite place, Germanic perhaps, European certainly. "You have become something of an irritant to me and I really have to insist that you start behaving yourself. You have already received one warning, no? And I do not like to give second warnings. You understand me?"

I nodded and mumbled that I understood before the man continued. "I guarantee there will be no more chances. Your girlfriend, Lucy yes? Perhaps she will no longer be so pretty. I advise you to go home and play happy families, my friend. If you want to have babies with Lucy stop meddling in affairs which are no business of yours! No more chances, Mr. Goldhawk."

"I am too soft, am I not?" The man asked his companion as they extricated themselves from the car and simultaneously slammed the rear doors shut. I did not hang around. Although they chose not to put a bullet through me, I still wanted to put a few miles between us as quickly as possible. A swift beer may calm the nerves I thought and headed for Southsea where I stumbled into The Red, White and Blue and ordered a pint.

It felt somewhat like being fired from a job; distressing in a sense and certainly a blow to the pride but also vaguely liberating. The threats to Lucy removed choice. There was nothing to be done other than withdraw my labour. Pull out, cease investigations, stop right there and then.

But of course it was not quite that simple. Problem one, how would that go down with Lucy and problem two, however much I wanted to believe that the meek would inherit the Earth I just didn't, so….what now? Another pint later I felt somewhat soothed and wondered back to Livingstone Road to contemplate the future.

My day hardly improved when I arrived home to find an elderly but concerned neighbour and his tail wagging dog on my doorstep. "William, I am so glad you're back, I've been waiting all day. I'm afraid you've been burgled." He said pointing out how the back door had been forced. "I've reported it to the police." He added looking every bit as doleful as the Labrador by his side.

"We were on our way out at about half past eleven and Sheba started barking and looking rather agitated. At first I ignored her but then noticed that your back door was ajar and banging gently in the breeze. Well, I thought, that's not like William so I had a closer look and saw that the lock had been tampered with. I didn't see anyone so went straight inside and Jean called the police. Here." He added handing me an envelope. "They want you to complete this form."

"Thanks Les, it's very kind of you and Jean to do that, I suppose I should go in and assess the damage." I replied feeling suddenly very tired.

It looked like a genuine burglary, plenty of mess and anything of value plundered. Not that I had much worth stealing just a little silver which had been passed down from my mother, some odds and sods of gold jewelry and a couple of French oil paintings which may or may not have been valuable. I would have preferred to have steered clear of the local constabulary but now it had been reported I felt obliged to complete the form which Les had passed to me.

I made a note of anything I could think that was missing and decided to drop it in at Kings Road police station the following day. As it transpired my trip was unnecessary as two uniformed policeman knocked on my door as I was clearing away breakfast the following morning. "May we come in Sir? I understand you reported a burglary yesterday morning?"

"Yes, that's right do come in." I replied trying my best to muster enthusiasm for their visit.

I invited them into the first floor sitting room and retrieved the form that I had completed the previous evening. After a brief conversation in which I explained how I had discovered the burglary the sergeant asked if it were alright for them to look around to which I agreed, trying not to show the irritation I felt. I decided to sit out their search and picked-up the morning paper which I re-read moodily waiting for them to leave.

Half an hour later I assumed they had completed their search as the younger of the two officers poked his head around my door and gave a little cough to bring me out of my daydream. "All done then?" I asked.

The constable was joined by his sergeant who strode into the room with a large canvass bag in his hands which he ceremoniously placed on the floor and opened in front of me. "Would these be your missing valuables, Sir?"

"Well yes but…er where did you find them?" I asked puzzled as I went through the content of the bag. "Everything seems present and correct, how very strange. Well thanks you gentlemen I really am most grateful."

"We found these hidden in your attic, Sir. Have you any suggestions as why a burglar would steal your valuables and then hide them in your attic. Rather…ah unusual behavior, wouldn't you say?"

"I have absolutely no idea!" I muttered quietly to myself.

"I am afraid, Sir, if you don't mind accompanying us? We have a few questions."

With my protests falling on deaf ears I ignominiously followed the two policemen to their car with the added woe of knowing that Les and Jean were watching my walk of shame from behind their lace curtains. How powerless I was in the face of my unseen enemy, I realised.

One hour later I sat in an interview room at Kings Road police station with only a watery coffee as company. It may have been ten years since I last smoked a cigarette but I could have murdered for one that minute, anything to quell my anger and calm my nerves. My blood boiled with the indignity of being out manoeuvred yet again but a small rational part of my brain ordered me to remain calm no matter what the provocation. And provoked I surely was.

Although hardly surprised when my arch nemesis Hanaho entered the room I groaned inwardly. Just looking at the expression on his face was enough to shatter my resolve to maintain my calm but I gritted my teeth, determined not to give him the satisfaction of seeing me rattled.

"Mr. Goldhawk I have your crime report here." He started, opening a folder and placing it between us on the table. "You were burgled you say?"

I went through the events of the afternoon for the second time trying very hard to give an impression of bored indifference. But

Hanaho was enjoying himself and had me exactly where he wanted me. "Bizarre behavior don't you think? Why would your burglar have stolen your valuables and then hidden them in your attic?"

I shrugged helplessly. "I really have no idea."

"Are you insured?" Hanaho then enquired.

"If you mean the content of my house, yes it is insured."

"Were you intending to claim for the 'stolen' items, Mr. Goldhawk?"

"I hadn't given it a moment's thought Inspector. It only happened yesterday!"

"Let's be clear, unless you have a good explanation we will be charging you for wasting police time with the intent to commit fraud. I can't imagine a judge or jury believing your cock and bull story, can you? Let's have the truth Mr. Goldhawk."

"It was just a few nick-knacks anyway hardly worth more than a few pounds. I would hardly put my career at risk for that, would I?"

"How much would you put your career at risk for?"

"That's not what I meant!" My hackles started to rise.

At that moment the door opened and a young uniformed constable entered with a large buff coloured envelope which he handed to Hanaho who looked like a cat that got the cream. He opened the end of the envelope and let the content slide slowly out and onto the table; a 32mm Berretta. I momentarily closed my eyes in disbelief before puffing out my cheeks and exhaling silently. How I was going to deal with this? I needed to think but realised it was hopeless. I had been well and truly stiffed.

"Does this weapon belong to you Sir?"

"Actually, no I borrowed it." I knew how utterly facile my answer must have sounded but was at a loss to contrive a convincing explanation without implicating Singleton.

"You borrowed it?" Hanaho looked at me theatrically. "And from whom did you borrow it?"

"I am afraid I can't say." I answered lamely.

"You can't say?" He smirked and I wanted to put both hands around his neck and throttle him but somehow kept an outward calm. "I assume you have a firearms certificate for this?"

"It's never been used I only ever intended…." I trailed off as I realised I was digging a deeper hole for myself.

"Yes? You'd only intended…. to what? What had you intended Mr. Goldhawk?" What are you a bloody parrot I wanted to scream but said nothing more.

"Have you anything further to say in your defense because as things stand it's not looking good. Would you like to call a solicitor, perhaps that long legged Miss Crawford? We enjoy entertaining her, don't we Dawson? She brightens up the place." He laughed directing his question at the young policeman.

I declined his offer on the grounds that I would be far too embarrassed for Helen to see me in my current predicament. "I am officially charging you with wasting police time with intent to defraud and also for possessing a firearm without valid certification. You will spend the night here with our compliments and may apply to the magistrate for bail in the morning. Good day to you Mr. Goldhawk."

With that I was led down to the cells and locked-up.

Twenty Two

When Lucy walked through the door the previous August with the news of Davenport's confession I never quite imagined it would lead to this; a night in a police cell, sitting on a stained mattress stinking of urine and staring at four grubby walls with only a chamber pot and a single wooden chair as companions. My beating at Flathouse Quay I could take, as it had no serious long term implications but this was different; a sobering wake-up call. What impact would a criminal record have on my well-ordered and comfortable life, I wondered?

The truth was accountancy was not the most exciting of professions and my 'Boys Own' extra curricula adventures had been something of a welcome distraction. But I had got involved *for* Lucy and now, *for* Lucy, I had to extricate myself before any serious damage was done. For a change of scenery I made the significant move from bed to the wooden chair where I parked my backside and used the old iron bedstead to rest my feet. Sound proofing was not a feature of my eight by eight cell and I had the dubious pleasure of listening to my inebriated neighbour retching and belching his way through the night, as I came to terms with the serious predicament in which I found myself.

As next of kin my father was informed of my arrest and to his credit arrived at mid-morning to post bail and drive me home. I cannot say he would have been my first choice to chaperone me away from the ignominy of a night in the cells and of course I was subjected to an obligatory lecture. I tuned-out somewhere after the third and well before the umpteenth time he told me what a disappointment I was to him. However, credit where credit is due, he did fork out the cash for my release and as a result I felt a grudging obligation to accept his invitation to one of his notoriously dull dinner party's later in the month at Liongate.

My father's antipathy toward the Cosgrove clan extended all the way down the line to Lucy and he allocated the bulk of his lecture toward a discourse on the reasons why I should ditch her in favour of my former fiancée, Helen. I had never quite got to the bottom of his obsessional dislike of anything to do with the Cosgroves. I supposed it was partly at least, based of snobbery. Certainly, he was a man with a Victorian view of the world and often reminded me that I was part of society's elite whilst Billy and his ilk were 'products of the proletariat', with the inference that they were an altogether inferior class of people.

He delivered his most vitriolic attack however, for my run-in with the police which he believed bordered on the subversive. My explanation was brushed aside and I was told in no uncertain terms that I should stop 'upsetting the applecart and to remember my station in life.' My behaviour embarrassed my father. As a JP he saw himself as a respected figure in Portsmouth society and he could not tolerate what he considered my refusal to accept the status quo. Although he was quite wrong; I was no rebel, I just wanted justice.

But if there was one thing my father had in abundance it was influence and before he dropped me home he told me that he would see to it that all charges against me were dropped. The *quid pro quo* was that I would immediately cease any activity which may cause him embarrassment and that included delving into the past. He was very insistent I should move on from my mother's death and get on with my life, a theme he repeated like a broken record.

Given my, albeit pitifully brief, stand against corruption it was shameful that I should accept without question my father's override of the criminal justice system but I did just that. God only knows what my mentor and friend Brian Surtees would have made of my complicity. I rarely stood up to the man and on this occasion I was grateful, if uncomfortable for his intervention. Of course I had been stitched-up by the police but I should have fought my own battle rather than relying on a counter stitch-up from my own father.

But I admit I slept easier the following night knowing that he had stepped in to save me any further harassment at the hands of Inspector Hanaho who, by then I realised was well out of my league as an adversary. I had no idea how my father went about getting me off the hook, I shut my eyes and blocked my ears. I did not want to know the grimy truth.

In retrospect it was perhaps unsurprising that the events of that weekend went someway to knocking the stuffing out of me. It is a moot point whether this interlude represented a time of soul searching and selfless refection on my part or whether I had just dropped into a self-pitying torpor. I liked to think that it was the former but in reality it was probably closer to the latter.

I avoided my responsibilities and steered clear of friends and colleagues alike. But worst of all I temporarily turned my back on the woman I loved. It must have been very obvious to Lucy that I had chosen to ignore her. I did not return her calls and had made transparent excuses about the pressure of work when she had suggested we met. The truth was I just did not know what to say to her.

I had thrown myself into work as a means to escape my responsibilities. I did not want to let Lucy down but felt I had been backed into a corner and could see no immediate way out. So, as was often the way, I buried my head in the sand and hoped for divine intervention which, of course, never arrived.

Winter limped on, the days imperceptibly lengthened and eventually I began to emerge from the malaise into which I had all too easily slipped. My father's dinner party at Liongate was my first social event of any description in a number of weeks and I hoped it would re-energise me and restore some semblance of normality back into my life. I took it as a sort of test of my resolve. If I could endure four hours in the company of my father and his cronies I must be on the road to recovery.

I donned a dinner jacket and bow tie and awaited my taxi which was due to transport me to Liongate. When I arrived my father was in a particularly effusive mood welcoming me almost as a father should welcome his son, with a broad smile and a firm handshake. Something was in the air. I was asked to receive the guests who started arriving just after 7.00pm, mostly from the higher echelons of Hampshire Society.

My father believed that success in the 'field of dinner parties' was measured by the number and seniority of the aristocratic, military or ecclesiastical titles on display. And as this particular dinner party included a Bishop, an Admiral of the Fleet and three knights of the realm I assumed my father would be moderately satisfied. Although the lack of a single Duke or Viscount would no doubt have irked somewhat. Certainly, as the only 'Mister' present I was in exalted company and knew my place.

The last to arrive were two people I knew very well, Sir Marcus Crawford and his daughter, my ex-fiancée Helen. Surprise must have registered on my face as Helen approached and gave my hands a squeeze before offering her cheek. I had almost forgotten how elegant and alluring Helen could be when she chose and there was no doubting that she stole the show that evening. Sir Marcus was his usual self, full of gruff Yorkshire charm, our past differences forgotten.

I suspected that Sir Marcus and my father were in cahoots in a less than subtle attempt at match making. It seemed that both were anxious to see Helen and I back together. It was not too long before we were engaged in conversation and although a little awkward at first the pre-dinner alcohol soon loosened our tongues and I asked Helen why she was alone.

"You were right about Michael. He really is an insufferable bore once you get beneath the surface. Honestly, his head is full of sawdust." With that Helen laughed and looked up at me. "So, in answer to your question....because I didn't want to be bored to death! What about you and the girl from the Library?"

"Lucy is her name as you know full well. She's fine but I confess I haven't seen much of her recently." I decided against further detail but suspected Helen would wheedle it out of me as the evening wore on.

"Have you missed me, honey?" Helen whispered in my ear, her breasts provocatively brushing against my arm. With the alcohol already beginning to affect me I had to work hard control the urge to submit to Helen's charms. My base instincts were powerful after nearly four months of celibacy and Helen's perfume and soft female touch was almost too much for me.

Helen knew me well but I resisted the temptation of being lead me down the path of no return and was relieved when we were joined by her father whose smile suggested he had misinterpreted my thoughts. Sir Marcus Crawford had moved down from his home City of Leeds to the Isle of Wight twenty years ago but still retained his Yorkshire bluntness as well as his north-country accent. Subtle, he was not but I liked his forthright approach to social interaction. There was certainly no-one else in the room who would have started a conversation as he did:

"Well I'm glad to see you two love birds making it up. I don't know what our Helen saw in that Michael... what's his name? A right pilchard if you ask me! Anyway what's this I hear about you being arrested William? Too many sherbets, me'be?"

Helen shook her head in disbelief at her father's subtle questioning before I went on to describe what happened. Helen took hold of my arm and looked concerned. "Hell, William you need to be careful, it's a dangerous game you are playing. By the way did you hear that Hanaho and his boss Superintendent Parker are under investigation? Our partners would love to see them nailed. It is common knowledge they are crooked but Hanaho is like the bloody Scarlet Pimpernel; as soon as you think you might have him, he's gone. Anyway, apparently there is an inspector from the Revenue in town at the moment, who's stirring up a veritable hornets nest. And by all accounts Hanaho and Parker are worried men."

"You young folks have all got it in for the establishment. There's naught wrong with Parker, I know 'im and he's just doing his job." With his contribution over Sir Marcus lost interest and moved away in search of more diverting conversation and left Helen and I to ourselves.

"Actually I have met the inspector, Singleton his name….Julian Singleton. He knows Brian Surtees and came along to our office trying to drum up support for his anti-corruption campaign. He's of the opinion that there was serious fraud centred in Portsmouth just before the War, defrauding the Admiralty and the Inland Revenue out of millions of pounds. So what have you heard about Singleton, Helen?"

"He reports straight into the Minister of State and is a trouble shooter, I gather. When official channels are blocked it's his job to unblock them. My guess is that the ministry knows that the police are not doing their job and Singleton has been sent in to deal with it. Dangerous work but he's a reputation for getting results. If he can't sort it out the Ministry send in the big guns; City lawyers and accountants and the establishment is pulled apart. Very expensive and politically divisive."

"So what's the consensus in your office about the local constabulary?" I said, still rankled about my arrest.

"We absolutely don't trust the buggers." Exclaimed Helen who took after her father in her use of colourful language. She went on. "We've no doubts that Hanaho and probably Parker too have been on the fiddle for years, despite what father says. But it's hard to catch people like them. They have friends in high places and it's a case of 'you scratch my back and I'll scratch yours'. They cover up for each other and close ranks."

I thought of my own father's role in my release but said nothing.

"Oh, by the way, now that Davenport is dead the police have closed the Stanley Jakes' file. Death by misadventure at the hands of a person or persons unknown is now the official line. So Billy is in the clear and if he ever surfaces he could sue the police for wrongful arrest, negligence and probably a lot more beside. And I'd be happy to represent him!"

"Singleton thinks whoever killed Jakes is behind a lot that went on in Portsmouth so we may not have quite heard the last of him yet." I added.

As the evening wore on I mingled with other guests and remembered quite how much I disliked my father's parties. His guests were mostly establishment figures over sixty and conversation more often than not, stilted and tedious. It was while I was trying desperately to extricate myself from the clutches of the insufferable Lady Hartridge who was intent of furnishing me with the life story of her equally insufferable pet Chihuahua 'Cindy' that my step-mother Elizabeth walked through the door.

Elizabeth was almost 30 years my father's junior and only a couple of years older than I was so perhaps I should not have been surprised when my beaming father announced that they were expecting a baby. The announcement changed the dynamics of the evening and as part of the family I was expected to play a role in toasting the happy event. I carried out my filial duties as best I could given my advanced state of intoxication.

Any opportunity Helen had to lead me into temptation was finally dashed when Sir Marcus decided it was time for them to leave. Before she left she kissed me on the cheek and gave me an inviting smile. Sir Marcus then proposed I joined him for a game of golf on the Island the following weekend. The soporific effects of the alcohol were not enough to prevent me from feeling that I was slowly being reeled in. I thought of Lucy as I had been for much of the evening and fervently wished I was curled up on the sofa next to her.

Twenty Three

After a desolate few weeks I felt somewhat energised, even if a little hung-over when I awoke the following morning. It was only when I recalled the Crawfords' pincer movement from the previous evening that I suffered a twinge of apprehension. Helen was an exceptionally easy woman to fall for as I knew from past experience but I was not ready to wind back the clock just yet.

Over breakfast I scolded myself for my recent lethargy and silently thanked Sir Marcus for dragging Helen away at exactly the right moment. My goose would have been well and truly cooked had I wondered down the wrong path with my ex fiancée. As it was, I felt sure that both Helen and her father where confident that I was back in tow.

But that was a battle for another day and frankly, the least of my concerns. I had developed a relatively thick skin and could handle the flak from the Crawfords. I was more concerned with Lucy and how to inveigle my way back into her affections without getting caught up in any more trouble. I decided to take advice and confide in Brian Surtees as he had never failed to provide me with sound counsel in the past. I knew too, that I needed to explain myself to Julian Singleton not least to cover the whereabouts of his gun.

Breakfast over, I went through my morning post and was surprised to find letters from both Julian Singleton and Sir Douglas Evill. I tore open the envelope from Julian which contained a short scribbled note asking me for an urgent meeting, suggesting The Sallyport as a suitable venue that evening. I was on my way out of the door so folded and popped the letter from Sir Douglas in my jacket pocket to read later. First, a chat with Brian to help me sort the wheat from the chaff and perhaps Sir Douglas's letter would offer an ideal excuse for me to re-engage with Lucy.

Brian Surtees was a bachelor and usually happy to accommodate me on a Saturday morning before his midday foursome at the local

Golf Club. I forewarned him with a telephone call and drove off to his home in the village of Rowlands Castle. Although Brian must have earned well over the years as a senior partner, he lived modestly in a small terraced house overlooking the village green.

I had a number of things I wanted to get off my chest but I knew full well all Brian would want to talk about was 'corruption'. As a Scottish Presbyterian and a man of principle he had a fierce sense of civic duty and he was right behind any campaign to root out the canker which had infested his adopted City. He wanted the firm to get behind Julian Singleton and hoped others, including me, would show the same commitment.

Once settled at the kitchen table over a strong coffee I went through my ordeal with the car hijackers and their threats to Lucy as well as the staged robbery and my ensuing arrest. I also admitted to my failure to inform anyone of the events of that weekend and the consequent fallout. Brian listened intently to my story and in typical fashion looked entirely unperturbed. If I were to shout 'fire-fire,' Brian would find time to offer an exposition of the day's play at a Lords Test match, before strolling off to call the fire brigade.

"You have behaved badly William and must rectify the situation by furnishing Miss Cosgrove with all the facts. It was unwise and most unfair to assume she would be unable to handle the truth. From what I have heard she is a resourceful young woman. Having come clean with Miss Cosgrove you must then talk to Julian Singleton and explain the facts to him. Don't you think that he would be more than a little interested in your experiences? I certainly do.

Now, off you go, I have things to do." With that, I was dismissed and shown to the door. My first reaction was to feel a little aggrieved at Brian's abruptness but as I drove away I understood the wisdom of his words and I knew that I had received exactly what I deserved; a metaphorical clip round the ear. It was strange how just a few words from Brian gave me the courage I needed to face the music from both Lucy and Julian Singleton.

It was close to midday when I arrived at Lucy's flat. I knocked on the door with Sir Douglas Evill's letter clutched in my hand as though this somehow gave my visit a validity that it would otherwise have lacked. Brought on my anxiety to reignite my relationship with Lucy my heart was pounding in my chest. I had decided to face the music with honesty and come straight to the point.

As a strategy it may had some merit but unfortunately my opening confidence lasted no more than a few seconds as I stuttered like a nervous five year old. "Hello Lucy, sorry I've been a bit…er. Well perhaps… we could ...er..."

"Spit it out William." Lucy's expression was halfway between amusement and despair.

Taking a couple of deep breaths and attempting to conjure up some clarity of thought, I started again. "Lucy, I know I have behaved badly. Can I come in and explain?"

Lucy looked perplexed but of course she was far too nice a person to offer any more resistance. So there it was, I was offered the chance of redemption and I took it with both hands. My apology was heartfelt and I was overwhelmingly happy to be back in Lucy's company. I vowed never to make the same mistake again. And meant it.

Over the next couple of hours we regained a measure of the warmth which I had so carelessly tossed away over the previous weeks with my thoughtless behaviour. Lucy understood my concerns for her safety and we agreed to steer clear of anything which could lead us back into trouble, at least until I had spoken again to Julian Singleton. I explained Brian's determination to help Singleton and the subtle pressure exerted to me to lend a hand.

A little later, when Lucy asked if I had made any progress tracking down my family in France I remembered the letter still folded in my inside jacket pocket. "Ah, I received something which may shed some light on that very subject only this morning. Let's see what Sir Douglas Evill has to tell us." With that I opened the envelope and unfolded the letter on my knee so that we could both read it:

Sir Douglas & Lady Edith Evill
Sycamore House
Uppington Hill
Winchester

Dear William

I trust this letter finds you well?

I thought I should let you know of a conversation that I had with a chap who worked with Barrington-Hope at Sopwith Aviation at Woolston. Alistair Buchman was an engineer and responsible for the design of the Camel and the Antelope.

We got talking about Hoppy and he told me that there were a number of people at Sopwiths who were less than happy with the verdict of death by misadventure. It seems that one man in particular was very vocal in his opposition to the coroner's report.

Of course, I have no way of knowing whether there is any substance to his claims but felt I was obliged to at least furnish you with the facts as they were presented to me. Mr. Buchman went on to say that the man who so strongly contested the official version of events was a member of Barrington-Hopes ground crew by the name of Arthur Swanson, who I understand lives in retirement in Southampton, at 33 Somerset Close, Highfield.

What exactly Mr. Swanson meant I really cannot say but I would be obliged if you were kind enough to keep me informed if you decide to follow-up this story.

Yours sincerely,

Douglas Evill

Nothing in my life it seemed was destined to be straightforward. "Looks like I'll have to prepare the Sunbeam for another outing. How's your diary Lucy?"

"Nothing would be me greater pleasure than to accompany you, Mr. Goldhawk." And the bewitching smile that lit up her pretty face gave me as much pleasure as anything had all year long.

Lucy had friends arriving for afternoon tea and I was politely pushed out of the door just after 3 o'clock which gave me a few hours to myself before meeting Julian. As I wandered home the first signs of spring were in the air; hardly warm but the sun was higher in the sky and fluffy cotton wool clouds gave a hint something more promising around the corner. The early buds where showing themselves on the hawthorns and I enjoyed a pleasant stroll through the streets of Southsea.

I had one more surprise in store for me when I got home. On my doorstep was Inspector Jack Hanaho, whose grinning countenance assaulted my vision as I walked up the front steps. Hanaho had a similar effect on my bowels to a hot curry; the mere sight of him gave me indigestion. What did he want this time I wondered?

"Mr. Goldhawk how very good to see you again. I trust you enjoyed your recent stay at our hotel and the *en suite* facilities were up to your usual standard? It's always a delight to have you staying and I am sure we will find further cause to offer our hospitality in the near future."

“What do you want Inspector?” I asked.

“I have come to return your gun …or should I say *your friend’s* gun?” The smile was replaced by a sneer as he continued. “Get a certificate or I’ll be down on you before you can turn around, understand? And Mr. Goldhawk.” he pushed his face uncomfortably close to mine before adding his final threat. “I owed your father a favour and now I’ve paid the debt so remember next time there will be no one to bail you out. I’m watching you Goldhawk.”

With that the Inspector turned and walked away.

Twenty Four

The sky was darkening as I walked down the High Street toward the Sallyport with rain now looking to be in the offing. The pub was quiet as I stepped into the entrance foyer, which like the rest of the interior was furnished in red velvet, dark wood with a particularly extensive assortment of brass knickknacks and historical prints which filled every square inch of shelf and wall space. But it was a cosy pub with dim lighting and plenty of nooks, crannies and dark corners; ideal for courting couples or clandestine liaisons. Julian looked a little out of place gulping back his pint in the inner sanctum of the lounge bar.

I was looking forward to an evening of camaraderie with Julian but felt a little uncomfortable knowing that my mission was to give him notice of my intention to quit. My priority was to protect Lucy and threats to her wellbeing left me with no option. It was not negotiable so there was no point in arguing the toss, I would tell him. In typical style as I walked into the comfortably furnished bar Julian clasped my right hand in his own and slapped me on the back as though I was the returning prodigal son. Slightly shaken but amused I took my seat.

It would be a mistake to underestimate Julian Singleton or to take his bluff persona as lacking in substance. His intellect was razor sharp and the more I got to know him the more in awe I became. He had a way of drawing you in and his powers to persuade were mesmeric. It was as though he reached inside your head and reconfigured your mind. Without even being aware you were agreeing with things that a few minutes earlier you had vehemently opposed. I am not saying that alcohol did not play a part but then Julian was well capable of intentionally using its effects to his advantage.

So perhaps it was no surprise that things did not go all my own way. I was given an early indication that our plans were not synchronised when I made to hand back his Berretta which much to my consternation he refused, telling me it was mine to keep. I had no option but to repeat the story I told Brian earlier in the day with the hope that would finally give me clearance to hand in my weapon. "So." I finished. "There you have it. I have to protect Lucy and that's just *not negotiable*."

I felt I had handled the difficult negotiations well and much to my relief Julian told me he totally understood and accepted my position. At least now we could relax and enjoy the evening knowing exactly where we both stood. "How's the investigation going?" I asked. "Have you made much progress?"

"I have quite taken to Southsea you know William. The pubs, the beer, the bracing sea air all agree with my constitution." Julian replied at a tangent and rubbed his stomach as if to prove the point. "What do you think of this Gales beer? Delicious isn't it?" He then gulped back what remained in his glass and handed it to me. "Same again please old man." He said, smiling before letting a sonorous belch escape his lips.

I returned from the bar a couple of minutes later with two pints of Gales HSB and plonked them on the table as Julian continued. "Things are going well. We're getting a small team in place and hope we may get our business completed by the summer. We have a few ideas and have uncovered some interesting bits and pieces."

"It's a shame I can't get involved. If it wasn't for Lucy I would…well you know. So what have you uncovered so far or is it all hush-hush?"

"Brian has given you the thumbs up and that's good enough for me. We had a bit of a chin-wag about you and you may be interested to know he assesses you as a competent but not top drawer accountant." A little surprised by the directness of Julian's tack and perhaps a tad hurt by Brian's assessment I tried to make light of it with a wince and an exclamation. "Ouch!" But before I had a chance to say more Julian went on:

"He thinks you get bored too easily and that's apparently not an ideal characteristic of a Chartered Accountant. In his humble opinion the aforesaid William Goldhawk is an extremely bright individual but prone to distraction. Could do better if he concentrated in class!"

"Well, I don't know about 'extremely bright' but he's got a point about concentration! The noble art of auditing is excruciatingly boring at times Julian. I don't think you'd stick it for five minutes!"

"I suspect you are right there, it may just drive me to drink. Talking of such matters I've almost come to the end of my second pint. My round I believe." And off he toddled to the bar to replenish our empty vessels.

With two pints down the hatch I had mellowed fast and as we had agreed that my voluntary contribution had run its course I felt the pressure was off. "So come-on Julian, what can you tell me? Have you got any ideas as to what's going on?"

"It's complicated but let's take one contract which serves to illustrate the nature of the beast we are dealing with. The Admiralty negotiated a contract for £4.7 million pounds for electrical supplies and services to the fleet to cover the period 1939 to 1943. The contract was awarded to the lowest bidder in a tender process which began in the bowels of Whitehall and was completed down here in Portsmouth when the final documentation was signed by both parties.

As you may imagine negotiation of contracts of this magnitude are complex and time consuming. During routine auditing in the late 1940's a number of anomalies were discovered. I can't go into too much detail but suffice to say that in the case of this particular contract the value of the goods and services supplied where calculated to be no more that £3.2 million. A big black hole of £1.5 million pounds!"

I sucked in my breath. "Wow! That's a lot of money. What were the other anomalies you mentioned?" I leant forward to catch Julian's whispered reply.

"Each contract is produced in triplicate. One copy is held by the supplier, one by the procurement department and one by the accounts department at the Admiralty. Neither of 'our' copies, the official copies are complete. Both are missing signature pages and the calculations on which the award of the tender was based. They have been tampered with. The evidence removed."

"What you are saying is that you suspect someone has creamed off the profit and then gone back to muddy the water so no-one can follow the trail?"

"That's exactly what I am saying, although more likely a syndicate than an individual. If one person organised and delivered a crime of this complexity he must be a latter day Professor Moriarty."

"Do you still see the Stanley Jakes' murder as relevant?"

Julian leaned back in his chair and removed a large cigar from his breast pocket which he lit with extravagant care before answering. "Yes, actually I am more certain that ever that Jakes had some involvement. I am guessing that he was trying to get in on the act and was probably murdered for his trouble. I think we will find that Stanley Jakes was attempting to blackmail certain individuals but did not have the nous to carry it through.

Imagine this William, Jakes has confidence to burn as he has made a killing through his extortion racket and gets wind of this contract. He feels untouchable. He tracks down the civil servants who are handling the administration of the tender and digs the dirt. He finds something with which to blackmail them; women, gambling, contraband, drink, who knows. And in return he wants information on the tender which he can sell to the highest bidder. Unbeknown to him there is already a far more powerful and sophisticated syndicate in town that does not need someone like Jakes marauding about like a recently castrated bullock." With that Julian moved his hand swiftly across his throat in a cutting movement to indicate the final demise of Stanley Jakes.

By this time I was enthralled and genuinely sorry I was to have no further involvement. I confess that I was surprised that Julian was so forthcoming. "You are getting a team together you said?" I encouraged.

"There will be four of us all told working down here in Portsmouth." Once again Julian had lowered his voice to ensure we were not overheard. "You will, of course meet the others in due course."

A double take. Did he really say I would meet the others in due course or was the alcohol affecting my hearing I wondered? I could not help but feel part of his team already but was unaware at the time how the master angler was skillfully reeling me in.

"Luke Elliott will be placed as a trainee policeman at Kings Road police station, reporting into none other than Inspector Hanaho. Elliot may be young but he has a cool head and I am hoping for enough to get Hanaho off the scene quickly. I haven't got anything solid on him just yet but have a hunch he could be trouble if we don't get shot of him soon. On the other side we have Margaret Philimore who has the task of running a series of meetings and lectures giving the city's accountants help identifying what to look for. Less glamorous but equally important. We want to ratchet up the pressure and hope this flushes-out our prey."

"I am behind you on Hanaho. There are a lot of people who would like to see the back of him." The beer had swelled my ego as well as my bladder as I sidled off to the gents with visions of swashbuckling adventurers swimming before my eyes. It was exciting stuff and I envied Julian as I contemplated the less than riveting prospect of a month-long audit at Jameson's Engineering in Farlington to look forward to.

When I returned to Julian, still with sword fights, espionage and intrigue swilling around my slightly befuddled mind I asked. "Four in the team you said. So you must be D'Artagnan, Luke and Margaret, Athos and Porthos. Who is the fourth musketeer? Who is your Aramis?" Wishing by this time that it could be me!

"The musketeers? A useful metaphor. We are looking for someone with local knowledge who knows his way around the City of Portsmouth. To extend your musketeer metaphor we want a fighter, someone like Aramis who is resilient and capable of handling himself. Someone who will blend into the landscape and whose financial training will enable him to spot a fraud or an inconsistency in a set of accounts from 100 paces. Anyone spring to mind?" Julian lent back on his chair exhaled a lungful of cigar smoke and stared at me in a disconcerting fashion that rather suggested he was referring to me.

I laughed. "Oh no! You won't get round me that easily. I thought we had an agreement? You told me but 30 minutes ago that you understood that my priority must be to protect Lucy."

"And so I do and so I do!" Julian agreed. "Of course we must protect Lucy. Our first priority, absolutely."

I felt bamboozled by a combination of skillful manipulation on the part of my companion and the beer which had left my brain functioning at less than 100% efficiency. We sat in silence; Julian looking as relaxed and innocent as the day was long whilst I struggled to keep my head.

"Why do I get the impression you are not being straight with me Julian?"

"William, please! You are concerned about Lucy and I am in agreement. Yes?"

"Yes, I suppose so." I agreed guardedly.

"So, we are singing from the same hymn sheet. I fail to understand your suspicions my friend. If you have any other concerns please tell me." He went on obtusely.

"Concerns about what exactly? I am not following you Julian." I said.

Another lungful of cigar smoke exhaled in my direction and Julian pulled a face giving the impression he was deep in thought. "As I see it and please correct me if I am wrong…you find your work a little tedious at times? Boring even and the idea of helping me bring to justice a criminal gang which has terrorized the area for twelve years is exciting to you. Right so far?" I nodded cautiously. "The reason you handed-in your spurs was because you need to protect Miss Cosgrove. So hypothetically, if I were to guarantee her safety you would still be on side. Yes?"

"Hypothetically, I suppose so…. But I have got a living to earn and bills to pay." I hedged.

"We protect Lucy, we handle your work commitments and we pay you lots of money…anything else?"

"Hypothetically, that sounds good but can you deliver?"

That was clearly enough encouragement for Julian to believe the deal was struck. He stuck out his hand asking me for my gentleman's agreement. We shook but I had very little idea what exactly I had agreed *to*. I sat back and wondered how on earth I had managed to get so well and truly mugged.

"I've not been totally honest with you William. I have been in discussion with Brian for a few weeks trying to secure your services and have also had you vetted in anticipation of you accepting our proposition. Our vetting procedure at Mi5 is thorough and takes time; and we haven't got much time. Brian has been helpful and indeed totally supportive of you and right behind our investigations. Tomorrow you will be travelling up to London to meet the Under Secretary for State at The Home Office, Timothy Whitten who will ratify your appointment and ask you to sign the Official Secrets Act."

"Mi5? You work for Mi5? I thought you were a tax collector working for the Revenue. You have got a lot of explaining to do! Are you seriously telling me that instead of reporting at Jameson's tomorrow morning in Farlington I'll on a train to London to meet a Government Minister?" My brain was spinning. I had so many questions but didn't know where to start.

For two hours Julian then filled in the yawning gaps and left me worried, disconcerted but most of all exhilarated. Before he left me he had one final surprise. "By the way William you may be interested in the name of the company which won the tender that we are investigating. It's Crawford Electrics."

Twenty Five

As I took my seat on the train to Waterloo the following morning I thought back to the events of the previous evening and what the implications were for me and for Lucy. Perhaps my overriding feeling was of disbelief. Disbelief that I could have signed-away the next six months after a 45 minutes conversation and four pints in a pub, disbelief that I was en route to meet a Minister of State to sign the Official Secrets Act and disbelief that I would be working for a branch of Mi5, albeit on a temporary secondment.

Julian had been thorough in his explanations but whether I had absorbed even half the information he had thrown at me I doubted. But I got the gist and felt comfortable enough with the options he outlined to protect Lucy and my own conditions of service (which were generous). Brian had agreed on a six month leave of absence but this was purely technical as for all intents and purposes I would continue in my post at Surtees, Hancock and Lampson but would be working 'undercover' for the Security Services.

I crossed the Thames at Waterloo Bridge and walked south along Victoria Embankment toward Westminster. With the sun shining and the air warming, London looked and felt almost back to its best after the ravages of the War. With Big Ben striking the hour the imposing Palace of Westminster soon came into view. I headed straight for the main entrance where I mingled with people of every age, dress, gender and nationality before finding a security guard at the gate who took my details and showed me into a waiting room.

I took a seat alongside an eclectic assortment of other visitors: mostly suited middle aged men with brief cases but also one informally attired young man who sat distractedly tapping the handle of his umbrella, a long bearded gentleman wearing a turban, a handful of women clustered in animated chatter around the tea urn and two impeccably turned out Army Officers. The room itself with its wooden seating, stone floors and high vaulted ceiling had an ecclesiastical quality about it which made me feel obliged to remove my hat and speak in a hushed deferential whisper when my turban wearing neighbour asked me for the time. For the non-religious it never seemed totally obvious why we felt the need to whisper in an empty Cathedral but we just *did*. And so it was here.

After a few minutes a chubby faced young man put his head around the door and gestured for me to follow him. Once out of earshot he introduced himself as a civil servant working for the Home Office and half way down a long corridor he showed me into the office of Undersecretary of State, The Right Honourable Timothy Whitten. Whether Mr. Whitten represented a typical Under Secretary of State I could not say but he was certainly very unremarkable to look at in his ultra conservative pin striped suit. He was seated behind a vast desk reading official looking papers when I entered but with impeccable manners he immediately put them to one side and welcomed me.

"Good morning William, very glad to meet you at last. I have just been reading your file." He smiled, in recognition I suspect of the surprise registered on my face. "One thing you have to get used to here is that we are very thorough, very thorough, indeed. This is Ernest Bannister by the way, who will be your liaison. If you need anything he's your chap." He gestured toward my rotund and cheery faced guide. Ernest grinned, nodded and pumped my hand enthusiastically.

"Have a seat William. I will soon leave you in the capable hands of Ernest who will deal with the formalities but I wanted the opportunity to say a few words today to impress upon you the importance of the work that you will be involved in. It's almost unprecedented that we recruit outsiders in this way but there are good reasons for this.

As well as the death and destruction caused by the bombs of the Luftwaffe and the guns and torpedoes of the Kriegsmarine there are many unseen and subtle casualties of war. One of which is the break-down of public administration and the rule of law. Many of the local records which bound the country together were destroyed by fires ignited by the incendiary bombs that rained down on many of our great cities. Hitler knew very well what he was doing; break the infrastructure and break the people. He didn't quite succeed but organised crime proliferated as a result and it's the Government's job to put the pieces back together again.

You were probably surprised to hear that an organisation like Mi5 is involved in parochial matters down on the south coast?" He looked up for a reaction and I nodded. "The truth is though." He continued. "It's a question of scale as well as national security. Various monetary values have been bandied about but I can tell you that we are now looking for fraud amounting to over five million pounds. Money effectively stolen from the Treasury and orchestrated, we believe, by one highly professional and ruthless criminal gang.

I want to impress upon you William, the need to always keep your primary objective in the forefront of your mind which is to catch whoever is behind these crimes. You may well have a very understandable grudge against that policeman and if he gets caught with his fingers in the till all well and good but frankly, the Department has no interest in Inspector Hanaho; we have far bigger fish to fry. Equally, you will want to protect Lucy Cosgrove, of course you will and rightly so but she must not get in the way of your work William. I want you to fully understand your responsibilities.

I have read your file and I am aware of course of the connection between the disappearance of your friend Billy Cosgrove and our investigations into the murder of Stanley Jakes. I want you to get to the bottom of this. If your friend is innocent who did kill Jakes? If we find his murderer, I have a hunch we will be closer to finding out the truth behind the Crawford's contract fraud.

The next point I would like to cover is the aspect of danger. Five million pounds is a lot of money by any standard and people will kill for it, so be on your guard and don't take unnecessary risks. Take your instructions from Julian and be vigilante. Neither should you under-estimate the obstacles you will face along the way. This will be no cake-walk be assured of that.

Now, Crawford Electrics." The Undersecretary paused. "It would be naïve on your part to imagine that your attraction to us was based purely on your track record and I am certain you are *not* naïve. No, your past work with the Admiralty during the War may be helpful but more importantly to us is your association with Crawford Electrics and the Crawford family, in relation particularly in your position as the company's auditor. Talk to Julian and he will fill in the gaps but I think you know the basic story. How did Crawford Electrics win a tender at nearly five million pounds which was worth little more than three million? A simple enough question and somewhere in their records must lay the answer. Find it William.

I understand you were engaged to Helen Crawford and that you have a long-standing and cordial relationship with Sir Marcus and Lady Sybil Crawford? Use these relationships to your advantage but do not over step the mark. Remember, no member of the Crawford family is yet implicated in any wrongdoing whatsoever so think of your job as uncovering the truth not as undermining your friendships. If Sir Marcus Crawford is innocent you will be doing him a great service by getting to the truth."

With that, the Undersecretary rose from his chair to indicate that the meeting was drawing to a close and asked if I had any questions for him, to which I replied that I indeed had one:

"This particular fraud took place during the war years and its now 1951. Are we just trying to uncover the events of the past or is there more to it than that?"

"A good question William but one to which I can give you only a partial answer. I can tell you that we have reason to believe that the syndicate still operates in some capacity and has connections to organised crime overseas. There are implications for National Security and hence our interest as well as my reticence."

My stay in the office of the Undersecretary was brief, no more than fifteen minutes before I was whisked off by Ernest Bannister to an another office in Pall Mall where my briefing continued. My new friend was Ernest by name and earnest by nature, a Cambridge Classics' scholar and a first class boffin he was nothing if not extremely thorough. By the end of the day my head ached from pure exhaustion, overloaded by facts, figures and procedures. If Ernest had his way it was clear that my cosy evenings with Julian Singleton in the Sallyport would be consigned to history. The protocol was that, except in emergency situations, team members should acknowledge their acquaintanceship with other team members in 'out of area designated safe house locations' only. I could not quite see Julian following that particular rule to the letter.

When I had sat in the Sallyport less than 24 hours earlier I could hardly imagine the twist my life was to about to take. All the work I was doing was 'classified' which meant I was to talk to no-one, not even Lucy about my position. Somehow I had to discuss the options to keep her safe without revealing why she was suddenly in need of protection. I got the distinct impression I had a bumpy ride ahead. It was pretty clear too that the Security Services expected a lot from their operatives, there was no molly coddling. We were expected to find your own way and pretty much anything was acceptable as long as our cover remained in-tact.

I was told to live as near a normal life as possible as a sudden change in lifestyle was likely to arouse suspicion which was to be avoided at all costs. It was something of a surreal day all round I thought as I headed back on the express to Portsmouth that evening. One thing that was not mentioned was the use of firearms so I assumed that my Berretta was a private arrangement between Julian and myself.

Twenty Six

Having signed a contract, the Official Secrets Act and half a dozen other assorted documents giving my consent to serve King and Country, I started to give some serious thought to how I was going to tackle my assignment at Crawfords without arousing suspicion. I needed free access to their archives and fancied that a formal letter from the Inland Revenue to the Crawford's auditors instructing us to perform a contract audit would provide the cover I needed. Ernest was unfazed by my request and promised an Inland Revenue letter of authorization would be in the post that afternoon.

With that in place I decided to confront the more delicate issue of Lucy and how to broach the subject of her personal security. I had little choice but to bend the truth and tell her there had been further threats made. It was a painful conversation for me but Lucy took it on the chin as I knew she would. After going through the options which included a temporary new life and identity in Canada, Lucy plumped for taking in a lodger; a lodger trained to cook, clean and shoot. Resigned but not entirely happy with the arrangement she also accepted my promise of a long weekend in Picardie to track down my family as small compensation for her discomfort.

Three days later I found myself on the Waterloo express train with colleagues Douglas Lampson and Michael Bridges, once again having to bend the truth, or more accurately tell an outright lie by passing off my Inland Revenue letter as genuine. I wanted to test its authenticity so handed it to Douglas who raised an eyebrow but said nothing before passing it to Michael who gave it no more than a cursory glance before returning his attention back to the Racing Post. No problems there.

The Crawford's audit was well underway now and Douglas seemed in the main, happy with progress. "On the whole the records are clean and the team at Spital Square has been accommodating enough, somewhat morose but accommodating! I do still have some concerns about these unusual transactions I mentioned to you a couple of months ago though. It's all very bizarre really but one minute there is nothing, a black hole with chunks of money unaccounted for and then out of the blue all the documents are in place, as if by magic!" Douglas explained.

"Really? That sounds a little odd." I queried.

"Well I was in the office on Monday with the intention of checking out those payments. You may remember I told you there was a bankers draft for around $56,000 with no supporting paperwork? Well Monday came and still nothing; no purchase orders, invoices, dispatch notes…not a dicky-bird in fact. I had a word with Benison who just nodded vaguely and said he would look into it and lo and behold, yesterday all the supporting documents were in place!"

"Well, that's good isn't it?" I asked hopefully.

"You would think so but it all smells a little fishy to me! I suppose we just do our job and let someone else worry about it but I don't know, I just don't know." He finished, shaking his head unhappily.

Once we arrived at Crawford's head office an hour or so later I left Douglas and Michael and went in search of John Benison the Chief Accountant. I can't say he was bowled over with enthusiasm to see me but greeted me cordially enough, at least until he caught sight of the letter from the Inland Revenue.

"What's this about then Mr. Goldhawk? More unnecessary paperwork?" He grumbled.

"Just routine." I lied. "It's really nothing to worry about. If you would care to point me in the direction of the archives I am sure I can satisfy the Revenue without getting you involved."

"You'll need to see Matthew Buridge. He looks after our records and he won't take kindly to you touching anything without his say so." With that, I was left to my own devises and walked off down the corridor in search of the keeper of corporate records, Mr. Matthew Buridge who I found consuming a sandwich and chatting to a posse of young women in the typing pool. Unfashionably long-haired but casually well-dressed Mr. Buridge was not amused by my interruption.

"Aren't I even allowed a sandwich without being hounded?" He winked at the girl nearest to him. "Come on then mate, I'll show you the archives. But don't go touching nothing without my say so, alright?"

It was not hard to get a measure of Matthew Buridge. "That's fine Matthew but remember I am authorised to examine any financial documents that I deem necessary so it would be in your interests to co-operate. Perhaps we could start with the archives covering 1938 and 1939?"

"Touchy! Keep your hair on fella' and follow me. It's down in the dungeon but we'll have to go via reception for the key." And off he set without a backward glance. The young receptionist sat filing her nails as we approached the front desk but preened when she caught sight of Matthew.

"Hello, my darling you are looking particularly ravishing this morning." It seemed complimenting girls half his age came naturally to Matthew Buridge but I decided that it may be judicious for me too to get to know the young lady so I smiled and introduced myself in a slightly less flirtatious manner.

Having secured the keys we set off again down a back staircase which led to the basement where the archives were kept. And something of an auditor's dream it was too, if you were that way inclined, as row upon row of neatly stacked and well-ordered box files met my gaze. All racked and identified by content, row and shelf number. I wondered down the first aisle with an over attentive Buridge at my shoulder.

“So what you are looking for? I might be able to dig it out if I know what you’re after.” He offered but without much enthusiasm.

“No need to trouble yourself, I just need to examine a few files. If you would just point me in the direction of 1938-39 archives as I asked, I’ll take it from there thank you.” Buridge seemed reluctant to do as I had requested and it was only on my insistence that he finally led me down a further flight of stairs to a second storeroom. Of equal dimension to the one above but far more cluttered and quite clearly containing records dating back to well before the war. The accumulations of dust and spiders webs indicated that the room had remained undisturbed for some years.

“This is all the pre-war stuff and I haven’t got round to sorting it out yet. But it’s on my list.” Buridge explained.

With no intention of settling down to work with Buridge hovering over my shoulder I told him (much to his evident relief) that I had seen enough. I would be back as soon as the opportunity arose but next time I would come alone. Julian was convinced that the contract fraud could not have been perpetrated without inside help and I needed time alone in the dungeons of Spital Square to prove him right (or perhaps wrong).

I decided to come back later in the afternoon, once the accounts department was closed for the day when I hoped to get a couple of hours of uninterrupted time to examine the records at my leisure. I chatted up the young receptionist, relieved her of the keys and by 6.30 I was ensconced in the lower basement with only a handful of scuttling spiders for company. The room was musty after years of neglect but seemed relatively dry and surprisingly warm so I was hopeful that the records would be in a readable condition.

Once I had gauged that the offices three stories up were closed for the night I started walking up and down the aisles trying to make sense of the rudimentary filing system. Unlike the order which characterized the floor above, the pre-war files in the lower basement were in a mixed assortment of boxes and folders, mostly identifiable only by a date and a scrawled hand written description, more often than not, illegible. I imagined I was in for a long session.

No more than an hour into my vigil, however, I heard the unmistakable sound of footsteps rattling down the cast iron steps, followed closely by two men whispering. My unexpected visitors were en route to the lower basement where I was holed up, a possibility that I had not foreseen. I gathered up my papers and stuffed them into the nearest box and quickly made for the door where I switched off the lights and crept quietly to the farthest corner of the storeroom.

I was squatting on my haunches out of view when the lights came back on and it took me no time to recognise my nocturnal visitors as Matthew Buridge and John Benison.

"Everything from 1939 should be down this aisle. Look for a large box with Admiralty Contract written on the side." Buridge was now moving down the aisle where I had been just minutes earlier.

"Is this the one?" I heard Benison ask.

"Yes, that's it I think." Buridge responded.

I could hear their combined struggle to remove a heavy box from a shelf and listened as they flicked through the contents. "This is what we want. Just go through the file and fish out anything that might incriminate us. And get rid of any reference to Lancier."

After a few minutes the two accountants had clearly finished their work as I saw Benison's head clear the shelving as he stood, before turning toward the exit. "Let's get out of here. I don't want anything that links us to this contract Matthew and I certainly don't want that auditor snooping around. Stick to him like glue if he ever suggests a further visit."

Within a few minutes of their arrival they were off and I was mightily relieved to hear their echoing footsteps receding into the night. I was equally relieved to find the coast clear so that I could make my own escape a few minutes later. I had decided that there was now nothing useful to be achieved in the basement so silently left the building by a side entrance and made my way back to Liverpool Street station. An interesting, if unexpected turn of events for sure but what did it mean I wondered? And what or who was Lancier?

"Lancier?" queried Julian after I had gone through the events of the day from a phone box at Waterloo Station. "No, I can't say it means anything to me. Interesting though, very interesting. We'll have to find out what our friends Benison and Buridge have been up to. Let me think on how we should proceed."

I was then given my assignment for the following day. "Tomorrow I would like you to track down Frank Gilbert if you can find him. I have been looking through Jakes' diary and there are a couple of entries I am particularly interested in and have a feeling Gilbert may be able to shed some light on them. One is in early October '39 and refers to a meeting with a Peter and the other a week later mentions an early evening meeting with Peter and Andrew C. This was the last entry before his death. Don't take any chances with Gilbert and make sure you have a few pounds in cash to loosen his tongue. Who are Peter and Andrew? I want you to find out."

Twenty Seven

I had a busy few weeks in store with a number of loose ends to tie up. My scheduled visit to the Isle of Wight would be a test of my mettle. As well as clearing up any misunderstanding with Helen which arose from our alcohol charged encounter at Liongate, I also intended a quiet word with Sir Marcus. It was difficult to gauge which way the wind may blow with Sir Marcus and I expected something of a stormy encounter. My aim was to exert just a little pressure by dropping the name 'Lancier' into the conversation and if that didn't bring forth the storm clouds my second bomb shell, that Crawfords was under investigation by the Revenue, surely would

On a personal front (and killing two birds with one stone) I had arranged to visit France with Lucy to trace my mother's family (my own family). At the same time I was hoping the visit would be a welcome distraction for Lucy who was finding life with an on-site bodyguard a little hard to bear. Her new companion Samantha Smith took her duties rather too seriously and Lucy was in need of a break.

As a means to prise Lucy away from Samantha for a day I had organised too, a visit to Arthur Swanson in Southampton. In a reply to my letter Mr. Swanson made it clear that he had serious misgivings about the Barrington-Hope verdict of death by misadventure and was more than happy to meet us and explain his reservations.

But my first task when I left the house the following morning was my rescheduled rendezvous with Frank Gilbert. I had been given an address in West Street, Havant and pulled up outside a three story redbrick Victorian semi-detached house around mid-morning to find Frank Gilbert half way up a ladder painting window frames.

Life is full of surprises, as the saying goes and Frank Gilbert was a surprise. I am not quite sure what I expected but it was certainly someone less accommodating than the smiling and agreeable man who greeted me. "Ah, I was expecting a visit about my former employer. Give me two minutes and I'll be down."

He stepped off the ladder and shook my hand. "Come inside and I'll make a cuppa. So, who do you work for? I heard through the grapevine that I may be getting a visit. Is this a police investigation?"

"I am a tax investigator working for the Inland Revenue. We are investigating the business dealings of your old boss, Stanley Jakes."

"You're about twelve years' too late old man! It seems to me rather like the horse has bolted." Responded Gilbert with a smile.

"That may be the case but we have a few loose ends to tie up." I replied giving the official line.

"I'll answer your questions but you need to understand that I am not and never was a criminal. Not really. The only crime I committed was turning a blind eye and that was down to fear. I was recruited in good faith by Jakes and I was unaware of his criminal activities until it was too late. I have done 2 stints in prison thanks to my former employer and as far as I was concerned his murder was blessed relief to me. Even today, twelve years on, I look over my shoulder not quite knowing if I'm safe, or if my past will catch-up with me. He was that sort of bloke, once he had you in his grip he wouldn't let go." Gilbert's earlier smiling countenance evaporated quickly as he recalled his experiences with evident displeasure.

He had clearly suffered from his association with Jakes and he did not enjoy reliving the memory but continued nonetheless. "Stanley's methods weren't subtle. He found out his victim's weakness, usually gambling, girls or drink and he'd give them the time of their lives. But once they were hooked he'd make 'em pay, big time. He ran crooked dog fights over on Portsdown Hill and was merciless once his victims got into debt. He'd hound them until they paid up, charging ridiculous interest rates.

And then there were the girls. He had a few working girls that he used to tempt the lecherous old men with and then he'd blackmail 'em. If you're interested in that side of his business activities you may want to consult a young lady who went by the name of Scarlet. Last I heard she lived down Ordnance Row opposite the munitions works. A real head turner she was and Stanley used her as bait. And believe you me they caught more than mackerel!

He had a more legitimate business as well, buying and selling to the ships but even that was underpinned by threats of violence as he didn't believe in competition. I kept his books for him and ran the office but tried to steer clear of the less savory aspects of the business so I can't really help you with the detail. The one saving grace about Jakes was that he did pay well. He figured, rightly as it happened, that the extra money bought staff loyalty."

As he came to the end of his story I asked him about the diary entries, Peter and Andrew C. "Peter and Andrew? No can't say their names ring a bell, sorry."

Disappointed I got to my feet to leave. I felt sorry for Gilbert, a young man whose time had been blighted by his affiliation with Stanley Jakes and hoped that it was not too late for him to get his life back on track. Before I reached the front gate I heard him calling me back.

"Wait a second… Pete and Andy, yes I do remember them! They were the two young chaps down from London who worked on the Admiralty contracts. Of course yes, they were only down here for a few months. It was their job to crunch the numbers and I know Stanley was very keen on getting them onside. I felt sorry for the buggers. He gave them such a hard time. I can't tell you where they are now but they disappeared back to London with their tails between their legs. Yes, it's coming back to me. Pete Taylor was a skinny lad but quite feisty, while Andy Cross was very young with a mischievous streak! Nice lads I seem to remember."

"So did you get what you wanted from them?" I asked.

"I didn't get involved in that side. Buchanan and Riley were the enforcers, I was only unleashed when Stanley needed to charm his victims rather than intimidate them. All I can say is that both Taylor and Cross were scared half to death when they realised what they'd done. Stanley asked me to deliver an envelope to each of them and they both looked like they would pass out when they opened them up. Exactly what was inside I couldn't say but it wasn't a birthday card!"

"Did Jakes have any dealings with two accountants from Crawford Electrics by the names of John Benison and Matthew Buridge?" I threw in on the off-chance.

"No idea I am afraid. But then I wasn't aware he had any connection with Crawfords either. But he did have his finger in all sorts of pies. I remember once a Rolls Royce pulled up outside the back of the office and a gentleman in a very expensive suit paid Stanley a visit. They were locked away in his office for hours. Not sure what it was about but you had to hand it to the bloke he had connections and got results."

"Any idea who the man in the Rolls Royce may have been?" I asked.

"There were rumours he was a politician but I never knew for sure."

"Have you any theories about who might have killed your former employer?"

"It's hard to say really. There were hundreds of people who wanted him dead I'm sure. Looking back it was inevitable I suppose that someone would do him in. He made a career out of other people's misery and he must have had more enemies than Genghis Khan by the time he was finished." And I could not disagree.

Ten minutes later I was back in the Sunbeam driving through the congested streets of Cosham toward Portsmouth trying to piece together what I had learnt. There was plenty of supposition but precious little substance. It was pretty clear that Stanley Jakes was involved in some capacity but I did not have enough information as yet to form a working theory. A serious crime was committed through Crawford Electrics that much was certain but who was guilty of a crime and who was an unwitting bystander was not so clear-cut.

It would certainly stretch credibility too far to suppose that the two junior civil servants, Taylor and Cross would have had either the experience or the authority to enable them to commit a crime of this magnitude, whether of their own free will or by coercion. They may well have played some role but I did not imagine for one minute that it was more than a minor one.

Sir Marcus Crawford on the other hand was surely up to his neck. After all he was the majority shareholder and Chairman of the company which stood to gain from the fraud. And Benison and Buridge? Hard to gauge whether they were guilty of serious fraud or minor misdemeanors, but guilty of *something* they certainly were. But I was not convinced that Julian would want me questioning the two accountants at this stage, arousing their suspicions still further. My gut feeling was that we needed to play our cards carefully and keep them close to our chest, at least for the time being.

But a telephone conversation revealed my total misread of the situation, or at least, my misread of the enigmatic Julian. "I think it's about time we put some pressure on Benison and Buridge, don't you? Why don't you collar Buridge and ask him about 'Lancier' and make oblique references to missing files. Make him aware we are on to him and what the consequences will be if he doesn't come clean. Make him sweat. I think that will yield results, don't you William? In the meantime I'll see if I can locate Monsieurs Taylor and Cross."

Twenty Eight

The following week was spent in London catching-up on routine matters relating to the Crawford's audit and with the weekend approaching I was looking forward to spending some time with Lucy. Saturday proved to be a beautiful spring morning and I decided to take a stroll over to her flat. As part of the new security arrangements we had had a telephone installed so I was able to warn her in advance to put the kettle on the stove. The elegant houses of Livingstone Road were resplendent, the ornamental cherries in full blossom and the sky deep blue. All in all, a perfect day.

So I was in good humour as I walked down Victoria Road South toward the sea front and hoped that Lucy was getting used to life with an armed lodger. I knew I would be in for a severe grilling and that it would be impossible to fob her off with vague half-truths. It was at the junction with Clarendon Road, I believe, that I resolved to tell Lucy the whole truth. I trusted her implicitly and although I would be in contravention of the terms of every contract that I had signed in London, I would tell her anyway.

Humming quietly to myself I wandered through the shopping area of Palmerston Road and down toward the sea front to Lucy's flat on Clarence Parade. I was surprised to find the front door ajar but pushed it open and shouted Lucy's name. Light from the front window flooded the hallway and illuminated the body which lay face up, perfectly still and stone dead. The single bullet which killed her had entered her skull between the eyes. There was no more than a thin trickle of blood running down her forehead. Although I knew she was dead my instinct was to search for a pulse which I did whilst keeping my eyes trained for her assassin.

"Lucy." I shouted urgently. "It's William." But my call was greeted by silence.

Lucy's lodger was past help so I stepped over her prone body and removed the Beretta from my pocket. I kicked open the door to the sitting room and peered inside before moving cautiously to the bedrooms but all was eerily quiet. Apart from the body of the unfortunate Samantha the flat was deserted. I picked up the telephone to dial 999 but had second thoughts and called Julian. As the phone line clicked open I heard the wailing of sirens closing in. The police had already been alerted. Julian picked up the phone and told me to sit tight, keep the gun out of sight and say as little as possible until he arrived.

Within seconds the police were hammering at the door. My immediate and only concern was Lucy and I was mightily relieved to discover that it was she who had called the police and was safe and well, currently under their protection at a friend's flat further down Clarence Parade. Julian arrived minutes later and took the Inspector to one side and after a few minutes of intense discussion he made his way over to join me.

"We must pick up Lucy and find somewhere quiet to talk William. Can we use your house?" Julian asked ushering me toward his car.

Twenty minutes later, key in hand I walked up the steps to my front door with a shaken Lucy at my side and a watchful Julian two steps behind. During the short car journey Julian had explained that as Samantha Smith worked for the Security Services the murder investigation lay outside the jurisdiction of the local police and we were to expect two officers down from London later that day. It was hardly surprising that Lucy was badly unnerved by the events of the morning and had remained silent on the back seat of the car.

Once inside we made for the sitting room and Lucy spoke for the first time. "That bullet was meant for me wasn't it?" She looked first at me and then Julian for an answer. It was Julian who replied:

"Yes, Lucy I think you were the target and you deserve an explanation. There are people out there desperate enough to kill to stop the truth coming out. You won't be surprised to know that there's money involved and a lot of it. Fraud on a massive scale and it's my job the bring those responsible to justice. But it's evident that they will stop at nothing to derail us. Miss Smith was collateral damage, caught in the crossfire. And I'm afraid to say, Lucy, the situation is not likely to improve until the buggers are caught."

"She was a funny old stick but I was quite fond of her." Whispered a distressed Lucy. "She took her responsibilities so seriously and I laughed at her for it! And now look. It's so awful to think she's been snuffed out… and for what? Poor Sam."

"It's not your fault Lucy. You are a victim too." I consoled her, before looking at Julian for support. "But we must take this threat seriously or you could be next. We really do have to get you away from here for your own protection."

"Oh no! I'm sorry William but I am not prepared to be shunted aside like that. This is my home and my battle just as much as it is yours." Lucy replied with a defiance I knew only too well.

"Let's have this discussion in the morning shall we? I think we should all stay here tonight William, if that's alright with you? I will organise an around the clock police watch on the house and we can make some decisions tomorrow." Julian interceded diplomatically.

During the course of the afternoon Julian and I were given a view of how the tragic events of that morning had unfolded and how Samantha Smith had been ruthlessly gunned down by an assassin on the doorstep. Lucy had been in the kitchen and oblivious to events only yards away. The gun's silencer had done its work and the perpetrator had made his or her escape unmolested and presumably untroubled by their conscience.

So shocked was Lucy on discovering Samantha's body that she left the house in her dressing gown and ran bare foot to her friends seafront house half a mile up Clarence Parade where, shaking with emotion, she dialed for the police. Although traumatised by the morning's occurrence, Lucy selflessly spent much of the rest of the day speaking to friends and relatives of Samantha, consoling and sympathising with every-one.

It was a sinister turn of events and put into perspective my own experiences. Surely there could be no doubt that whoever was behind the shooting of Samantha was also behind, both my beating at Flathouse Quay and later abduction by gun point on my own doorstep. Why, I wondered had I twice been spared? Had the shooting of Samantha been a consequence of our enemy having finally lost patience? I reflected on my own good fortune and with remorse, on the crucial, albeit unintentional part that I had played in Samantha's death.

I knew now with an unerring certainty that I had reached the point of no return. My inexorable destiny was to see this through to the bitter end. The shooting was a brutal declaration of intent and I had little choice but to confront it head on. It was midnight when I finally followed my guests up to bed and later still before I slipped into an uneasy sleep. The catastrophe of the day spilled over into my dreams in which I was tormented by a beguiling and dangerous predator. I could not see it or touch it but could sense its all-pervading presence.

I awoke with a start and the reality of my nightmare came instantly to mind. Our enemy knew us but we did not know our enemy, an invidious and dangerous situation to find yourself. The morning brought little respite and certainly no resolution to the thorny issue of Lucy's protection. She was adamant that she was not leaving Portsmouth, let alone England and once Lucy had made up her mind she was a hard person to shift.

Mid-morning came and we had a visit from the police but we were able to tell them very little. No-one, it seemed, had so much as glimpsed the killer and clues were scant to the point of non-existence. The sum total of clues from the scene was a very ordinary size 9 shoe print which may or may not have belonged to Miss Smith's assassin. In summary, the killer may (or may not) be a man with a very average shoe size. Hardly enough to get the pulse racing. I somehow doubted our colleagues from London would have a successful sojourn on the south coast.

After responding to interminable and repetitive questions from our thorough Inspector from the Met we were finally left along just after midday. There followed an afternoon of much brow beating and teeth-gnashing, mostly, it has to be admitted, on my part. I was more than a little concerned by the recalcitrant Lucy's determination to ignore the danger she faced. Beyond all other considerations I wanted her safe.

"These people are ruthless Lucy! You saw what they are capable of only yesterday." I said with no attempt to hide my exasperation.

"So tell me William, why is it that you think it's alright for you to stay but not me?" Lucy countered defiantly.

"Well, let's face facts Lucy I think I have rather more in the way of physical attributes to look after myself than you do!" I slung back, a little too vehemently.

"Oh, I get it. You are the big hero and I'm just a weak and defenseless woman! So a bullet would just bounce off you I suppose?"

At this point Lucy threw a cushion in my direction and Julian laughed. "Now, now children no more fighting please. You won't win this one William. However much I agree with you, the lady isn't going anywhere and I think you will have to accept it."

We eventually reached an uneasy compromise which meant Lucy moving in upstairs from me. Normally a scenario which would have left me purring with pleasure but in the current circumstances by no means an ideal option. But what choice did I have? As Julian reminded me I could not force her to accept my more extreme alternative and exile to a foreign land for a girl who had never crossed the Channel was by any standards an extreme measure. But now, it would be incumbent on me to keep her safe; a new complication I had to factor into my already complicated life.

Julian was insistent that wrapping ourselves in cotton wool was not the answer and that we should maintain the normal patterns of life albeit with a few extra precautions. Some form of normality was to be restored the following day as we all agreed that Lucy and I should keep our appointment with Arthur Swanson in Southampton. After all, moping at home would not help anyone, least of all the unfortunate Samantha.

Twenty Nine

It was with mixed emotions that I drove out of Portsmouth with Lucy the following day contemplating the circumstance which had so unexpectedly thrown us together. In one sense I was overjoyed to welcome Lucy as my new lodger but after the shooting of her companion this was tempered by an intense worry about the danger that she faced. A danger that hitherto had been somewhat theoretical but seeing Samantha with a bullet between the eyes brought it home all too graphically.

Our progress that morning through Fareham and Titchfield slowed to a crawl thanks to roadworks and the tension in the car was stretched taut. Things had been voiced in the heat of the moment over the previous 48 hours which would have better been left unsaid and perhaps in sympathy with the traffic conditions our normal chatter ground to a halt.

The killing of Samantha brought into focus the fragility of life and prompted the need for me to articulate my deeper feelings to Lucy but I had long been afraid that any declaration of love would not have been reciprocated. Had the intensity of the last two days injected some much needed backbone into me, maybe I would finally have plucked-up the courage to express how I felt but characteristically I spurned the opportunity and botched my lines.

"Lucy, I hope you understand my reasons for wanting to send you away yesterday?"

"I think I do yes. I am a thorn in your side and you want me out of the way." Lucy replied with feeling.

"It's not like that Lucy I just… want to keep you safe." I kept my eyes firmly on the road ahead hoping that somehow Lucy would interpret my half spoken words as I had intended and at some level I think she did as she took my left hand from the steering wheel and gave it a gentle squeeze. Lucy was incapable of holding a grudge for long.

"So William do you know where you are going or shall I consult the road atlas?" Lucy had decided it was time to draw a line in the sand and rummaged around on the back seat in search of the Michelin map. In typically stoical style she tried hard to lift the gloom and concentrate on the reason for our visit. "Do you know any more than Sir Douglas wrote in his letter? Arthur Swanson worked with your Dad at Sopwith's but had doubts about the verdict of accidental death. Is that right?" Lucy had taken to calling Major Barrington-Hope 'my dad' and I had ceased to contradict her on the basis that soon enough we should learn the truth, one way or the other.

"That's pretty much as I read it, yes. I think we have to turn soon don't we?" I asked as we approached a set of traffic lights on the outskirts of Southampton. A mile or so further I turned into Highland Road, a residential street with modern crescent bayed, semi-detached houses lining both sides of the street as far as the eye could see. We soon found Somerset Close and the abode of Arthur Swanson which was tucked into the far corner of the cul-de-sac.

Arthur Swanson was a trim and sprightly septuagenarian and even in retirement he dressed in a jacket and tie and welcomed us both with a firm, formal handshake. "Please come in and have a seat. You must be William? You won't remember me, of course but I met you and your sister on a number of occasions when you were young children. That was a long time ago, twenty-five years or more. How is your sister?"

As I had made it a habit of late, I then went on to summarise the confusion of my life story and could not fail to catch the bafflement in our host's eyes. "Well that's extraordinary! I am sure that you are the Major's son. The similarity between the two of you is uncanny. I saw it the minute you walked through the door."

The third person, I realised, to draw the same conclusion just by looking at me.

We spoke for some minutes more about the circumstances behind our visit and the conflicting evidence which Lucy and I had so far gathered together. Arthur Swanson listened as I explained about my mother's death, my upbringing at Liongate, the confusion about the circumstances and date of Barrington-Hope's death and my birth certificate which was at odds with rest of the evidence. I also gave an explanation of our visit to Sir Douglas Evill and how this led us to Southampton. I finished by asking why he had been unhappy with the official verdict of accidental death.

"Unhappy! I was more than unhappy. To this day I am convinced the Major was murdered but when I voiced my concerns I was treated as a bit of a nutcase. Well, let me tell you what happened and why I believe he was murdered. See what you think. Firstly, Major Barrington-Hope was unquestionably the finest pilot I ever had the pleasure to work with. He was a perfect gentleman and even with one arm he could fly any plane as if by God-given instinct. I never knew a man before or since who had an easier rapport with his craft and I would have trusted him with my life (as I often did when accompanying him on test flights).

The Antelope which he flew on the day he disappeared was prepared by me and she was in perfect order. All checks were completed on the morning of the flight and I was totally satisfied with her. I am aware that accidents happen but the events I witnessed that morning convinced me that this was no accident."

Arthur Swanson was certainly adamant but I hoped that his reasoning had not been disturbed by guilt. Was it possible that he had made a mistake in preparing the plane or that his oversight had led to the tragedy? If that were the case it would hardly be a great surprise that he would convince himself of an outcome which pointed the finger of blame elsewhere, especially as he obviously held the Major in such high esteem.

“Are you suggesting that the plane was sabotaged?” Lucy asked echoing my own thoughts.

“No, absolutely not, the plane was is perfect working order when he took her up.” Swanson replied leaving no room for argument.

“But you said he was murdered, how can that be?”

“Well, this is what happened. It was the middle of the summer and the Major came in early, around 7am, which was not unusual. I saw him being dropped at the gates by his wife - your mother- and start to walk toward the main hanger where I was completing the final checks on the aircraft. When he saw me he raised his hand and waved and shouted out to me asking if I wanted a coffee. I waved back and nodded, and watched as he changed direction and crossed the tarmac toward the canteen.

Just before he got to the door another man approached him from the direction of hanger number two and laid a hand on his shoulder. I didn’t recognise the man and was mildly concerned as there were restrictions in place for visitors and we saw very few strangers within the compound. I could see them talking for a short while before they both disappeared inside.

After an hour or so there was no sign of my coffee so I decided to clean up and walk over to the canteen myself. The day was warming up and it looked like another scorcher so I removed my overalls and wandered across the runway toward the double doors which were open. Even this early it was so bright outside that my eyes could not immediately adjust to the gloomy conditions in the canteen.

Had my eyesight been better I too may have been a pilot and I may also have been able to identify the man I believe killed Major Barrington-Hope. As I entered, the man sitting beside the Major quickly stood-up, patted him on the back in a gesture that I could not readily interpret and walked out of the far door. I wandered across the room toward the Major who looked uncharacteristically flustered and out of sorts.

'Are you alright sir?' I asked him.

'Yes, thank you Swanson. I'll be out shortly. Is everything ready?'

I had known the Major for three years and he was the most reliable and easy going man you could ever wish to meet. He was never moody or distracted or difficult in any way. But something had got to him that morning. A little later after I had taxied the Antelope out of the hanger and onto the runway I saw the Major walking toward me tugging at his artificial arm in a very nervy way that suggested something was not quite right. His normal calm demeanor had deserted him and as he approached I could see that he was sweating and muttering to himself.

I tried to dissuade him from flying but it was no use. I should have insisted but of course it's easy in hindsight. I remember he was twitchy and wouldn't look me in the eye and slurred his word as though he'd been drinking. He said 'Clear the chocks old boy.' Something I had never heard him say in all the time I'd known him. He clambered aboard and off he went. Not his normal smooth take-off I might add and that was the last I saw of him."

"Very curious but hardly murder surely? Whatever this mysterious fellow said may have affected his judgement but you can hardly accuse him of murder, can you?" I asked.

"When the Major climbed into the cockpit he was back in the war. I am convinced he was hallucinating and had no idea what he was doing or where he was. He simply was not himself. In my book it was murder."

Lucy's brow furrowed and she shook her head in disbelief. "What are you suggesting Mr. Swanson that this man drugged him or laced his coffee? A bit far-fetched isn't it?"

"That's exactly the conclusion that the inquest drew but I saw it with my own eyes. Yes, I believe he was drugged. I can see no other explanation and I've had twenty five years to think about it."

Visions of Clive Davenport's story floated into my mind but I quickly dismissed them as unconnected. "This mysterious man, was he ever identified? And what was said at the inquest?" I asked in puzzlement.

"Your mother saw him as she drove off but like me could offer no explanation nor had any idea who it may have been. Well that's what she said *at the time*. The canteen was deserted and no-one else had any recollection of seeing anyone or anything unusual. The inquest accepted my story but concluded that it had no relevance to the accident. I tried my best to get them to investigate but I was a lone voice."

"Is there anything else at all you can tell us which may help us identify this man? The Major had no enemies that you know of, or any reason to want him dead?" I asked, although at the back of my mind I understood what a thankless task it would be trying to track-back over twenty-five years. I was no more than going through the motions.

"I can't tell you much. He wore a light coloured suit and I had a feeling he was not a local man. I only heard a couple of words he spoke but I am sure I detected an accent and he called the Major 'Hoppy,' so I suspect he knew him from the war. I cannot imagine anyone taking against the Major as he was such a gent. I kept in touch with your mother until she became ill and like me she was convinced that her husband had been murdered. Just before she died I received a letter from her which you may care to read."

With that Arthur Swanson handed me the letter which was written in my mother's hand. The second paragraph brought home to me the personal aspect of our mission that day. Somehow, even though we were investigating the possible murder of a man who may have been my father I still felt two steps removed. It was hard to feel personally involved until I read my mother's words.

Dear Arthur

I count you as a dear friend and know the esteem held for you by my late husband Geoffrey who often spoke to me about you, always with affection and high praise for the standards you kept.

As my time approaches, I often wonder if it is possible to die from a broken heart; I now believe that it is indeed so. I have found life hard to endure without my beloved Geoffrey. So for myself I care not that death comes calling but for my beautiful children, I worry so much. I have made what provision I am able but must leave it in God's hands to take care of them both.

The reason for my letter, as well as to thank you for helping me in my darkest hour, is to commit to writing something that has weighed heavily on my mind since not long after Geoffrey's death. You asked me once whether he had any enemies and I dismissed the idea out of hand.

Perhaps I should have given the matter more thought as he made one enemy, thanks to me. Just after the war finished I was working as a nurse in a British Military Hospital in Paris when I met a young British officer who I only ever knew as Harry. He was charming and very kind to me at first and we became friends. In time though I saw an altogether different side to him and cared little for his 'tastes'. He was cruel and sadistic.

I became very frightened of him until Geoffrey came to my rescue. Of course, Geoffrey shielded me from the details but he successfully kept Harry away from me until we left Paris in the autumn of 1920. Through some French friends I later learnt that Geoffrey had followed Harry and caught him mistreating a prostitute and had threatened to report him to the authorities for which he could have been shot.

Geoffrey never breathed a word to me about Harry until after we left Paris but I have often wondered whether Harry could have been responsible for his murder. I can only speculate, of course but just maybe one day the truth will emerge.

I do not expect you to act upon this information but just keep it safe.

Affectionately yours,

Catherine

My mother had been dealt the poorest of poor hands in the card game of life and tears welled in my eyes as I thought of her suffering. The good times for my poor mother had been in short supply and my heart bled. I handed the letter to Lucy who also found it hard to control her emotions and we both sat still and quiet for some minutes digesting the sad story that the letter told before I decided it was time for us to leave. I thanked Arthur Swanson for his help and courtesy but mostly I thanked him for befriending my mother in her time of need.

It seemed extraordinary how death and intrigue had followed us around and at each turn we were thrown more questions with very little in the way of answers. Surely there could be no connection between the apparent murder of my father (I had now to believe that he was indeed my father) and the death of Stanley Jakes and yet both stories had this same very unusual dimension. I needed time to think and suggested we drove down to the New Forest for lunch. Lucy was quiet beside me, wrapped in her own thoughts but that was often her way. I was sure once she had assimilated the events of the morning she would have her say.

We took a scenic route through the Forest and found ourselves in Brocken Hurst where we discovered a quiet tea room on the High Street. "I think you need a conversation with Sir Edward, William. In your heart you must now believe that Geoffrey Barrington-Hope is your real father and that you have a sister called Claudine. It's about time you learned the truth once and for all."

Of course Lucy was right. The weight of evidence was heavily against Sir Edward being my biological father and the time was right to confront him. Why the pretence? Why go to the trouble of forging a birth certificate to re-enforce a lie? Solutions to so many of the riddles which entwined my life were, it seemed, out of my reach but this one was tantalisingly close if only I could extract the truth from the man I had believed was my father.

Your life is your life and it was very difficult to imagine how it could have been, had chance taken a different turn. My childhood at Liongate was abject, lonely, sad ....and I could have easily conjured up another half a dozen adjectives to describe my misery. So to imagine how different it should have been, had chance smiled kindly, was impossible. The picture I evoked was a blank. There was no happy family snapshot to remind of what I had missed. I guessed that the ache inside me was something only the bereaved or those who had experienced extreme loneliness could fully understand.

It had been a defining day in my life as it was the first time that I truly believed that Major Barrington-Hope was my father and that I had a living, breathing twin sister, my own flesh and blood. I wanted to share my feelings with the woman I loved but somehow the words would not flow. My emotions had left me drained and temporarily at least, mute.

Instead, we sat in silence for a long time, before eventually I returned to a less demanding subject. "What did you make of Arthur Swanson?"

Lucy pursed her lips before answering. "I wasn't sure at first, I wondered if he saw a conspiracy where there was none but by the end… I don't know. He seemed genuine and I suppose I wanted to believe him. Sometimes not knowing is the worst thing. That's just how I feel about Billy. I just want to know even if the truth hurts."

We then shared a plate of unpalatable ham sandwiches and a pot of tea and reminisced about Billy and our life before the war. Slowly, as the afternoon wore on the tension from earlier ebbed away and we began to relax in each other's company. We left the café and wondered onto the grassy area, kept trim by the forest ponies which separated Brockenhurst from the woods to the north of the village. The day was fine but with a keen breeze and we made for the shelter of trees.

"Do you remember the twins, Oscar and Harry?" Lucy asked as we reached the woods.

"How could I forget? Oscar with his polio and the 'chariot' that Billy made for him. What I remember most though was his encyclopedic knowledge of footballers and his hundreds of cigarette cards. He could hardly read and yet he memorised every detail of the players and was so proud of himself. Billy was good to those boys, almost like a surrogate father to them. If anyone ever dared bully or laugh at them, Billy was straight to their defense. That's why I liked your brother so much. He pretended to be a tough guy but really he was such a softy."

Lucy smiled at the memory and wistfully appealed for me not to forget Billy and our commitment to find out what happened to him. "I know you have a lot on your plate but don't forget him will you William? He was my beloved brother and I owe him."

I assured her that I had no intention of giving up on my long lost friend and how I hoped my investigations elsewhere may just shed light on his story. We walked further into the forest and watched the late afternoon sun set from the vantage point of an old wooden footbridge crossing a forest stream. Somehow the tranquil setting and the emotions expended during a previous few days was the catalyst I needed to finally put my arms around Lucy, draw her close to me and kiss her gently on the lips.

Thirty

The car journey home was an altogether happier occasion than the tense drive out. Lucy laid her head on my shoulder as I drove and for the first time in months I felt truly at peace. The frenetic pace of my life over the recent weeks was far from conducive to a tranquil and peaceful existence and I had felt nothing but frustration at my failure to develop my personal relationship with Lucy. But then I was a product of an English public school so perhaps my reticence on the emotional side was not altogether surprising. Certainly, that was Lucy's view and I was in no position to disagree.

It was early evening by the time I pulled the Sunbeam up to the kerb outside the house and I had little time before departing for my next engagement. After the shooting of Samantha Smith our team had been placed on 'amber alert' which meant a more rigorous security regime. Team meetings were now arranged by HQ and our weekly assignments arrived in code. The cypher I had received earlier that day described my instruction for the evening which was to take an eastbound train from Fratton Station before alighting at Emsworth to meet a driver.

I left Lucy reluctantly and arrived at Emsworth Station as the sun disappeared below the horizon, before locating my onward transport, a black Morris Eight parked-up in nearby Bridge Street. For the first time my activities felt they belonged within the pages of a spy novel as I gave and received a coded password before being granted leave to take a seat in the rear of the car.

The night was drawing in as we drove through the village of Westbourne and up into the rolling hills of the South Downs. Within a few minutes the skies had darkened sufficiently for me to lose track completely of where we were and after a further twenty minutes or so my hitherto silent driver pulled the Morris into a layby. Although unquestionably a man of few words he did explain at this point that a five minute stop was part of our new security arrangements to ensure we were not followed.

After the allotted time my driver executed a three point turn in the narrow lane and we retraced our outward journey for about a mile before turning off into a narrower lane still. The dim headlights forged a yellowish path through the black as the car slowly edged up the rutted track. After a short while I saw ahead a sentry post and an armed guard, a surreal sight in the heart of the Hampshire countryside. The driver provided the necessary documentation and we were granted entry.

The Morris pulled-up alongside a motley assortment of other vehicles parked on the hectare of tarmac that surrounded the run down and forlorn stately home which now served as 'a home from home' for the Security Services. It was a ramshackle and sadly neglected country retreat. The inadequate lighting added to a gloomy aspect and once parked I was led inside through a deserted and dingy entrance hall. Julian later told me that it was once the ancestral home to the Earl of Birleston who died with no heir so bequeathed it to the nation on his death in the 1920's. Not quite knowing what to do with it, Birleston Manor was eventually passed to the Security Services thanks in main to its remote location. Not a single farthing, I guessed had been spent on maintenance since.

Julian Singleton's temporary office based on the first floor resembled a bomb site with papers, files and other debris scattered to all corners. It seemed that I was the last to arrive and Julian approached with his usual bonhomie and outstretched hand. I was introduced to the other members of the team, Luke Elliot, broad shouldered, tall with a friendly confident manner and the sharp witted but diminutive Margaret Philimore.

Despite the tragedy of the previous week Julian was in ebullient mood as he launched straight into the business of the evening. "The shooting of Samantha Smith on Friday night has put a proverbial rocket up our backsides' and we have no choice but to push through our plans more quickly than I had anticipated. I was of the mind to let things unfold gradually but the consternation that the shooting has caused in Whitehall means this is no longer an option. They want to see action and so action is what we will give them.

It's clear to us all that the crimes we are investigating would not have been possible without the collusion of the local police, magistrates and possibly even some elements within the judiciary. If we undermine the system which has supported the corruption, the edifice will surely crumble. We start with the local constabulary, Ladies and Gentlemen. We start with Superintendent Nigel Parker and Inspector Jack Hanaho. Luke, tell us what you have discovered about the two men. Keep it short and to the point."

"Superintendent Parker is 64 years old and only months from retirement. In all but name he has already passed the reins to his more dynamic second in command Jack Hanaho. He's a lame duck spending his days practicing his putting skills on his office carpet and drinking rather too much whisky. I can't see Parker as a threat but he is certainly guilty, of at the very least, gross negligence and incompetence. He must be aware what is happening on his watch but chooses to ignore it. Parker is weak and ineffectual. Is he corrupt? I'm not sure.

Inspector Hanaho, 44 years old, runs the show and is a very different character; highly intelligent, brash, tough and uncompromising. We've had him under surveillance for weeks and his fingers are everywhere. He is corrupt but so far untouchable. He uses a combination of bribery and bullying to quell unrest. Jack Hanaho is a powerful enemy with influential friends. He is the lynchpin and we need him out of the way and out of the way, fast."

"So, how do we do that Luke?" Julian pushed.

"We have already collected plenty of evidence from our surveillance but we need to turn it into something which will stick. Photographs, witnesses…make a strong case. Get the press involved perhaps." Luke replied.

"A good plan but I want Hanaho out by the end of the month." With that Julian crossed the room and consulted a wall calendar. "I want a copy of his resignation letter in my hand by …when shall we say, the 27th April? That's one week this coming Friday."

"With all due respect Sir, I don't see Inspector Hanaho as the resigning type." Luke countered.

"Tell us about Chen Yung." Julian then asked ignoring, for the moment, Luke's assessment.

"Ah, yes Sir, we've been keeping an eye on the Golden Dragon on the London Road in Northend for a while now and they have a small but busy counterfeiting operation behind the shop. Hanaho has been aware of it for months and yet has made no move to shut it down."

"Now, why's Hanaho done nothing about it do you think?" Julian asked, doing his school teacher impression and pointing at me.

"I guess you are going to tell us he's being paid off?" I offered, hoping for a gold star.

"Ten out of ten, William. What more do we know about Chen Yung and the Golden Dragon?" Julian asked again, this time turning to Margaret.

"They have a small letterpress behind the shop but their most valuable asset is a Chinaman known only as Li, with a talent for creative design. Generally, he uses a legitimate document, usually a birth certificate or passport and re-creates it to order with a new identity. But recently they have become more adventurous and print certificates which Li personalises by hand. A very profitable little business when you consider they charge up to £25 for a birth or marriage certificate which he knocks out in an hour."

"That's all very interesting but let's put that to one side for a minute. I will be using this intelligence when I ask for Hanaho's resignation but now let's turn to a little scheme that I have in mind. I think William that you will rather enjoy what I have in store for your friend the Inspector. Your job is to bring the press; your chap from the Portsmouth Evening News, and you Luke have the simple task of ensuring that our duplicitous Inspector receives this note by 10.00am on the morning of the 27th April. Just as a failsafe to ensure he is fully committed. By lunchtime I conjecture that Jack Hanaho will have tendered his resignation."

Luke shook his head. "I'm sorry Sir but I know the man and just can't see him going quietly!"

"I feel a little wager coming on." With that Julian extracted a ten shilling note from his wallet. "Ten bob says that he has resigned by midday on Friday 27th April."

"You're on, Sir!" Luke agreed with a confident air as Julian turned to me and raised an enquiring eyebrow.

"I think I'll sit on the fence if you don't mind, Julian. So what devious plot have you hatched up?" I asked trying to imagine what on earth could be done to so quickly induce Hanaho to resign. It seemed unlikely but then Julian was a man you underestimated at your cost as Luke, I suspected, was about to find out.

"At 9am sharp on the morning of Friday week I would like you William, Margaret and our friends from the press to meet me at the Camber Dock. Look for a fishing vessel by the name of The Fair Isabella and you will find me aboard. Thank you ladies and Gentleman for your time. We need to go over your assignments for the coming week but I'd rather do that in the Crooked Billet around the corner, a hostelry with an extremely obliging landlord who will provide us with the snug all to ourselves!"

Within fifteen minutes we were ensconced in the altogether more cheerful surroundings of the Crooked Billet. The rotund and smiling publican locked the door behind us and left a pitcher full of ale on the table which to my surprise, even Margaret helped us drink.

"I didn't put you down as a beer drinker Margaret!" I said. "Cheers!"

"I have worked with Julian for three years and it did not take me long to work out that if you can't beat him, you may as well join him." Explained Margaret.

"It's an outrageous slur on my character Miss Philimore." replied Julian. "I am as sober as a judge and an upstanding member of the community."

"So you won't want that pint of Courage Best then?" Luke asked.

"Well just one perhaps and give me a ciggy I'm in need of a nicotine fix." Julian gestured.

With that Luke, pulled a packet of Gold Leaf from his pocket and offered them around. Margaret pulled a face before scolding the smokers for their bad habits. "You oughtn't to be smoking at your age Luke and you shouldn't encourage him Julian. It's a bad habit, and it's addictive."

"Addictive, eh? Well I've never heard that one before Margaret." Julian replied looking unconcerned.

"The nicotine gets into your bloodstream and your body craves more and then you can't stop." Margaret continued with authority.

"You don't want to believe that old rubbish, Margaret." Julian laughed.

The banter gave way to more serious business and the next hour was devoted to trying to piece together all we had so far learnt. In my view it all seemed so dispirit and I found it difficult to see where we were going but Julian was his usual upbeat self. "I think we are making good progress and once we get shot of the Inspector things will start to fall into place." He went on to furnish us all with a dossier put together by Ernest Bannister with our assignments for the following week.

Looking in my direction, he continued. "Ernest has discovered the current whereabouts of Peter Taylor and Andrew Cross, the body of the latter, unfortunately, resides in a cemetery in northern France but Peter Taylor is alive and well and living in Camberwell with wife and three children. He now works as a depot manager for a haulage company just off the Whitechapel Road. I have a feeling that Peter Taylor will prove our most compelling witness so far. He will have experienced Stanley Jakes doing what Stanley Jakes did best; intimidate and extort.

Now William, this interview must be conducted with care. We want to understand how the fraud was perpetrated, the role that Stanley Jakes played (if any) and all other people who had any involvement. Taylor will have to turn Kings Evidence so he can divulge all without fear of prosecution. I hear you are off next weekend to France William, so I would like you to get straight on to this on Monday and report back before you leave."

The beer flowed freely and after a time the conversation degenerated into general chit-chat which gave me the chance to get to know my new colleagues on a more personal level. Although from the outside we must have looked something of a strange mix I felt comfortable with my new team. It was nearly midnight before we staggered out of the Crooked Billet and after 1am when my long suffering driver finally dropped me home.

Thirty One

Despite the late night and the beer I woke fresh and early the following morning looking forward to what I hoped would be a crucial week in the investigation. I had booked a room at the Russell Hotel overlooking leafy Russell Square for four nights as I would be spending a good deal of the week at Crawford's City office and I would be looking to catch-up with Peter Taylor in Camberwell. On my insistence Lucy had agreed to spend the week with her mother in Worthing.

First stop was Crawford's HQ where I would be stirring things up a little with Benison and Buridge. I was on the Circle Line heading east toward Liverpool Street, reading of the death of Ernest Bevin in the Daily Telegraph when I glanced up and to my surprise, saw that the man sitting directly opposite me was none other than Sebastian Harris. I folded my paper away and attracted his attention. It took him but a second to recognise me, smile (that urbane smile) and register his surprise. "William Goldhawk, well, well! What brings you up to the Capital?"

"Just a tedious audit I am afraid. Nothing to get the blood racing! How about you? I dare say you spend a lot of your time in London?" I ventured a little awkwardly.

But as was his way he soon had us chatting as relaxed as could be. Mostly we talked about the of the news of the day, the death of indefatigable Bevin, the up-coming Festival of Britain and even the prospects of the FA Cup final between Newcastle United and Blackpool. I didn't see Harris as a football man but he seemed genuinely excited at the idea of the 'magpies' coming to Wembley and recalled his childhood visits to St James's Park. I hardly registered that the Oxbridge educated Harris was then, a Geordie by birth.

After a long delay at Tower Hill we both left the train at Liverpool Street and Harris suggested a coffee before we went our separate ways. We found a suitable establishment on Bishopsgate and ordered coffee.

"As a Chartered Accountant you must have heard about the investigations into corruption in Portsmouth? I attended a lecture by two investigators from the Revenue, Singleton and Philimore. It was interesting I thought. What do you make of it all?" Harris asked once we were seated.

Sebastian Harris came from the same mold as Brian Surtees and it was difficult not to talk freely to a man with such an easy going charm. But although I trusted him I felt obliged to keep my own council and hedged my reply. "We've had them at the office and Singleton seems a decent sort of chap. I gather he's investigating pre-war fraud on a pretty massive scale. Millions of pounds I believe. What do you make of it Mr. Harris?"

"In my book the twelve years since these supposed crimes were committed will surely have washed the evidence clean away. After all there was a war in between and the chaos that left behind will hardly help their investigations. No, I wish them luck but I am of the opinion that they would be better-off packing their bags and heading back to London. But then I am a cynical lawyer who has been around the block a few times!" He finished with a rueful smile.

The last time I had met Harris was at his Emsworth office when he had recounted how he had found the body of Billy Cosgrove. The shock had been such that I had felt unable to probe the solicitor about his relationship with my mother but perhaps now was an opportunity. So I reminded him of that long ago conversation when he had revealed that he had met my mother in Paris.

Sebastian Harris was incapable of looking flustered but I got the distinct impression that he was, at the very least, uncomfortable with my question. He peered at me over his gold rimmed spectacles and leaned forward in his chair before replying:

"William, sometimes things happen in life which are less than ideal but you are forced to make the best of a bad job. Now, I am indeed aware of much of what happened to you when you were a young child and the circumstances which have, in a very circuitous way, led you to ask me the questions that you have today. I suppose that my hope (and I am sure that of your father) was that this day would never come. But you are an intelligent and inquisitive boy so perhaps it was inevitable."

"What…." I started but Harris held out a hand to indicate he had more to say.

"Your father has done what he thought was right to protect you. The more you scuttle about uncovering things from your past William, the more trouble you will heap upon yourself, I promise you that. I fully understand your curiosity (it's only human nature) but please for your own sake don't delve too deeply. Things are not always as they seem."

For the second time in two meetings, Harris had left me floundering and unable to articulate the many questions that I was desperate to ask. But clearly I was to get no more that day. "Until we meet again William. I hope that the audit is a success." And with that he stood, shook my hand and walked from the café.

With plenty else on my plate I shook my head in disbelief and parked the new information I had received in the far corner of my brain for later processing. If I dwelt too much on Harris's revelations I knew that I could not concentrate fully on the job in hand. I finished my coffee and made the short walk to Spital Square and up the stairs to the accounts department on the first floor.

I found a spare desk and could not help but notice that Matthew Buridge was keeping his head down and avoiding eye contact. Amused, I felt inclined to play a little game with the nervous

Buridge, just to crank up the tension somewhat, so I nonchalantly wandered in his direction. "Ah, Matthew I've been looking for you. There are a few problems that we need to discuss."

He looked up, alarmed. "What about? Surely it's Benison you want to talk to?"

"Why should I want to talk to Mr. Benison?" I enquired.

"Well, he's the chief accountant isn't 'e?" He fidgeted uncomfortably in his chair.

"This is in relation to archived materials Matthew which I believe is your jurisdiction, is it not?"

"Well yes I suppose. What is it you want to know?"

"I am up to my neck at the moment Matthew, shall we pencil in a meeting this afternoon for 2pm?"

"Er, well what's it all about exactly? Shouldn't we get Mr. Benison in on the meeting too?" He asked, his discomfort now displayed in a sweaty brow.

"Oh, I don't think that will be necessary." I replied smiling. As I made to leave, I theatrically turned back toward him one time more. "One thing Matthew I will want to look at is the Admiralty Contract of 1939 and could you bring the Lancier file with you please? We'll meet in the auditors' office at 2pm."

I could only imagine the anguished look on his face as I walked across the office.

I had apologies to give to Sir Marcus as the events of the previous weekend had forced cancellation of my planned visit to the Isle of Wight. All things considered, a blessing as the total lack of contact from Helen was evidence enough that she too felt our relationship had well and truly run its course. In our hearts I think we both understood that an Isle of Wight rendezvous would just have been embarrassing for us both.

I anticipated an awkward confrontation as I walked up the stairs to the Directors' suite, so steeled myself as I knocked on the Chairman's door. "Ah, William lad, how good to see you. Awful business at the weekend! A tragedy and no mistake. She was nought but a young gal. Have they caught anyone?"

"Not that I am aware. It seems that it may have been just a random act of violence and the poor girl was just in the wrong place at the wrong time. All very sad and such a waste." Julian and I had agreed a strategy to keep a lid on the real reason for the shooting.

"How's the audit proceeding, William? I trust my staff is giving you what you need?"

"All going well Sir Marcus but I have a couple of questions which I would like to ask about your tendering procedures and who took responsibility for submitting bids. I am particularly interested in the large contracts you won just before and during the War."

"We're in 1951 lad, why are you interested in contracts awarded so long ago? I hope this has nought to do with these fraud allegations that I've heard about recently? We are an honest business lad and the last thing we need is for our customers to think we are under investigation." Sir Marcus answered gruffly, just about keeping his notoriously short temper in check.

"I am going to be blunt Sir Marcus. These investigations will take place here and at every major firm in the sector whether or not you give us your co-operation. We are legally bound to look into the award of a number of Admiralty contracts, two of which were awarded to Crawford Electrics. I am totally confident that the firm has acted in good faith so you will have nothing to worry about but investigate we must."

“Ah, that’s all very well but it’s all such a waste of our valuable time! So what do you need from me William?”

“Who was responsible for the 1939 contract negotiations?”

“It was our Finance Director Eric Rowe who has long since retired and died a couple of years back. Much of the work was done by Benison and his team but it was Rowe’s signature that appeared on the bottom of the contract.”

“What was Benison’s role?”

“It was ‘is job to put the tenders together at a price where we were likely enough to win ‘em and make a fair profit into the bargain. He was champion at that kind of thing and we won some very lucrative business on the back of his work. That’s why he’s paid well above the going rate for a Chief Accountant.”

“Lancier?”

“What’s that lad? What’s Lancier?” Was it genuine bafflement I saw on his face? I wasn’t sure.

“Did you use consultants to help you with the tenders?”

“I believe so, but I left that to Eric and John. That was their domain.”

“Thanks Sir Marcus, that’s been very useful.”

Sir Marcus Crawford was a consummate and experienced professional, hardly likely to panic under my questioning and I found him difficult to read. As I turned to go though, perhaps his last contribution to our conversation was the most compelling. “By the way William, I am not sure if you were aware that we moved into Spital Square in ’43 after our office in Cannon Street was damaged in a bombing raid. We lost a good deal of our records. I…er, just thought I should mention it."

***

I was hardly surprised when 2 O'clock came around to see Chief Accountant John Benison stride into the room with a worried looking Matthew Buridge on his coattails. Benison gave me an out of character ingratiating smile. "Mr. Goldhawk, I trust you had a pleasant weekend? Matthew tells me you have a few questions?"

"Yes, gentlemen please have a seat. Matthew have you got the Lancier file please?" I asked holding out my hand in anticipation.

"Landseer, Sir? Who's Landseer?" Asked the obsequious Benison, giving more than a passable impression of Uriah Heap.

Landseer then, not Lancier! Ah-ah progress, I thought!

"Of course you know to what I refer Mr. Benison, please do not take me for a fool. I want everything you have on the 1939 Admiralty Contract on my desk by first thing tomorrow. That's all gentlemen."

"Now look here Mr. Goldhawk I am not sure I like your tone. And neither, am I sure you have the authority to tell me what to do! I'm Chief Accountant here and you are our guest; an unwelcome one at that!" Benison blustered with Buridge trying hard to hide an insolent smile of satisfaction.

I looked-up from my chair behind the desk. "Hiding or withholding evidence in a criminal investigation is a very serious matter. I am part of a team investigating a number of extremely serious cases of fraud. If you wish to proceed on your current path I think it is more than likely that you will face criminal charges. On the other hand if you tell me the truth....well, put it like this, your chances of salvation will be improved. So, gentleman, I strongly recommend you make a clean breast of things before you get yourselves into further trouble. Do you understand me?"

I could see the indecision in Benison's face. He really had no idea whether or not I was bluffing so I put him out of his misery. "You may wish to return any documentation you have on Landseer to the box from which you removed it last week. I'm leaving early tonight but will expect to see you in the morning, gentlemen." With that I looked down and continued to scrutinise my papers but not before I glimpsed the shocked surprise on the faces of the two accountants. I had little doubt that they would be back in the morning.

***

My plan for that evening was to intercept Peter Taylor on his way home from work and steer him toward a local hostelry for refreshments. A beer, I found generally worked as a lubricant for the vocal chords and usually gave me a sound investment for my shilling. As it turned out Peter Taylor was a hard nut to crack. He was easy enough to track down at the transport depot where he worked, tucked just off the Whitechapel Road on the Mile End border but convincing him to accompany me for an early evening beer was more of a challenge. I fell into step beside him as he left the yard at 5.30, a thin wiry man in his late-thirties, curly brown hair and a jaunty step. "Peter Taylor?" I asked.

"That's me, Gov'nor what can I do yer for?"

"How about joining me for a beer? On me." I asked in a friendly tone.

"That sounds like an offer that's hard to refuse but I knows there's gunna be a catch, right Guv'?"

"I'm after information about your time in Portsmouth."

"Must have the wrong man, Guv'. Never set foot in Portsmouth."

“Look Peter, I know exactly who you are and when you worked in Portsmouth. You were there for six months in ’39. I just want to find out what went on.”

“Common enough name. Now I’m jumping on this bus!” He grabbed the hand rail as the bus sped up and jumped aboard leaving me stranded on the pavement. As I walked back to Aldgate Station I decided to leave Peter Taylor until another day. Maybe by the middle of the week he’d be in a more reception frame of mind having received a subpoena from the Courts.

I called Lucy from a phone box and we talked until my change ran out. My mind strayed forward to the end of the week and our trip across the channel. Apprehensive about what I may find but delirious at the prospect of an uninterrupted four days in Lucy’s company.

Thirty Two

It was no surprise to find a dusty box by my desk when I walked into the auditors' office the following morning. After a quick rummage I was satisfied that the two accountants had come to their senses and restored the documents they had earlier removed. Rather than spend unnecessary time in a detailed examination of the contents, first I wanted to hear it straight from the horse's mouth and I did not have to wait long. Within a few minutes John Benison and his shadow Matthew Buridge stood at the doorway.

As anticipated the bellicose manner of the previous day had more or less evaporated and the two men were contrite and worried as they took their seats opposite my desk.

"Let's return to 1939 shall we?" I asked. "The Admiralty Contract: explain to me the whole process from receipt of the documents from the Admiralty to being awarded the contract in November."

Rather than launch straight in, Benison wanted assurances. "Look Mr. Goldhawk, we were acting under instruction and if I tell you everything I'd like to feel you'll feed us some slack. Our jobs could be at stake if we are, well you know .... misrepresented."

"I'm not sure you are in a position to negotiate terms with me Mr. Benison. Whose instructions were you working under?"

"The Finance Director, Eric Rowe. He signed the Contract."

"...who's rather conveniently now dead? I have no axe to grind with you two but I want the truth, the whole truth."

Benison pulled a face which I took as grudging acceptance of my terms. "The tender arrived sometime in the summer of '39 and it was a monster, well over 200 pages and very involved. They wanted to know everything; labour rates, the countries where we sourced our materials, square footage of factory space, an inventory of machinery, quality and calibration procedures, relationship with Trade Unions, how we would continue to manufacture if our plant was destroyed by an act of God or by a German bomb. And so it went on and on and on.

To be honest we were pretty gloomy at the prospect of the work involved. It was early summer, I had just got engaged and this tender meant the prospect of six months of twelve hour days and the sort of pressure we could have done well without. But it had to be done and the silver lining was a big fat bonus if we won the contract.

Anyway a few days after we had started working on it, Mr. Rowe asked to see me in his office. He was quite ill by this time and his mental faculties were declining. Sir Marcus knew he was a lame duck but out of loyalty I suppose, he kept him on. He bumbled on about this chap who had come to see him and promised to deliver the contract for a commission. The long and short of it was that I agreed to meet the man. He was from a firm of specialist consultants with their UK base in the City called Landseer. The parent company was from Chicago and I was to meet an American by the name of John McDermott.

Our office was in Cannon Street at that time and the suave McDermott arrived with his impeccable credentials, testimonials from around the world and a scheme that sounded just too good to be true. He proposed to take on the entire management of the tendering process for a commission, only payable if the tender was won.

A good deal but it got even better. The commission was structured so that nothing at all was payable unless the contract delivered 'excess' profit. The proposition was that once the bid was agreed by us, Landseer would submit the contract at a higher price and we were to pay 80% of any excess profit as commission. He was very convincing and it seemed we could hardly lose. We were paying for their expertise and specialist knowledge; they had 100's of researchers based in New York and Chicago whose job was to analyse the market and had detailed knowledge of the competition which allowed them to assess exactly where to pitch the prices. Apparently, this type of market analysis was normal practice in the States.

Nothing was payable up-front and the terms of the contract had been passed by our legal boys so I was happy to sanction the arrangement and forwarded the contract to Mr. Rowe to sign. Landseer delivered as promised and …well the rest is history."

I scrutinised Benison's face as he hastily averted his gaze and looked in vain at the moody Buridge for support. "That's not quite true is it Mr. Benison? If it were, you would have had no reason to hide the evidence. Let's hear it as it actually happened, shall we?" As I spoke I picked-out the contract from the box beside my desk with Eric Rowe's signature alongside that of a representative of Landseer.

Benison was not a convincing liar and I suspected he was not a serious conspirator; my gut feeling was that the pair of them were no more than sprats in an ocean full of sharks. As I looked down at the contract in my hand I had intuition that something was not quite right. Perhaps I would not have worked it out at all had I not seen the anxiety on the face of Benison and the hostility in the eyes of his colleague.

I then stood and examined the signature of Eric Rowe more closely under the bright light of my desk lamp. Gently moving my finger across the lettering I could feel and see the telltale indentation made by a tracing. Although, no expert on the subject I held a shrewd suspicion that the signature was forged.

"Now Mr. Benison, Mr. Buridge, let's have the whole truth. I'm no Sherlock Holmes but even I can tell this signature is a forgery." I bluffed, hoping I sounded more confident than I felt.

I obviously did, as Buridge caved-in. "For god's sake John, tell him the truth. He'll work it out in the end anyway."

Benison puffed out his cheeks. "Alright, alright you win; it was not quite as simple as that. I went to Rowe but he refused to sign the contract and told me to take it to the Chairman for a signature. But Sir Marcus too refused to sign it on the grounds that it was the responsibility of the finance department. For us it was all a bit of a nightmare as we had glimpsed the forbidden fruit and then had it plucked from our grasp. You see Landseer proposed to take the tender and prepare it themselves which would leave Matthew and me with a very easy summer.

When we gave the news to John McDermott that our Directors were not prepared to sign, he would have none of it and just told us to, get our 'butts in there and get it signed!' And he offered us £100 a piece to deliver the signed contract to his hotel room by Friday evening. We heard Rowe was retiring before the tender was due to be submitted so we took the chance and forged his signature."

"Let me get this right." I interrupted, putting aside the admittance of the forged signature. "The Contract between Crawfords and Landseer passed the responsibility of the management and submission of the tender from you to Landseer. You were to agree a base price above which Landseer was to earn a commission of 80%?"

"That's about it, yes. Effectively, they did all the work and in real terms it cost us nothing! We only paid them out of excess profit so I thought it was a good deal for the Company."

"Oh, I see, it was philanthropy on your part was it?" I asked letting my exasperation show. "Let me enquire, how much did you honestly expect Landseer to earn from their work? £5,000 or £10,000 maybe…? Not let me hazard a guess £1.4 million? Did it not occur to you that something was not right? That their profit was somewhat excessive! For god's sake you are accountants, you must have known!"

Benison looked into his hands, mumbled an indecipherable grunt and shrugged his shoulders. His hitherto silent partner Matthew Buridge then made a rare contribution to the debate. "Yes, alright we were suspicious but didn't really know the market or our competitors so had no grounds to justify an official investigation. After all what could we say? There was a signed contract and Landseer fulfilled the terms and by the time we got an inkling of what was going on it was done and dusted. We had very little choice but to accept it."

"So tell me, once you had been notified by the admiralty that you had been successful how did you pay Landseer? Did they issue a single invoice for the total amount which I suppose was what, 80% of £1.7 million?"

"Yes, a single invoice which was paid in four instalments over twelve months as per the terms of the contract. You'll find their invoice in the box along with a copy of the completed tender." As he spoke Benison dug out the invoice from the box and passed it to me: £1.36 million pounds for consultancy services.

"Wow, so you just wrote four cheques for over £300,000 each to a company that you knew virtually nothing about for consultancy services." As a Chartered Accountant I was genuinely shocked at their flagrant disregard for procedures to safeguard the Company's money. "What was Sir Marcus's reaction to be presented with an invoice of this size?"

Buridge looked at his senior colleague for an answer but Benison just shrugged his shoulders again before eventually admitting that he had used the illness of Eric Rowe to hide the truth. "Sir Marcus was unhappy at paying out such a huge commission but believed it was a *bona fide* contract signed by a Director of the Company so he felt bound to honour it."

Although I had little sympathy for Benison and even less for his surly partner Buridge I could not help believing that neither was guilty of more than crass stupidity. Whether the Courts would take such a lenient view was not at all clear however, as the forgery was technically a criminal offence and a serious one at that. The real criminals though, I felt sure were elsewhere, perhaps on the other side of the Atlantic Ocean. I doubted that John McDermott or Landseer Consultants would be quite such easy targets as Benison or Buridge. In fact I had severe doubts as to whether we'd find them at all.

"John McDermott, the American; tell me about him." I demanded impatiently.

"I met him three or four times, he was bearded and dressed quite conventionally. If you ignored the whiskers he was more of a City gent than an American. Grey suits, glasses and was perhaps average height. I suppose he was forty years old or thereabouts. I'm not good with accents but he said he was a native of Chicago. To be honest he was a charming man." Benison then looked at his colleague and asked, "Didn't you meet him at his office once Matthew?"

"Yeah, I dropped some papers off there." Buridge offered begrudgingly.

I was feeling particularly irritated with Matthew Buridge whose earlier contrition had given way to a moody unhelpfulness. Thinking I had been too soft, I tried to pull him back into line. "How do you think you are placed currently Matthew? We are investigating one of the largest frauds committed on this Island and you are implicated up to your neck. How about trying to help yourself by treating my questions seriously? Where did you meet McDermott?"

It seemed to do the trick and pulled him, at least temporarily from his lethargy. "Banner Street near Old Street tube station, I can't remember the number but it was on his business card which is clipped to the invoice. It was just a temporary office whilst they were in London, nothing grand." Buridge then dug out a folder and placed it on the desk. "Have a look at their corporate brochure. It shows their offices in Chicago and gives a load of statistics about the business and what they did. All very impressive."

I looked at the brochure and guessed it was probably a work of fiction, produced for the sole purpose of pulling the wool over the eyes of the likes of the two gullible accountants sitting opposite me. "Did you check the facts on this brochure? Perhaps contact your counterparts in the Mid-West of America to ascertain the credentials of Landseer Consultants. Verify the number of researchers they employed and ascertain if this skyscraper pictured actually belonged to them?"

A look at their faces told me all I needed to know. It had been a painful interview which had left me feeling frustrated and angry. Once again progress could be measured in inches and every inch we moved forward we uncovered yet more questions. Rather than finding the expected link between Crawford Electrics and Stanley Jakes I find a connection with another party altogether, based four thousand miles away! I could see no sign of the murky waters clearing.

Thirty Three

I spent the next three days going through the box by my desk which contained the records relating to the contract and made endless enquiries about Landseer Consultants and John McDermott, both in London and across the Atlantic in New York and Chicago. It came as no surprise that I drew a complete blank. The only Landseer I found was a property developer in Bedford. The global Landseer brand as portrayed in the promotional brochure with hundreds of researchers and a fifty story office in downtown Manhattan simply did not exist and it never had.

I made enquiries with the New York Stock Exchange, the FBI and numerous other agencies but on every occasion I hit the same brick wall. And the American embassy confirmed the only two non-military US Citizens with the name of John McDermott who had officially travelled to Britain in 1939 were John G McDermott, aged 14 and John-Wesley McDermott aged 61 who holidayed for two weeks in August.

The only clue that I was left with was 44 Banner Street the temporary office let to Landseer Consultants by the Property Management Company Carstairs which still traded in Holborn. Slim pickings but a lead I needed to follow-up nonetheless. It had not been a good week and I had a foreboding that things may not improve with my second attempted interview with Peter Taylor.

With the weekend fast approaching and Julian's deadline with it I could not afford a further set-back. I would try the same routine as on my last visit and catch the reluctant Peter Taylor as he left the depot but this time I would not take 'no' for an answer. It was just after 6pm when he strode out of the main entrance and along the Whitechapel Road, cigarette hanging from the corner of his mouth and a copy of the Evening Standard folded under his left arm.

When he caught sight of me on the corner of New Road he quickened his pace and shook his head to register his irritation. My rehearsed speech lacked coherence as I puffed to keep pace. "Peter, listen... please ....it's pointless ignoring me." I panted. "You'll only get subpoenaed if you do and that will be worse for you in the long run."

He suddenly stopped dead and I thought he was about to swing a punch at me. "Look 'ere mate, I told yer last time, I don't want to talk, alright? Not now not never. Just fuck-off, will yer?" He growled swatting me with his rolled up newspaper.

"Woah." I gestured for him to calm down. "Look, just hear me out. A couple of minutes that's all I ask."

"Two minutes and that's yer lot." Taylor stuck his chin out and his eyes bulged as though he was about to explode. There was no doubt his nerves were frayed.

"Look Peter, I can talk to you off the record now and if we need you to go to Court you may have the option to turn the King's Evidence which means you will be immune from prosecution. Now, if you ignore me and walk away we will return with a subpoena forcing you to attend Court. If you choose that route the chances are that you will be prosecuted."

"Yes I know what a fuckin' subpoena is! Come on then let's find a boozer. End of the day I can't see I've a lotta fuckin' choice!"

We walked a further 100 yards or so up the road until we came to the Kings Arms, a large uninviting looking establishment on the busy junction with Vallance Road. I followed Taylor in through the revolving doors to the saloon which was quiet except for a huddle of hardened drinkers standing at the bar postulating loudly on the world's affairs particularly in relation to the fortunes of West Ham United. I hazarded that the Kings Arms attracted the serious drinker and doubted if the Landlord stocked much in the way beverages of the non-alcoholic variety.

In keeping with traditions of the pub I bought of couple of pints of bitter and steered Taylor across the sawdust covered floor boards to a quiet corner. I attempted to put him at ease by explaining that he was, as far as I was concerned, no more than an innocent victim and that I would do all I could to keep him out of trouble. After lighting another cigarette and gulping back a couple of swigs of his beer he visibly relaxed and I began to hope for a favourable outcome to my evening after all.

"I was a very different bloke before the war. My Dad and older bruvver were dockers but me mum, god rest her soul, knew that weren't for me. I was always a bit weedy- well look at me I still am- but quite smart. Did well at school like and came out with me school certificate. Me ole' mum had scrimped and saved and bought me something of an education, not a posh school but she paid this old boy, Mr. Dalrymple to teach me at 'ome in the evenin's. And when I left school I went to work as a Civil Servant and ended-up at the Admiralty. I was always good with numbers so they put me in the administration and finance department which looked after procurement and contracts.

To be honest it was fuckin' borin' but pretty undemandin' and I earned fair money. I worked out of an office in Southwark Street and one day I noticed they was looking for recruits in Portsmouth…wherever the fuck that was. I just wanted a change so I applied and bugger me if I didn't get the posting. There were two of us, myself and a lad named Andrew Cross. Chalk and cheese we was! He was prim and proper from Hampstead and he spoke posh but liked to pretend he was one of the lads, into beer, girls and especially football in a big way.

We arrived at Portsmouth 'arbour Station one Monday afternoon. We may as well 'ave bin on Mars! I'd hardly bin out of Walthamstow in 24 years and can you believe that I'd never set eyes on the briny sea? Crossy had been to the Isle of Wight once, so I considered him something of an 'ardened international traveller. Anyway, at first I fuckin' loved it! No-one lookin' over me shoulder, the pubs were fuckin' brilliant and we 'ad the seaside on our doorstep!

And Crossy was hilarious! He was just like a little kid in a sweet shop and what's more the boy had plenty of cash, much of which he chucked in my direction. Poor old Crossy never made it made back from Dunkirk. Anyway, one evening we found ourselves in a crowded boozer called the Pembroke Arms, half way between the dockyard and our digs in Kent Road. Crossy supported The Arsenal and was getting a bit rowdy, singing songs and the like. Before long a couple of local Matelots started jessing him. No more than a bit of friendly banter about Pompey beating the Arsenal but old Crossy took it a bit too seriously and just wouldn't leave it alone!

After a while with the beer flowing freely, out of nothing fists started flying and the whole place erupted. A full scale brawl ensued and old Crossy got a good battering. Before things got too out of 'and these two blokes who'd bin standin' at the bar waded in and sorted things out. Well-dressed gents, tall and not the sort you'd wanner argue with, if you get me drift? Stanley Jakes and Norman Buchanan introduced themselves and brought us both a beer.

Well, we was a wee bit wet behind the ears and thought nothing of it, just two blokes being chummy. It didn't occur to us that the likes of Jakes and Buchanan would never mix with blokes like us without a fuckin' good reason which eventually, to our cost we found out! For twelve long fuckin' years I've worried about the consequences of what we done back in '39. This King's Evidence business; is it true like that I could get immunity from prosecution? I've always somehow thought I'd end up in the nick for what we did." Taylor stared into the half empty beer glass in his hand and sighed. "I'm glad me old mum's gone and won't have to witness me shame."

I wanted Peter Taylor as an ally and at the same time sympathized with his plight so did what I could to console him. “These boys were professionals and you and Andrew Cross were just young lads. I think you are being too hard on yourself. Tell me what happened next?”

“We were sucked in good and proper, that’s what ‘appened next! When the boozer closed Jakes invited us to his Club, Uncle Sam’s Bar just off the Hard. It was a seedy old place with a jazz band playing American rag-time but it was packed to the rafters with sailors and women of dubious morals, if you know what I mean. Jakes kept plying us with booze and acting like we were his best mates. Why the fuckin’ ‘ell I didn’t twig I’ll never know but there you are.

Next thing I know these two dolly birds come sidling up to us and before you know it we’re up on the dance floor. The girl dancing with me was a looker, make no mistake and she was all over me. I thought all me Christmas’s ‘ad come at once to be honest and looking at the expression on the face of Crossy he weren’t no different.

After a while, this bit of crumpet took hold of me and dragged me off the dance floor through to what I took to be Jakes’ flat, behind the Club. It was a plush set-up and before you know it I’m on a double bed with me trousers round me ankles. I’d like to say I enjoyed meself but to be honest I was that drunk I couldn’t tell yer! Within a few minutes the evening came to an abrupt halt. One minute I have this dolly in me arms and next, Crossy and me are on the street staggerin’ back to Kent Road.

A week later this well-spoken gent knocks on me door and hands me an envelope. I didn’t recognize the bloke but he said he had een sent by Mr. Jakes. I wondered if p’raps I’d left something at his flat which he was returning. I wished! Instead, inside the envelope was two photographs of me and this dolly, stark bollock naked! I got the shock of me life and wondered what me mum and me girlfriend back in Walthamstow would make of ‘em. Crossy got the same treatment and we spent the next week sweating, waiting for somethin’ to ‘appen.

Didn’t take a genius to know that we was going to be blackmailed and sure enough Jakes eventually arrived wearing a smirk as wide as the fuckin’ Thames Estuary. To cut a long story short he wanted us to rig the tender. Otherwise…well you can guess! We told him it wasn’t that easy and our work would be checked by our supervisors but he’d ‘ave none of it. ‘Do it boys and these photographs will be history but if you fail… well, need I say more?’ I tried to brazen it out by pretending not to be worried about the photos but Jakes just laughed. He knew exactly how we really felt.”

“So he wanted you to rig the tender in Crawford’s favour, then?”

“No, no…Jakes was backin’ another ’orse! There was four companies involved, three from England and one from America. The American bid was by far the cheapest but the Admiralty weren’t keen and wrote the terms of the tender in such a way that scuppered the Yanks bid before it got off the ground. So that left Crawfords, ELC Components based out of Birmin’ham and MARCOS what ‘ad factories all over England and Ireland.

It was MARCOS who Jakes was backin’ which was a double problem for us because they was the dearest. Well, with no obvious alternative, Crossy and me decides just to do our jobs and see what turned up but to be ‘onest it was hell! Jakes or Buchanan was on our case every other bleedin’ day and the only respite we got was when we visited factories with old ‘Smiler Jones’ our boss. The only thing going for us was ‘Smiler’ was a timid bugger and me and Crossy could always get one over him. When we went visiting factories, ‘reality’ and our report bore very little resemblance. Old ‘Smiler’ would point out the discrepancies but we’d growl and he’d soon back down. After round one, thanks to our creative reporting, MARCOS was definitely in the driving seat."

I was left scratching my head. "MARCOS? But Crawfords won the tender, I am confused Peter. I thought you fiddled the figures in favour of Crawfords not MARCOS?"

"That, my friend is because you've only 'eard 'alf the story!" Taylor answered dramatically as he downed his second pint. Lighting another cigarette straight from the butt of his last he wagged his finger. "This is where it gets interestin'!"

To heighten the dramatic effect Peter Taylor smoked his cigarette, supped from his third pint and stared at some unidentifiable spot on the far wall for a good two minutes before resuming his story. "The summer passed and we was close to wrapping things up. We was worried because at the end of the day the price was the crucial element in deciding which company would be awarded the contract and we knew we'd 'ave to fiddle it somehow, unless we wanted an un'ealthy dose of Jakes and Buchanan.

Crossy was all for goin' to the police but I didn't fancy that would solve our problems, just the opposite in fact so I talked him out of it. And as it 'appened, that was a good decision from yours truly because our 'guardian angel' visited me that very next evenin'. I was walking back from the dockyard past the Garrison Church when I sees this well-dressed geezer sitting on a park bench by the railings. It's getting pretty dark by this time and there's a nip in the air so I was a bit surprised but not 'alf as surprised as when the man said, 'Peter Taylor, please have a seat I have some good news for you.' Well, you could 'ave knocked me down with a feather!

'Who the fuck are you?' I asked, or words to that effect. Well, next thing you know I'm sitting on the bench next to him and he starts talking about me as though he'd bin sittin' on me shoulder for the past 6 months. He knew every fucking thing that 'ad gone on; about the contract, about Stanley Jakes and his threats, the photographs, Andrew Cross, even old 'Smiler' got a mention. I swear to god he was fuckin' psychic.

Anyway, I sat there amazed not really knowin' how to respond when he asked me if I would like the photographs destroyed and Jakes off my back. Of course I'd like 'im off my back but what was the catch I wondered? Anyway the long and the short of it was, like Jakes, my new friend wanted me to rig the tender! But unlike Jakes he knew what he was on about. He was organised and gave me strict instructions about what to do and how to go about it. He'd done his 'omework that was for sure and seemed to 'ave every angle covered.

I 'ave to say the thought of getting Jakes off my back was more than a little appealing to me but I didn't know this gentleman geezer from Adam so wanted assurances. I Says, 'Alright Guvnor so if I do this 'ow do I know that you'll get Jakes off me back?' He looked up from under his hat and just said in that funny voice of 'is, 'I am a man of my word Mr. Taylor. By the time I meet you here in two days' time, Stanley Jakes will no longer be a threat to you. If you do as I say your problems will be behind you but cross me, and they have only just begun.'

So, of course next day I wakes up to find ol' Jakes has 'ad his head cracked open with an 'ammer! I didn't quite know whether I should be laughin' or cryin' but on balance I can't say I was sorry to see the back of the man. But on the other 'and, I couldn't help thinkin' Crossy and me was sinking deeper into the mire. Jakes murdered and this gentleman wanting us to fiddle the tender! I can't say it didn't cross me mind that we'd jumped neatly from the frying pan into the fire. The gentleman may have been more respectable and educated that Jakes but just as fuckin' ruthless.

Crossy and me had a confab and we thought the safest bet was to do as the man said and 'ope he was as good as 'is word. So over the next week or two, me and the gentleman fixed the tender. He revised all the prices and I got 'em signed by 'Smiler' Jones and they were submitted to the Board for 'due consideration'. To be honest I never thought it would take twelve years for the authorities to catch up with us."

The good professor surely! "Can you describe this man Peter?" I asked, my excitement rising.

"Of course, I only met him after dark and he was very careful to keep his identity hidden. He wore a hat and scarf and I never really got more than a glimpse of the man. He gave me the impression that he was well groomed if you know what I mean? Smart dark suit, expensive overcoat...like he belonged to the upper classes. He 'ad a funny voice, like posh but somethin' added maybe Irish, Welsh I'm no expert but he didn't sound like he come from Portsmouth. You know, nothing like Jakes."

"Spectacles? Did he wear them?"

"Now you mention it, he did. Round gold ones, as I recall." Hardly conclusive but another small piece of the jig-saw in place.

I was sure there was more to come from Peter Taylor but I was satisfied with my evenings work. We spoke for a few minutes more, mostly about the details of how the fraud was committed before we went our separate ways with a promise on my part to do what I could to help keep him out of custody.

Feeling buoyed by what I had learnt I walked south along the Whitechapel Road back toward the City. For the first time I felt progress had been made and now harboured little doubt about the Davenport confession. The professor did exist, I was certain and he had mixed a potent cocktail of hallucinogenic drugs to induce Davenport to murder Stanley Jakes. And this was a by-product of an elaborate plan to defraud over a million pounds from the Admiralty. I felt a surge of adrenalin as I made the connections.

But I still needed to understand the intricacies of the relationship between John McDermott and the professor. They were in cahoots, of that I was certain; one manipulating the Admiralty and the other, the supply chain. John McDermott was responsible for persuading Crawford Electrics to sign the contract which would deliver the commission while the professor took charge of controlling the award of the contract through Peter Taylor and Andrew Cross. Jakes had been a side issue, no more than a minor irritant. He had seen an opportunity but possessed neither the wit nor the finesse to exploit it. But his uncontrolled marauding did constitute a threat to the carefully laid plans of the master conspirators and for that he was murdered.

Billy Cosgrove was a convenient scape goat which led me to make a further connection, between the police (most probably Hanaho) and the conspirators. Otherwise why would they have been so keen to pin the murder on Billy? And why so strenuously resist investigations into Clive Davenport's confession? It seemed clear to me that it was because they wanted to remove any possible link between the conspirators and the death of Stanley Jakes. There was no doubt in my mind we were dealing with not only ruthless but highly sophisticated criminals.

And criminals who had Police Inspector Jack Hanaho on their unofficial payroll; a potent force and a hard nut to crack. I wondered exactly what Hanaho got from the arrangement but squeezing information from a hardened operator like the Inspector would be next to impossible. That could wait for another day though, I thought to myself as I made my way toward the underground.

Thirty Four

Forty eight hours later I stood arm in arm with Lucy and watched the Sunbeam being loaded onto a cross channel ferry at Dover. The stevedores expertly attached the chains to the car's chassis and a huge crane hoisted it into the air before it was lowered gently onto the deck to be released and man-handled into its final position for the journey. There were several dozen cars to be loaded and we watched, fascinated as they manoeuvred one after the other onto the deck and into the tiniest of spaces, squeezing in far more cars than seemed physically possible. After a couple of hours, with the majority of vehicles safely on board the gangplank was finally clunked into position and we gratefully took our place in the queue and made our weary way up to passenger deck. It had been a long day.

I had not seen a great deal of the world in my thirty years, at least that I could remember, having only completed two sorties from my homeland as an adult; travelling by train through western Europe to Italy on a 'voyage of discovery' and a BOAC flight across the Atlantic on a short holiday to the USA but for Lucy this was the first time she had ventured abroad.

We had hardly got ourselves settled on the upper passenger deck it seemed before the coast of France came into view on the horizon, lights twinkling out of the early evening gloom. We peered through the half-light as we approached the docks at Calais and could not help but compare it with our recently departed home. The straits of Dover were an insignificant stretch of water but the sights and sounds which greeted us in France, offered a sharp contrast to those on the English side of the channel.

The Hotel de Calais was situated within a stone's throw of the docks and we had arranged to leave the car at the quayside until the following morning. The light had faded completely as we disembarked and our walk was illuminated only by the dull and misty glow of the street lamps. Lucy's eyes sparkled as she took in the differences and appeared delighted by everything she saw. Even the mundane and ugly took on the mantle of the foreign and exotic. Calais was hardly the most French of French towns, with its mercurial history but its differences were enough to capture Lucy's imagination with the abundance of the small Citroen cars, the shuttered and slightly shabby terraced dwellings abutting the pavements and the pungent smell of Gauloise cigarettes which permanently hung in the air. The excitement radiating from her face was contagious and I loved watching her eyes, wide with anticipation, flitting from one new experience to another.

We strolled, hand in hand down the Rue Descartes toward our hotel before discovering a cosy restaurant en route, the perfect setting for our first continental liaison. As we entered *Le Coq Noir* I searched my mind for the fragments of schoolboy French which somewhere lurked within but was relieved to find that Lucy had clearly paid more attention than I, to French lessons in school. She took over and I sat back, soaked up the atmosphere and perused the wine list.

A delicious four course meal slowly unfolded before us, washed down with a bottle St. Emillion. But before we got too engrossed in the delights of the cuisine Lucy wanted an update on the investigation which we had purposely put to one side during out journey. I was happy to oblige with the hope that Lucy would provide a different perspective to my own. Of course, she still harboured hopes of finding clues to the death of her brother and having had an attempt on her own life, she was justifiably anxious to know what progress was being made. Lucy, as was often her way absorbed my comments without immediately replying.

But then, halfway through the starter she suddenly asked. "Are you sure William that the professor and John McDermott are not one and the same?"

It took me a few seconds to grasp her point but my immediate reaction was to disregard the possibility. "Oh no I don't think so." I started but then opened my mind. "But then um, I suppose ….the American connection, the accent, the beard…." I trailed off as I realised how all of these things could have so easily been mimicked. "Well I'll be damned yes; I suppose it really is possible! I wonder…I just wonder." I smiled at Lucy.

I made a mental note to myself to ask Ernest Bannister to run a cross check on witness statements relating to meetings with the Professor and John McDermott to see if there were any matches.

Whilst I mused on the intriguing possibility of our man being a master of disguise, Lucy brought me back to the present by asking whether I still had the time and inclination to investigate the circumstances behind Billy's death. She worked very hard to keep Billy's memory alive and gently cajoled me at every opportunity to keep my promise to leave no stone unturned.

During the car journey from Portsmouth Lucy had told me she had received a note from Catherine Salter, the adult version of the girl who witnessed Billy being abducted outside the Red White and Blue in 1939. Our previous attempt to speak to Catherine had been aborted by the instincts of an over protective mother but it now seemed mother had been overruled. I agreed to add a meeting with Miss Salter to my busy agenda for the following week.

It was close to midnight before we reluctantly left *Le Coq Noir* and ambled back toward the hotel. Our passage and hotels were booked under the names of Mr. and Mrs. Goldhawk and Lucy had enjoyed the shocked looks we received when our passports revealed our true status. "The English are so old fashioned." She had exclaimed with a laugh. "You can bet the French will have no such qualms!" And she was right.

The reception at the Hotel de Calais had long since closed but our passports were exchanged for keys and towels by the concierge who showed us to our room and made us welcome with a Gallic shrug and a knowing grin. I had hardly given a thought to the reasons for our visit to Picardie and it was only lying in bed with Lucy asleep next to me that I finally opened my mind to what may lay in store for us. I had made enquiries from England with a Notaire in Fontaine Notre-Dame about the *Reneaux famille* but got nowhere. The local bureaucrats were hard to pin down and despite enthusiastic promises and plenty of exclamations (Mais Oui, mais oui..pas de problem!) I soon gave up in a tangle of red tape and decided my best chance was to visit in person.

So here we were, on the threshold I hoped of at last getting to the truth about my past. It was a two hour drive from Calais to Fontaine-Notre-Dame but we planned a stop at St Omer where the Flying Corp had been stationed for much of the First War and where Captain Barrington-Hope made his miraculous reappearance. Before venturing out, however, we spent two luxurious hours in bed taking full advantage of the laissez-faire attitude of the French to *affaires de la coeur*. Even the smell of fresh croissants from the boulangerie opposite could not entice us from bed early that day.

It was mid-morning when we finally threw back the covers and pulled open the shutters to a gloriously sunny day before making the short walk back to the quayside to retrieve the car. It was well into April and there was a genuine feel of spring in the air. We found our way easily enough through the quiet streets of Calais and drove along the D26 southeast toward St Omer. If we had expected a museum or even recognition of the Flying Corps' role in the town's history we were to be disappointed. Perhaps it was unsurprising that the local population preferred to forget about the War which had ravaged their countryside and taken so many of their young men.

After an hour of fruitless searching we continued on my way toward Fontaine-Notre-Dame a further 50 kilometres south. We crossed the Western Front at some indeterminate point near Neuve-Chapelle but found little to suggest the trauma suffered only a generation earlier, except for the yellow daubed munitions which were dumped at the roadside at regular intervals.

Fontaine-Notre-Dame was a small town but far more than the village that I had somehow expected. We drove slowly up the main street which was, in typical French style, shut for lunch. Shops closed, shutters pulled to and not a person to be seen. How very different from the bustle of an English town in the early afternoon. Time was on our side so we parked-up and went to explore on foot. It was not an unpleasant town but neither was it remarkable. It lacked an obvious centre but was equipped with the essentials, la boulangerie, la charcuterie, la pharamacie, le Tabac and la Poste. It was strange sensation walking through the empty streets but I could not help but imagine the extravagant family lunches being served with the ubiquitous carafe of *vin rouge* behind the closed doors of the houses which we passed.

As we walked, soaking up the warmth from the sun, Lucy asked me about my family and how much I knew. In truth, it was very little but the question helped me focus on the day ahead. "My mother had a younger sister, Marie and a brother Cedric. And then of course there was my twin, Claudine. As you know the family lived on a farm somewhere near here. But that is pretty well all I know and it's perfectly possible that the family have moved on." Before adding pessimistically. "So we could be wasting our time."

After several minutes of aimless wondering we had caught our first glimpse of life in the town, an elderly lady in black some way in front of us hobbling slowly along with a stick in one hand and a shopping bag in the other. A well-fed dog of mixed breeding trotted happily along beside her. We quickened our pace to catch-up and got to her just as she reached her front door.

"Excusez-moi, Madame, je suis à la recherche de la maison de la famille Reneaux. Pouvez-vous m'aider?" Lucy asked, putting me to shame with her easy French.

The old lady awkwardly turned to face us and with a quizzical look answered. “Augustine Reneaux lives at number twelve rue Victor Hugo.” She replied and pointed down the street. “It is the next street in that direction”.

“Augustine Reneaux, let’s go and find out if he’s part of the family, shall we?” Lucy asked grabbing hold of my hand and pulling me in the direction of the rue Victor Hugo.

Within a few minutes we stood on the pavement outside number 12 rapping on the door which was answered by a fastidiously dressed elderly gentleman in a suit and tie.

It transpired that Augustine Reneaux was my great uncle, the brother of my mother’s father who had died some years earlier. His delight at the sudden reappearance of his niece Catherine’s son was evident but with his memory and his hearing failing, coupled with my indifferent French, it made for difficult conversation. His long term memory was intact however and his recollections of my mother still vivid. We listened as best we could over a cup of coffee and a slice cake but I was anxious to find the farm, my aunt and most importantly to discover the whereabouts of my twin so we thanked my newly acquired relative and made ready to leave.

We were pointed in the direction of *Le ferme au Moulin du vent,* a few kilometres outside the town and walked quickly back to the car following the diagram drawn by Augustine. South along the main D26, left across the valley and up the brow of a gentle slope back toward Cambrai. Butterflies invaded my stomach as I tried to envisage the forthcoming encounter. I had come a long way in every sense to finally arrive here on my day of reckoning. Was this out of the way farm in Picardie, my first home I wondered? These people who were my own flesh and blood, were they the family I yearned for when growing up in the cold and unforgiving Liongate? I was soon to find out.

The property was easily found on the right hand side of the road, a large, ramshackle stone farmhouse surrounded by a tumbled down barn and other out-buildings in varying states of decrepitude. There was a rusty collection of old and disused ploughs and other unidentifiable farming paraphernalia dotted around the yard, some, almost certainly relics of the last century. What a great playground for a little boy I thought!

I pulled the car up between two old window-less Citroen vans now serving as chicken coops and a muddy pond populated by a noisy collection of geese and ducks which mistook us for bearers' of their afternoon snack as they arrived at the car enthusiastically honking and quacking. The farmhouse itself was an ancient looking building brought to life with early flowering shrubs, pot plants and lichen covered stone ornaments. All in all it was a chaotic, vibrant and lively scene.

No sooner had I turned off the engine and engaged the handbrake when a middle aged, grey haired lady with floral dress and piney appeared from the side door and shooed the voracious birds away from the car. As I stepped out the lady peered at me and frowned. "Guillaume? Est-ce vraiment toi? Ce n'est pas possible." She hurried toward me, staring hard into me face.

"Mon Dieu! Cedric." she called. "Son Guillaume, le fils de Catherine. Il est ici!"

With that she burst into tears and hugged me for all she was worth. I reciprocated, feeling moved and not in the slightest part awkward. My aunt then stepped away and looked at me for several seconds. "You look so much like your father, William. Please, introduce me to your friend and come and meet your uncle Cedric." She smiled and walked to Lucy and kissed her on both cheeks. "Vite, vite inside please… we have much to talk about."

With that we were ushered inside to a large farmhouse kitchen where Cedric also, in the Gallic tradition, kissed us both ceremonially on each cheek. He then pulled out chairs from under the huge wooden table for us to sit on. Beaming, Cedric then shook his head and muttered, "Alors, Son Guillaume, I cannot believe it. After all this time!"

Once settled with coffee my aunt took my hands in hers and asked. "William why has it taken so long for you to come to us?"

Feeling unaccountably guilty I explained how, had it not been for the eagle eye of Lucy, who had interpreted the photograph of my mother and father which resided on my mantelpiece, I may never have come at all. During my story my aunt sat in rapt attention, hands clasped together and elbows resting on the table edge. Her eyes were moist and the emotion showed in her face.

"Why did Sir Edward keep you in the dark, William? I do not understand."

And neither did I but I intended to find out. But my more immediate concern was to understand why and how I had become separated from my twin and been consigned to the misery of life at Liongate. So rather than answer her question I asked one of my own. "Tell me about Claudine? Was she brought up here with you?"

"It was difficult William but before your mother died she took the decision to separate you and Claudine. It broke her heart but she thought it was for the best for you both. Geoffrey, your father, wanted his son brought up and schooled in England and Catherine thought it best for Claudine to stay here with us. It was a terrible decision for her to have to make. She married Sir Edward as a…how do you say in English, a marriage of convenience? She knew she was dying and he seemed a kind man and treated her well in her last weeks. We had hoped that he would be a good father to you William. But perhaps we were wrong?" She asked looking at me for confirmation.

“When did Claudine first hear that she had a brother?” I asked not really wanting to be drawn into the rights and wrongs of my mother’s final arrangements.

“When she got the letter on her eighteenth birthday. But you know she never forgot you.” Cedric chipped in, in his strongly accented English.

Lucy glanced in my direction and I knew exactly what she was thinking. “What letter Cedric?” I asked. But I already knew the answer.

“Why, the letter from your mother of course. She instructed us to give it to Claudine on her eighteenth birthday. She wrote to you both but you must know that.”

I knew immediately that it was the very same letter torn from my grasp by my father all those years ago. “What did the letter say, Cedric? What did the *letters* say? I never had the chance to read mine.”

“Ah, mon dieu! So that is why it had taken you so long to arrive on our door step! We saw the letters, one to Claudine and one to you. They explained what Marie has just told you. Why you were separated and your mother’s very last wish that the two of you should be together again once you both reached eighteen. The letter to you William gave you this address and asked you to make contact with your sister. We waited but you did not come. We were very sorry but Claudine was …well very angry.

It is important that you understand William that your sister believes you abandoned her; that you did not want to know her. She thinks that you had your life in England and wanted no part of your *famille en France*. She has erased you from her memory and as far as she is concerned you do not exist. She was hurt, heartbroken. That is how it is but I hope you will be able to talk her around.”

I was stunned. Having spent no more than half an hour in their company I knew already how much happier my childhood could have been on the farm with these kind people. My emotions where yo-yoing from self-pity to bewilderment. My most basic instinct though was the need to find and make peace with my sister. "Tell me more about my sister. Where is she now?" I asked.

"Of course William. But first I want to show you the farm and where you played when you were a little boy. You loved it here you know? You and Claudine were a real handful running around the place, clambering over anything and everything in your path. Claudine was such a tomboy. Anything you did she was not far behind. Do you remember anything about your time here, William?"

I confessed that I did not but strangely, as I took in the scene around me I was struck by a feeling of déjà vu so perhaps deep in my subconscious the memories were still alive. It was surreal and frustrating experience delving into the innermost recesses of my mind trying to recall any fleeting memory which may help bring to life my earliest years. Lucy was convinced that the traumas I suffered at Liongate were responsible for my inability to remember and I had no reason to doubt her insight. As we followed my aunt up a pathway toward the largest of the three stone built barns which surrounded the farmyard it was difficult to suppress my feelings of melancholia. I could almost hear the happy sounds of children playing and exploring; could see in my mind's eye my own self as a four year old, running unrestrained through the vineyards with Claudine close on my heals.

I was brought back to the present by my aunt's voice. "Cedric, do you remember the time William fell into the duck pond?" She giggled and looked back to me. "You were chasing the chickens and tripped over a flower pot. You were maybe three but you didn't cry. You pulled yourself out the water, soaking wet and just went on chasing the chickens. We all laughed so much. They were very happy days!

You were a confident little boy William and your sister idolised you. She would have followed you to the ends of the Earth. It is strange that you do not remember. Claudine remembers. She recalls you clearly and you know I don't think she ever really recovered from your separation. She lost her spirit the day they took you away. Claudine was always a very clever girl though and is now a doctor working with children in Paris. We are very proud of her.

This barn here is where we put your father's plane. Your mother and I were in the yard when we heard the sound of engines and your father's plane clipped the top of those trees there; they were not so high then. The plane turned over and landed in the field over there. Come I'll show you."

We edged through a gap between the barn and the apple orchard and down a gentle incline toward an irregular shaped field still muddied from ploughing. "We ran down from the yard and your father was hanging upside down from the cockpit covered in blood. Do you know the first thing that he said to us? 'Good afternoon ladies, I'm sorry to drop in without an invitation. You couldn't possibly lend a hand getting me out of this bally contraption could you? Only I'm somewhat stuck!' You know William, your mother and I both fell in love with Geoffrey instantly. He was so full of charm and humour. Such a gentleman. And of course your mother was so beautiful too. A match made in heaven as you English say! And look at you William, so much like your father."

Although something of an emotional rollercoaster it was a magical afternoon for me exploring the farmyard, wandering through the apple orchards and the outlying fields of maize beyond and hearing stories of my long forgotten childhood, of my mother and father and of my twin sister. It was difficult not to compare the warm, homely chaos of the farm to the cold order of Liongate. As a boy my heart had yearned for the simple pleasures of family life, a life so evident in every nook and cranny of the Reneauxs' magical helter-skelter home. From the photographs on the wall, the children's drawing taped to the cupboard doors to their ornaments, mementoes and keepsakes, all treasures of a close family life. A family that by rights I should have been a part.

For the rest of the day and into the evening my aunt and uncle filled in many pieces of the jig-saw which made up my early life. Much of what I had learnt about my father from Sir Douglas Evill and Arthur Swanson was confirmed and my heart swelled with pride as I listened and understood the true caliber of my parents. There was no doubting that they were a selfless and gallant couple. I could have talked all night but others around me flagged so in the early hours we finally retired upstairs to bed and I quickly fell into a deep contented sleep.

Thirty Five

Within a few hours of retiring we were awoken by Napoleon, the farm's French Cockerel who took his dawn alarm duties very seriously. The previous day we had enjoyed watching the pugnacious Napoleon as he strutted around the farmyard, his demeanor belying his diminutive stature but we could have done without his early morning exuberance. The enthusiasm of his morning call matched his feisty temperament which served him so well in the battle for kitchen scraps in the post breakfast scramble. Napoleon most definitely ruled the roost at *Le ferme au Moulin du vent.*

But it was another glorious day so, in truth, an early rise was not an unpleasant experience. Less so still, once we smelt the fresh baguettes, croissants and coffee already awaiting us on the kitchen table. Despite looking somewhat bleary eyed, Cedric and Marie welcomed us warmly and once again I contrasted the happy scene with the lonely breakfasts I endured at Liongate, staring at the back page of my father's Daily Telegraph, where conversation was definitely not part of the morning ritual.

Lucy and I were booked onto the afternoon ferry from Calais and I had planned an early start with a detour via Paris to visit Claudine but the consensus of opinion had been against me. The women held sway and insisted a more subtle approach was required. I generally deferred to Lucy on such matters anyway so was persuaded that Claudine should be afforded time and space to adjust to my sudden re-appearance in her life.

So it was to be left to my aunt to explain to Claudine the circumstances behind my re-appearance. Much too quickly for my liking midday arrived and our time on the farm was over, so reluctantly, Lucy and I bid farewell to our wonderful hosts and started back toward Calais. My aunt cried and Cedric insisted that we visited again in the summer which we enthusiastically agreed to do.

It was a painfully slow journey north with every farmer in Picardie on the roads transporting livestock and spring vegetables to market, but the *joie de vivre* that I felt having rediscovered my family kept me in good spirits. Sadly, my elation served only to emphasise the contrast in fortunes between Lucy and I. Whilst I revelled in the luxury of my new found family Lucy still struggled to come to terms with the death of her brother and the guilt she felt about the shooting of housemate Samantha and although she tried hard to share my excitement she was unable to hide her underlying despondency.

I could not bring Billy or Samantha back from the dead but I was determined to intensify my efforts to deliver some sort of closure for Lucy who needed answers, however unpalatable, in order to move on with her life. The irony that it was Lucy's eagle eyes which had set me on the path to discovering my own roots was not lost on me.

Thirty Six

The following day I was back to work and my first port of call was the office in Landport Terrace to catch-up on events at Surtees, Hancock and Lampson. It had been three weeks since I had set foot in the building and there was a certain comfort in being back but as I sauntered up the stairs and through the main office I wondered if I could ever be wholly satisfied with my old life back again. Could I slip back into the profession like I would slip my feet into a pair of comfortable carpet slippers? Probably not I thought but time would tell and I was happy enough to let the future take care of itself.

I knocked on Brian's door and popped my head round to find him in conversation with Douglas Lampson. "Ah, the wanderer hath returned. Come on in William." Brian gestured for me to come in and close the door.

"Douglas and I were talking about Crawfords. How's your investigation going?"

So I explained about Landseer Consultants and the role of the two accountants, Benison and Buridge. Brian stroked his chin in thought and asked. "Do you believe them about Sir Marcus or do you think they may have been in cahoots? It's all a bit of a concern. We don't want to get embroiled in anything which could damage the reputation of the firm."

"They lied through their teeth initially but my impression is that they told the truth in the end, albeit under duress. Their final version certainly tallies with what I heard from Peter Taylor. Someone nobbled Taylor and bribed the two accountants but they weren't in it for the money they just wanted an easy summer. It seems extraordinary that Sir Marcus did not see what was going on under his nose but I have no evidence against him. It maybe that he became aware of the corruption after the event and brushed it under the carpet. If so, it was certainly unethical but whether he committed a crime I am not entirely sure."

Douglas then looked at Brian who raised an eyebrow before speaking. "Last Friday William, I had a phone call from a very irate Sir Marcus Crawford complaining about your conduct and to quote, 'your underhand methods'. He claimed you went well beyond your brief and delved into matters which were of no concern of yours as well as unsettling his staff. He wants you taken off the team."

"Oh, really?" I was genuinely shocked. "He is apt to fly off the handle on occasions but that is fairly extreme I must say."

"Yes indeed! I told him that he should be grateful that the investigation into corruption is non-chargeable but I am not sure he was listening!"

"But William." Douglas chimed in. "We are in an invidious position having racked-up over 800 billing hours during the course of the audit. What do we do? Antagonise the man and risk a fight in the courts to recover our money?"

"It's a problem I admit but we can't just roll over and let him trample over us, can we?" I asked.

Forever the pragmatist, Brian's solution was to play the whole thing down and soothe Sir Marcus's dented ego. "I'll drop him a note calming the waters. If he genuinely has nothing to hide he will come around. If, on the other hand, he *does* have something to hide....well...we'll cross that particular bridge, when and if we come to it, shall we gentleman?"

There was no argument from me. Any further objections from Sir Marcus would only increase my suspicion but I was well aware that he was a man who blew hot and cold at the best of times and perhaps this latest outburst was no more than venting steam. But nonetheless I would need to keep a careful eye on him.

***

By the middle of the afternoon I felt I had paid my dues and left the office in search of Catherine Salter. I had telephoned the bakery where she worked in Elm Grove and had been informed that she clocked-off at 3pm on a Monday. It was only a short walk from the office but I received a good buffeting from a gusty wind as I walked up Kings Road and past the building sites which offered the people of Southsea their daily reminder of the devastation caused by German bombs a decade earlier.

As I arrived at the intersection which marked the boundary between Kings Road and Elm Grove, I could make out the doorway to Crofton's Bakery a little further up the road on my left. It was a few minutes before 3 o'clock so I slowed my pace and looked out for a tea shop or other suitable venue for our meeting. Catherine Salter was evidently not the sort to dilly-dally as she briskly left the bakery barely 60 seconds after the church bell had struck the hour. I caught her attention and she offered me a surprised and nervous smile but agreed to talk.

A few minutes later I were sitting in the window of Mrs. Hubbard's tea room in Castle Road with a clearly uncomfortable Miss Salter who sat awkwardly staring down at her hands and nervously drumming her fingers on the table top. It took a good few minutes of small talk before she would even look me in the eye but eventually I took the plunge. "So tell me what you saw that night Catherine?"

"I saw these men put Billy in the back of a van and drive off."

"Are you sure it was Billy you saw?"

"Oh, it was Billy all right." She replied with a hint of a smile.

"How can you be so sure Catherine? It was dark and it was a long time ago. You were only, what eight… nine years old?"

"All the girls had a crush on Billy, me included. It was Billy alright. I'd have known him anywhere."

"So what happened exactly?" I asked sipping at my tea.

"Well, as I said he came out of the pub and this man put a blanket over his head and two other men bundled him into the back of the van."

"Did you recognise any of the men?"

"Well yes, as I told the police there was Mr. Barlow who I often see around the shops in Fawcett Road. He must live around here somewhere; a big chap with a limp. It was the same van that came round most nights and picked-up the drunken sailors."

"What, do you mean the provost van? Billy was taken away by the naval provost?" I asked, amazed.

"That's right didn't you know that? I told the police. It was all written down and I signed-it." Catherine looked almost as surprised as I felt. There was no mention of the naval provost in the statement that I had read.

"You are absolutely sure it was the provost that took Billy away?" I asked again, shaking my head in surprise.

"Yes, I saw the van most nights (everyone knew the naval provost van) and it was the same driver and his mate, the two that put Billy in the van, like. The third one was older and dressed in a long dark coat."

I pulled a carbon-copy of Catherine Salter's statement which Lucy had retrieved from the police files, from my pocket, unfolded it and laid it on the table between us. "There's no mention of the provost here Catherine."

"That's not my statement! And that's not my signature! Where did this come from?" Catherine looked alarmed. "My statement was two sides long and I gave them much more detail than that." Given what I had discovered about Hanaho's methods it came as no surprise to me that the police had tampered with the evidence. I was looking forward to Julian's confrontation with Hanaho later in the week and hoped that at last we may be able to put the duplicitous Inspector in his place.

I was not sure whether my status was enough to grant me access to the Provost Marshal's headquarters but one way or another I wanted an interview with the officer in charge, Commodore Henry Cockburn who, by chance I had encountered before at one of my father's dinner parties. Taking my leave of Catherine Salter I retraced my steps to Landport Terrace and put a telephone call through to the Commodore and I was pleasantly surprised when I heard his gruff voice at the end of the line:

"Mr. Goldhawk, well, well and what can I do for you, young man?" He asked and I could almost see his moustache twitching.

So I explained the circumstances behind my call and put it into an official context by connecting the disappearance of Billy with enquiries into the fraud perpetrated against the Admiralty. I had read the Commodore correctly and once he grasped the possible link between what happened outside the Red, White and Blue and the crime, he proved to be most obliging.

"We'll certainly do what we can to help. Our records are generally pretty tidy so please come on down, *now* if you like and we'll see what we can dig out for you. If you ask for me at the gate they'll put out a call and I'll give you clearance."

Feeling pleased with my unexpected progress I jumped in the car and drove the half-mile to Whale Island where the Commodore, as promised met me at the gate and escorted me back to his office. During our short walk my host gave me an overview of the operations of the Provost Marshal's office and pointed out the salient features of HMS Excellent where their offices were housed. We entered the administration block on the furthest corner of the compound and I was introduced to a young lady in the uniform of the Royal Navy.

"This is Warrant Officer Sylvia Banks who works for the purser and knows our records better than anyone. And this is William Goldhawk part of the team investigating some fairly serious fraud going back to before the war. Please give him what assistance he requires."

Turning back to me the Commodore bid me good afternoon. "I'll leave you in the capable hands of Warrant Officer Banks but please put your head around the door before you leave if you don't mind."

"How can I help Mr. Goldhawk?" Sylvia Banks asked, as she tidied her desk in anticipation of a change in her afternoon routine.

"I'm trying to track down the movements of a Billy Cosgrove who disappeared in 1939. You may remember the case?"

"Ah yes, I read about it in the Evening News a few months back when his sister organised a protest outside the police station. So he has not turned-up then?"

"No, I'm afraid not. What we have discovered though is that he was abducted outside the Red, White and Blue in Fawcett Road and thrown into the back of the naval provost van. That was the last anyone saw of him. Do you have records of your drivers going back before the war by any chance?"

"I can do better than that. Nigel Barlow has been driving for us since the year dot and he's working today if you want a word?"

After weeks of paralysis suddenly my investigations seemed to have taken a leap forward in every direction. I had hardly expected to be speaking to one of the men responsible for taking Billy Cosgrove so soon. Sylvia Banks explained that Nigel Barlow was a former rating but had lost his sea legs in the 1930's and had worked as a handyman on the base ever since. We found him ensconced in the boiler room with his afternoon cuppa, reading the Daily Mirror.

"I have a visitor for you Nigel." Sylvia said before making a diplomatic exit. "You know where to find me, Mr. Goldhawk."

Nigel looked none too pleased with the interruption but grunted an invitation for me to be seated on one of two garden chairs which, alone with a milk crate pressed into service as a coffee table, made up the basic furnishings of his hideaway.

"Have you heard of Billy Cosgrove, Mr. Barlow?" I asked as I sat down on the less rickety of the two garden chairs whilst keeping a close watch on Nigel Barlow's face.

"Billy who? Coswell? No never 'eard of him."

"Cosgrove, Billy Cosgrove." I repeated slowly, my eyes still trained on his face.

"No never 'eard of no Billy Cosgrove." He replied returning his gaze to the Daily Mirror.

"Let me remind you Mr. Barlow, Billy Cosgrove disappeared on the 14th October 1939. At the time there was a warrant out for his arrest for the murder of Stanley Jakes. Ring any bells?"

"What's this gotta do with me? You come barging in here without so much as a by your leave. Who'd you think you are? I don't have to answer your questions!"

"No Mr. Barlow you are absolutely right, you don't have to answer my questions. But let me tell you something that just might interest you. You were seen bundling Billy Cosgrove into the back of your van outside the Red, White and Blue on the night he disappeared. It's now twelve years since Billy went missing and we have applied to the coroner to have him declared dead. So by this time next week we will have a murder investigation on our hands and who, Mr. Barlow, do you think will be heading up our list of suspects?"

The colour drained from Nigel Barlow's ruddy cheeks as he took in the implications of what I had said. "How do you know he's dead? I never killed him! I was trying to help him!"

"Perhaps you'd better start from the beginning. What happened that night Nigel?"

Looking genuinely shocked Nigel Barlow blurted out. "Alright, alright! Yes it was me and Reg Cubit who put him in the van. It was a spur of the moment thing really. We had been drinking in the Royal Exchange a couple of nights earlier and heard a rumour that there was a plot to get Billy out of the country. We'd all grown up in the streets around Southsea and knew the Cosgrove family well enough. They were decent people and Billy was a nice lad. We didn't want him going to the gallows especially on account of that bastard Jakes. Anyways, to cut a long story short, me and Reg agreed to lend a hand.

It was our job to get Billy down to the docks. We drove the provost van most evenings and were well used to hauling drunks out of the pubs so it was the perfect cover. We drove in and out of the docks regular like so there were no questions asked. That night we drove through the main entrance as usual and backed up just the other side of the pontoon where there was no chance of being seen. It was as simple as that. I had hoped Billy got clean away and had a vision of him living in Australia or somewhere like that."

"Or did you knock him over the back of the head and throw him in the harbour, Mr. Barlow?"

"No I did not! I am no murderer."

"Who was the third man involved in Billy's abduction?"

"Abduction makes it sound like a crime. It wasn't like that. We were trying to help him escape the hangman's noose! I don't know the name of the bloke but he was, like the brains behind the operation or so we gathered. Me and Reg just helped out so to speak. My missus reckons he might have been from the anti-death penalty brigade…you know, maybe the husband of that Gloria Steadman who'd been making speeches, ranting on about what a sin it was to take someone's life, even a murderer's. Anyway, the man didn't say a lot but once we got Billy into the van, he got in the back with him and then, like I said we dropped them down at in the dockyard. And that was the last I saw of either of them, god's honest truth."

"I need to know who this man was Mr. Barlow. It's your neck on the line here so think hard." I replied.

"Look I really don't know. I'd help you if I could. All I can tell you is he was sort of upper class. You know, posh. A bit like you if you don't mind me saying. Wore a suit and long dark coat but he didn't want to be recognised. He was careful not to show his face and used a strategically placed scarf and hat to hide his identity. He'd arranged it all with Jack Spicer at the pub but I don't know if they ever actually met face to face. I think it was sorted out over the telephone, at least that's what I was told. When it was all over like, we talked about it in the pub but no-one had a clue who the man was."

"What was his build? Slim, tall…how would you describe him?"

"He was quite stocky I seem to remember and not as tall as you. About my age maybe but it was a long time ago…maybe Reg will remember. I only met him very briefly like."

"So the plan was… what exactly? To get Billy out of the country?"

"Yes that what we thought but none of us really knew for sure. We just assumed he was going to be smuggled aboard one of the ships in port. As I remember there were a few ships in that night, a couple Royal Navy frigates and a handful of merchant ships."

I spent a further ten minutes probing Nigel Barlow but was satisfied I had got all that I was likely to get from him. My gut feeling was that he was telling me the truth but to make absolutely certain I would be looking for corroboration from his partner Reginald Cubit and would also be paying a visit to the landlord of the Royal Exchange. My next port of call though was the records office at the dockyard. But before leaving the care of the Provost Marshal, the Commodore gave me a letter of introduction to the Vice Admiral's office at the Naval Dockyard's HQ which looked after the archives detailing the movements of all shipping in and out of the harbour.

Thirty Seven

I drove down Queen Street, parked the Sunbeam on the road outside Brickwood's Brewery and made my way on foot down to The Hard and through the Main Gate toward the administration offices of the Royal Dockyard. If Nigel Barlow was correct and Billy had been whisked abroad by some unknown benefactor to avoid the gallows it was logical to assume he would have left the country by one of the ships docked in the harbour on the night of his disappearance.

But according to Sebastian Harris, Billy's decomposed body had been pulled from Prinsted Harbour in early November which meant he must have died within a few days of his abduction. Was his mysterious 'benefactor' in fact his killer then, I wondered? It seemed likely. Logic told me that Billy had been murdered on the night of October 14th 1939 and his body dumped into the harbour and washed-up a couple of weeks later ten miles down the coast but without proof I would never be sure.

With my letter of introduction from the Provost Marshal I was welcomed by Captain Andrew Brewster who, although somewhat thrown by my unexpected appearance, found time to listen to my entreaties and pass me over to his assistant Beverley Traegust who he was confident would be able to furnish me with the information I was after. The austere Miss Traegust, prim, efficient with round tortoiseshell framed glasses and hair made-up into in a bun seemed to have an encyclopedic knowledge of the Royal Dockyards at Portsmouth. She pulled out a ledger and turned the pages to reveal the names of the vessels in dock on the night in question.

"There were three merchant ships in the harbour that night Mr. Goldhawk, two flying the British Ensign and one American cargo ship. In addition there were several ships of the Royal Navy but only two on active service, The Exeter which was en route to the South Atlantic and the Archimedes which sailed for the Mediterranean the following day. The others were in port for refits or longer term assignments. The merchants were all in port for another week at least. Only the Exeter sailed that night."

"Let's start with the merchant ships shall we, Miss Traegust?"

"It was actually very quiet in the harbour that particular week as a patrolled convoy had crossed the Atlantic a few days earlier. Of course with the U-boat threat there was very little movement of single ships outside British waters. Of the British merchant ships in the harbour that day, one belonged to Fyffes' which had just delivered a consignment of bananas and the other was a fuel tanker The Hibernian which spent most of its time, by the look of these records, transporting fuel around the coast of Britain; Glasgow, Liverpool, Bristol, Plymouth, Portsmouth, London. The American ship the Denver Star was a bulk cargo transporter which had been due to cross the Atlantic with the convoy but had some technical problem which had delayed her sailing. Yes, it was an unusually quiet night in the harbour which at least narrows your search somewhat."

"What was the story with the Exeter?" I asked.

"Well, this looks more interesting. You said your man Cosgrove was a dockyard electrician, didn't you? Have a look at this." She said, pointing to the ledger. "She'd had some long standing electrical problems according to the Captains log. They took on board three electricians from the dockyard here in Portsmouth." Turning back to the shelves the redoubtable Miss Traegust removed a slimmer volume and after a two minute search came up with the names. "There was a William Brown of Eastney, a Terrence Pritchard also from Eastney and an Irishman by the name of Patrick O'Reilly. Unfortunately, both Brown and Pritchard were killed when the Exeter came under enemy fire during the Battle of the River Plate. O'Reilly returned to Portsmouth via The Falkland Islands in 1943. There was also a David Armstrong a dockyard shipwright who joined the ship at Devonport who also survived and came ashore in Portsmouth with O'Reilly in '43."

“So these chaps were not enlisted in the Royal Navy but worked on the ships as civilians?” I queried.

“That’s exactly right. Particularly when there were minor technical problems and they did not want to delay the sailing they offered the dockyard workers free passage. It was generally considered something of a perk, at least before the war. Although how it was viewed in late 1939 with the peril of the U-boats I could only guess.”

I puffed out my cheeks in exasperation, knowing the hopelessness of my task. It was difficult to know where to go next. “No ‘Billy Cosgrove’ listed anywhere of course?” I asked with no expectation whatsoever.

“No, but I’ll keep looking Mr. Goldhawk. If you want my opinion I would guess it most likely that he left under a false identity. Forged ID’s were rife on the black market in that period.”

“Well let’s start by trying to track down someone aboard the Exeter. It’s a long-shot I know but we have to start somewhere. Can you help me? Give me a few names of ratings or officers who live locally?” I finished passing her a calling card with my telephone number.

I did not know quite what I had expected but felt disappointed on Lucy’s behalf nonetheless. Lucy was away visiting her mother and I had hoped to surprise her with some news on her return but after hitting the latest in a series of brick walls I decided to keep my investigations to myself for the time being at least. That morning I had got off the blocks at quite a pace and had optimistically anticipated a successful conclusion to the day’s work but in reality, I had to remind myself, Billy was dead and there could be no happy ending. I tried hard to push aside negative thoughts and focus on keeping my investigations on track.

Thirty Eight

With no further progress to my enquiries into Billy's final journey, Friday could not come soon enough. I had spoken at length to my Mi5 liaison officer Ernest Bannister and got the gist of Julian's plan to oust Inspector Hanaho. Julian believed that by undermining the foundations we could bring the whole edifice crashing down. The theory went that without the support of the local police and Hanaho in particular, cracks would to start to appear and with the help of a few well directed hammer blows the structure would crumble. A fine theory no doubt but what of the practicalities I wondered.

Hanaho was a wily old fox and not likely to be easily snared and even if he was, how would he react? It would be safe to assume he would not accept his fate meekly. And looking further ahead, if Hanaho was forced to resign what next? Would our quarry run to ground or as Julian hoped, break cover? Run to ground and we may lose their scent or break cover and who knows what the consequences. We had already received notice of the ruthlessness of our enemy and Julian's actions would undoubtedly be interpreted as provocative.

I was glad that Lucy was out of harm's way at her mother's, I reflected as I walked along the High Street with keen anticipation down toward the Camber Dock. It was early, a little after 7am but as I rounded the corner I could see the dock was already alive with fishermen unloading their catch from the previous night or preparing their boats for the day ahead. The overpowering smell of fish, mixed with the pungent fumes of the motor oil which belched from the exhaust pipes of the grubby diesel engined vessels made for a heady perfume. And as the fishermen and market traders went about their business and the herring gulls swooped, squawked and fought over scraps of fish offal thrown from the boats it added-up to an intoxicating atmosphere.

Boats were moored three abreast in the narrow gully which formed the entrance to the Camber Dock and over the water I could see that The Bridge Tavern was doing a brisk trade even at this early hour. I eventually spied the Fair Isabella tucked away in the furthest corner of the dock, her red hull catching the light of the early morning sun. On board, a disheveled looking man was loading boxes and crates into the hold. I smiled when I realised the scruffy individual was non-other than Julian himself, already in character for the action to come later in the morning.

"Ah, the first to arrive! Come on board William and I'll show you around." Julian called looking very much like he had spent the previous week under the arches at Waterloo Station. A stubble of four days, an old navy blue fisherman's jumper, threadbare and several sizes too large and hair which had not seen a comb for a week completed the look.

"You look fabulous Julian. Is this the new spring collection you are sporting?"

"I'm glad you like it! Grab a couple of those crates will you and help me down stairs and I'll give you a tour of the Fair Isabella. She's quite a boat."

She was indeed an impressive vessel, with an array of gismos and technical gadgetry designed by some of the brightest scientists in Britain to help counter the threat of the Cold War. Julian was clearly proud of his new toy but in typical fashion made light of it. "It took all my powers of persuasion to get her down here for the week! She cost thousands to develop and they don't trust me with her?! Can you credit that, by jingo?!"

The main cabin was piled high with boxes of 'contraband', mainly spirits and cigarettes but also an array of cigars, ports and vintage wines. "Don't get any ideas William. I'll have to account for every bloody bottle and every last cigarette!" Julian moaned with an exaggerated shake of the head.

I looked around the cabin and at first sight it was typical of the interior of an off-shore fishing boat, scruffy, oily, and messy with junk piled high in every corner. But on closer inspection there was more to it. "You see those two mirrors William? Well come and look at this." With that, Julian felt for a concealed handle and slid open the door to the rear bulkhead behind which was a room, crammed full of electrical equipment. At first glance it looked like a mini television studio with cameras, microphones and an assortment of other electrical components and cables. Once inside, the mirrors took on the appearance of clear glass and we were able to look back through into the main cabin.

"A one way mirror, rather clever, eh? Developed by our friends across the pond. You and the boys will be safely locked away in here during my little chat with the Inspector. It is lined with lead so almost totally sound proofed which means you can talk normally and we won't hear a thing. It's a bit disconcerting until you get used to it. And with a switch of a button everything Hanaho says will be recorded in both sound and vision. Oh I do hope the Inspector is in a chatty mood!"

Over the course of the next hour the rest of the crew arrived; Simon Griffin the editor of the Evening News who could hardly contain his excitement as he anticipated the final curtain in his long running saga with the local constabulary, Nigel Morton a freelance journalist and defender of the subjugated classes, Simon Williams a local solicitor, of course Margaret Philimore and two police constables from the Met'. Julian decided that Hanaho was unlikely to react well to discovering his young lieutenant was a spy, so under sufferance Luke was to sit the morning out.

The bait had been set by the Harbour Master who had been primed to call the police station and report the arrival of a suspicious boat at the Camber Dock crammed full of contraband. He accepted his bottle of whisky gratefully in payment for his contribution and announced that Hanaho had taken the bait, hook line and sinker. So we were all set to go and took our positions in the studio.

The morning dragged and it seemed an inordinately long wait in which time we'd resorted to discussing football and Pompey's chances of retaining the Championship when at last I heard the familiar voice of my nemesis, Inspector Jack Hanaho. "Police." He growled. "I'm coming aboard." We watched as the bulky framed Inspector edged down the steps into the forward cabin. "Are you the owner of this vessel?" He asked Julian.

"Yes, she's my boat." Julian answered in a slightly less than convincing West Country dialect.

"Have you any objection if I have a look around?"

"Well…er actually I …"

"Tough. I'll look anyway and you are Mr……?"

"Braithwaite, Mark Braithwaite. I'd like to see your search warrant Sergeant." Julian ventured but Hanaho ignored him and pulled open the first cardboard box he came to.

"A little bit of care please Sergeant, its valuable merchandise!"

"*Inspector*, Mr. Braithwaite." Julian was corrected. "*Inspector* Jack Hanaho. Customs and excise clearance papers, please." He continued, clicking his fingers and holding out a hand.

"Oh, come on Inspector it's just a few bottles! Be reasonable."

"A few bottles? I'd say we've got £500 worth of booze here Mr. Braithwaite." With that Hanaho ripped open another box, pulled out a bottle and examined the label. "I'm no connoisseur but this looks like twelve year old single malt, an expensive vintage Mr.

Braithwaite? Craggan mor, 1938? What can you tell me about this wee scotch?" And with that he unscrewed the top and took a sip.

"Too peaty for my palate." Hanaho shook his head and walked across the cabin and poured the entire content of the bottle down the sink. I saw Julian involuntarily wince.

"No, please Inspector." He implored, with no need to act.

I sat spellbound as I watched the opening salvos. Margaret, Simon Griffin and I sat in the chairs with our noses up close to the one way mirrors whilst the others stood to the rear too engrossed to notice the whirring of the two strategically placed cine cameras and the intermittent feedback from the microphones. We talked in whispers despite assurances from Julian that this was unnecessary. Everyone in the room willed Julian to bring the bellicose and arrogant Inspector to his knees but it was by no means a foregone conclusion. Hanaho was a tough and resilient opponent even for someone as accomplished as Julian Singleton.

It was clear that Inspector Hanaho was enjoying himself as he pulled one box after the other from its hiding place and inspected the content. In most instances he removed a bottle and unscrewed the cap or pulled the cork before pouring the precious liquid down the plug-hole. Julian sat on the bench seat, head in his hands looking miserable.

"Look Inspector, surely there is something we can do here! I have tied every penny I have in this gear and I can't afford for you to pour it all down the plug hole. I'm already in hock for the boat and I have two little'uns at home."

"Perhaps you should have thought about that before you got involved in smuggling." Replied the hard hearted Inspector as he reached under the seats and removed several cartons of cigarettes. "Ah, now these I would happily take off your hands Mr. Braithwaite."

Sensing an opening Julian played his cards carefully. “Look Inspector, I don’t want any trouble, I’m sure we can come to some arrangement. Just tell me what you want.”

“How much did you pay for this little lot?” Hanaho’s body language softened just a smidgeon and I guessed he was thinking how he could best profit from the encounter.

“I paid in Dutch Guilders, so it’s hard to be precise but about three hundred quid.”

“Must be worth what, eight hundred on the black market?”

“It might have been before you poured that whisky down the sink! Yes, well something close to £800 maybe.”

“And how often do you make the trip?”

Julian looked askance, and muttered his reply. “I’ve never done this sort of thing before. It’s just that we needed the money. It was a one-off.”

“You’re lying Mark and that means no deal. Looks like we’ll have to impound your boat and confiscate the booty after all.” With that the Inspector turned toward the steps and without looking over his shoulder added. “I’ll be back with a warrant.”

“No, please Inspector...I’ll do whatever I have to but don’t impound the boat for god’s sake. I’ve nothing else!” There was panic in Julian’s voice and I could not help but admire his acting skills as the Shakespearean tragedy continued to unfold before our eyes. Margaret whispered in my ear. “Hanaho is going in for the kill now. He has Julian on the ropes. What an actor that Julian is, he should be on stage!”

Sure enough Hanaho turned around and faced Julian. "You wanna cut a deal Mark?"

"Yes, I'll do whatever's necessary Inspector but don't cripple me please, I have a family to support."

"Sit down and listen. I need you to understand a few basic rules about cutting a deal with Inspector Hanaho. You don't mess with me. You do as I say, when I say it. And you talk to no-one. Do I make myself clear?"

"Yes, yes Inspector, of course."

"Good, I like *regular* business Mark and if you scratch my back I'll scratch yours. Two hundred pounds cash per trip is my terms. For that I will keep the dockyard police and the customs off your back. Does that sound fair enough?"

"Two hundred quid! That's daylight robbery!" Julian blurted out.

"Unfortunate terminology don't you think? I am not sure you have fully come to terms with my rules, Mr. Braithwaite! My revised terms are two hundred and fifty pounds!"

"Alright, alright…just tell me what I do." Julian's face was a picture of misery.

"Right, first thing is that I need the deeds to your boat as collateral and a non-refundable deposit of, let us say, £100 which secures your free passage today. Don't ever cross me Mark or I will issue a warrant for your arrest for the smuggling of contraband before you can say Jack Robinson."

Julian looked about to argue the toss but Hanaho put a hand up to discourage further discussion and continued. "Think before you speak Mark; remember it's always best to accept my first offer." With that Inspector Hanaho sat down, smirked and removed half a dozen packs of John Player's from a box at his feet and stuffed them in his pockets. "Oh, I think I'll take these just to cement our partnership. The deeds and the money please, my friend."

With that, Julian made a charade of opening the safe and withdrawing the deeds and the cash which he carefully counted and passed note by note to the Inspector and for the benefit of the camera added. "Right, Inspector here's your £100 in lieu of services as agreed. In return you agree to make sure I get a free run in and out of the harbour and you keep the customs and the dockyard police off my back. Yes?"

"A deal and thank you Mark, I think that concludes our business for the day." replied the policeman making ready to leave.

"Not quite, Inspector there is something else I want to show you before you go." As Julian turned toward us he gave a theatrical wink and pulled out two Newspaper proofs which Simon Griffin had produced for him and placed them face-up on table. "Perhaps you would care to caste your eye over these Inspector and tell me which you think is more appropriate for this evening's edition of the Portsmouth News?"

It was a sweet moment as the Inspector took in what was laid in front of him. 'Shock' comes nowhere near to adequately describing his reaction. He twitched violently and looked around the cabin as though hunting down an annoying fly. His brain seemed to take in what he had read but could not quite make sense of it. This was our cue to enter the fray and incredibly I almost felt sorry for the loathsome Inspector as he turned an ashen shade of grey. He fumbled desperately for words as Julian calmly began his explanation:

"Everything you have said this morning Inspector was recorded using the highest quality sound and vision equipment supplied by His Majesty's Government. Furthermore, just in case you harbour hope that this evidence may be inadmissible in court we have a file this thick with surveillance photographs and witness statements cataloguing your practice of extorting money and accepting bribes as well as your failure to follow procedure and comply with regulations." With that Julian threw a thick pocket wallet crammed full of papers on the table. "Shall I go on Inspector, because this is just the tip of the iceberg and there is plenty more where this came from?"

Quite suddenly the mood changed and Hanaho tried to re-assert his authority by grabbing Julian by the lapels and shaking him violently. "You won't get away with this." And then it was as though a light bulb was switched on in his brain. "Christ I know who you are! You're that bloody investigator, Singleton, aren't you? I've got friends in high places and I promise you that you will regret having crossed me."

But Julian was in no mood to be cowed and before either of the policemen from the Met could intervene he levered Hanaho's hands from his coat and pushed him firmly back into his seat. "That is good Inspector I look forward to meeting your friends. Now please listen carefully, I want you to be thinking straight. We have enough evidence against you to put you away for a very long time but as you were prepared to cut a deal with me so I am prepared to cut a deal with you."

I had read somewhere that as a defense mechanism in cases of extreme anxiety, the brain, shuts down certain of its functions. It happened in war and provided the mental condition under which soldiers in the trenches were able to charge into no-mans-land to face almost certain death from enemy machine gun fire. To me, Hanaho looked as though he'd reached that point. He was totally oblivious to his surroundings and focused all his attention on Julian, with murder in his eyes. The Inspector had been top dog for such a long time his swagger had become permanent and his fall from grace so sudden and unexpected that his brain was simply unable to cope.

In contrast Julian was the personification of calm. “Inspector, you have a choice: either you can resign your position, with immediate effect and take a long vacation abroad, or you face the immediate consequences of your actions and we publish a full expose in the Evening News. This will include a transcript from this morning’s conversation when you attempted to extort money from me (or should I say Mr. Braithwaite) as well as photographs of the money changing hands. If, on the other hand you choose to resign there will be a small article which describes your resignation as ‘unexpected’ but leaves your reputation intact. A courtesy you do not deserve, I might add but one we are prepared to offer so long as we neither hear from you, nor see you until our work in Portsmouth has come to an end.”

“Resign? You seriously underestimate me Singleton! You will not force my hand!” Hanaho shouted as he stood and walked toward the steps.

“Before you go Inspector please would you empty your pockets? I believe you have the deeds of the Fair Isabella, £100 and half dozen packets of cigarettes that don’t belong to you. And perhaps you’d care to take this with you; it’s a copy of your resignation letter. Sign it and hand it in at the front desk of the Portsmouth News by midday and we won’t publish. You’ve been a policeman for twenty years so you don’t need me to spell out the consequences for you if you don’t. Good morning to you Inspector.”

It was a dramatic end to the morning as Inspector Hanaho heaved himself up the steps and stalked away hurling abuse at us all as he went. But had Julian’s bid to dislodge the Inspector failed I wondered. If Hanaho was true to his word, resignation was the last thing on his mind. But the look on Julian’s face and the confidence in his voice suggested he had no such qualms.

“Well I thought that went well except for the sacrilege of pouring all that claret and whisky down the drain. The man’s a heathen as well as a first class bully!”

“It looks rather like the Inspector does not intend to play ball though, doesn’t it?” The solicitor Simon Williams said, following my line of thought.

“Inspector Hanaho will come to his senses before the deadline. He has far too much to lose, I guarantee it.” Countered Julian confidently.

“I hope you are wrong Julian! I’d love to run that story. It makes my blood boil to think he might get away with this.” Simon Griffin retorted angrily.

“He’ll get his comeuppance in this life or the next, don’t you worry about that.” Julian offered in consolation.

Thirty Nine

Julian and I spent the rest of the morning outside the Bridge Tavern anxiously sipping beer awaiting news. Well at least I was anxious and sipping; Julian was his normal self, unperturbed, gulping and apparently without a care in the world. But with confirmation of the Inspector's resignation even the enigmatic Julian managed a whoop of delight and he immediately got to work organising a party of celebration which started before the sun went down and continued until the early hours. Luke paid up on his bet and with it, the stock of Julian Singleton rose still further. He had an uncanny knack of making the right call whilst those around him floundered in indecision. It was an emotionally charged night and one that I was never to forget. For us it was the last of its kind.

Inspector Jack Hanaho had signed his resignation letter and left a copy at the head office of the Portsmouth Evening News in Commercial Road a few minute before the midday deadline as Julian had predicted, so Simon Griffin's hopes of an expose were dashed. I never saw the Inspector alive again but the ramifications of his relinquishing the reins took on a momentum of their own. In one sense at least his resignation had the desired effect of flushing out our enemy. They came alright, hunting retribution which was both swift and brutal.

When I awoke the next morning my head told the story of the evening's revelries and my first stop was the bathroom cabinet to locate some aspirin. Lucy was still away but I did not have the house to myself as I had given a spare room over to Julian who had decided against rolling up drunk at his B&B and suffering the wrath of his puritanical landlady. Despite his state of intoxication and the lateness of the hour when we finally fell into our beds, he insisted I was to wake him at 7am, leaving only four hours of sleep to recharge our depleted batteries. After a bath, a shave and a restorative coffee I dutifully climbed the stairs to the third floor and knocked sharply his door.

I received no immediate response but that hardly came as a surprise. "Come on Julian, it's after seven." I shouted through the door. Still nothing, so I turned the handle and pushed the door open to find the room empty. Puzzled, I had just turned to leave when I noticed a scribbled note propped up on the bedside cabinet. In typical style, Julian left me wondering:

'Sorry old chum had to dash, something rather urgent. Will call, Jules.'

True to his word the telephone rang before I'd even made it to the bottom of the stairs and Julian's voice boomed from the earpiece reminding me of the delicate state of my head. I was summoned to drive up to the Meon Valley forthwith, picking Luke up en route to Bay Tree House. I pulled a road atlas from a kitchen draw and was driving out of Southsea by 7.30 towards Luke's Milton flat.

"What's all this about William?" Luke asked a few minutes later as he lowered himself into the front passenger seat of the Sunbeam.

"I really have no idea." I replied. "But you know Julian, always one for the unexpected!"

Bay Tree House was a large, modern detached residence set in a half acre of garden. I pulled the car into the drive and stopped alongside a conservatory style extension which housed the billiard room. There were two police cars in the drive and a number of uniformed officers milling around which told me that we had been summoned to crime scene.

Julian rounded on us as we stepped out of the car. "Follow me. I hope you have strong stomachs." Julian said as he led us through the front door. "Brace yourself, it's not a pretty sight." And with that we were shown into a study where slumped forward on the desk was the body of Jack Hanaho with half his brains blown away. A gun was still in his hand.

"My god." Luke whispered. "Suicide?"

"Not much doubt. His wife heard shots just after midnight and this is what she found." The Inspector in charge cut-in.

"I didn't even know Hanaho was married. Surely this wasn't his house? He lived in a flat in Old Portsmouth, didn't he?" I asked, puffing out my cheeks in an attempt to purge myself of the gory image in front of me.

"He did indeed own a flat in Old Portsmouth, as well as a substantial town house in Mayfair and of course this place here, plus I have discovered a substantial property portfolio abroad. He was a wealthy man. On a policeman's salary, it doesn't really add-up does it? But then that hardly comes as a great shock." Julian said.

"I wonder why he bothered to resign only to shoot himself a few hours later." I mused.

Julian gave an imperceptible shake of the head, meant clearly for my eyes only and very quietly whispered. "It wasn't suicide. Hanaho was murdered." He then added in a louder voice, for general consumption. "He probably came home last night and considered his options and didn't like what he saw. He'd presumably got used to the high life which would have come to an abrupt end without the perks of the job. Did he really think he'd get away with this forever? I suppose we'll never know."

Then turning back to Luke and me, he said. "Anyway, gentlemen I didn't invite you over here just for you to witness the sad end of Inspector Hanaho. Let's find a suitable place to talk. The events of the last twenty-four hours will have repercussions and we need to prepare. William?" Julian asked looking in my direction. "How about the Seven Stars at Petersfield, I am sure they can rustle-up some coffee to keep us awake."

An hour later, strong coffee to hand Julian for once looked serious. “It’s hard to feel too much sympathy for a man like Hanaho and I won’t pretend that I’ll lose any sleep over his demise but nonetheless his passing is a set-back. If there was one person who knew the identity of the elusive professor and John McDermott then it was the Inspector.”

“What makes you think Hanaho was murdered?” I asked when we were safely out of earshot in the farthest corner of the bar.

“Well if he wasn’t it was a mighty elaborate suicide! He was shot twice through the head; the first through the side of the head the second through the mouth…to make it look like suicide. They will figure it out sooner or later of course but I am quite happy with a suicide verdict for the time being. Hanaho became a lame duck the minute he handed in his resignation and his ‘employers’ had no further use for him.”

“But why kill him?” Luke asked.

“These people are ruthless and the minute Hanaho lost his job he became a risk. The simplest way to eradicate the risk was to kill him. I am afraid it’s really that simple.

So gentlemen, we have Hanaho dead, we have a fairly good understanding of how the frauds were perpetrated, we know the professor had Stanley Jakes killed to prevent him derailing his plans, we surmise that Billy Cosgrove was framed to suppress any further investigations into the murder of Jakes but we still do not know the identities of either the professor or of John McDermott. And just to add to the puzzle you have been assaulted twice William and we’ve had Sam Smith murdered in the belief she was your girlfriend.

But it begs the question, why William, were you spared? These people are ruthless killers, we know that and yet twice you were apparently at their mercy and got away with a warning. Why? Were you just lucky or is there more to it?"

"What are you suggesting?" I asked, although it was a question that I had wrestled with for weeks.

"Humour me for a minute. Just suppose Sir Marcus is the professor. He's known you for years and you were even engaged to his daughter. You are almost family. He can't quite bring himself to kill you so what does he do?"

"He threatens him I suppose." Luke answered.

"Well its possible isn't it? It's a working theory at least." Julian postulated looking at me.

"I don't know about that." I answered noncommittally.

"Well, why not? You admitted to me you had a good relationship with the family."

"Well yes but I can't see Sir Marcus …." I trailed off.

"Wouldn't it be the perfect crime? Sir Marcus points John McDermott at Eric Rowe the feeble minded Finance Director because he knows he's losing his judgement and when Benison steps in, Sir Marcus is presented with the perfect alibi. His company wins the contract and he shares the profit from the fraud with his partner in crime, John McDermott. And if ever he is questioned he pleads ignorance and Benison and Buridge carry the can."

"But Sir Marcus is a rich man. Why would he want to do it?"

"Greed, William, greed! I've yet to meet a poor man who doesn't want to be rich or a rich man who does not want to be richer still. It's sometimes referred to as human nature." replied Julian.

I hoped that Julian was wrong as I did not want to see the family that I had come to know so well over twelve years pulled apart but it was hard to suppress my inner doubts and Julian had an unerring ability to pick-out the wood from the trees. Was it my imagination or had Sir Marcus's behavior been even more erratic than usual of late? Was his attempt to suspend me from the audit team in character or did it smack, just a little, of desperation? I thought back further to many after dinner conversations I had had with Sir Marcus and to his robust defense of the local constabulary. I knew that Sir Marcus counted Chief Superintendent Nigel Parker amongst his personal friends but could this have been more than just friendship? The more I thought the more uncomfortable I became.

"We'll come back to Sir Marcus in a minute. Tell me William what else have we got on John McDermott? What of his accent? Was he a genuine American?"

"We've not got a lot to go on certainly. I found no trace of Landseer from any of my contacts in the States, or John McDermott for that matter but there's no surprise there. I have traced the property agent which let the office near Old Street to Landseer and I'll be following that up. As for McDermott's American accent, well, neither Benison nor Buridge questioned it but I can't vouch for their credentials as experts in the dialects of America's Mid-West."

Julian looked thoughtful, leaned forward in his chair and addressed us in a conspiratorial whisper. "We are closing in on our target gentlemen but we must take extra care. If Inspector Hanaho was the means by which our gang had been able to operate outside the law who knows what they may unleash now in revenge. I would like you to keep Lucy out of the city if possible William and for you both to be extra vigilante. We could well be in for a rough ride.

William, I also need you to keep the pressure on Sir Marcus and the two accountants. Make them feel uncomfortable. If they are hiding something this will at the very least make them sweat. I want you to keep looking for Billy Cosgrove. Not that I expect you to find him but I don't want our enemy to know that."

Slowly the meeting wound down and we agreed to meet up again the following week. The three of us all had plenty on our plates so were happy to make a move.

As I drove back home I decided on a detour to Liongate for my long overdue confrontation with 'my father'. It was a meeting I was not looking forward to and hence had avoided for far too long. I dropped Luke off in Southsea centre and headed-off toward the seafront and parked the car outside the six foot high brick wall which sealed-off Liongate from the outside world. I mentally steeled myself, walked through garden under the shade of the old cedar and up the stairs to the front door where I rang the doorbell.

Sir Edward was working in his study and greeted me with a smile and a formal handshake. I could not help but be aware that my erstwhile father had showed distinct signs of warming toward me in recent months. Always so cold and aloof as I grew up he had genuinely thawed since he had met his new wife Elizabeth. But I pushed aside any personal feelings which may have side-tracked my ambitions and launched in. "I was in France last week visiting my mother's family and as you can well imagine I got a few surprises. Would you like to explain why you chose not to tell me the truth about my past?"

Sir Edward slumped down on his chair. Although I was sure it was hardly a total surprise he nevertheless had the good grace to look contrite. "Alright William, take a seat and we'll talk."

I sat on the same sofa I had all those years ago when I had had the letter from my mother torn from my grasp. Sir Edward looked a different man now, somehow smaller, almost vulnerable and far from the austere and frightening figure he presented when I was younger. But he was far too shrewd a man not to have anticipated the possibility of this meeting and therefore I guessed he had a rehearsed speech tucked away in his locker.

After a sip of coffee from the cup on his desk, he started to talk. "I met your mother just after the Great War in Paris where she worked as a nurse in a British Military Hospital. Catherine was kind and beautiful, a seductive combination especially in the aftermath of war and I was one of a number of would-be suitors who fell madly in love with her. But unfortunately for me she chose another. Your real father as you now know was a gallant and dashing young Major in the Flying Corp, Geoffrey Barrington-Hope; a flying ace and a decorated war hero, it was not hard to see why your mother fell in love with him.

Later that year my own mother died and I came home to Liongate to take over the reins here and heard very little from your mother or the Major for the next year or so. But out of the blue your father contacted me again in the summer of 1920 asking for my help in securing a position for him as he wished to return to England. He was a charismatic and able man even with one arm so it was easy for me to find him a suitable job. Sopwith's were delighted to have him on board and your mother and father moved into a house in the New Forest later the same year. We met-up on occasions and I remember how very happy your mother was when you and your sister were born. She had all she wanted, a dashing husband, two beautiful children and a lovely cottage in the Forest.

We had only just had our first telephone installed when I received a call from your mother to tell me that the Major had been killed in a flying accident. She was devastated, of course but I still loved your mother and did what I could to comfort her. She was inconsolable and it was only you children who kept her alive. I am convinced it was the shock of your father's death that eventually killed her.

When the cancer took hold I married your mother and cared for her during her last weeks. It was her wish that you be educated and brought up in England and I gave her my word I would treat you as my own son. I know that I was not a good father to you William but sadly it's far too late for me to put that right. And that's about the gist of it. Claudine your sister went back to France and was looked after by her aunt and uncle."

"But I had a right to know! My sister was waiting for me in France and you kept the truth from me! Why? I still do not understand." I tried to control my temper but I wanted to scream at this man who had robbed me of my childhood and then he robbed me all over again as a young adult. I wanted answers but there were none. No answers, just excuses.

Sir Edward attempted to justify his behaviour by telling me that he had done it for my benefit and that he was protecting me from the pain of losing a mother and father at such a young age but I was in no mood to listen and my emotions got the better of me. All the anger and bitterness which had formed over the years came out as I railed against all the injustices I had suffered at his hands.

When I finally walked out of Liongate I wondered if I would ever return. There was nothing left for me there but sad and painful memories. I felt betrayed and mistreated by the man in whose hands my mother had placed her trust. I came home to an empty house and wished that Lucy had been there to offer her calm counsel and sooth my shredded nerves.

Forty

I arrived home to a note from Beverly Traegust the Naval Dockyard archivist asking me to call her. Glad of an excuse to keep myself occupied I telephoned to find that the dedicated Beverly was still at her desk even though it was past knocking-off time on Saturday afternoon.

"Mr. Goldhawk, thank you for calling me back I have a couple of names for you. You could try Oswald Davis who was a midshipman aboard the HMS Exeter. I can see from his file that he was an electrician by trade so if Billy did end up on board he may well have run into him. Or there is Samuel Baldwin, a rating who lived in Southsea not too far from Billy's home in Jessie Road. Is it just possible that they had known each other before the war?"

Still seething with indignity following my rendezvous at Liongate I needed something practical to get me out of the house so grabbed a notepad and pen and headed straight for the door. I had no luck with Samuel Baldwin who had, I learnt from his wife, since joined the merchant navy and was away at sea so I made my way down to the Hard to catch the ferry across to Gosport.

Oswald Davis lived within a stone's throw of the ferry terminal and after accepting directions from the local newsagent I was soon rapping on the door of his terraced house. Mrs. Davis tried hard to put me off and it took all my powers of persuasion to get me through the front door but eventually, after promising not to keep him too long I was shown into the sitting room. It soon became apparent why she wanted to protect her husband's privacy.

The disfigurement of his face was quite terrible to behold. One side of his head was a mass of scar tissue, raw, pink and ugly. The fact that the left side of his face was almost untouched served only to parody the grotesque nature of his injuries. His clothes covered the full extent of the damage but it was easy to imagine that his life was consumed by the physical and mental pain of the injuries he suffered.

His attractive wife Sylvia explained that Oswald had received his disfiguring burns on board the Exeter at the Battle of the River Plate when the engine room exploded after receiving a direct hit from the German battleship, The Admiral Graf Spee. "Oswald had been left for dead but made a miraculous recovery. The pain never goes away though Mr. Goldhawk. He lives with it day and night."

I felt immediately guilty bringing my seemingly trivial questions with me but the expression on both their faces betrayed a willingness to help. Although they had seemingly been abandoned by God there was defiance in their eyes which suggested they were far from defeated. Once we got talking I realised that like me earlier the same morning, they were only too glad of a distraction to take them away from their own struggles, even if it was just for a short time.

"Mr. Davis, I understand that the Exeter had electrical problems and that was the reason she docked at Portsmouth before sailing off to the South Atlantic?" I asked first, looking for confirmation of what I had been told by Beverly Traegust.

"Well yes." Oswald Davis rasped slowly in a whisper. "The whole ship was dogged by electrical faults from day one. She was laid down in the 1920's and they made a mess of her wiring. One night I remember in particular we were in convoy in the Atlantic keeping lights low to avoid being spotted by enemy aircraft and all of a sudden the whole ship lit up like a bloody Christmas tree. You know we never really did get to the bottom of the problem but I spent every minute of every day painstakingly checking and replacing the wiring."

"Do you remember any 'dockyard mateys' coming aboard at Portsmouth to help out with the electrics?"

“Thing is Sir, there were always people milling around doing this and that and you never really took a lot of notice. And the navy boys didn’t have a lot to do with the civilians anyway. There were a few ‘mateys’ on board I recall but I never got to know ‘em. Sorry I can’t be of more help.”

“Do the names Pritchard, Brown, Armstrong or O’Reilly mean anything to you?” I asked without much hope.

“Actually I do remember William Brown and Terry Pritchard but only because they were killed on the River Plate and the names of all the dead are etched in my mind. They are just names though; I can’t remember them as living people.” A wistfulness came into the voice of Oswald Davis as he went back in his mind to the fateful day.

“We were in the River Plate estuary off Argentina chasing this German battleship and I was down in the engine room when the first shell struck. Next thing I remember is looking around to see a ball of fire coming straight at us down the corridor. There were ten of us down there that morning and we didn’t stand a chance really. It was a miracle that I got out with my life. I wedged myself between two pillars and somehow it kept me alive.”

Sylvia clearly wanted to shake her husband from his thoughts so asked me about Billy Cosgrove and the reason that I was trying to track him down. I explained as best I could without mentioning murder or intrigue but Mr. and Mrs. Davis were avid readers of the local press and were not easily fobbed off. I was interrogated to a depth that I had hardly anticipated and when I finally finished my explanation Sylvia turned to her husband.

“What about that young lad you wrote to be me about Oswald? The one who you said should have been on the stage? You know!”

“Oh yes, Joey! You know I’d forgotten all about Joey!”

My ears immediately pricked-up. “Who was that? Tell me about him Oswald.”

“Yes, Joey. Young Joey. He was an electrician. I dunno where he came from but he was a civilian. He may have come aboard when we docked in Portsmouth.”

“What did he look like Oswald?” I asked, my pulse starting to rise.

“He was a good looking lad. Tall, strong, straw coloured hair I seem to recall. He was always telling stories about this and that and making people laugh. He was good for moral.”

“What sort of stories did he tell?”

“Mostly funny stuff. Impersonating the Marx bothers’ and Laurel and Hardy! Everyone liked Joey. Yes, I’d forgotten all about young Joey!”

“He didn’t have a tattoo on his arm did he Oswald?” I asked holding my breath.

“Now you mention it, he did. Yes, I remember now. It was the Pompey sailor. He was a mad keen on Portsmouth football club.”

“My god that’s Billy!” My pulse rate was now through the roof. I pulled a very old and dog eared photograph of Billy and Lucy from my wallet. “Could this be Joey?”

Oswald took the photograph and peered at it closely. “I think that’s Joey. Yes, I do.”

“Tell me Oswald was Joey aboard the Exeter during the battle of the River Plate on the thirteenth of December 1939?”

“Oh yes, he was in the Atlantic with us. Of course I have no idea what happened after that. I was transferred to the Ajax and then to an American ship and ended-up in hospital in Los Angeles before being shipped home in '45. So Joey was Billy Cosgrove. Well, well that's quite something isn't it Sylvia?"

So Billy Cosgrove's body was not dragged from Prinsted Harbour in the autumn of '39 after all. Could he still be alive? A tantalising possibility.

"Do you know if Billy survived the battle?"

"Well yes I am sure he did. He was nowhere near the engine room. As far as I remember he was helping the gunners so he was not likely to have been in any danger unless he was very unlucky and hit by a stray bullet. And anyway he wasn't on the casualty list, I'd have remembered."

"So what happened to the Exeter after the Battle of the River Plate, Oswald?"

"She limped into Port Stanley where she underwent emergency repairs before returning to Devonport for full repairs and then she was back on convoy duty. She was finally lost in the Java Seas where she was sunk by the Japanese in '42."

"Is it possible that Billy was still on the Exeter when she was sunk?"

"I couldn't tell you that, Sir. It's certainly possible. If you haven't heard anything from him since before the war....well, it's hard to be optimistic. Not many of my comrades returned Mr. Goldhawk." By now Oswald Davis was showing signs of distress, his breathing laboured and his brow sweating. Sylvia looked at me anxiously which I took as my cue to leave. I could not help but admire this brave couple who offered such an example of human fortitude in the face of extreme adversity.

I walked back to the ferry terminal with a new energy and determination to track Billy down. The logical part of my mind tried and failed to assert itself. William, it said, even if what Oswald told me was correct and Billy survived the Battle of the River Plate he probably perished during the six years of hostility which followed. But the cerebral portion of my brain would have none of it and was desperate to believe that Billy was still alive. I resolved to find out, one way or the other and also to keep my discovery to myself, as giving hope to Lucy would only serve to hand her a new and unnecessary anxiety.

The other question which seared into my brain concerned the body found in Prinsted Harbour. Was it from the German submarine after all? And what of Sebastian Harris had he purposefully misled me? Surely not but where did Billy's watch come from? Perhaps it was another elaborate attempt by the professor to throw us off the track. If Billy was *assumed* dead it would serve the same purpose as if he was *actually* dead. His guilt would have been taken for granted and further investigation into the murder of Jakes called-off.

Forty One

Perhaps it was because my mind was too engrossed trying to work out my next move that I failed to spot the tell-tale signs at my backdoor. Too absorbed in thought to notice the shadow cast by my assailant as I fumbled my door key into the lock. He hit me hard, very hard I discovered when I came around a short while later laying on the floor of my front room. To say my head ached, came nowhere near doing justice to the throbbing pain which exploded behind my eyes. Alongside the pain came the stomach cramps and the nausea as I wretched and groaned, spitting out blood and bile and gasping for breath.

I wanted to close my eyes and slip back into the sanctuary of unconsciousness but instead my vision slowly cleared and the familiar setting of my sitting room swam into focus. Bound and trussed like a Christmas turkey it was all I could do to rock onto my back in a futile attempt to make myself more comfortable. But all I managed was to bring forward a fresh wave of nausea.

It was not until he spoke that I became aware of the man sitting in the corner of the room.

“Your whisky is good! I would have asked before helping myself but you were somewhat indisposed. I hope you will excuse the liberty?” It was a heavily accented voice.

With that the man rose from his chair, grabbed me by the lapels and hauled me into a sitting position. Although shot through by a further spasm of pain it felt better sitting and the nausea started to recede. Returning to his seat, the man picked-up his whisky before very deliberately pulling a long barrelled handgun from his coat pocket.

“Where’s Singleton?” He asked, pointing the gun at my head.

"Who are you?" I whispered hoarsely trying to ignore the potential of a bullet between the eyes.

"I think you know already who I represent. My employer does not take kindly to your interference and it is my job to deal with the problem. But let's not get ahead of ourselves. I asked you a question and I strongly advise you to answer. I repeat, where is Julian Singleton?"

"We've met before haven't we, Grigor?" The name, I invented but his Eastern European accent made him easily identifiable as the man who had hijacked my car at gunpoint earlier in the year. "I thought I recognised that ugly face and the stink of your garlic breath."

I got a size ten in the mid-drift for my troubles and hacked-up more blood in the resulting coughing spasm. Given my state of utter helplessness perhaps provocation was not the best tactic on offer but some inner demon had got hold of me and I did not feel like playing ball. "You are a tough man aren't you Grigor? How about picking on someone in a position to defend himself?"

Another hefty kick in the ribs and this time my assailant pushed the barrel of the gun into my face. "You think you can play games with me eh? I ask you one last time, where's Singleton?"

"Singleton you say? No, I am sorry Grigor I don't know anyone of that name. Is that the gun you used to kill Samantha Smith? Shooting a defenceless girl between the eyes from three feet, wow you are a tough guy aren't you Grigor? You are the shit on my shoes Grigor, no more." I whispered spitting more blood onto my Persian carpet.

Instead of the expected retaliation this time the man sat down and sipped his drink. "Very well William, we will play it your way. With or without your help I'll find Julian Singleton and I will kill him just as I will kill you. Once I have put a bullet in Singleton's head I will hunt down that girl of yours. My employer likes to have fun with the girls and once he's finished with her it will be my turn. Do you know what I like to do William?"

"You bastard! You lay a finger on Lucy and you're a dead man!" Game and first set to Grigor.

"I love you English! You are so predictable, always rushing to the aid of a damsel in distress! In my country women are not important. We use them only for having fun and for breeding." With that Grigor laughed and sat back in his chair with obvious satisfaction.

"So who sent you Grigor the Russian?"

"Yes, I am a proud Russian but I am not sure you are in a strong position to interrogate me. Maybe I tell you just before you die, we shall see. But I am getting bored William so if you have nothing to tell me…maybe it is time?" He waved the barrel of the gun in my direction.

With the prospect of a bullet getting closer my instinct to survive jolted into action. The best idea- the *only* idea- that came to me was to encourage my new friend to keep drinking. It would not take much of my best single malt to dull the brain so maybe, just maybe, too much Glenlivet would provide me with a chance to wriggle free somewhere along the line. With my options all but exhausted, it was worth a try.

"Look, before you do your worst how about sharing some of that whisky?" I rasped and to my surprise, Grigor pulled a tumbler from the drinks cabinet in the corner of the room, poured a large measure and handed it to me. Drinking was not easy with my hands tied but I managed to bring the glass to my lips and take a sip. The temptation was to down it in one but I figured my slim chances of survival depended on me keeping my wits.

“Thanks Grigor, perhaps we can be friends after all.” I said with heavy sarcasm. “So you want Singleton, eh?”

“No-one stands in our way. If they try we will eliminate them. It is very simple.”

“Perhaps I can help you after all. The truth is that Singleton is no friend of mine.”

My captor looked at me hard. “Talk to me.” His eyes looked hungry but distrustful.

“He’s a double crossing bastard. I took him as a friend but he stabbed me in the back!”

“Go on, my friend.” Grigor sat forward in his chair hardly able to contain the snarl in his voice. I knew how little red riding hood must have felt.

I made up some cock and bull story about how Julian and I had fallen out over a promotion at work and that although we worked together I had never really forgiven him. Most of the whisky in my glass had found its way into a pot plant on the hearth but I did my best to give the impression that it was the drink that was loosening my tongue. Grigor was amused but intent on discovering what he could before he left in search of Julian who was the prize scalp. I was no more than a means to an end as far as the Russian was concerned.

Another whisky surreptitiously disposed of and I began to slur my words. I hoped I was not over doing it. But as Grigor had already polished off a third of a bottle himself I doubted his judgement was at its best. My next task was to lead Grigor down the garden path away from Julian and Lucy in the hope that this would buy them enough time to escape his murderous attentions. As far as I knew Julian was still holed-up in his lodgings in Southsea but I pointed Grigor toward London and Julian’s favourite watering hole, the

George and Dragon in Clapham. Whether a sober Grigor would have seen through my subterfuge I am not sure but certainly a Grigor soaked in whisky seemed convinced.

Searching for something else to keep the conversation flowing, I asked Grigor the question which had perplexed Julian. "Why was I spared Grigor? You had me on the ropes and you let me go, why? You put a bullet in the head of a defenseless girl but not me. I can't imagine it's because you like me."

"Ah, xnmnk. The English are sentimental fools! But not the Russians! If we Russians were in charge there would be no sentiment." With that Grigor pointed the gun at my head and pretended to pull the trigger. I flinched and screwed my eyes shut and Grigor laughed.

"An Englishman you say?"

"His father was a good Russian exiled from his homeland and his mother an English whore! I am bored William and your whisky is sour." With that Grigor delved into a canvas bag at his feet and pulled out a reel of tape. Pulling a length he walked across the carpet toward me and firmly stuck it across my mouth. I was helpless to resist and sat back, heart pumping ferociously, waiting for the coup de gras.

It came but not as I had expected. Rather than the bullet Grigor carefully removed a syringe from his bag and stuck a needle in my arm.

"Courtesy of Xnmnk. It will take the pain away."

And so it did, temporarily at least. My next conscious thought was the sensation of being hoisted into an ambulance and watching two red fire engines furiously pumping out water in an attempt to control the raging fire which engulfed my house. I became dimly aware of lying in a hospital bed with an oxygen mask clamped to my face as I slipped in and out of consciousness with disconnected voices and the shadowy faces of doctors and nurses adjusting my apparatus and taking my blood pressure. And at some point too, watching another man (a policeman I thought) standing at the foot of my bed. I guessed he was speaking but I could make no sense of his words as I drifted back into a state of morphine induced oblivion.

It was Monday morning, 48 hours later before I fully regained consciousness and was able to piece together the events which had led to my current state of acute discomfort. My throat was raw, my breathing laboured and my head pounded as though it had lost a head butting contest with a double decker bus. But at least my mind had cleared and my memories had for the most part reconnected. A doctor sat on the side of the bed taking my pulse:

"You're a very lucky young man! I thought we may lose you when they bought you in but you've made remarkable progress. You'll find talking painful for a while yet, until your lungs heal but I'm hopeful you'll make a full recovery in time. How are you feeling?"

"Alright… considering!" I whispered between rasping breaths. "Bloody sore throat though, I could do with some water." I spoke with a hand on my chest as though this may somehow ease the pain from my scorched lungs.

"What happened, Doctor, besides the fact that my house was burnt to the ground and I was given a fearful whack on the head by a very hard object that is?"

"Clinically, you were admitted with minor burns to your hands, bruising to your arms and torso, severe smoke inhalation and as you rightly diagnosed a very nasty bang on the back of the head. It's not for me to talk to you about how it happened though, Mr. Goldhawk. I'll leave that to the police. Er and one other thing, you had a near lethal cocktail of very unusual drugs in your bloodstream."

By the afternoon I was feeling stronger and able to shuffle around the ward unaided and by early evening I was already foolhardy enough to be thinking of how best I could engineer a premature exit. Dr. Lee's insistence on a ten day convalescence break was an indulgence I had no intention of accepting and had my smoke damaged clothes not been tossed into the incinerator I would have already been on my way. With a dangerous Grigor, together with sore head and bruised ego after his failure to nail me, still on the loose my main concern was for Lucy and Julian. My brief lunchtime encounter with Chief Inspector Steven Clayton, the replacement for Hanaho left me worried. Hanaho may well have been 'bent' but Clayton was a witless individual and whilst I urged immediate action to locate the Russian assassin he was intent on charging me with insurance fraud for setting fire to my own house.

A little while later, sitting in blue hospital issue pyjamas, drumming my fingers on the arms of the chair in an empty day room, I thought about my latest lucky escape. Whereas I had previously been 'warned-off' on this occasion there no getting away from it, they meant me dead. As Julian had forecast, with the removal of Inspector Hanaho their patience had finally snapped. The rules of the game had shifted and the stakes risen.

I could only assume that my desperate attempt to encourage Grigor's drinking had saved my life. Surely, had he been sober he would not have let me off the hook so easily. I found out later that my curtain twitching neighbour Les had watched Grigor's escape and phoned the fire brigade. Thanks Les.

My thoughts were interrupted as the door swung open and I was delighted to see the familiar face of Julian Singleton sail into view and happier still to see Lucy following in his wake. "Glad to see you up and about William old boy!" Julian exclaimed as he pumped my hand enthusiastically before heartily clapping me on the back and causing me to erupt into a spasm of painful coughing.

With an equal measure of warmth but somewhat less exuberance Lucy embraced me. “Oh, William I wish you’d stuck to accountancy! You’ll get yourself killed one of these days. Look at you!” It was wonderful to have Lucy back in my arms and I could feel the sting of tears as my own tension evaporated in the emotion of our reunion. Pulling back and looking me in the eyes, Lucy then whispered solemnly. “They meant to kill you William. Please don’t let them take you. I’ve already lost a brother and I don’t want to lose you too.”

Julian listened with rapt attention as I explained the details of my encounter with Grigor and his face showed alarming signs of satisfaction. He gave me the strong impression that Grigor’s attentions were not totally unexpected and in fact the satisfactory culmination of a well laid plan. Feeling somewhat uneasy and trying to read his expression I gave a Julian a quizzical look.

“Why do I get the feeling you are holding something back Julian?”

He pulled a face and held up his hands in mock defeat. “Tell me William.” He asked as he removed his wallet from his inside jacket pocket and pulled out a photograph. “Is this by any chance Grigor?”

I nodded. “That’s Grigor.”

“Igor Vasilyev, KGB operative for the Russian Ministry of State Security and on the most wanted list of the CIA and MI6. He’s a very intelligent, well-educated and ruthless man. What brings Igor to Portsmouth I wonder and who’s he hooked up with?”

“You rattled their cage Julian and they didn’t like it. He’s certainly dangerous and you need to watch your back.” I warned, speaking slowly to avoid worsening the pain in my chest. “There’s something that Grigor, or I should say Igor said, Julian. He’d drunk some whisky and I was a dead man in his eyes so maybe his guard was down. He referred to his boss as shmick, or schimmick.

Russian I suppose and also that the man's father was a Russian patriot and his mother an 'English Whore'."

"Well, well we're making progress. I'll find a Russian translator and see if we can shed any light on this. Shmick, you say? The professor, John McDermott and now Igor Vasilyev....what's going on?" Julian whispered to himself. "Suddenly our British affair takes on an international flavour."

With that thought hanging in the air Julian diplomatically retired outside for a cigarette, giving Lucy and me some time alone together. But any chance of intimacy was dashed when the ward sister arrived with my medication and the best we could do was sit hand in hand as Lucy gave me a status report on the house which I was relieved to hear had withstood the flames better than I had expected.

Julian returned a few minutes later with a sizable box under his arm which he dropped on the chair next to my bed and announced that it was my bedside reading for the duration of my stay. The argument which ensued was testy but as I was in a minority of one I grudgingly accepted defeat and mentally prepared myself for a few more days of incarceration. My protestations which I delivered between bouts of uncontrollable coughing that I was in the rudest of health fell on deaf ears.

"I think we are missing something William, something obvious." Julian threw in. "We have information coming out of our ears and it's been sifted and analysed endlessly by the boffins but I'm not satisfied. Somewhere in this box is a clue, I am sure of it. And I want you to find it."

"Thanks Julian I thought I was on sick leave!" I complained.

Ignoring my plea Julian continued. "We are looking for connections. Is there something which connects Sir Marcus Crawford, a Russian assassin, the professor and Landseer

Consultants? It's a bit like looking for a virgin in a Parisian brothel…oh sorry, Lucy I mean a needle in a haystack. Piles and piles of paperwork but somewhere buried deep, is the answer. It's about statistics and probability."

I scratched my head trying to decipher Julian's baffling exposition on statistical probability when Lucy piped up. "So Julian, what you are saying is that somewhere in this box will be a clue to identifying a virgin in a Parisian brothel?"

"Not so much *identify,* as to offer the probability of finding a virgin in a Parisian brothel."

"You don't need statistical probability theory to establish that Julian!" Lucy countered, laughing.

"Alright, perhaps the Parisian brothel metaphor wasn't the best." Julian conceded before finishing, "The point is I have a strong hunch that we are staring the obvious in the face."

I agreed to take on the thankless task because, despite my protestations, I agreed with every word that Julian had said. It was only left to discuss a way to keep Lucy safe and out of reach of the Igor Vasilyev. After much hand wringing Lucy eventually agreed to hide out with my family in Picardy for the immediate future and I watched with a heavy heart as Julian escorted her out of the hospital to make arrangements for her exile.

Forty Two

Over the next three days I got stuck into the box that Julian had left which was painstaking work but every now and then something would crop-up to keep me interested. The banks, coerced into cooperating had provided financial information on individuals and companies under investigation and I was shocked to find Sir Edward Goldhawk high on Julian's suspect list. He had accumulated a fortune over twenty five years but it seemed there was little evidence of how he had acquired it, justification enough it seemed, for closer scrutiny.

As a child growing-up I had no reason to question my privileged upbringing nor the two gleaming Rolls-Royces parked in the garage. Although hardly a model father I went along with the consensus that, away from family life anyway he was a philanthropic and generous man, who went out of his way to help the poor and the disadvantaged. On one hand it seemed absurd that Sir Edward could be involved in murder and subterfuge on this level but then he had surprised me before and as I had learnt to my cost. He was a man with deep secrets.

I also learnt of the long standing personal relationship between Sir Edward and Sir Marcus Crawford who had been at Oxford together. My professional mentors, Brian Surtees and Douglas Lampson had also been up at Oxford during the same period just before the First World War, nothing suspicious in itself but nonetheless information I felt I should tuck away for future reference.

As the days drifted by my health returned and I became increasingly bored with the clerical task I had been set but even more by my confinement to a hospital ward. During the course of my stay I had endured the dubious pleasure of two more visits from the new Chief Inspector and it took all my powers of persuasion to convince the beak nosed policeman that my house fire was not an insurance scam. And I also failed completely in my bid to cajole him into releasing resources to track down Igor Vasilyev but at least, I concluded, Chief Inspector Clayton did not possess the guile to emulate the criminal activities of his infinitely more resourceful predecessor.

One morning I was sitting-up in bed, brooding and planning my escape when I received an unexpected break through. After months of hard graft in which the investigation had ebbed and flowed, something precious washed up with the tide. The break-through came in the guise of a visitor who was waiting for me in the day room. Glad for an interruption I scurried down the corridor and found a man of similar age to myself, who introduced himself as an old acquaintance of Billy Cosgrove. He was of medium stature with sharp features wearing an old, ill-fitting suit and I guessed that he had been recently de-mobbed from the armed services.

"Mr. Goldhawk?" he asked as he removed his cap from his head.

I nodded and the man went on. "I'm Frank Lewis, Oscar Davis told me you were making enquiries about Billy Cosgrove."

"If you have any information at all about Billy I would be glad to hear it Frank." I encouraged.

"Well, like Oscar says it doesn't seem too likely he's still alive or he'd have been in touch, wouldn't he? But I can tell you he did survive the Battle of the River Plate. The last I saw of him he was on the Falkland Islands."

"Tell me how you can be so sure it was Billy Cosgrove, Frank?" I asked hoping that he was not an opportunist looking for an easy way to earn a few shillings at my expense.

"I was in the Royal Navy for the duration and on the Exeter when she engaged with the Admiral Graf Spee in the estuary of the River Plate. I got to know Billy quite well. He was good lad and very popular with the crew. He had a way about him of relieving the tension when things were at their worst.

Billy wasn't what you'd call a hard drinker by any means but one night after a few beers he told me in confidence how he had been stitched-up and framed for a murder he didn't commit. He'd been smuggled aboard the Exeter to get him out the country."

With a few sentences Frank Lewis had talked me around. He had known Billy. "Did he tell you who was responsible?"

"No, he didn't tell me but *he* knew alright. Whoever it was put the fear of god into him and told him to keep away or they'd come after his family. Of course I didn't know him as Billy Cosgrove, he was Joey Duggan to me. He hadn't come aboard at the same time as the other dockyard workers but then the Exeter was always blowing fuses and so an extra electrician was a godsend. As far as I knew, there was never a question of him not being a legitimate member of the auxiliary staff. He had his papers and he was a good worker."

"So, as I understand it, after the battle the damaged ship limped to the Falkland's for repairs. And what next, Frank?"

"There were no dry docks in Port Stanley (at least large enough to take a cruiser the size of the Exeter) so it was just a question of getting her sea worthy before steaming back to Devonport for full repairs. Billy was a free agent and decided to sit out the duration in the Falklands. At least that is what I supposed. They were looking for men to work in the docks and as a British base there was nothing to stop him from staying on. It was a god forsaken hole really, unless you were a sheep! But then Billy had good reason to stay, didn't he?"

He did indeed, I thought. "So that was the last you saw of him?"

"I never saw or heard of Billy again. But if you want to find out what happened to him you might want to try a chap called O'Reilly, Patrick O'Reilly who was an Irish shipwright who became very friendly with Billy. He was originally from Dublin I think but ended up in the north of England somewhere. Liverpool, Manchester….I'm not sure. But I'm certain that Billy and O'Reilly stayed on the Island when the Exeter left for home just before the Christmas of 1939."

Billy Cosgrove had been alive and well albeit half way around the world at Christmas 1939 and had a compelling reason for staying away. I had believed Billy to be dead because I could see no logical explanation why he had not returned home after his arrest warrant had been withdrawn. But Frank had given me a reason, a reason to hope that maybe, just maybe Billy was still alive.

There was nothing that would keep me in hospital for a minute longer. I strode back to the ward, dressed and with a spring in my step walked out of the hospital without so much as a backward glance. Free at last I hailed a cab and set-off to find Beverly Traegust.

I felt fully rejuvenated as I strode through the Main Gate and into His Majesty's Dockyard toward the administration block to find Beverly and give her the news. After a double take from a surprised Miss Traegust which reminded me how gaunt I had become after my brush with Igor we got down to business.

"Follow me William and we'll see what we can find."

Working in silence Beverly pulled out ledger after ledger from the shelves before finally sighing and admitting defeat. "Nothing here I'm afraid William, on either Joey Duggan or Patrick O'Reilly. The next step is a cable to the Governor's office in Port Stanley. I'll probably get an answer in a few days. Where will you be staying?"

Disappointed but resigned I gave Beverly a phone number of the Grosvenor Hotel in London where I was to meet Julian that evening. After ten days incarceration I felt in need of some fresh air and although an unseasonably cold and blustery day I decided to walk back along the seafront and cut through central Southsea to Campbell Road and home. It was good to feel the wind in my hair and it gave me time to consider my options. Given the information I had received from Frank Lewis my inclination was to go in search of Billy but I still had no clue where to start looking and anyway needed to speak to Julian first.

One thing was certain, hanging around Southsea was an option to be avoided until such time as my friend Igor was off the streets. His details had been circulated to the police, airports and ports but given the fact that he had eluded British justice for ten years did not give me grounds for much optimism, particularly if Chief Inspector Clayton was representative of the quality of our law enforcement.

I was relieved to see that the builders had already begun work on my fire damaged house and reassured to see a pc plod outside keeping a guard. Whether police constable Bert Wilson would have had the wherewithal to deal with Igor Vasilyev I was more than a little doubtful but Lord be praised, I suppose I should have been thankful for small mercies! Having packed a bag I climbed the stairs to my study and made a withdrawal from my safe. The Berretta handgun went into my briefcase alongside a dozen rounds of live ammunition. No longer would William Goldhawk be a soft target. It was time to get serious.

In two minds about whether to take the car I eventually plumped for the train and made my way up Fawcett Road toward Fratton Station and the express to Waterloo. I arrived at the Grosvenor in the early evening to find Julian in the lobby awaiting my arrival in an excitable mood. Without even his usual enthusiastic handshake and slap on the back he launched in.

"You've caused quite a stir William after your encounter with Igor Vasilyev! His is a scalp Mi6 have long been after and the minister wants a chat with you tomorrow. Vasilyev only gets involved when the stakes are high and it's pretty clear now that the Russians have a serious involvement in our affair. We have been aware for some time that they've been grooming young undergraduates from Oxford and Cambridge Universities. They are mostly naïve young men and women with a social conscience who are seduced by the idea that the communists are freedom fighters battling against the tyranny of European fascism. Whereas for most it's a short term infatuation for a few it sows the seeds for something more sinister. In the most extreme cases defection and espionage.

It rather looks like the little local skirmish that we have uncovered is rather wider reaching than we at first thought. It's pretty clear that a good portion of the money stolen from the Admiralty has been syphoned off by the Russians with the help of local communist sympathisers. So, once again we return to the same question we've been wrestling with for the last three months; who is the professor? What have we learnt of the elusive godfather in these latest political shenanigans?

He's obviously an educated man and probably went to one of our top universities. He's almost certainly multi-lingual and likely to speak Russian amongst a host of other European languages. Igor talked of the professor having a Russian father and an 'English whore' as a mother but our boys don't think this should necessarily be taken as a literal translation. The Russians are apt to use parental metaphors and we don't necessarily believe that the professor was spawned from the loins of a Russian. More likely, we think, his defection was taken, figuratively as a rebirth and hence the idea of a Russian father.

When I started this investigation I assumed the motivation for the crime was greed but it seems I was wrong and in fact it was politically motivated. The professor has played out most of his adult life fighting in a war for the Russians against his homeland.

What sort of man does that? Someone with strong convictions for sure but more to the point someone twisted by fate; someone with a reason to hold a grudge against his own country. Surely we are looking for a man with a tortured past?

It seems more than likely that the professor holds down a responsible job and has a position of some status within the local community. For a long time I wondered if he may even be a Doctor after learning of the cocktail of drugs he used to induce Davenport into his hypnotic state, not to mention the drugs pumped into your system last week. A Doctor is usually above suspicion, a perfect cover. But unwittingly Igor Vasilyev has pointed us in another direction. Shimuck, William. My Russian pronunciation may leave a little to be desired but I think we know they call him 'the chemist'.

A strange nick-name don't you think? Even if you are a chemist by profession you would not usually be so called would you? So it begs the question does is not? I would guess that the man we call the professor has an unusually strong interest in drugs; possibly the sort that sell for high values on the black market.

So, we are looking for an educated man who probably works in a professional capacity and has a standing in the local community; possibly with a job or a background as a chemist. Likely to have shown early signs of 'left' leaning politics and probably a communist sympathiser. Involvement in the Spanish civil war would be consistent with the politics of our man and possibly even a conscientious objector during the Second World War."

"How would that fit?" I asked. "Surely, if he was anti-fascist he'd have no cause to object to us fighting the Nazis!"

"Strange, I know but the communist values are sometimes hard to fathom. The Marxists believe in the inevitable struggle and eventual triumph of the working man over the establishment and the Britain class system, supported by its government is every bit as pernicious to them as the politics of the Nazi Party."

"All this seems so far away from the disappearance of Billy Cosgrove! Can it really be connected?" I felt the investigation slipping further from my grasp and needed to bring the discussion back to my own experiences so I explained to Julian about my meeting with Frank Lewis.

Julian closed his eyes in thought. "You know William if our enemies had shown less interest in our search for Billy Cosgrove I'd be apt to see it as a side issue. But right from the start they made their displeasure at our enquiries abundantly clear. Why were they so keen that you did not pursue this particular line of enquiry?"

"Yes, that's pretty much what I thought. You know for the first time I'm beginning to believe that Billy may still be alive and if so, I am sure he holds the key. But if that is the case, Igor and his pals will be doing all they can to hunt him down before we get to him."

"That, William, in a nutshell if why I think you should make it your number one priority to find Billy Cosgrove. If he's alive find him! In the meantime I've got Luke and Margaret up here in London out of harm's way. It will be our job to trawl through all the information we've collected and narrow down our suspect list. The professor is in our grasp William, I'm sure of it." Julian's jaw was set in a determination I was unused to seeing in my normally enigmatic boss.

Before the evening was up I wanted to confront Julian about the pre-eminent position that Sir Edward Goldhawk occupied in his suspect list. It was strange but even after half a lifetime when my surrogate father and I had failed to connect on any level there was still some deep buried instinct in me to fight his corner. The truth was that despite everything, I did not want to believe the man who had made such a hash of bringing me up was capable of cold blooded murder.

"What's the basis of your suspicions about Sir Edward, Julian? I grant you my relationship with my ex father is at an all-time low but I can't see him as a killer."

"That must have come as something of a shock to you but Sir Edward's past is something of a closed book and given his wealth it makes him *de facto* a suspect but I hope we'll be able to rule him out soon enough. I wouldn't worry. I have purposely kept you out of the loop when it comes to Sir Edward but if you wish to volunteer any information which may be relevant please do. He wasn't a communist by any chance I suppose?"

That was about as tactful as Julian was likely to get and I declined to talk more on the subject except to say I had no cause to suspect 'my father' of anything more than being a bad parent. Despite Julian's reassuring words I was not completely convinced his suspicions were just down to Sir Edward's unexplained wealth. Something in Julian's demeanor suggested there was more to it. We left things at that and spent the rest of the evening sipping anxiously at our beer and trying to avoid any subject connected to our investigations. But the conversation about Sir Edward had in some way placed a barrier between us and unusually, in what had become a close friendship, our conversation dried up.

Before retiring to my room I made my way into the lobby to locate a telephone to call Lucy and was glad to find her in good spirits. Claudine was to pay the farm a visit the following weekend and I got the feeling it was by way of dipping a toe into the water before our first meeting. My aunt had brushed aside my anxiety at Claudine's reluctance to meet me by telling me that it was the lady's prerogative to take her own time. With plenty to occupy my own thoughts I said my goodnights to Lucy and went upstairs to bed.

Forty Three

The following morning I was met by Ernest Bannister and whisked off to the office of the Right Honorable Timothy Whitten in Pall-Mall. If I had ever been under the illusion that I was an important cog in the governmental machinery constructed to bring the Admiralty fraud to a satisfactory conclusion then I had been deluded. The parochial world in which I existed hardly registered on the radar of Timothy Whitten who was focused only on national security and the position of the UK Government on the world stage. My search for Billy Cosgrove seemed absurdly insignificant in the context of the political manoeuvring which he laid before me.

However, I was amused to realise that I had assumed something of a celebrity status as the only operative to have survived an encounter with Igor Vasilyev. My tactic, born from desperation, of encouraging the Russian to 'drink' had, somewhere along the line, been elevated to the status of a brilliant piece of operational field work. And who was I to disagree? But I was under no illusion that the real reason I had been summoned to the office that morning was to furnish my masters with every last detail I could bring to mind about Vasilyev. Everything else was bunting.

I felt more like a grubby and ill-informed street urchin than an Mi5 agent in the presence of the Undersecretary but I did my best to answer his questions with a modicum of authority and to make my search for Billy Cosgrove appear to be a logical extension to my work. Timothy Whitten was the personification of good manners and if he doubted my decision making he showed no sign. One thing I remember from my previous visit though was that superfluous chitchat was not *de rigeur* and within fifteen minutes of walking into his office I had been politely shown to the exit.

I returned to the Grosvenor Hotel to find a message waiting for me from Beverly Traegust asking me to call her and with no desire to spend a minute longer than necessary kicking-my-heals I made for the telephone kiosks in the lobby. On the third ring I heard the line click and the familiar voice of Miss Traegust on the other end.

"William, I have not heard from Port Stanley but I have some news which may help you. I've been doing a bit of digging. Joey Duggan was originally from Leytonstone in East London and was reported missing by his mother in August 1939. Now, according to the police interview Maureen Duggan, Joey's mother, claimed he'd been in and out of trouble as a lad and ended-up living rough on the streets but since that summer had dropped out of sight completely. A few months later, Mrs. Duggan herself was killed in an air raid and the file on her son closed.

It seems that Billy Cosgrove's ID card, apprenticeship debenture and passport were forged using Joey Duggan's identity. Who was responsible for the forgery or where they procured Joey's details from, heaven only knows. It seems likely that a desperate Joey sold his soul for a few shillings. He had probably never set foot in Portsmouth but according to the official records had a twelve-year service history as a dockyard electrician. Easy then for Billy to step into Joey's shoes. He just had to be himself in a work context but assume a new name and personal history which of course, he could pretty much make-up. There would be no one around to argue with him. None of that will help you trace Billy but I can also give you something on Patrick O'Reilly which may turn out to be more useful.

Patrick Seamus O'Reilly was, contrary to popular mythology originally from Belfast and not Dublin. He was nominally a Catholic but religion was not an important part of his life. When he turned eighteen he jumped on the nearest ship and steamed-off to Liverpool to seek his fame and fortune before finally rolling up on the other side of the Pennines in Yorkshire. According to his passport and identity papers, before the War he lived at 22 Pearson Grove, Hyde Park in Leeds."

"You are a marvel Beverly but how could you possibly know that religion was not an important part of Patrick O'Reilly's life?" I laughed.

"You are not the only detective around these parts, William Goldhawk! On his passport dated January 1936 he describes himself as Catholic and four years later on his ID card he claims 'no religious affiliation'."

"Ah, ah! Yes, good for you! A real amateur detective. Leeds it is then. I was rather hoping for a small town in the Home Counties but never mind, at least it gives me something to work on."

***

With the summer solstice fast approaching it was still daylight as I steamed into Leeds Station just after 9pm that evening. Leeds was a large industrial but relatively prosperous city, with an array of impressive shops and municipal buildings as well as its famous covered market. Grimy black with coal dust, the not unpleasant smell of coal hung in the air as your permanent companion.

My evening's destination was the Queen's Hotel just a hop, skip and a jump from the station. A young lad with a strong local accent helped me up the stairs with my meagre baggage before I offered him sixpence for his trouble. I felt genuinely relaxed as I contemplated a walk and perhaps a pint of frothy bitter at a local hostelry before the sun went down. My state of calm did not have time to ferment however, as I was hailed by the receptionist on my way down the stairs and given a message to call Julian Singleton as a matter of urgency. Instantly put on my guard I dialed the Grosvenor and was quickly put through.

"Bad news old chap. I'm afraid you have company in Yorkshire. Igor has been on your tail and persuaded Miss Traegust to spill the beans on your whereabouts. I suggest you check out of the Queen's and find a nice cosy Bed and Breakfast somewhere away from the crowds. The local police have been alerted and we'll be sending a couple of agents from London so there will be a reception party waiting for him but don't take anything for granted. He's dangerous William, as you well know so be on your guard."

'Bugger', that certainly put the mockers on my relaxing evening stroll. But I reckoned that the Russian must be, at a bare minimum, a couple of hours behind me so at least I had some time to find alternative accommodation. I repacked my bag and left the hotel with the intention of picking-up a cab outside the station. Headingley seemed as good a destination as any, with the cricket ground the only Leeds landmark that I recognised from my street map.

My taxi dropped me outside the Original Oak public house on Headingly Way opposite the junction with St Michael's Road. The Original Oak offered rooms but I wanted something further off the beaten track so wondered into the back streets of Headingley to see what I could find. Eventually a distinctly unappealing B&B caught my eye. The perfect hideaway I thought. Even if accompanied by a pack of bloodhounds with my scent in their nostrils I could not imagine Igor Vasilyev tracking me to the Rose in June.

Despite its cheery name it was a dark and dingy Victorian red brick property with but one virtue. It was indistinguishable from 100 other similar establishments dotted around the City of Leeds. I felt safe, at least until the following morning.

My sleep that night was punctuated by nightmares involving long barreled hand guns and murderous Russian assassins. As I came to the following morning I sincerely hoped that Igor had been intercepted by the local constabulary but needless to say he had not, as I discovered after making a telephone call to London. No sign of the elusive Igor Vasilyev anywhere. So it was with some trepidation that I stepped out onto the pavement and followed my map to Pearson Grove.

22 Pearson Grove, the last known address of Patrick Seamus O'Reilly, was only a short walk and I berated myself for not checking with Julian whether Beverly Traegust had shared that information with the Russian. Was I to expect the assassin to be waiting for me on the street corner? It was a risk I would have to take as I wound my way through the labyrinth of terraced streets in search of Pearson Grove. My fingers were tightly wrapped around the handgun in my pocket and I could not help but compare my small, toy-like Beretta to the gun of choice of Igor Vasilyev. In a gunfight at Pearson Grove I guessed my chances would be somewhere between slim and non-existent.

I brought my heart beat under control and knocked firmly on the door at number 22, a three story back to back terraced house. The man who opened the door was unshaven, bald and sported a string vest which could hardly have achieved less as a means of covering his huge belly. It was a warm day and already a sheen of sweat glistened on the man's forehead.

"Aye, what do'ou want?" He asked, clearly annoyed at the interruption to his morning.

"I'm looking for Patrick O'Reilly who used to live at this address just before the War. I wondered if you might know what became of him."

"Patrick O'bloody Reilly! You an' me both! If I ever catch that bastard I'll string 'im up. He put ma Gloria up t' duff and then fucked off without paying 'is rent. I'd skin the bugger alive if I ever laid my 'ands on 'im."

"When was that Mr.....?"

"The name's Brian Baker. It were ..." and with that the huge man turned his head and shouted. "Brenda, when did that bastard Patrick fuck off?"

With that, Brenda appeared trudging up the corridor. Hardly of model proportions herself, she looked diminutive next to her obese husband. "It were '39 just as War started weren't it?" She looked at me without expression or interest before slowly turning and walking back down the passage.

"Do you know what happened to him?" I asked.

"Brenda, luv." Brian called out again. "What 'appened t' bugger?"

Brenda came trudging back to us for a second time. "He join't Royal Navy didn't 'e, Brian. Sent Gloria a card from Malta or some such place."

Before Brenda had the chance to leave us again I asked if they knew whether O'Reilly had returned to Leeds after the War but I knew I was whistling in the wind. I sensed that the Bakers were going to give me nothing more. I asked whether they had heard of Joey Duggan but predictably they had not. The only morsel I prised from them was that Patrick O'Reilly favoured the Four Horseshoes as a drinking hole and that daughter Gloria lived in south Leeds. The only consolation I derived from the dismal doorstep interview was the anticipation of a probable meeting between Igor Vasilyev and the bovine Bakers. An occasion for which I dearly wished I could be a fly on the wall.

I would pay a visit to the Four Horseshoes that evening but my plan for the afternoon was a trip to Leeds Town Hall to see if I could track down Patrick O'Reilly or Joey Duggan through official channels. The Council maintained a register of rate payers and voters on the electoral roll which would cover most adults living within the City's boundaries. Without being particularly optimistic I knew I had to go through the motions, after all backing long-shots had got me this far. A very helpful Gordon Thompson walked me through the records and between us we came up with a handful of suspects dotted around the City. Shoe leather would likely be at a premium over the next few days.

With an hour or two to kill I decided to make a couple of house-calls en route back to Headingley in order to get a preview of what I had in store. The Duggan's of Bentley Lane had never heard of a Joey Duggan but nevertheless could not have been more accommodating; I shared tea, cakes and the life story of the Duggan family before retreating to the streets to walk-off the excesses of their hospitality. The Duggans' of Brewer Street on the other hand informed me in no uncertain terms to 'bugger-off back from where'st I'd come'. Either way, neither the Bentley Lane Duggans' nor the Brewer Street Duggans' had any connection with Joey.

It was when walking back through Meanwood later in the afternoon that I caught a glimpse of Igor Vasilyev and was forced into taking evasive action by diving through a draper's shop doorway and hiding behind a rack of curtains. On the good news front the fact that Igor was still roaming the streets of Leeds suggested that he had faired no better than I in running Billy Cosgrove to ground. But on the other side of the coin my job, already difficult enough would become nigh on impossible with the Russian so close on my heals.

The British weather came to my immediate rescue. The rain came tumbling from the sky and as shoppers took cover I pulled my collar up to my chin and darted out of the shop before walking briskly back toward my B & B. A phone call with Julian left me in no doubt how seriously London was taking Vasilyev's appearance in Leeds. Suddenly, finding Billy Cosgrove had assumed the highest priority. But were we all chasing our tails I wondered? My grounds for tracking Billy to Leeds were tentative but enough to alert Igor, who in turn had brought the Security Services scurrying up the spine of England. As I replaced the telephone hand-set onto its cradle another metaphor sprang to mind which included the words 'wild goose' and 'chase'.

My visit to the Four Horseshoes that evening proved fruitless but with a sting in the tail. I enjoyed the company, the darts (which I lost convincingly) and relaxed with a few pints of excellent Yorkshire ale. I had turned-up just after 8 o'clock and it had been laughingly easy to spot Perkins and Butler who sat self-consciously in the far corner of the bar sipping bitter shandies. The two agents wearing London issue tailored grey suits could not have offered more of a contrast to the rag-bag collection of men that made up the rest of the clientele of the public bar. At least it drew the focus away from me as I had struck up conversation with a boisterous group of darts players.

Before the beer had gone too far to impairing my judgment I had brought Joey Duggan and Patrick O'Reilly into the conversation by pulling photographs of the pair from my wallet. There were no takers, not a spark of recognition from anyone. I meticulously navigated the public bar, the lounge bar and the snug but in all cases was greeted by the same shake of the head. I played every card trying to jog memories but dispiritingly got nowhere. I finally admitting defeat as last orders were called and meandered out into the night to a near deserted Headingly Way.

Despite the disappointment the beer had kept me in good spirits. As I had walked slowly down the street humming to myself I remember feeling a little sorry for the two out of place agents, Perkins and Butler. While I had relaxed and shared a beer or two with the congenial locals the agents had sat all evening, stiff-backed and uncomfortable. At least, that was how I had felt until the light-bulb in my brain illuminated and I got an instant fix on reality. Until that moment I had assumed that Perkins and Butler were present at the Four Horse Shoes to protect me. But when the reality hit me, it fairly slapped me across the face and brought me out of my befuddled complacency.

I was bait. No more than a lure to catch Igor Vasilyev. Perkins and Butler did not drive 250 miles from the Capital to protect me! They came to catch the Russian. My drinking made me easy prey and I very quickly grasped what a fool I had been. It was a realisation that probably saved my life. Rather than blundering down the road appreciating the fragrant smell of roses in the warm summer evening I forced myself to keep my wits about me. And I needed to.

I gave myself a metaphorical slap across the face in an effort to re-focus and took a look around. A hundred yards back from where I had just come I saw the two agents walking swiftly and then start to run in my direction. Their body language, at first suggested anxiety and then panic as they gesticulated and shouted in my direction. That was more than enough for me. Instinct took over and I ducked onto my haunches and dived head-long into the recessed entrance of a shop long closed for the night. I was aware of the almost simultaneous crack of a fire arm and the smashing of glass behind me.

As I sat up and pushed my back into the doorway trying to keep out of sight I pulled the Berretta from my pocket. Although not really in a fit state to contribute to a gun fight I could hardly be seen cowering in a doorway when my associates were in the thick of the action. Peering around the side of the recess I could make out Vasilyev on the other side of the road crouched low behind a parked car. The streets were thankfully quiet and with the sound of gun fire the few people who had been loitering, quickly fled into the night. With Vasilyev focusing on Perkin and Butler I had for an instant, a clear shot and let off a round. The bullet ricocheted off the car and the Russian ducked out of sight.

Perkins shouted across the road in an attempt to persuade Vasilyev to surrender his fire arm but that was never likely to happen. The Russian, even with odds of three against one fancied his chances and cracked-off another couple of rounds in my direction. More glass shattered behind me and splinters of wood ripped from the door frame just above my head. Igor could shoot but that was no surprise. I was well out of my depth but decided I may just have a role in creating a nuisance whilst the real marksmen fought it out. So I kept plugging away hoping for a lucky shot.

It soon became something of a stalemate and the firing became sporadic. But from the corner of my eye I saw movement and watched with horror as a very drunk young man wandered into the line of fire. I shouted but too late. Igor jumped out from behind the car and grabbed the man around the neck pushing the barrel of his gun firmly into his temple. The man spluttered and waved his arms in protest but Igor was quickly in control and the man stilled.

"I want Goldhawk." Shouted Vasilyev in the direction of the agents. "Or your friend here is a dead man."

With that the man whimpered and I swore silently under my breath. Perkins and Butler were five of six doors down from me crouched low behind a garden wall and there was no chance of a quiet confab to discuss tactics. I had to act alone and the prospect of another personal encounter with the Russian was distinctly unappealing. What was my choice? I could see no other option but to comply with Igor's wishes. However, the beer gave me some bravado.

"Alright, I'm coming out." I shouted as I stepped out with my hands held high.

The two agents broke cover and slowly followed with their guns trained on the Russian. "Nice and easy Igor and no-one will get hurt." Perkins shouted as he found a vantage point in the middle of the road.

I knew I was as good as dead if I let the exchange take place but I was equally conscious that a wrong move would mean a bullet for our uninvited guest. As I approached I could see the terror in the man's eyes as he pleaded with Igor not to harm him. I was now within ten paces of Vasilyev and willed the agents to keep him talking. Whether Perkins anticipated my move I never found out but just at the right moment he spoke.

"Now Igor, let's not make any false moves here. Let the boy go and Goldhawk is all yours." Both agents had their guns at arms-length pointed at the Russian. For an instant Igor's attention shifted from me to Perkins which was all I needed. I dropped my right arm quickly to my side and let the Berretta hidden in my sleeve slide into my hand. At the same time I moved sharply to my left and dived behind the car the Russian had previously used for protection and simultaneously fired into the air to cause a distraction.

I dared not fire directly at Vasilyev but as I had anticipated my move created the opening for Perkins and Butler. As Vasilyev followed my diving body he exposed his right side to the two agents and I heard the crack of gun fire. By now I was on my haunches peering over the bonnet of the car and could see the Russian had been hit. I jumped out and grabbed the unfortunate hostage and pulled him to safety. Vasilyev had only been winged and scrambled off down a side street shooting as he went.

Butler followed the Russian and Perkins strode over to us. "Smart move Goldhawk you may just have saved your own bacon." He then turned to look at the man by my side who was shaking uncontrollably and understandably in a state of shock. "Get him home, give him £10 and tell him to keep his mouth shut. No police. I'll catch-up with you later." With that Perkins followed the other two and left me to negotiate a way out with our inebriated friend. I got clear just as the sirens approached and gladly avoided an awkward confrontation with the local constabulary.

Forty Four

Much to my relief I found out from Julian the next morning that Vasilyev had finally been caught after being cornered in a school playground and was already on his way back to London for interrogation. It would make the rest of my stay in Leeds more comfortable but my hopes of a significant break-through were dashed with Julian's gloomy assessment:

"Don't expect much from Igor, he's been well trained. We'll get little or nothing and within a few months he'll be shipped-off back to Mother Russia in exchange for one of our boys. And who knows, in another year or two, we'll as like as not, have the pleasure of his company again!"

"Bloody hell! Are you telling me he won't even be tried in a British Court?" I was horrified.

Julian laughed. "You have a lot to learn William. We are pawns in a game of chess in which the reputations of the world's most powerful countries are the stakes. We have no influence I'm afraid. And one thing you will learn is that politics always takes precedence over justice."

"And what of loyalty?" I asked bitterly. "I am sure you were behind setting me up as bait to catch Vasilyev last night!"

Julian laughed again and boomed down the line. "Don't take it personally William. I knew you'd pull through and we got our man didn't we?"

"You bastard! I could have been killed. You could at least have brought me in on your little deception!"

"But would you have been as convincing if I had?"

Another harsh lesson learnt. There was no sentiment in this game and in my heart I knew Julian was right. My anger subsided and was replaced by a rueful smile as I considered just how far I had come under his tutelage. I was no longer the nine to five company man I once was and I knew with absolute certainty that I never would be again. The adrenalin rush from the previous night would see to that. My admiration for Julian Singleton, already high, ratcheted up another notch. I chuckled to myself at the realisation that the die had been cast and my new career established. There was no turning back.

***

Although I fully expected an interminably long and tedious day I went about my work with a fresh determination. My task was to chase through all the Duggans and the O'Reillys in the vicinity to establish if Joey or Patrick were amongst them. It was another warm day with little in the way of breeze as I travelled about Leeds using a combination of my aching feet and public transport. By lunchtime my stamina was sapping and by mid-afternoon I had pretty much exhausted all hope of finding Patrick O'Reilly let along Billy Cosgrove. I had always known it was a long-shot but as I walked away from the last house on my list I had to accept that I was at the end of the line.

I would certainly not forget my brief interlude in the north. The theatre of war had been relocated from the south coast to Yorkshire and we had finally caught the Russian assassin Igor Vasilyev. But as far as my original objective, I had got nowhere. In many ways, perhaps I had fallen into the trap of allowing my own feelings to influence my decisions instead of taking a rational look at the evidence. I wanted to find Billy for personal as much as professional reasons and as I was learning, such sentiment was unwise.

But before returning to the Rose in June guest house and packing my bags, on impulse I decided to make one last visit. I pulled a scrap of paper with the address of Gloria Baker from my pocket and consulted my street map. As I thought, 17 All Saints Road was within walking distance so I apologised to my blistered feet before heading back up the hill toward Middleton. Having not exactly taken to Brian or Brenda Baker I had so far avoided their daughter out of blind prejudice and was not particularly looking forward to chewing the cud with her that afternoon.

However, as it turned out, even if parents Brian and Brenda possessed certain bovine characteristics, Gloria did not. She was a very attractive woman, I guessed in her late twenties with long luxuriant auburn hair and a friendly open smile.

"Gloria Baker?" I asked in surprise when the door opened.

"As was, yes. Baker was my maiden name. Can I help you?"

"Yes, I hope so. I am looking for Patrick O'Reilly and I understand he was a friend of yours?"

"Yes, well perhaps he was a little more than a friend. My little Jimmy's dad. What do you want with Pat? Nothing wrong I hope?"

"No not at all. Actually I am searching for a friend of his, Joey Duggan and hoped Patrick may know where I could find him."

"Joey Duggan, you say?" Gloria replied a little too quickly.

"Do you know him?" I asked, watching Gloria's reaction closely.

"Oh, no I don't think so…um what did you say your name was?"

"William Goldhawk. I was once Joey Duggan's best friend." I smiled and thrust out my hand.

"Um, I am sorry I can't really help you William." Gloria smiled weakly.

"Well perhaps you could give me Patrick's address? And a telephone number if he has one?"

"Oh, right, yes…. I'll get them for you." Rather than inviting me in Gloria pushed the door too and disappeared up the corridor before returning a couple of minutes later looking flustered. "Look I am sorry but I don't seem to have his address. He lives in London somewhere but I haven't seen him for a couple of years."

I was unconvinced. "The name Joey Duggan is an alias, his real name is Billy Cosgrove. He was my best friend and I am here to help him. His life is in danger. Does the name Billy Cosgrove mean anything to you?"

The expression on Gloria's face betrayed anxiety and indecision and with a heavy sigh she finally relented, opened the door and led me into her comfortable sitting room. Whilst I sat, Gloria stood by the doorway and fumbled open a packet of cigarettes.

"Alright, I do know of Billy Cosgrove but I was sworn to secrecy. As far as I know he lives abroad…somewhere I don't know where. He was a friend of Pat's but got caught-up in some trouble so didn't come home after the war. That's about all I can tell you. Pat was very insistent that we never betrayed his confidence."

"So you've never actually met Billy?"

"Um, no I've not met him." Gloria drew heavily of her cigarette. "What did you mean when you said his life was in danger?"

"There are things in Billy's past which have caught up with him and I need to find him before he lands himself in more serious trouble."

"Oh, I see." Gloria whispered quietly to herself as she finally sat down. "So who's looking for him and what do they want?"

"It's a long story and I won't bore you with the details but a gunman on his trail was arrested in Leeds only yesterday."

"A gunman in Leeds, surely not?" Gloria asked looking both flabbergasted and alarmed.

I pulled a rolled-up copy of the Yorkshire Post from my jacket pocket, unfurled it and held it up for Gloria to see the front page. 'Gun Fight in Headingley', ran the headline. "Yes, it's hard to believe I know but Billy inadvertently got tangled-up with some serious criminals. And he has some information which they want buried. The man caught last night in the Headingley gunfight is a Russian agent by the name of Igor Vasilyev."

"That's crazy I can't believe it!" Gloria protested. "Surely if you are right we should go to the police?"

"The police are aware but if Billy is abroad as you say he should be safe enough.... for the time being anyway." I answered.

"Yes, I suppose you are right. Well, Mr. Goldhawk I'm sorry I can't be any more help to you. If I hear from Patrick I will be sure to let you know." With another smile caste from granite Gloria showed me to the door.

I took my leave but rather than my original plan of returning to the Rose in June to collect my belongings I made my way down the front steps and looked out for a convenient hiding place with a view of her front porch. Opposite the house was a dry-stone wall which ran down the hill and separated the street from adjacent fields and a little further down a brick-built bus shelter. I walked around the block to check the coast was clear before hopping over the wall and hiding behind the shelter.

As I suspected I did not have to wait long. Within minutes I saw the door to number 17 open. Gloria looked flustered as she peered first left and then right before locking the door and striding purposefully down the hill. A multitude of chattering and laughing children on their way home from school provided some cover as I jumped back over the wall and followed the agitated Gloria down the slope from a discreet distance.

In the valley at the bottom of the hill stood the picturesque church of St Jude's and as she approached Gloria squeezed through a gap in the hawthorn hedge and into a churchyard. Rather than follow I stayed on the other side of the hedge as she walked along the path which skirted the graveyard. Although I was only yards away I was well protected by the overgrown hedge and was able to glimpse Gloria as she came to the cemetery and an area of recent burials where she stopped in front of a grave stone and knelt down with a small bouquet of summer flowers. I was shocked to realise that the grave belonged to four year old James 'Jimmy' O'Reilly.

As Gloria arranged the flowers I peered through a gap in the hedge and noticed two men clambering down a ladder propped up against scaffolding which clung to the side of the church. Neat piles of new tiles on the scaffold walkway told me they had been replacing the old stone roof. Gloria looked up and smiled as one of the men approached.

It was the unusually blond hair which first attracted my attention and as he drew nearer I saw the familiar smile light his face. Billy Cosgrove. A surge of euphoria swept through me as I thought of Lucy. I strode back up the road to the gap in the hedge and squeezed through. Twelve long years had elapsed since I had last laid eyes on Billy but as he stood before me, the same mop of slightly disheveled hair and only the faintest signs of aging, the passing years melted away. Still handsome and square shouldered he placed an arm affectionately around Gloria's shoulders before turning toward me.

"Mr. and Mrs. Cosgrove I presume?" I asked grinning like a Cheshire cat.

"William Goldhawk." Billy said but with no hint of a reciprocating smile or even the offer of a hand shake. "Well, you're here now so you'd better come up to the house."

Hardly the exuberant welcome I had hoped for but perhaps Billy Cosgrove would rather bury the past. With his jaw set firm he trudged back up the hill with Gloria at his side while I followed-on behind. How often I had dreamed of finding Billy but never had I imagined a reunion quite like this. In my mind's eye I had visions of back slapping, laughter and celebration. But for Billy, my dream looked more like his nightmare.

A few minutes later, feeling awkward and anxious I was seated in the Cosgroves' sitting room with Billy opposite. "I'll make a pot of tea whilst you two talk." Gloria said before catching my eye and mouthing 'good luck' as though she expected trouble. She then disappeared into the kitchen and left Billy and I alone.

"Twelve bloody years to find me William! Twelve long years!" A simmering anger was displayed on his face as well as in his words. But checking himself he asked. "Anyway, that's as it may be, how's my Lucy?"

"She's well Billy. Did you read about her in the paper? She cleared your name. You know you are free to come home?"

"I don't read papers but yes I did hear she had cleared my name and I'm grateful. Tell her I'm grateful." Billy looked down at his hands as he spoke. Despite his attempts to remain aloof it was easy to see the turmoil bubbling beneath the surface. "I've missed my kid sister that much I will tell you."

"Billy what happened to you? There are people out there who want you dead. Why? What happened all those years ago?"

"You bloody tell me William!" Billy's eyes blazed.

"I don't know! That's why I'm here!" I shot back my own hackles starting to rise. "Why didn't you come home? What were you so afraid of Billy?"

"You don't know? You seriously expect me to believe that *you* of all people don't know?" Billy growled through clenched teeth.

I was baffled. "I've spent months tracking you down so I could find out. Treat me as an idiot by all means but please don't treat me as the enemy."

"You are the enemy as far as I'm concerned. I've had enough of this conversation. It's time you left! Go home William and leave us in peace."

"Alright, if that's the way you want it Billy. But what shall I tell Lucy? What do I say to her? Your sister Billy, who's been grieving for twelve years?" With that I stood up and made a show of walking across the room but as I got to the door Gloria barred my way.

"No, William don't go…sit down." And turning to her husband she said firmly. "That's no way to treat your old friend Billy. William, if Billy's life really is in danger I want to hear about even if Billy doesn't. What happened? Billy never talks about his past."

So I told my story with Billy sitting mute in the corner. From the murder of Stanley Jakes and Billy's arrest warrant, to the day that Lucy knocked on my door the previous autumn, my run-in with Inspector Hanaho, the confession of the dying Clive Davenport, the mystery of the professor, the massive fraud at the Admiralty and the Russian connection. I then went on to explain the inadvertent part played by Billy and why he had become a target for murder.

“You see Gloria, Billy was set-up by the police who planted the murder weapon in his bedroom. Inspector Hanaho was on the payroll of the criminals and they expected Billy to hang. But they reckoned without the determination of his sister or the death bed confession of Clive Davenport.”

Billy sat silently through my explanation, his expression giving little away but I hoped our conversation would draw him in.

“But why frame Billy?” Gloria asked.

“He was a convenient scapegoat, that’s all. There was a long-running feud between Stanley Jakes and Billy ever since a drunken Jakes tried to force his attentions on his sister Lucy. If you were looking for someone to frame he was the obvious candidate as the bad blood between them was well known.”

“So what happened? Was Billy arrested?” Gloria looked first at me and then Billy.

“No, just before the police came knocking he disappeared and Hanaho publicly accused him of absconding to avoid the gallows. His disappearance just confirmed his guilt in the eyes of the police; and the public for that matter. And we’ve had all sorts of conflicting evidence thrown at us since. I was even told by a reliable source that Billy’s body had been washed up in Prinsted Harbour a few miles from Portsmouth six weeks after he disappeared. We thought you were dead, Billy.”

“So how did you find me?” Billy at last entered the conversation.

“An eight year old girl watched you being bundled into the back of the Naval Provost’s van and I tracked down the van’s drivers Nigel Barlow and Reginald Cubit. From there I worked out you had almost certainly been either knocked on the head and chucked into the harbour to drown or bundled aboard a ship. Eventually I tracked down a junior officer by the name of Oscar Davis who served on the Exeter and remembered you. From Oscar Davis to Frank Lewis and eventually to your friendship with Patrick O'Reilly and his connection with Leeds. From there to Gloria's parents and finally to you here.

Nigel Barlow was under the impression that he was part of a plot to get you out of the country to save you from the hangman. But I think the exact opposite was true. I think you were abducted so you couldn't stand trial and had no chance to defend yourself."

Billy offered a non-committal grunt and I finally asked the question I had waited so long to ask. "Who was it Billy? Who was with Nigel Barlow and Reginald Cubit the day you were thrown into that van outside the Red, white and Blue?"

I held my breath as Billy looked-up, gave a humourless smile and shook his head. "It was your father William!"

It should perhaps not have come as such a surprise as I was aware of Julian's suspicions and I had good reason to form many of my own. But nevertheless a shock it was. Perhaps it was because I did not want to believe him capable of such deeds that I had pushed the possibility from my mind. Instead of scrutinising the evidence as I surely should have I had skated over it. In the recesses of my mind I was aware that I did not know much about 'my father's' past nor did I know how he had accumulated his fortune but rather than finding out more, I had rather too conveniently turned my attentions elsewhere.

What a fool I had been! So much for forging a career in British Intelligence. How would I explain this to the politicians who paid my salary? With the shock still registered on my face I looked up at Billy.

"My god, you really didn't know did you?" he said with a just a hint of a smile on his lips. "I have spent 12 years cursing you

William! It never occurred to me that you didn't know your father was behind this."

"So tell me exactly what happened that night Billy." I replied struggling to come to terms with what I had been told.

"There's not a great deal to tell beyond what you already know. I was in the Red, White and Blue having a pint when a lad ran in with a message from Lucy telling me to scarper as the police were onto me. As I left the pub by the front door a blanket was chucked over my head and I was bundled into the back of a van. Next thing I know I'm handcuffed to the seat, the blanket removed and your father sitting opposite me.

Well he was a magistrate....a part of the establishment so I assumed that I was under arrest but I was put in the picture as we drove down to the docks. It was not so straightforward. He handed me a passport and papers and told me the only way I'd escape the gallows was if I assumed the identity of Joey Michael Duggan and never set foot in Hampshire again. I tried to explain that I wasn't guilty but he wasn't interested. He just kept repeating that if I wanted to live I had to keep well away. What clinched it was when he started on about Lucy and my mother. He told me that if I were ever to contact them again I'd be signing their death warrant.

I had plenty of time to ruminate on his threats as within hours I found myself on board the HMS Exeter cruising off to the South Atlantic. There were a few non-naval personnel on board but the others came up from Devonport so I was taken for Joey Duggan with no problems. And to the rest of the world I'm still Joey Duggan. It's only Gloria who knows any different."

Once he accepted that I was ignorant of 'my father's' part in his abduction Billy thawed and the oppressive atmosphere lifted. The sullen individual who had sat brooding through my explanation became alert and questioning, wanting to know everything that had happened during his enforced exile. So far I had only given the sketchiest of outlines but with Billy's new found enthusiasm I slowly started filling in the gaps.

By the time I finished my audience was goggled eyed and I seriously wondered whether they took me for a delusional crackpot. Even to my own ears my story seemed pretty far-fetched; the shooting of Samantha Smith, the largest financial fraud in British history, Russian espionage not to mention my own role working for Mi5. For reasons I am not sure I am able to explain I revealed nothing of my personal circumstances, neither my relationship with Lucy nor the road I had travelled to uncover the truth about my real family. That, I decided was for another day.

Gloria was the first to speak. "So you think your father is the 'professor' do you?"

"It's beginning to look that way. Why else would he have warned off Billy and threatened his family? Nothing else makes sense."

"But why not just kill him as he had Jakes? Surely that would have been far simpler and safer than the elaborate plan to give him a new identity?" Gloria asked.

"Maybe but they did not want another murder on their hands which would require further investigation. This way Billy's guilt was taken for granted and the case was closed. Much neater." I replied applying a healthy dose of guesswork.

"What I can't understand is the connection between the fraud and Stanley Jakes? Why did they want Jakes dead in the first place?" Billy then asked.

"Stanley Jakes worked for these people but wanted a larger piece of the pie not just the scraps he was being fed so went into direct competition. But he was well out of his league and the professor and his associates were never likely to put up with him muddying the water so had him removed; permanently. You, Billy, just happened to offer a convenient excuse for them to pin the murder elsewhere."

"Yes I see it's beginning to fall into place. I had always imagined that my bust up with Jakes was the reason for my arrest but nothing else really made much sense to me. And what about the Russian connection?" Billy asked next.

"We don't really know for sure but Julian's guess is that the fraud was politically motivated. Someone with communist sympathies or with a grudge against this country perhaps? I don't know a great deal about 'my father's' politics but apparently he had communist leanings when at Oxford, although I can't really imagine it."

"So what next, William?" asked Gloria.

"I really have no alternative but to confront 'my father'."

I could not help but think again about the shooting of Samantha Smith and my own good fortune. If 'my father' was behind the killings it would make a sort of perverse sense. He was not quite prepared to inflict the *coup de gras* but wanting to scare me off. It still felt all very far-fetched but one way or the other I knew I had to get to the truth before anyone else suffered the same fate as the luckless Samantha.

"I'm coming with you William." Billy said leaving no room for discussion.

"Come on then Billy, it's time to get our lives back." I replied.

Forty Five

Sir Edward Goldhawk was the only father I had ever known. How I would have loved to have raided my childhood memory bank to find the dashing Major Barrington-Hope playing sword fights with me on the lawn or lifting me into the cockpit of his Sopwith Camel and reliving stories of heroic dog fights with 'the Hun' but sadly that was not to be. With not a single first hand recollection I found it difficult to revel in the glories of the man who had provided the seed to bring me into the world. Without memories how could I conjure up the genuine emotions necessary to forge a father and son bond? The answer was I could not. Despite everything, on a subliminal level I still thought of Sir Edward, the man who had made such a shoddy job of bringing me up as my father. However much I may have wished otherwise it was his mental image lodged in my memory.

So, perhaps that was why I had no intention of following Security Services' protocol and handing the intelligence I had gathered to my masters in Whitehall. I knew very well that Julian would have made his own enquiries and drawn the same conclusions as me anyway and I wanted to reach Sir Edward before he did. Even with the weight of evidence firmly against him I took it as my filial duty to extract a confession before plunging the dagger into his back.

Although Billy deserved the chance to confront the man who had so grievously wronged him, in one sense at least, I regretted agreeing to let him accompany me. I needed to control the encounter with 'my father' which would be easier alone. Still, the decision had been made and Billy and I were heading back to the south coast together. With the capture of Vasilyev, Lucy had decided (against my advice) to return home and my immediate thoughts were of her reaction at seeing Billy alive. The sensible thing would have been to prepare her for the shock of her life but both Billy and I were seduced by the drama of the reunion and common sense had been cast aside.

The train journey home was in many ways a godsend as it allowed us to bridge the inevitable gap which had opened between us. Listening, gave us both a deeper understanding and empathy for the other. Whilst I had already guessed at the inner turmoil that Billy had suffered I had to that point paid it scant attention. His emotional wellbeing had come in a distant second to my obsessional quest to find him. Billy had taken a buffeting alright: he had been scarcely nineteen when he was whisked away from his family and friends and for twelve years he wrestled his conscience, never quite knowing if he was doing the right thing and having no one to guide him through.

As the train pulled out of Nottingham Victoria Station we had the carriage to ourselves and Billy leaned toward me. "You know William, after our stint in Port Stanley, Pat and me managed to hitch a lift back to Blighty on an American cargo ship. We had decided to join the Royal Navy and persuaded the Governor to sign our papers. We arrived home and docked in Liverpool in September and whilst Pat came back to Leeds I had a week to kick my heals before joining the Ark Royal at Devonport.

I remember it so clearly. It was a typical drizzly English day and it felt bloody good to be home. I yearned to see my family and friends in Southsea and I managed to cadge a lift from a lorry driver heading down to Southampton docks. He dropped me at the train station early evening and within an hour I arrived at Fratton. I pulled my collar up and my hat around my ears and waltzed down Fawcett Road with every intention of paying a surprise visit to mum and Lucy.

I got as far as the Red, White and Blue where I stopped off for a quick drink but as I sat and supped my pint my courage drained away. I positioned myself near the window and watched the street opposite hoping to catch a glimpse of Lucy but of course I didn't. All the 'what ifs' floated back into my mind and I couldn't do it. So instead of going home I just drank too much and ended-up on the next train to Plymouth. I've had nightmares about that evening ever since. The thing is William, I felt like such a coward."

For the rest of the journey to London we shared stories and by the time the train pulled into St. Pancras any residual unease between us had drifted away. It was a liberating journey which started with mutual suspicion but ended with us re-connecting and sharing a common goal. We both wanted answers but most of all we wanted the chance to lead a normal life. Billy had lived in the shadows for too long and I was desperate to give Lucy her freedom back.

I had phoned Julian before I left Leeds and we arranged to meet in the bar at the Russell Hotel at six that evening. Julian had been in an excitable mood and was far more interested in talking than listening which had suited me well. He assured me that arrests were only days away and that he had one last crucial job for me which (praise the Lord) involved a visit to 'my father'. As I had suspected the noose was tightening around Sir Edward's neck even without the evidence from Billy.

When we arrived in London Billy disappeared off to find a suitable hostelry to while away the evening whilst I jumped on the tube to Russell Square where Julian awaited me in the hotel bar, a half empty pint glass in his hand. Before I even had time to remove my soaking raincoat Julian launched in.

"Well William, we've had quite a week. With the arrest of Vasilyev, the Russians have kept out of our way so we've had time to delve far deeper into the lives of our chief suspects. Your father, William...." Julian peered up from his pint to assess my reaction but I was too intent in wrestling off my wet coat to register. "Sir Edward Goldhawk...you've told me you know nothing of his history, of his politics or how he accumulated his fortune?"

"Very little. He's a private man and keeps his business to himself. I suppose I always imagined him to be a Conservative.... of the old school. He certainly seems to possess a sort of Victorian paternalism and always wants to be involved in helping the less fortunate. But how much that has to do with benevolence and how much to do with bolstering his social standing I wouldn't like to say." I added, somewhat uncharitably.

"Let me tell you what we know. Your father went up to Oxford in 1908 where he read Chemistry at New College and shared digs off the Cowley Road with his closest friend Marcus Crawford. You were right about his political affiliations, in those early days anyway, he was a member of the Conservative Party but neither Marcus nor your father showed signs of being particularly political.

But all that changed when your father befriended a young Spaniard named Juan Marquez who awakened his social conscience. Marquez was an interesting character. He came from a rich and well-connected Spanish family but was an idealist, heavily influenced by the writings of Karl Marx and Fredrick Engels. It seems your father drifted away from Marcus Crawford and became close friends with Marquez sharing a new political fervour.

At the end of his first year the young Edward swapped his 'practical' Chemistry degree for Philosophy, much to the apparent exasperation of his father who threatened to disinherit him. Fortunately for Edward he had already inherited a considerable sum of money so the prospect of being disinherited did not overly concern him. Politics began to play a more and more important part in his life. He joined a fledgling Communist Party which Marquez had formed at Oxford and according to his tutor Malcolm Forster he moved from mainstream to revolutionary almost overnight. He denounced the Conservatives as 'bourgeois' and made a public show of resigning his membership during a meeting at the Oxford Union. He even wrote a letter to the Times predicting the overthrow of the Tsarists in Russia and an uprising of the workers of Europe. His essays showed all the signs of his new political affiliations."

With that Julian pulled a couple of old photographs from a file and handed them to me. “That.” Julian pointed. “Is your father and with him is Juan Marquez.” I stared in surprise at the three young men pictured. They were dressed as working men with large caps and dusty old grey suits. “Now look at the contrast with this photograph taken 12 months earlier.” A more conventional Oxford undergraduate picture of Edward with his friend Marcus in light coloured blazers and boaters.

“So who’s the third man?” I asked peering closely at the first photograph. Julian indicated for me to turn it over. I read the inscription aloud. “J, self & H. So do we know who H is?” I then asked at the same time as I trawled through my memory bank.

“No we have no idea. That’s one for you William. But before we get ahead of ourselves, what about the link between your father and Marcus Crawford? It’s all something of a coincidence don’t you think? Good friends at Oxford and then both finishing-up on the south coast with pots of money. Perhaps I’m being too cynical but there are rather too many coincidences for my liking.

Anyway, after the War it seems your father’s business flourished and by the early twenties he was a rich man. He got involved in any number of worthy causes giving large sums to various local charities; on the face of it not the behaviour of a greedy and selfish man.

Then, seemingly out of the blue in the autumn of 1935, £20,000 was transferred from your father’s bank account to a bank in Spain and over the course of the Civil War he made a number similarly large deposits. It seems more than probable that these were political donations. So perhaps we’ve been barking up the wrong tree. Is our ‘professor’ politically motivated rather than money motivated?

My bet but I have no proof, is that Juan Marquez was the recipient of this money on behalf of the communists. We’ve tried to track

Juan Marquez but like so many of his compatriots he disappeared during the war and has not been heard of since."

"So you think Sir Edward may have been a communist?" I thought of the life I led as a child watching a procession of the wealthy and the titled coming and going from Liongate. Was Sir Edward an actor using his lavish dinner parties as cover for his political designs? Surely not! There would have been clues; young spirited men and women and fighting talk. Working men, Trade Unionists, clandestine meetings in the shadows, hushed, whispered and passionate speeches. But there was none of that, just establishment figures from the upper echelons of society more likely to be talking about cricket than politics.

If 'my father' was a communist, I supposed he was more likely a Russian spy using his influence to infiltrate the power brokers of the British Navy. It all seemed so very unlikely but then again I had first-hand experience of the Russian connection so perhaps it was not impossible.

And throw into the mix that 'my father' trained for a year as a chemistry student and where did it lead? As Julian had said there were a string of coincidences which were hard to ignore; plenty to suggest that 'my father' was, indeed, the professor. Had it been Sir Edward, I wondered who had drugged Clive Davenport and precipitated the murder of Stanley Jakes? And *what of* the connection with Marcus Crawford? I certainly recall that Sir Marcus as a regular visitor to Liongate throughout my childhood. Were they, as Julian suspected, in league? A marriage of convenience, both wanting money but for different reasons?

Julian gave me a few minutes to assimilate what he had told me before going on. "We have plenty of circumstantial evidence against your father and Sir Marcus but what worries me is if we arrest them now they will wriggle free. We need proof, William. We need to know for sure that they committed the crimes. We need evidence of a financial link between Sir Marcus and your father. They were in this together William; I can feel it in my bones. You need to dig around, be a little imaginative William. Find that link!"

I was beginning to wonder what I was letting myself in for. If Sir Edward really was the person that it appeared he may be I felt an impotent force. He had controlled me all my life and somehow I wondered if I had what it took to stand up to him now. With an involuntary shiver I tried to quell the unrest which had wormed its way into my head.

***

With no mention of Billy, I left Julian before closing time and jumped on a number 37 bus to Waterloo Station. My friend was waiting on a bench with a bottle of brown ale as company. "The train leaves in 10 minutes Billy." I said pulling him to his feet with a surge of good feeling, very glad of his company. Confronting 'my father' seemed more daunting the closer it became and despite my previous reservations I needed Billy to stand by my side. Billy was no side issue. He was as much a part of this as I and we needed to face it together.

We planned to catch the slow mail train home and arrive at the crack of dawn with the hope of catching-up on some much needed sleep en route. But as the train pulled out of Waterloo I wanted first to go through a plan of action with Billy which I hoped would help focus my mind on the events to come. My old friend though had a rather different idea. Billy Cosgrove, the street fighter of old, the confident, swaggering teenager of 1939 was long gone. He had been replaced by a more thoughtful but uncertain man. Despite an understandable bitterness he showed surprisingly little desire for revenge. He just wanted the chance to reclaim his old life without fear of the repercussions. Tired of running, he craved normality, a family life and to introduce his wife Gloria to his sister Lucy. He wanted to walk the street unmolested. And my attempts to draw him into discussions about confronting ‘my father’ were gently re-buffed.

Despite the nervous energy which had been my companion for the previous forty eight hours I dropped off to sleep surprisingly quickly, propped up against the window using my rolled jacket as a pillow and did not wake until the sun made its first appearance as the train shunted into Havant Station, a few miles short of our final destination. Billy too had slept and sounded both excited and anxious about the prospect of the day ahead.

“What’s the plan then William? I am in your hands. I don’t even know where Lucy is living? I hope my reappearance won’t give her heart failure!” He rattled off, combing his hair with the help of a reflection from a train window.

“Breakfast first and then we’ll go and surprise Lucy I think don’t you?” Lucy had often chastised me for my insensitivity and I wondered if introducing Billy back into her life with no warning may be my crowning glory. But on the other hand I was about to deliver to her a present of unimaginable value and I wanted us all to enjoy the moment.

Lucy was staying at my house but I could see no benefit in explanations yet. Breakfast was a hurried affair in a café on Albert Road, both of us eating only as a means of killing time. We were too agitated to fully appreciate the lavish fry-up and talked of anything but what was on our minds. We had agreed earlier to give Lucy time to surface before making our entrance. Time weighed heavily but finally the clock on the café wall struck 9 o’clock and gulping back the last dregs of coffee I stood, threw a florin on the counter and walked out of the shop with Billy in step beside me.

Within five minutes we were walking-up Livingstone Road and I turned to Billy with an encouraging smile. “That’s the house up there on the left so are you ready?” Billy puffed out his cheeks and grinned back.

Forty Six

But as it transpired neither Billy nor I were ready for the surprise in store for us. After I opened the front door it took only a fraction of a second for my brain to register a problem. Lucy's suitcase lay on its side unopened, the hat-stand by the door had been toppled as had a small corner table which had deposited the telephone and a pot plant on the floor. There was a framed painting askew on the wall and large man-sized muddy footprints across the hallway carpet. I feared the worst. Bounding-up the stairs I called Lucy's name and searched room by room. But predictably there no sign.

My shouts alerted Billy who came hurtling through the front door and up the stairs with alarm written across his face. He too instantly guessed the fate of his sister. "She's been taken hasn't she? They knew I was coming. This is my fault, I should have stayed away!"

"Come on Billy let's go and find her." I said striding for the door and picking up my car keys on the way out.

Billy looked dazed. Following me out of the front door he asked plaintively. "But where do we start?"

"Liongate." I answered emphatically, jumping into the driver's seat of the Sunbeam. Miraculously, even though the car had sat idle for a week it started without the need for the crank-handle. I revved the engine hard to iron out the misfiring as the car spluttered and coughed its way up the road. I wanted to scream out loud partly at my stupidity for not foreseeing the obvious and partly out of fear for what they may do to Lucy. Any semblance of rationality gone I was in a dangerous mood as I drove recklessly through the streets of Southsea toward Liongate. Whether or not 'my father' was directly responsible for Lucy's disappearance I felt like ripping him limb from limb.

Billy, stunned, sat staring vacantly out of the windscreen saying nothing. I screeched to a stop outside the back gate of 'my father's' house and yanked the handbrake on so hard I felt the cable snap. Hauling myself from the car and slamming shut the door behind me I pulled open the gate and ran up the garden path. I rang the door-bell at the same time as frantically searching through my pockets for a key. After what seemed an eternity the door was opened by a member of 'my father's' staff and I pushed past him and strode up the stairs heading for the study.

Without knocking I flung open the door to find 'my father' sitting behind his desk surrounded by a mound of papers. I had the impression his first reaction was to smile but thought better of it once he gauged my mood. My anger had not subsided. I was heartily sick of being a pawn in a game I wanted no part in. Whatever 'my father's' role I had every intention of wringing the truth from him.

"Where is she?" I shouted aggressively placing my hands on the desk and menacingly pushing my face to within inches of his. He looked genuinely shocked as he raised his hands in submission. "Sorry William, I am not sure who you are talking about. Slow down and explain."

"Lucy! Come on, no more lies! Where is she?" I demanded coming close to grabbing him by the lapels in my frustration.

"William, calm down and tell me what you are talking about. Lucy has gone missing?"

"She returned home from France yesterday and when I got in this morning she wasn't there. There'd been a struggle. She's been taken…kidnapped! Come on father I know what you've been up to!"

"I have nothing to do with this but….. I might just know where she is." 'My father' whispered thoughtfully as he stood and walked across the room to a filing cabinet from which he pulled out an Ordnance Survey map. He carefully unfolded it, laid it flat on his desk and peering through his bifocals he traced his index finger up the A3 into the South Downs.

“Here William, look.” He tapped his finger on an area designated as forest right in the middle of the Downs close to the village of East Harting.

“You think Lucy is being held there?” I asked, incredulous.

“You are owed an explanation, William and you will get one. I promise you that but first we must rescue Lucy.”

“There have been so many lies! Why should I believe you father?” I simmered trying to keep my rage in check.

“Have you come here with Billy Cosgrove?” ‘My father’ then asked calmly.

“You know then? Yes, Billy’s down stairs.” I replied guardedly.

“I guessed as much. That’s why Lucy has been taken. She’s an insurance policy.”

Before I could question him further ‘my father’ turned away from his desk and unlocked a set of large wooden cabinet doors from which he pulled a rifle. Holding it in one hand he heaved it across the desk for me to catch.

“Know how to handle one of these William?”

I looked down at the old Lee Enfield and nodded.

“Good, now listen carefully. I know who is holding Lucy and I am pretty sure she’ll be here; East Harting Timber Company.” He said pointing at the map. “Harry Devereaux, to give him his real name owns the business as well as the woodland and uses it as a hide-away. There's a saw-mill here and behind it is Harry's place. It's an old stable which he's converted to use as a base. He's dangerous, William, very dangerous. You'll need your wits about you." And with those words of warning he searched a drawer and pulled out a box of ammunition which he placed in my open hand.

"Come on father, you are coming with us. I want insurance too."

"No, that would be foolhardy. We need to get Harry away from there before you go in. Just hold your horses for a minute whilst I make a telephone call." My father gestured for me to sit as he thumbed through an address book on his desk and dialled. In short time I heard the click of the line opening and caught the muffled sound of a man's voice.

"Harry, it's Edward. William has been in touch. He's found Cosgrove." I could not make out the words on the other end of the line but 'my father' nodded several times before replying.

"That's water under the bridge Harry. We can't rewrite history we have to deal with the cards we have…." But Harry it seemed, disagreed.

"No…no, of course not."

"Yes…alright."

"William is bringing him here to Liongate." 'My father' said. "They should be here at midday. You know the score Harry, if I go down you come with me. So I strongly advise you to get in the car and drive over here now and we deal with Billy Cosgrove together. But no guns, Harry."

A few more undecipherable grunts from 'my father' and the conversation was over. Turning to me he gave a taut smile and said.

"He's on his way so that leaves you with a clear run. You and Billy get up there and get her out. The property may be guarded but I don't think Harry will be expecting visitors so if you are careful you may catch them unawares. Call me when you're away and then I think it's time for you to meet Harry."

Why was it I always seemed to be dancing to someone else's tune, I wondered? I came determined to control the confrontation with 'my father' but as usual, he effortlessly wrestled the initiative from my grasp. What choice did I have but to take his word for it? Lucy's life was more important than my pride so I grabbed the map from the desk and ran back down the stairs, gun in hand and into the street like a marauding cowboy. Billy was leaning against the car looking lethargic but jumped too when he saw what I was carrying.

"Christ William! I Hope you haven't shot him!"

"Get in Billy and I'll explain."

Hardly convinced myself, I then tried to justify my decision to a sceptical Billy. The more I tried the more hollow my own words sounded. Was I really so gullible as to believe we would find Lucy in this back of beyond location? Surely we were on a fool's errand, 'my father' getting me out of the way so he could make good his own escape or put some other devious plan into action?

Pushing aside my negative thoughts I gritted my teeth and put my foot to the floor hitting the A3 at 75mph. The adrenalin rush precipitated by my reckless driving seemed to lift Billy from his lethargy and he too now looked ready to face whatever lay in store. He proved a more than useful navigator and had us quickly through the wooded South Downs close to our final destination near East Harting. It was an out of the way location all right and hardly recognisable as southern England. The roads were rutted and barely passable and dwellings of any sort few and far between.

As we approached a junction Billy told me to slow and look for a place to pull over which was difficult only because the lane was so narrow. With rather more to worry about than a minor breach of the highway-code I pushed the front of the car into the bushes as best I could before retrieving the Lee Enfield from the back seat and my Berretta from the glove box. Billy meanwhile, studying the map walked across the road to get his bearings.

"It looks like if we go this way, straight through the trees we should intersect the track which connects the saw-mill to the main road. But don't hold your breath because this map is 30 years old and I've no compass." And with the sun high in the sky and no obvious landmarks we would have to proceed with care or could end up back where we started.

We plunged into the wood and kept up a reasonable pace for about 20 minutes before coming to a barbed wire fence which followed the course of a stream and marked the boundary between two tracts of woodland. If the barbed wire was insufficient deterrent to dissuade a casual visitor the grim warning signs surely were not. Rather than the familiar, 'Trespassers will be prosecuted', a sign nailed to a tree on the opposite bank warned of 'Danger of Death- Keep Out- Designated Shooting Area'. The stream offered only a minor obstacle but the barbed wire was a different matter. With no bolt cutters and only summer clothes to protect us from the sharp barbs it tested our resourcefulness to the limit.

But once on the other side of the fence it took barely five minutes before we hit the track leading to the saw-mill and keeping just within the line of the trees, we followed it north. We saw no sign of life but there was evidence of fresh car traffic along the rutted, dirt track. Neither Billy nor I acknowledged what was inevitably preying on our minds. By focusing on the task at hand we were able to believe in our mission although the doubts, spawned from the lies we had both been fed, smouldered just beneath the surface.

As the track swept away to the right we caught sight of the saw-mill with its corrugated barn like roof and ragged assortment of brick-built and prefabricated outhouses. Although it looked deserted there were three trailers piled high with cut-logs and other evidence which suggested a working mill. Keeping our eyes peeled and using the trees as cover we left the track and skirted the perimeter. We decided our best option would be to make our approach from the north which would give more cover and a better view of the converted stable where we hoped to find Lucy.

"Billy, how are your shooting skills?" I whispered as I pulled out the Beretta from my trouser pocket and handed it to him.

From our vantage point we had a view of a cobbled courtyard enclosed by the 'L' shaped stable, the rendered rear wall of the saw-mill and six foot high brick wall protected by broken glass cemented along its top edge. In the corner of the courtyard, ears twitching and nose sniffing into the wind, was our first problem. The German-Shepherd, I guessed, had already caught our scent as it excitedly yelped and growled its way around the courtyard. Starring down from our position just inside the tree-line I watched as the middle of three doors on the stable block opened and a man emerged. He had been alerted by the whining of the dog and came prepared with a gun in his hand. He looked in our direction but after a few seconds it seemed he was satisfied it was a false alarm and after shouting a few expletives at the hapless 'Bruno' he went back inside.

"And how are you with dogs?" I asked quietly under my breath. "If you can get yourself down to that gate on the far side of the courtyard and keep the dog occupied I can sneak through the iron gate down here and hide behind the door. When matey boy comes out to see what the commotion is he'll see old Bruno and head straight for you. Meanwhile I can come-up behind him and...crack!"

Billy looked thoughtful. "Might work but what if there's more than one of them?"

"I'll take the handgun and you take the rifle." I then demonstrated using Billy as my model. "I'll grab our friend around the neck, like so and push the Berretta into his temple, voila! I'll then turn back toward the door and if there's an accomplice I have a hostage and you covering me with the rifle."

"Eat your heart out the Duke of Wellington! Could this be Goldhawk's Waterloo?" Billy asked with a smile.

Within a few minutes and after loading both guns we put our plan into action. I waited and watched as Billy edged his way across the slope and around the front of the saw-mill. I caught his signal as he reached the far side before starting back toward the gate. Billy was now up-wind of Bruno and so far the dog showed no sign of alarm. It was my turn to move and I slid as quietly as I could down the hill. Within 90 seconds I had reached the gate and signalled to Billy to start the diversion.

The dog looked-up in surprise as Billy approached and hurled his muscled body at the bars of the gate barking furiously. It was an easy task for me to slip open the side gate and take-up my position behind the door. With no chance of a false alarm this time the door flew open and the man we saw earlier charged out, his gun pointing directly at Billy as he yelled at the dog to 'get down.' Without even a warning he let off two quick rounds in Billy's general direction but the bullets harmlessly ricocheted off the stable wall as Billy ducked. As the man set himself for another shot I got to him but rather than the prescribed neck-brace I chopped hard at the back of his neck in anger and he crumpled to the floor. That piece of stupidity left me exposed and when his accomplice entered the fray I was a sitting duck.

I saw him from the corner of my eye as he raised the long muzzle of his hand gun and pointed it straight at my chest from no more than 15 paces. I was done for. I heard the crack of gunfire and waited for the thud. But it never came. It was my assailant who dropped to his knees with a red patch spreading fast across his white shirt. Billy stood on the other side of the gate, the Lee Enfield at his shoulder.

Apart from the frightened yelping of Bruno, cowed and terrified by the gun fire, all was now quiet. The first man was out cold and his accomplice surely dead. Billy entered the courtyard through the main gate still cautious and covered me as I walked across the yard to the open stable door. Once my eyes adjusted I took in a large and well-ordered working office. With the exception of the vaulted ceiling it looked to have more in common with an office in the City than a stable block in the back of beyond.

There were three interior doors on the ground floor as well as an open wooden staircase which led to a mezzanine floor. I gestured to Billy to take the ground floor whilst I made my way upstairs to the living quarters. No sign of Lucy but before I had the chance to fret I heard Billy shouting:

"William down here!"

I sped down the stairs and across the office to find Billy holding a prostrate Lucy in his arms. Fear gripping my chest like a vice I quickly reached for her wrist to check for a pulse. Strong and steady, thank god. Looking down at her arm and seeing the puncture marks it wasn't hard to guess how she had been subdued. Looking around I found the vial and a needle which I pocketed for later analysis.

"She'll be fine Billy. She's been drugged but her pulse is strong." I said with a certainty born from knowing I could accept no other outcome. She had received a heavy dose but her breathing and pupil dilation suggested she was slowly coming round. I wanted her checked over nonetheless and my immediate thought was to get her home to Southsea.

"Let's see if her captors have left a car for us so we can get her out of here quickly." Before we left I also needed to attend to a few chores such as securing our friend in the yard and finding a temporary home for his dead chum. The man I hit was still unconscious and rifling through his pockets I found a wallet and a key fob emblazoned with a Mercedes emblem. Although his papers confirmed his identity as Alf Connor I had serious doubts. Neither man looked quite British, dressed in what seemed to me like pre-war Russian suits, I strongly suspected both were compatriots of Igor Vasilyev.

***

The four litre Mercedes glided over the rough terrain and with Lucy lying on the rear seat with her head on Billy's lap, I was not quite sure whether I should be worried or euphoric. My mind was eased as I saw Lucy through the rear view mirror sitting-up, disorientated and oblivious to her surroundings but at least slowly regaining consciousness.

Feeling relieved I turned my attention back to road. The powerful Mercedes got us home in good time and whilst Billy carried Lucy through the front door and up the stairs I telephoned, first 'my father' to tell him to expect me within the hour and then Julian. I was not ready to hand over the reins just yet so kept selected details to myself as I gave him an abridged version of the morning's events. With a strong recommendation that he should make the trip to East Harting Timber Company I hoped to be afforded the time I needed to conclude my business with Harry Devereaux and 'my father'.

I gave myself just long enough to watch Lucy's face as she came too and recognised Billy. A moment at savour. Hardly surprising in the circumstance but Lucy was half convinced she was dreaming and she had to hold Billy's hand and stroke his face with the back of her hand over and over again before she was finally convinced.

The look on her face was wonderful to behold and made me more determined than ever to complete the task at hand and give these people their lives back.

Forty Seven

I have some vague recollection of sitting in the back of a classroom one summer's day listening to Professor Hendreich droning on about Thomas Hobbs and Immanuel Kant and the philosophical concept of free will verses determinism. It pretty much passed me by but as I sat in 'my father's' study that hot afternoon in June 1951 I wondered whether Billy's disappearance had set in motion a chain of events over which we had no control. It was easy to imagine our destiny floating on the tide; all of us just flotsam washed-up wherever the great ocean gods decreed.

'My father' promised me earlier that day a full explanation and he was true to his word. Before the sun went down that evening both men who had shared their stories with me were dead and I knew the whole grisly truth. As I understood it the doctrine of determinism asserted that someone's personal history determined their actions and that free-will was no more than an illusion. Perhaps that was the case with Harry Devereaux. Certainly, it was easy to see how his life of crime developed after being hit so hard, so young by misfortune. Was his path through life pre-determined by the unique combination of circumstances which shaped his early years? Perhaps it was.

Having left Lucy and Billy together for what was bound to be an emotionally charged reunion, I arrived at Liongate in the middle of the afternoon. 'My father's' study was a sumptuous affair with an antique oak-desk, built-in bookcases crammed full of interesting historical and learned books as well as an eclectic collection of ornaments and knickknacks he had collected from his travels around the world. A *Turner* took pride of place above the fireplace and it was comfortably furnished with a leather sofa and armchair to match. As I walked through the door 'my father' introduced me, although the introduction was superfluous as I was already acquainted with Harry Devereaux albeit by his contemporary persona.

For once 'my father's' desk had been cleared of its clutter. All that remained was a black, old fashioned table-lamp and a revolver resting in the palm of his hand pointing in the direction of Sebastian Harris who sat unmoved on the armchair in the corner of the room. Sebastian Harris, a man I had learnt to respect and admire for his easy going charm and his worldly wisdom. A man ahead of his time, both cultured and suave and a man of whom I had always felt in awe. I said nothing but just sat on the sofa and waited for proceedings begin. A court room with 'my father' the prosecuting barrister and me the presiding judge.

"I have a story to tell you, William." 'My father' started. "It's a long story and I hope that Harry will feel able to contribute. It began at New College Oxford in the autumn of 1908 when we met as chemistry undergraduates.

Harry was a quite brilliant scholar with the world his oyster but fate dealt him a severe blow. Mother, father and sister all died in an accident when he was at Oxford. Bad enough, of course but humiliation followed when it emerged that his father had squandered the family's investments in a life of debauchery and drunkenness the extent of which he had successfully hidden from those close to him.

As if he had not suffered enough, Harry then had to swallow the indignity of borrowing money from me to pay his university fees. Whilst he had lost everything I inherited a small fortune from an uncle who had lost his life in the San Francisco earthquake of 1906. At first, my once carefree and good humoured friend was not quite sure who to blame for his plight and he fell into a state of depression. I tried as best I could to lift him but he needed an outlet for his anger and frustration.

It came in the form of Juan Marquez who arrived in Oxford in January 1909; confident, handsome, rebellious and Spanish, the perfect antidote to the public school toffs who Harry came to blame for his ill fortune. Marquez provided the ammunition to feed his simmering anger. The Spaniard was a young man with great charisma and Harry needed someone to believe in, to fight his corner against the rich and privileged. We all revered Juan to some extent and many of us ditched our political roots to join his fledgling communist party but for most it was no more than a short term infatuation.

Indeed, I was as besotted as any and threw my weight behind the cause which Marquez so eloquently espoused. We were all brothers in arms and enjoyed the togetherness it engendered, swaggering around the streets of Oxford talking to anyone who cared to listen of liberty, equality and fraternity. I even swapped my degree subject to be in step with Marques! It was a fun time but ran out of steam when the prospect of real life beckoned.

But for Harry it was different. He was an outsider, an impoverished student from the north surrounded by a sea of privilege. The seed planted by Marquez grew quickly and strongly within Harry and his communist convictions flourished. Whilst I and others dabbled, Harry was deadly serious. He became a disciple of Karl Marx obsessed with the notion that the bourgeois middle classes would eventually fall to the sword of the working man in a mighty pan-European workers' revolution.

Harry's passion for politics was matched only by his dedication to his studies. He brought flair to the otherwise mundane subject of chemistry. Whereas for us more pedestrian students, study was no more than a means to an end, for Harry it was genuine love affair. His interest was not just academic either, he had an obsession about how the mind could be affected and manipulated by chemicals. He locked himself away in his bedroom for hours at a time mixing and experimenting with drugs of all description. He was christened 'professor chemical' by his corridor in recognition of his 'soirées' as he liked to call them which became legendary and in one case, at least, deadly.

As Oxford students we were supposed to be the cream of the crop but could be perversely stupid. Harry's idea of Saturday evening entertainment involved injecting his guests with a cocktail of chemicals and recording their behaviour. On one particular occasion a young man, Jack Fischer, jumped from his window on the third floor to his death after one of Harry's 'soirées'. It was hushed-up but we knew very well what drove poor Jack to his death."

Harry then spoken for the first time. As though taking part in a philosophical debate he gave a measured explanation for the demise of the unfortunate student.

"It was something of a surprise when Fischer jumped to his death, I had not before then understood the susceptibility of the weak minded to hallucinogens. Of course Fischer was typical of his class, in-bred and feeble minded. Important research nonetheless."

Once it was clear Harry had nothing more to add 'My father' carried on with his story.

"Harry duly collected his first class degree before moving down to London University to study Law in which, by all accounts, he also excelled. Our paths did not cross again until 1916 when we were thrown together in France. The War suited Harry and he built a formidable reputation as a legal representative and defender of the subjugated Tommy. He by no means shirked his responsibilities toward the war effort either, far from it. He helped develop countermeasures to combat the effects of chemical warfare and was credited with designing the first genuinely effective field gas mask.

It wasn't until a few months ago, almost 35 years later that I realised how I was duped by Harry in Flanders fields. Strangely enough William, it was you who was indirectly responsible for my discovery. I read your transcript in the Evening News of Clive

Davenport's confession and I was transported back to that fateful day on the Somme."

"Yes, Harry I may be slow but I worked it out in the end. How did you do it, a little something in my coffee? It was the first day of the Somme offensive in July 1916 and I was due to be one of the first over the top, as our job was to clear a path through the barbed wire before the dawn attack. I always assumed that I had suffered some sort of mental breakdown or shellshock because I never made it. I was picked-up two hours later wandering aimlessly a couple of miles behind our own lines. I could offer no explanation and faced a Court Marshall for cowardice."

"You seem to have forgotten I saved your life Edward." Harry interrupted. "Perhaps you should explain to William what happened to your regiment? Am I not right when I say it was all but wiped out that morning and here *you* are, alive and well thirty five years later? Don't you think you owe me a debt of gratitude Edward?"

"Harry is right of course, he almost certainly did save my life." 'My father' then paused before asking. "So *how* did you do it, Harry?"

"It was an interesting experiment. You know my methods Edward but actually in this case it was mind games, the power of suggestion. It helped that you were dog tired and I grant you, I did ease you along with a mild sedative which you rightly guessed was dropped into your coffee. Once you were relaxed and on the verge of sleep I hypnotised you and ordered you, in the guise of your commanding officer, to withdraw. It was quite interesting how very eager you were to do my bidding as you disappeared into the night.

Now the really clever bit was the combination of mainly opiates I injected into your bloodstream which so perfectly mimicked a severe flu virus. Within hours you were delirious, thrashing about in your bed as though you'd contracted Yellow Fever. It was beautiful to behold and my job in defending you became a simple matter. Of course, the toffs in charge didn't like shooting officers anyway so getting you off the hook was easy enough. It was simply a question of demonstrating that you were out of your mind with delirium. Had you been a Tommy with a thick northern accent I am sure it would have been a very different story though."

"At the time I knew nothing of all this and just felt an enormous debt of gratitude to Harry Devereaux, the brilliant lawyer." 'My father' continued. "So when I bumped into him again after the War outside the British Officers' Club (which we christened the Piccadilly Club) in Paris I was delighted to take him under my wing. Like many young army officers of the day I gravitated to Paris after the Armistice because there was so little to draw me back to England. Paris was run-down after four years under siege but still offered an exciting alternative. Harry had just arrived in France whereas I had been knocking around for a few weeks and already had formed a small circle of friends. Among them was your mother Catherine Reneaux.

In a world which had largely lost its charm, Harry was both charming and worldly-wise and I was proud to call him my friend. He had a broad breadth of topics on which he could discourse intelligently, leaving me and most of my other friends in the shade. He spoke French like a native and his socialist ideals were all the rage with the Paris set. Harry became popular very quickly at the Piccadilly Club, so perhaps it was hardly surprising when he caught the attention of the beautiful Catherine Reneaux. Your mother, William, was a lady of immense beauty, gentleness, and intelligence. She was guileless to a fault and was easily lured by the charming Harry.

The first I knew of trouble brewing was when a tall and dashing man came charging into the Piccadilly Club asking for Harry with murder in his eyes. It was my introduction to your father and he was incoherent with rage. From what I pieced together Harry had tried something ungentlemanly with your mother and when she spurned his advances he took his frustration out on a prostitute slashing her with a knife. When I questioned him he seemed to believe his actions were perfectly legitimate on the basis that the woman was a traitor and had prostituted herself to German soldiers during the war.

It came to light that this was not an isolated incident and Harry had a penchant for mistreating prostitutes. Of course I was shocked by his behaviour but convinced myself that the years on the Western Front somehow effected his mind so rather than leaving him to the wolves I helped smuggle him back to England with a new identity. Harry Devereaux became Sebastian Harris. I explained my theory and actions to your mother and father who were just happy to get him out of the country."

I got the impression that, perhaps because he had never before had the opportunity to share his triumphs with an attentive audience, Harry enjoyed his afternoon in the limelight. Rather than protest his innocence and contest 'my father's' version of events he seemed proud of his accomplishments and totally devoid of remorse or empathy for his victims. I was at once shocked at his callousness and oddly disappointed at his apparent lack of conviction. In truth Harry Devereaux was nothing short of a deranged and psychotic megalomaniac. I shuddered at the thought of Lucy at his mercy.

"The newly invented Sebastian Harris settled in Emsworth and borrowed enough money from me to start a law practice with a small office in North Street. I went on with my life and I hoped the unseemly business in Paris was forgotten. With his dark side temporarily, at least, buried, Sebastian reverted to his charming, urbane self and once again inveigled his way into my circle of friends. There was little sign of further trouble until I heard that your mother and father where thinking of returning to England and asked for my help in securing your father a job.

Sopwith's agreed to take Geoffrey on as a test pilot and I tried my best to smooth the waters and persuade the couple that Harry Devereaux alias Sebastian Harris was a reformed character and the trouble in Paris was nothing more than an aberration, a result of three years on the front line. Your mother, characteristically forgiving, managed to coax her husband into letting bygones be bygones so Harry's secret remained in-tact and I became his unwitting apologist

By the mid-twenties, using his Marxist connections Harry turned his attention away from Western Europe towards Russia where, with corruption rife, money making opportunities were easy to come by. Whilst the ordinary Russian suffered under Stalin many of his officials did very nicely and they clamoured for a share of the luxury goods coming out of America. Harry provided the means. He used his contacts to arrange the import of consumer goods, particularly anything American from cars to televisions and many other things besides.

I was roped in as Harry's unofficial banker but gratefully accepted a 100% return on my money and it was only later that I realised what a fool I had been, leaving myself open to a charge of business malpractice or worse. Harry used my discomfort to draw me further into his murky world. Rather than do the sensible thing and get out before the damage was too great I let him persuade me to fund further shipments almost all of which provided a healthy return. But I was well aware that the money used to pay for these goods was syphoned illegally from public funds. I can offer no excuses.

I was in it up to my neck and Harry had no intention of letting me off the hook. His schemes became more and more outlandish as time went by and he lost his grip on reality. His ambitions knew no bounds and nothing would stand in his way. Any attempt on my part to extricate myself from his madness was brushed aside. Out of desperation I lodged documents with a London solicitor containing evidence enough to put Harry inside for a very long time, to be made public in the event of my death. A life insurance policy if you like. So for thirty years Harry and I have been inextricably bound to each other, neither able to wriggle free of the other's grip.

Harry's business thrived throughout the twenties and thirties and he became almost a celebrity in Russia meeting Stalin himself on a number of occasions. Because of his new found status I had a relatively easy time of it until the onset of the Spanish Civil War when I was asked to contribute large sums to the anti-fascists. I was surprised to find Harry was still in contact with Juan Marquez who was back in his homeland fighting against Franco. I got the strong impression that by this time Harry was under the control of the Russians and my money was doing little more than propping up the communist sympathiser Juan Negrin as prime minister of the Popular Front. Stalin was desperate to prevent the right wing taking control of another European power and as far as I could see, was using Harris as a sort of political fundraiser.

It must have been the autumn of '38 when Harry came to me with the outline of his plan to defraud the Admiralty. It was a bold and foolhardy plan even by his standards and I wanted no part in it. But unwittingly I got dragged in to save your friend Billy Cosgrove from the noose. Harry's henchmen were, in those days local riff-raff and Stanley Jakes was hand-picked from the gutter. Harry recognised a like-minded character with no scruples but of course it was bound to end in trouble. Jakes stepped out of line and Harry had no hesitation in arranging his murder."

"Why the elaborate measures Devereaux?" I asked. "Why not a bullet in the head?"

"Experimentation, my dear William. I was testing myself and my latest concoction to see if it were possible to turn a mild mannered man into a killer. An interesting and if I may say so a very successful experiment."

"And you were prepared to let Billy Cosgrove hang for a crime he didn't commit?"

"It was for the greater good, William. You must understand that sacrifices have to be made in the pursuit of progress. Why get so het about one individual? There are 2 ½ billion people on our planet, William. Why jeopardise so much for one? It makes no sense."

It would, of course have been pointless arguing with the man who, somewhere along the line, had lost touch with reality. His values were those of a madman. Harry Devereaux was unhinged and very dangerous and on one level I wanted to escape his presence as soon as possible. But on the other hand I sensed that this may be the only opportunity to draw from him a complete picture of his warped life of crime. It seemed unlikely he would cooperate with a police investigation so rather than rise to his bait I kept my cool.

He had been immensely proud of the Admiralty fraud which from his perspective was easy to understand. The sheer audacity of the crime was breath-taking as much as its execution was brilliant. Harry Devereaux was a master tactician and how he pulled all the threads together was nothing short of astonishing. What struck me most forcibly was that Harry had committed this gargantuan fraud alone. There *was* no John McDermott, Harry had choreographed the entire production and played all the parts himself. He demonstrated his American accent to me which would have fooled all but the most discerning critic.

'My father' then continued. "Harry paid Inspector Hanaho in return for his cooperation and Billy Cosgrove was framed for the murder of Stanley Jakes. Unwittingly the Cosgrove boy made powerful enemies and I knew would likely hang without my intervention. So I arranged to get him out of the country and warned him to stay away. It was the best I could do."

"Your sentimentality is your weakness Edward. It was a big mistake letting that boy go." Harry interrupted sharply.

In an age which saw the rise to power of both Adolph Hitler and Joseph Stalin perhaps we were lucky that Harry Devereaux had steered away from political ambition. Certainly his deranged mind had plenty in common with the men he revered. The implications of the story which unfolded that hot June day were massive and perhaps the sheer enormity of it all dulled my senses and I could not quite bring to mind something which niggled at me all afternoon. There were a hundred questions I wanted answers to but knew I would need patience and that it would take weeks or even months before everything came to light.

"When your father died William, I spent more and more time in the company of your mother helping her to come to terms with her loss. She was bereft and agreed with my proposal that we should marry for the sake of her children. She wanted financial security for you both and asked me to grant her husband's wish that you be educated in England. I confess I was in love but it was no more than a business arrangement for your mother."

Up until that point the atmosphere in 'my father's' study had been strangely muted; no anger, no raised voices and very little disagreement. Harry Devereaux seemed happy enough with 'my father's' interpretation of his life's story and treated the event almost as an academic exercise. But then quite suddenly it changed. My own objectivity left me as I dredged from the far recesses of my mind the connection, the very obvious connection which had, until that point, remained obstinately hidden.

Of course, Arthur Swanson was right all along. Major Barrington-Hope, my real father, had been murdered and Harry Devereaux was his killer. The mists of time had all but eroded the possibility of discovering the truth behind the Major's death but then, quite miraculously it was laid before me, crystal clear. With the realisation my temper flared and my inclination was to take the gun from 'my father's' hand and shoot Harry Devereaux dead.

"Devereaux." I started as I struggled to keep my vocal chords from constricting. "Can I ask you a question? Did you meet my real father, the Major, again after Paris?"

Harris just looked at me and smiled. The cold merciless smile of a killer but he did not reply. He had no need to reply. His eyes danced with delight and my urge to strike back became overwhelming.

"You bastard!" I shouted as I launched myself across the room in his direction. Harry Devereaux may well have been over 60 but was still tough, sinewy and quick with his reflexes. As I made to grab him he brought his elbow up and cracked me across the bridge of the nose. Before I could recover 'my father' pulled me by my collar and nudged me back toward the settee.

"That was stupid William!" Sir Edward said before asking. "What's that about?"

"He murdered my father! He contrived to make it look like an accident but actually he drugged him before a test flight." I spat, resuming my seat and wiping a smear of blood from my nose.

I think Sir Edward was about to argue the point when he turned and looked into Harry's eyes, saw the truth and slumped back into his seat, stunned. It was then Harry's turn to take centre stage.

"Well gentlemen that was an interesting afternoon but I have a plane to catch. Let's get down to business shall we?"

Astounded by his audacity I laughed. "You are hardly in a position to make terms Devereaux!"

"Well I have to disagree, William. When was the last time you saw your girl, Lucy? We talked about insurance early in the afternoon you may recall? ... and I am always… always well insured." A smile flickered across Harry Devereaux's face.

"Your insurance policy has just expired Devereaux. You should have checked the date before you booked your flight." And with that I pulled the driving license I had taken from the pocket of his henchman at the saw mill and flung it at him. "Alf Connor has a severe headache Devereaux and Lucy is alive and well under police protection. No insurance pay-out I'm afraid!"

For the first time Harry Devereaux's mask slipped and a trace of surprise or was it fear swept across his features.

Sir Edward then stood and looked out of the window. "The police have arrived William. Please show them in."

As I made my way down the stairs and out into the garden I just had the time to look around one last time and take in the splendour of my surroundings which I had taken for granted for most of my life. The magnificent 150 year old cedar dominated the upper terrace whilst the rest of the garden was mostly laid to lawn, all lovingly tended by 'my father's' gardener. My eyes moved to the colourful summer bedding plants in full bloom and the purple clematis and passion flower creeping over the red brick wall which separated the grounds from the surrounding streets. And the grandiose Thomas Owen designed house; all in all a tranquil and delightful scene. My home for nearly twenty years.

I heard the gun shots as I approached the side gate, one, followed 30 seconds later by a second.

For the record the official version showed that 'my father' shot and killed Harry Devereaux at 6.47pm on June 18th 1951 before turning the gun on himself.

Yes, for all of us just flotsam, washed up where the great ocean gods decreed.

Epilogue

July 1952

The case never went to trial. "Well it wouldn't would it?" Julian explained. "The British Government is hardly likely to broadcast to the world that it had been duped out of millions of pounds by the Russians. No, the Official Secrets Act will ensure that we are wiped from the pages of history!" Not that Julian cared a jot. He was far too busy chatting up my sister Claudine.

The occasion was a summer gathering of friends and family in Southsea. My aunt Marie and my uncle Cedric from Picardie were guests of honour as we celebrated new beginnings and freedom from the lies that had hitherto blighted our lives. Claudine had become a regular visitor to our home and already Lucy and others had noticed the almost…well, twin-like rapport which existed between us. Memories of my early years at *Le ferme au Moulin du vent* started to return and I was told my French accent improved almost overnight.

It had been a year of discovery for me as I had slipped back into the tranquility of auditing without so much as a backward glance. Nothing too taxing, if you'll excuse the pun and absolutely no Russian assassins or murderous villains anywhere in sight. Lucy and I were engaged to marry and Billy and Gloria had moved into the next street. Life had returned to the humdrum normality which we had all craved. Well that was the consensus view and for the sake of others I was determined to go with the flow, at least for the present.

Twelve months had passed since the shootings and plenty of water had flowed under the bridge since. Although there had been no trial that did not mean investigations had ceased. Far from it, Julian for one had spent most of the year sifting through the debris before submitting a bulky report to the Ministry (even if it had been quickly confined to gather dust within the bowels of Whitehall). It had been a little while since I had spoken to Julian and I was itching to prise him away from Claudine for an update. As I had turned over the events of that tumultuous year in my mind I had unearthed many things which I still did not fully understand.

Sir Edward had written a full and detailed confession which had been posted to me on the morning of his death. The shootings were pre-meditated and in 'my father's' case the price he felt compelled to pay for his involvement in the crimes. It was hard not to feel sympathy for a man who was more victim than villain. Not by nature a corrupt or selfish man he had devoted much of his life and a great deal of his personal fortune to helping those less fortunate than himself.

Sir Edward had been dragged unwittingly into supporting Devereaux's criminal activity and had neither the strength of character nor the guile to haul himself clear. His fatal mistake was his need to see the best in Harry, when there was no 'best' to see. And of course once Harry had woven his web of deceit tightly around him there was no escape.

I finally managed to tempt Julian away from Claudine by waving a beer under his nose and steering him out into the garden toward two free chairs under the shade of the apple tree.

"I received a letter from 'my father's' solicitor last week and you were right to say he was a wealthy man. I'm not quite sure what to do with my share but I am glad that Elizabeth has decided to take up residence at Liongate after all. It has hardly good memories for me but somehow I wanted the house kept in the family. I just hope it will prove a better home for baby Tom than it was for me. So tell me Julian, you've had a chance to examine his business dealings by now, how *did* he make his money?"

"Simple, he was a very shrewd business man. He invested all over the world and managed to buck the trend of low returns through the 30's and 40's. As far as we can see his business dealings were as clean as a whistle except for a couple of salvos into Russia which Devereaux orchestrated. Not my business maybe but I don't think you should feel guilty about accepting your inheritance William. I think Sir Edward owed you something. You've been through the mill on his account."

"Well maybe, we'll see. I've not really given it much thought yet but there are still a few things I want to know." I answered. "Tell me about the two men at the saw mill? Billy shot one dead and he can't sleep at night as a result."

"Yes, we have identified the man Billy shot as Dimitri Bukov from the Ukraine, an evil bastard if there ever was one. He was a Russian agent working for Devereaux and believe me, Billy should not fret. Bukov made Vasilyev look like the Archangel Gabriel by comparison. It was he and not Vasilyev who was responsible for the shooting of Samantha Smith and Jack Hanaho."

"Really! So you were right, Hanaho's death wasn't suicide." I replied.

"He was executed by his former employers and must have seen it coming the minute we exposed him."

"My god! Well you were right there as well. You said Hanaho would get his comeuppance!" I exclaimed. "And Devereaux?"

"Yes, Devereaux, an interesting and complex character. I don't believe that he ever really came to terms with his father's humiliation. It must have unhinged him. When he had come down to Oxford he had felt proud of his achievements and expected to mix with his intellectual equals and had visions of being surrounded by the brightest young minds in the country and talking long into the night on subjects of weighty import. Instead he found his peers to be largely self-indulgent and spoilt.

At one level he wanted to conform, to be invisible, part of the crowd and he shed the skin that identified him as a boy from a lower middle class family in a northern city. From a position where he had felt crushed and socially inferior Harry Devereaux created a new image for himself. He re-invented himself as something of an international citizen without carrying the baggage of social class. By his second year at university his new persona was established and he and Juan Marquez became the leaders of their particular pack.

The very people who he had despised, he befriended. He made a point of inviting the titled, the rich and the privileged to his infamous parties. The same people who he believed had sneered at the 'old' Harry Devereaux. But of course, Harry still loathed these people for what they stood for and his soirees were no more than a means to exact revenge. He mocked and ridiculed anyone unable to compete with his razor sharp intellect."

"How did he get into bed with the Russians in the first place?" I asked. "I don't see that his communist convictions were genuine, do you? He had no compassion for anyone."

"It was after the First World War that he gravitated toward Russia and was right behind the revolution which he hoped would be the first of many uprisings against inherited wealth and privilege. He despised Western European democracies which he believed sustained the class system (particularly in Britain) and put power in the hands of the few to the detriment of the many.

He had felt impotent as a young northern undergraduate arriving in Oxford and spent all his life fighting back, wanting to prove himself. Did he really believe the new Bolshevik Russia was some kind of political Utopia? Who knows? Perhaps, he did or perhaps he was motivated by a hatred of the class system in his own country.

But either way the Russians must have recognised an opportunity in Devereaux. He was highly intelligent, prepared to betray his country and easily flattered. So they gave him status, inviting him to dine at the top table, eventually with Stalin himself. Devereaux was overwhelmed by the attention and as we have since discovered, repaid his hosts in spades."

"What I can't understand is how did he manage to get away with it for so long?" I then asked with a shake of the head.

"He had a network of high ranking officials on his payroll who were well rewarded for their services but more importantly were ruthlessly dealt with for any breach of discipline. Stanley Jakes was a prime example. Devereaux's unbreakable code was anonymity and discretion and no sooner had Jakes started to shout his mouth off than he was 'removed'. Devereaux maintained control by keeping his disciples in perpetual fear of each other, a technique he had learnt from the Russian Security Services."

"What will happen to all these people? Will they ever come to trial?"

"No, I suspect not. Most will be quietly shunted to one side with a polite request that they should retire to sunny climes forthwith."

"And Sir Marcus Crawford? Guilty or not guilty?" I then asked, having received a call from an agitated Helen only the previous evening.

"I am not sure he has emerged from the investigations smelling of roses exactly! Let's start with his friendship with Harry Devereaux. Devereaux, as we know, did not really have friends in the conventional sense and yet had a long association with Marcus Crawford so for a while I did wonder if they had plotted together. It seems such an obvious alliance but the further I delved the more convinced I became that Devereaux or should I say Sebastian Harris just used Sir Marcus by exploiting his position as

Crawford's solicitor to manoeuvre his way into the business without arousing suspicion. By the time he had finished, Harris /Devereaux understood the inner workings of Crawford Electrics better than Sir Marcus himself.

Sir Marcus was something of a business maverick who often sailed a little close to the wind and although Crawford Electrics became a huge company it was his 'baby'. Or at least that was how he viewed it. He founded it and although eventually raised capital through a share issue he never quite got the hang of the idea of 'shared' ownership. As a result he had something of a free and easy attitude to the company's cash. If he needed money for a holiday, or a new car he saw nothing at all wrong with using the company's cheque book and hence the holes in the accounts which were highlighted by the audit.

When I gave the news to Sir Marcus that Devereaux was behind the Admiralty fraud his shock was genuine. Like many people, Sir Marcus was somewhat in awe of Devereaux and had often taken his advice on business matters. In one sense Sir Marcus is a lucky man. Had this gone to court he would surely have been prosecuted for complicity. He knew something was not right but chose to turn a blind eye. Although he was not in cahoots with Devereaux he was far too shrewd not to realise that his company was profiting from an underhand deal. I strongly suspect he will get away scot free, especially with Helen representing him!"

As the afternoon wore on Lucy, Billy and Gloria wandered out to join us. "I hope you are not offering William any further careers advice Julian!" Lucy asked with a smile.

"Heaven forbid!" Julian countered winking in my direction.

"How's the investigation going? I hear from William that you've submitted your report." Lucy asked as she linked an arm with mine.

"It's all done and dusted and any crumbs that remain will be swept under the carpet. But I'm glad I have caught you all together because I did want to give you an insight into Sir Edward's behaviour. I think you deserve an explanation."

"I always felt Sir Edward held a grudge against us Cosgroves but William tells me that he had good reason." Lucy said.

"That's true, misguided perhaps but the lies he told were designed to protect William. He wanted to remove any possibility of William inadvertently stumbling across Devereaux. The Cosgroves were connected to Devereaux by virtue of the feud between you Billy, and Stanley Jakes. Sir Edward knew that Devereaux planned to frame you for the murder and wanted to keep William well away and out of harm's way. All that stuff about class differences, social position and so forth was baloney. He didn't mean a word of it. It was just a ham fisted attempt to keep you two apart."

"I wish I could have known the real man behind the mask. It sounds like he was tormented by Devereaux for most of his life." Lucy said.

"That's certainly true. And of course far from being the villain of the piece he saved your life Billy. Devereaux wanted you off the scene permanently and Sir Edward knew your best chance…perhaps your only chance was to leave the city for good."

"Yes, it took me twelve years to work that out. How different things may have turned out if I had known the truth. But I suppose that every cloud has a silver lining and I may never have met Gloria if things had been different." Billy said putting an arm affectionately around his wife.

"And so say all of us." I agreed.

As the wind freshened and the evening drew in we all made our way inside and I could not help but reflect on the part that chance had played in my life. Had I not stumbled on Billy Cosgrove and Stanley Jakes feuding outside the Albany Tavern that summer afternoon in 1939 where would my life have taken me I wondered? I looked around with satisfaction at the seven people who had become the most important in my world; Lucy my beautiful fiancée, Claudine my exotic twin, my aunt and uncle from Picardie, my best friend Billy and his wife Gloria and my mentor Julian Singleton. It was all too easy to imagine but for the chance encounter which triggered the chain reaction of events which ended in such dramatic fashion in 'my father's' study the previous summer, none would ever have crossed my path.

The End

Printed in Great Britain
by Amazon